BLUE MADAGASCAR

ANDREW KAPLAN

PRAISE FOR ANDREW KAPLAN

"Unrelenting suspense." –*Booklist*

"Kaplan's writing is reminiscent of the best of Ian Fleming, Robert Ludlum and Tom Clancy." –*Readertoreader.com*

"A smashing, sexy and unforgettable read." –*Publishers Weekly*

"ELECTRIFYING . . . a searing, ultimately satisfying entertainment with energy, passion and moral resonance." –*Kirkus Reviews (*Starred review)*

"Flawlessly conceived . . . The characters are unforgettable. Kaplan is up there with the best." –*Readers Favorite*

"Matches the best work of the late Robert Ludlum and then surpasses it." –*Suspense Magazine*

"In a word, *terrific* ... The pace is blistering, the atmosphere menacing and decadent, and author Andrew Kaplan is in marvelously smashing form." –*New York Daily News*

"Kept me up well into the Late Show hours . . . paced like a ride on the Magic Mountain rollercoaster. Hollywood, please copy." –*Los Angeles Times*

"Superb and original." –*Nelson DeMille*

"One of the smartest, swiftest and most compelling spy novels I've read in years." *–Harlan Coben*

"Excellent ... pulsates with intrigue and dramatic suspense. A powerful read." *–Clive Cussler*

"[Kaplan's] characters and locales are brilliantly etched . . . the plot is riveting." *–London Times*

"Andrew Kaplan represents a gold standard for thriller writing." *–David Morrell*

"Brimming with action." *--Washington Post Book World*

"Successfully blends sex, suspense, sustained action, an exotic location, and historic plausibility . . . a superior thriller that is a memorable and entertaining reading experience." *--Library Journal*

"Wow! More heart-thumping twists and turns than *Day of the Jackal* and *The Spy Who Came In From the Cold* rolled into one. . . a textbook example of how to write a great thriller." *-- Katherine Neville, NY Times bestselling author of The Eight*

"A highly suspenseful page-turner. . . I hate to use the cliche but it's true: I couldn't put it down". *-- Brian Garfield, Edgar Award-winning author of Death Wish and Hopscotch*

"With rapid-fire narrative and a complex plot, Andrew Kaplan gives readers a truly intriguing and engaging spy thriller." *-- Freshfiction.com*

"A killer pacing that never lets up . . . This is an action thriller that will leave you breathless." -- *Mystery Matters*

"Andrew Kaplan is one of the few among spy writers' community who writes with a large sense of authenticity . . . You can really feel the atmosphere . . . In the case you like Tom Clancy books or Bourne series, you will love this book." -- *Mystery Tribune*

"Grabs readers by the collar and does not let go until the very end. Action-packed and filled with mystery, betrayal and excitement . . . I loved this book! It just blew me away and had me furiously turning the pages to find out what happens next." -- *Night Owl Reviews*

"Be careful where you read this thriller. There's a real danger here you will become so engrossed . . . you'll lose all track of the time. So be careful!" -- *Bookloons*

"Steamy, erotic, spellbinding fiction with more twists and turns than Hitchcock and Graham Greene combined." -- *Roderick Thorp, author of Die Hard and The Detective*

"Andrew Kaplan surpasses the genre... a suspenseful, breathless story." -- *Warren Adler, author of War of the Roses*

ALSO BY ANDREW KAPLAN

Homeland: Saul's Game
Homeland: Carrie's Run
Scorpion Deception
Scorpion Winter
Scorpion Betrayal
War of the Raven
Dragonfire
Scorpion
Hour of the Assassins

ISBN:978-1-7368099-1-4 (paperback)
ISBN:978-1-7368099-0-7 (ebook)
ISBN: 978-1-7368099-2-1 (audiobook)
Library of Congress Control Number: 2021910157

Smugglers Lane Press, U.S.A.

First Smugglers Lane Press printing: June 2021

Visit Smugglers Lane Press on the World Wide Web at www. smugglerslane.com; visit Andrew Kaplan at www.andrewkaplan.com

For my son Justin, who makes things happen and makes them better.

AUTHOR'S NOTE

A complete list of *Jessica's Rules* is provided at the end of this book.

"Death solves all problems – no man, no problem."

JOSEPH STALIN

"*Or maybe not.*"

JESSICA "JESSIE" MAKARENKO

"THE INVISIBLE WOMAN"

SHE EXISTS for five and a half seconds. Face a white blur in the headlights, head turned away from the camera, impossible to identify as she disappears into the night shadows. And gone.

The notorious Lazaro cell phone video shot by coincidence – although dozens of conspiracy theories would later claim otherwise – through the windshield of a car on Key Biscayne's Crandon Boulevard hours before the news broke. Yet nowhere is there a record of her visit at the exclusive Key Colony enclave where the fatal encounter with presidential candidate Governor Jeffrey "Win with Jeff" Smullen – at that moment, up seven and a quarter points in the polls and favored to be the next President – supposedly took place.

No witnesses. No confirming testimony from any of the guards at the gate-guarded community or the Secret Service assigned to guard Governor Smullen. Not a single second of video from even one of the security cameras at the complex. Nothing to substantiate the rumor that she was there, that she was a part of what happened, which was why the media dubbed her, "The Invisible Woman."

When the Lazaro video emerged, the first evidence she actually existed, and the instant object of a bidding war between ABC, Apple News, Fox and MSNBC, the media wolf pack's feeding frenzy went as one commentator put it, "Full Metal Psycho." Lacking other targets, the spotlight turned on those who first broke the story: WFOR, the local CBS TV affiliate in Miami, and on the man who made the call, its news director, George Rees, who always swore he didn't know a damn thing more than anyone else.

That night. Prime time. Digital clock on the screen counting down 4 days 11:36 hours to the election. On-set on-camera, one second there was Mace Cottrell, silver-tongued campaign manager for Governor Smullen smoothly repeating his talking points for the two-millionth time, when an aide rushed out and whispered something to him. Without a word, mid-sentence, Cottrell abruptly stood up – give the devil his due, talking head analysts would say later, no change in expression, he gave nothing away – yanked off his mike and pulling his cell phone from his jacket, bolted from the set as if, one liberal talk show host would later snarkily observe, "he had a bad case of diarrhea about to explode."

In the control room, George Rees, middle-aged, salt-and-pepper hair and a Dad belly that betrayed an expense-account affinity for good restaurants, was about to signal his attractive blonde female anchor – Florida, after all – Julianne Marsh, to improvise for thirty seconds, when his iPhone vibrated. The one he reserved strictly for emergencies.

Rees took off his headset and put the phone to his ear. Afterwards, those present said his jaw literally dropped open in shock. As the technicians around him chattered, he made a set of vicious cutting signs to his neck to shut them up.

"Christ! Is this for real? You shitting me?" Rees said into the phone. It was later revealed that the person on the other end was Pete Flynn, a lieutenant on the Miami-Dade PD, who'd always been a good mutual backscratching source. A result of WFOR's lucky location, on NW 25th Street in Hialeah, close to MDPD headquarters; ideal for after-work schmoozing with cops at the Longhorn, the local bar and grill.

Rees stared wide-eyed through the glass at the set, where Julianne – not exactly the highest IQ in a business that in Rees' view had dumbed down to the point where a shot of chimpanzee DNA would be an improvement – was doing her best to tap-dance over the dead air time. She and fellow talking head, GOP strategist Lawrence "Tax cuts will solve everything" McHenry were speculating about what might have caused Mace Cottrell, not known for erratic behavior – certainly not for tossing away even a millisecond of free TV air time – to suddenly take off.

"Get back to me as soon as you can. And hey, I owe you, man," Rees said, finishing the call while simultaneously checking the AP feed on his laptop. But it was the usual crap. New polls. Smullen up nine and a half in Ohio. Campaign stops by surrogates. Blah. Blah. Nothing. Nothing. Smullen was here in Miami, due to head tomorrow to Orlando and Tampa; Florida as always the ultimate swing state.

Rees put his headset back on and punched a button on his console to get Hailey, his on-the-scene reporter at the Smullen campaign HQ in downtown Miami. Around him, the noise level rose; newsroom phones started ringing, people talking. Something was happening.

"What? Hailey I can hardly hear you. What's going on?" Rees listened. "Jesus! It's impossible. Can you confirm? Wait, who's with you? Let me talk to him." He snapped his fingers several times for quiet, looking at the people around him, at this point all staring back at him.

Rees spoke into the headset mike again. "Jared, listen. Can you get inside? I need visuals. Anything. Inside, if humanly possible. Even if it's inside the men's room. If we can't, I want Hailey standing outside the hotel; steps, front entrance, whatever. Get the hotel logo. I'm putting her on the second you've got a spot to point the camera. And get confirmation!" Pause. "From somebody, anybody. The fucking janitor! Put Hailey back on." He waited. His staff was dead silent, eyes on him, ignoring the images on their computer screens and monitors. "Hailey, listen. We're going with it. Get what you can and get ready to go on in exactly two minutes. This is it, kid. We're going to you live, so be ready. C'mon, now. This is history."

He turned to his crew and the set window and hit a button to talk to Julianne through her ear bud, eyes darting at a monitor to confirm they still had about thirty seconds on the bladder drug commercial – Florida! – that was running.

"Julianne, we have breaking news," he said into the headset. "You need to stress it has not yet been confirmed by either the campaign or the Miami-Dade Police Department. I mean you have to make the non-confirm very very *very* strong so we're legally covered or we're in deep shit. Nod if you understand how serious this is."

He watched her nod.

"Okay," he said, taking a breath. "You need to stress there has been an unofficial report, which we cannot, I repeat *not*, confirm, but it's been reported that Governor Jeffrey Smullen, candidate for President and currently ahead in all the polls, is dead." Julianne's eyes went wide. "Right now, that's all we have. Hailey's at the scene. You'll cut to her as soon as she's ready. I'll cue you to go to her live."

1

As they started the network's "Breaking News" music and visual, Rees' emergency iPhone buzzed again. He grabbed it.

"Yeah, Pete," he said. "For real? Did he leave anything? I don't believe it. Not for a second." He listened again. "Okay, thanks. And Pete, I owe you forever. Whatever you want. Jack Daniels Twenty-seven, my first-born kid. I mean it, man, thanks."

Rees looked around for an available reporter. Cody Robinson was talking to a female intern. "Cody!" Rees bellowed. "Get your ass and a camera over to the Key Colony Club on Key Biscayne! Now! Get over there. I don't care if you get twenty speeding tickets." And when Cody Robinson hesitated, shouted, "Go! Run!"

On the set, Julianne motioned McHenry into silence, faced straight into the camera, solemn as a church and shocked – not having to act for once – knowing her announcement would be played and re-played all around the world because they were scooping everyone in the universe, as the camera light lit, made the announcement.

"We interrupt our scheduled programming to bring you the following important breaking news regarding the Governor Smullen campaign in Miami. WFOR CBS Local News has received an unconfirmed report, and I must stress that as yet, this report is *un*confirmed," Rees behind the glass giving her a thumbs-up for that, "that Governor Jeffrey Smullen, the heavily-favored candidate for President, is dead. We have no further details. To get more on what's happening, we're switching live to our reporter on the scene, Hailey Squires."

"Up on two," Rees said and a technician brought up Hailey, who was standing, microphone in hand in the middle of a crowd, many with orange and white "Smullen for President" signs, on the steps in front of the Four Seasons Hotel in downtown Miami.

Many in the crowd looked confused or stunned, having just heard the rumor. A number of women were crying, holding each other. One man with a sign on a stick repeatedly smacked it against a streetlight pole until others grabbed him. People milled about. No one seemed to know what to do. Several on-lookers shoved towards Hailey, who stood in an open space, spot-lit in the darkness by her cameraman, Will. The crew's PM, Jared motioned people back to give her space. Two Miami-Dade PD officers watched, batons in hand, openly glaring at the TV crew.

Hailey brushed a stray hair from her forehead, looked straight at the camera and started: "Julianne, I would like to repeat, we have no official confirmation from either the Miami-Dade police or the Smullen campaign. In fact, there's been no announcement and when I tried to speak to Campaign coordinator, Jack Applegate, who was going somewhere in a hurry, all I got was – and I quote – 'No comment. We have nothing to say.' Those were his exact words. Although the fact that he did not immediately deny the story is telling.

"Nevertheless, I have to tell our viewers, that we have an unconfirmed source who has indeed reported that Presidential candidate Governor Jeffrey Smullen died approximately one half hour ago, which would make it around," glancing at her watch, "eight oh seven PM Eastern Time." At that, a woman in the crowd cried out. "He died at a friend's townhouse at the exclusive Key Colony Club in Key Biscayne. No one from the Smullen campaign has come forward to either substantiate or deny this claim. Now, and this is new – there's a second very shocking report. The same unconfirmed source – I can't say whether it is from inside the campaign or not – has reported that the cause of the Governor's death was as a result of a gunshot by his own hand." There was a murmur, an almost animal groan from the crowd. Someone gasped "Oh no!" as if what happened wasn't real until she said it.

"Hailey," Julianne broke in. "Are you saying Governor Smullen committed suicide?"

On-camera, Hailey holding her hand to her ear-receiver, nodded. "Julianne, that's my understanding. Impossible as it seems, just days before an election that he appeared to have a good chance of winning, that's exactly the information I've received. Again, let me stress, no one in the campaign or the MDPD is officially confirming anything, though" she looked around her, "as I said before, it's telling that we're not seeing or hearing anyone from the campaign contradicting this report. At the moment, they're not talking – to us or anyone."

At that moment, Julianne defined her career forever, making a statement that achieved the most-viewed score in YouTube history with nearly two-and-a-half billion views. She stared in blank confusion at the camera and simply blurted out loud what everyone else was thinking: "Why," she said, "would someone about to be elected President kill himself?"

In the frenzied days that followed and as both parties scrambled to deal with the unprecedented situation of a major party suddenly without a candidate days before the election, Republicans calling for the election to be postponed, Democrats declaring that law and precedent made delay impossible, public curiosity more and more centered on "The Invisible Woman" on Crandon Boulevard. She had changed the world, though no one knew how – or why – or if she was even involved? Deemed a "person of interest," there were sightings of her in cities from Vancouver to Buenos Aires. All proved false.

Nonstop chatter, tweets, and tens of thousands of images,

real and Photoshopped, ping-ponged between the blogos-
phere, Twitter, the cable TV talkathons and Facebook threads
thick as ship's hawsers, many declaring with absolute certainty
that she was a spy, an assassin, a pregnant mistress, or that she
had nothing whatsoever to do with it.

Despite all the speculation, as George Rees himself told
the FBI agents who questioned him: "The fact is, not one
person has offered a plausible explanation to either of the two
central questions: Why? Why'd he do it? And how is it
possible with all the media attention that no one's been able
to identify this so-called 'Invisible Woman?' More to the
point, who is she?"

PART ONE

SIX WEEKS EARLIER

"Chance happens, but evil is a hunter. You can either be prepared or prey."

JESSICA "JESSIE" MAKARENKO

CHAPTER ONE

NICE, FRENCH RIVIERA

"FIFTY-THREE SECONDS," said Vincent the Cat. A final reminder. Fifty-three seconds from the instant Lucas crashed the stolen BMW SUV through the jewelry store's locked front door, triggering the silent alarm, till they were back inside the SUV, Lucas already backing away. They'd be cutting through traffic before either the private security or *les flics*, the cops, could even begin to react to the alarm.

Vincent pulled the *balaclava* over his face. The others in the stolen BMW SUV, Lucas behind the wheel, Patrice, Nabil the North African, already had theirs on, their faces holes for eyes in black hoods. They hefted pistols and heavy hammers to smash the glass display counters cased two days earlier, so they knew exactly which diamonds to take. All wore latex gloves to leave no fingerprints or DNA.

Vincent made a final visual check. His gaze swept the checkerboard walkways and sidewalk cafés in the Place Massena. The day was sunny, warm; the sky the endless blue that had drawn artists like Matisse and Chagall to the Côte d'Azur; the air with a uniquely Mediterranean scent of mingled sea air, garlic, and diesel fumes.

People were out enjoying the weather: students on bikes, chic "*bobo*" mothers pushing strollers, African migrants hawking "genuine French" souvenirs made in China, gypsy teenagers running the gold ring scam on late-season tourists, "Did you drop this ring, Monsieur? Looks like real gold." Vincent ignored them. He was looking for parked vans where they shouldn't be on the Avenue de Verdun, lone men or women standing around, pretending to read a newspaper or mobile phone. So far so good. Still, he was jumpier than usual. Something wasn't right. "Even the best plan can go wrong," Remy, his old cellmate in La Santé prison had told him once. "Otherwise none of us would be here."

A man sat alone at an outside café table, watching the Place Massena with an air of someone with nowhere to go. But he wasn't a *flic*; Vincent could always tell. A man looking for something to break the boredom. What was unusual about that? Vincent paid more attention to the street surveillance cameras as they neared the target on the Avenue de Verdun. Almost there.

"It goes?" Patrice asked. Vincent didn't respond. The Cat never did anything without thinking things through.

They called Vincent "*le Chat*" because of his icy half-smile under a mustache, large nose, and his convict trick of never blinking or looking away when his brown eyes stared at you, usually more than enough with his rangy one-meter-eighty-five (six foot one) body to intimidate any *mecs* who tried to challenge him. Others said he got the name because of his reputation for keeping cool, for always landing on his feet even when things got hot.

Vincent glanced at his watch. Fourteen minutes to noon when the jewelry store, like many French stores closed for lunch. For three days running they'd done a visual drive-by. Almost never any customers in the store at this time; the jewels practically begging to be taken. Besides, Vincent told himself, they'd done the most dangerous part the previous night.

The jewelry's store's security –an armed private guard, internal and external surveillance cameras, secret alarms to simultaneously alert a private security firm and the police, steel window shutters that automatically closed, locked steel and bulletproof glass front door designed to look less intimidating to customers by the store's expensive gray stone façade – were minor concerns for their type of "smash and grab" assault. The biggest obstacle was the row of steel sidewalk posts placed by the Nice municipality to prevent cars from parking on the sidewalk. Those steel posts could stop them cold.

Late the previous night, three-thirty AM, the Place Massena deserted and ghostly with streetlights, they came around the corner dressed in blue municipal workers' coveralls and caps and hands shielding their faces. Nabil, the youngest and most agile of them, climbed Vincent's body like a monkey. Balancing on Vincent's shoulders, he taped over the jewelry store's outside security camera with black electrician's tape, after which they taped the cameras of the adjacent buildings on both sides of the store.

Patrice lit a 55-amp plasma torch and kneeling, cut two steel parking posts off at their base. Vincent then reattached the posts upright with daubs of low-silver-content solder for a weak bond. The posts looked solid and upright as before, but now a child could knock them over. Nabil followed with quick-dry black paint, rendering the fix invisible. They removed the electrical tape from the security cameras and were gone. The entire operation took less than five minutes.

Now they were back on the Avenue de Verdun in bright sunshine, a picture postcard day, moving to the target. Vincent nodded to Lucas; the go-ahead. His heart rate ticked up. Always that rush, like a soldier in the final instant before battle when every pore in your body is electric and you've never been more alive. Ready, he shoved aside the feeling that something was about to go wrong.

Lucas hit the gas, swerving first into the left lane, then abruptly right. The SUV accelerated, aimed straight at the store's front door. The SUV hit the sidewalk, the bumper sending the parking posts flying. They smashed into the jewelry store's front door, knocking it off its hinges, the front of the SUV plowing into the store itself.

A woman employee screamed as the three of them jumped out, guns pointed at the security guard and the others, screaming *"Bouge pas!"* Don't move! Patrice stuck his gun in the guard's face, grabbing the man's gun from his holster. Vincent and Nabil smashed the glass display cases, rapidly scooping up the jewels along with bits of broken glass into plastic bags. Everything like clockwork, except . . . *Merde.* Shit, Vincent thought. There were two customers in the store.

One was an old man, in his seventies at least, with a tanned pitted face like an unskinned potato. He wore plaid-style slacks that only a foreigner would wear and a purple-colored – Purple! – Hawaiian-style shirt. With him, was a slim young woman in a red leather mini-skirt. A dark-haired beauty – she could've been a super-model, *Alors*, a rich old man with a sexy young woman. Hardly a novelty on the Riviera or anywhere in the world for that matter, Vincent mentally shrugged as he shoveled handfuls of diamonds and jewelry into the plastic bag. Twenty seconds and done, he thought. At that moment, everything went off the rails.

Instead of finishing grabbing the jewels, Nabil stuck his gun into the old man's face and demanded his wallet. The old man, who'd no doubt been in there to buy something for his *petite amie* and even had the wallet in his hand, wouldn't give it to him.

"Leave it. There's no time! We came for the diamonds," Vincent snapped at Nabil, but it was already too late.

"Here," said the old man, holding out folded money in his other hand. An American; he spoke American-style English, not French. "I need the wallet."

Nabil did what anyone would do. He smashed the American in the face with his pistol and grabbed the money *and* the wallet.

"Enough of this stupidity! *Allons, vite,* let's go!" Vincent said, thinking that was the end of it, when the young woman stepped away from the American. She grabbed a handful of the diamonds from the last case they'd broken, but hadn't finished because of Nabil's idiocy, and said to Nabil in French, "Take me with you."

Just like that, the two of them like a gangster Romeo and Juliet. Vincent wanted to shoot them both, but all he could think of was the time. Their fifty-three seconds were past! Deal with it later, he decided, grabbing a final handful of diamonds, good ones, along with some ruby and sapphire rings and earrings from the last case.

"*Allez! Allez!*" Go! Go! Vincent shouted. But as Nabil turned to go, the American grabbed at his jacket to get his wallet. Nabil turned and shot the American in the face. For an instant the crack of the shot froze them like a photograph.

"Are you insane?" Vincent screamed at Nabil, but it was too late. The American was on the floor, one eye a grisly mess, blood pooling from the back of his head. The store employees stared, wide-eyed. One of them, a woman whimpered, then clapped her hand over her mouth. Vincent checked at his watch. *Merde!* They'd already been in the store too long – nearly two minutes! If they didn't leave at once they'd be caught.

"*Imbecile*," Vincent muttered, shoving Nabil ahead of him. They leapt into the SUV, the girl too. Even as the doors slammed shut, Lucas was already reversing back out to the street. He whipped the SUV backwards towards the Place Massena, ignoring the honking of an oncoming car, then spun 180, tires squealing to a stop. Lucas slammed the vehicle forward, wheels skittering on the tram tracks as they cut across the Place Massena and onto Boulevard Jean Jaurès. Behind them, they could hear the wail of a police siren back on Avenue de Verdun.

The quick moves by Lucas had bought them a critical few seconds, Vincent thought in the midst of his fury at Nabil. It might also throw off the *flics*, who would expect them to go one-way on Avenue de Verdun towards the seaside Promenade des Anglais.

They pulled off their balaclavas, glancing around at the traffic and each other with dazed, sweaty faces. Lucas headed towards the parking garage where they'd hidden the switch cars. Vincent stared at Nabil and held out his hand. Nabil handed him the plastic bag containing the jewels he'd grabbed along with the wallet from the American.

"The old man, he . . . " Nabil started to say.

"Shut up," Vincent said, seething. Thirty years, all he could think of. The penalty for murder during a robbery. Thirty years in a bottomless pit of *merde* like La Santé, filled with Arab *racaille* scum who'd stick a blade between your ribs for saying *bonjour*. He couldn't do it. Not again. The girl said nothing. She would have to be dealt with, Vincent thought.

What on earth made Nabil do it, he wondered. It made

no sense! A *coup de foudre*? Love at first sight, a *thunderbolt*. Was it possible? How could it be that without a word, in less than half a minute the idiot could fall in love with a woman he'd never seen before? And yet, how else to explain it? Only now because of it, they were *foutu*, all of them screwed. There would be an intense manhunt. Vincent hadn't been so furious since that time in La Santé when that son-of-a-whore Yanis sold him out just three months before he, Vincent was due for release and he'd had to gut the little rat.

Lucas turned onto the side street off the Place Garibaldi and drove into a building garage with a *Parking Privé* sign, motioning to the watchman, a Corsican, they'd bribed to keep his mouth shut. The Corsican opened the electric gate and they drove up the ramp into the structure.

Vincent got out of the SUV. He backed a blue Peugeot out of a parking space; Lucas parked the SUV in its place. Patrice, Nabil, and the young woman climbed into a second get-away car, a stolen Renault. The plan was for Patrice and Nabil to leave the Renault in the Nice airport parking where Nabil had stashed his old Clio. Patrice would lay low in a rented room in St. Laurent-du-Var. Nabil was supposed to stay in his cousin's empty flat in L'Ariane, a heavily North African district in northeast Nice. Only now Nabil had the girl with him.

Vincent got out of the Peugeot and rapped on the window of the other car. Nabil rolled the window down. "The *chatte*'s seen our faces," he said, using the vulgarity for the girl. "Keep her with you. Don't let her out of your sight."

The woman stared at him, her pretty face a mask, impossible to read. He sensed she understood how close she was to death. Better to cut her throat now, Vincent decided, reaching for his knife.

At that moment, the two-tone wail of a police siren

echoed off the garage's concrete walls. Vincent froze, then eased as the sound began to fade. They were running out of time. The *flics* would be setting up roadblocks all around the city while he stood there hesitating like a fool. He grabbed the young woman's hair, twisting her head to make her look at him, pricking her under the jaw with his stiletto.

"Give me your mobile," Vincent said. She handed it to him. He pressed the tip of the blade into the skin, drawing a drop of blood. "You've seen our faces. If you want to live, you don't leave, you don't talk, you don't piss without permission until we get back." And to Nabil: "If she makes a sound, tries to call anyone or get away, kill her – or we kill you."

CHAPTER TWO

ALPES-MARITIME PREFECTURE, NICE

JEAN-PIERRE BROCHARD KEPT GLANCING at the dashboard clock as he inched through traffic. He was running late. It was the *five-to-seven* time of day, the sun turning the windows of buildings and shops along the Promenade des Anglais to gold.

Normally at this hour, he would be having a stop-off *pastis* at a local café with one or two fellow judges before heading home. These days, mostly with his boss, Chief *Juge d'Instruction* Guy Mazeaud. There was a rumor that Mazeaud was about to be offered the post of President of the Court of Assizes, in which case, Mazeaud hinted he would recommend that he, Brochard be named Chief *Police Judiciaire* Prosecutor for the entire Alpes-Maritimes department.

Athletic, dark-haired, handsome, a graduate of ENS, the highly-selective École Normale Supérieure, and the equally exclusive Pantheon-Assas University, Brochard a rising star, a *procureur*, or investigative criminal prosecutor to keep one's eyes on. And though he had expressed no immediate interest in politics, he'd already been approached by political parties from both the right and the left to run for the National Assembly.

Only today, it was imperative he get home on time. Last night, he and his wife, Gabrielle, Gabi, had been up late, decorating their apartment for the party. It was his daughter, Juliette's, fourth birthday and all her little friends and cousins and their parents were on their way to his place. Instead, here he was driving in the opposite direction to the Préfecture near Nice Airport to look at a corpse; the man murdered in the Avenue de Verdun robbery. He'd gotten a last minute call from *chef de group*, Kurt Giroud, chief detective of the homicide and crime squad.

"Jean-Pierre, you better get over here," Giroud said. They'd worked together enough that Giroud called him by his first name and used the familiar "*tu*".

"Can't it wait?" Brochard had asked.

"No. This requires the *Procureur*. There's something about this corpse. You better come," Giroud said. Later, Brochard would wish he had never picked up the phone, had cut his hand off before he answered it. Though even he could never have imagined that it would up-end his life, endanger his family and force him to reconsider everything he believed in.

He turned up Route de Grenoble along the Var River, exiting a side street into the parking area for police officials. The gendarme on duty recognized him and waved him through the metal detector. He took the stairs down to the lower level, where Giroud was waiting in the coroner's examining room. As ever in France, the walls were a faded institutional gray; the room smelled of disinfectant.

With Giroud and Dr. Romain Lemoine, the salt-and-pepper bearded medical examiner in his white surgical scrubs, was Marie-Laure, Giroud's number two, her blond hair pinned back with a clip. The naked body of an older man, late-sixties or early seventies, presumably the man killed in the jewelry store robbery, lay on the examining slab. The cause of death was obvious, Brochard noted, glancing at the destroyed eye where a bullet had entered.

"What's so important it couldn't wait till tomorrow?" Brochard said impatiently.

"This," Dr. Lemoine said, lifting the dead man's right hand and separating out the thumb. "See the ridge on the skin around the nail down to the first joint?"

"What about it?" Brochard asked.

"I've only ever seen something like it once before," Giroud said. "A fingerprint transplant," nodding to Marie-Laure, who now that the *procureur* was here, took the hand into her own latex-gloved hands and began fingerprinting the dead man's fingers, starting with the thumb, that she notated as a transplant. "The thumb and index finger of both hands too."

"Really? What about ID?"

Giroud shook his head. "The robbers took his wallet."

"So our victim could've been a criminal too?" Brochard said. "Could he be connected to the robbery?"

"Impossible to say," Giroud shrugged, a Gallic gesture old as Charlemagne. "The store employees say not. They say he was shot because he wouldn't hand over his wallet to one of the *malfrats*." The slang word for criminals. "Or perhaps because of the girl. It's curious. In the store security video, she and the *malfrats* seemed not to know each other. Then in a matter of seconds, one of them grabs the wallet, the girl joins him and this one is dead," gesturing at the corpse.

"Perhaps she was in on it. Perhaps they both were," Brochard said.

"A feud between rivals? A possibility. The store

employees said the woman was pretty enough to be a model or an actress. Maybe they were fighting over her?" Giroud said.

"Then why the business with the wallet? It's not her. There's something else." Marie-Laure shook her head.

"So, our victim does not want to give anyone his wallet, even at the point of a gun, and had changed his thumb-print. You really did not want anyone to know who you are, did you, *monsieur*?" Brochard said to the corpse. "Do we have any information on who he might be?"

"He's an American," Marie-Laure said.

"How can you be so sure?"

"His dental work is American. The store employees said he spoke American-style English, not French, not English-English. Also, the appalling bad taste in clothes," she said with a half-smile. "Even for a rich American."

"And we know he had money because . . . ?"

"Buying diamonds on the Avenue de Verdun for a young woman forty years younger? Hard to imagine he was so great a lover," Marie-Laure shrugged.

"If he's a foreigner, it should be easy enough to track down who he is," Brochard said. "What about these *typique* American clothes? Do we know where they were purchased? See if a credit card was used."

"We're checking. We're also checking all the hotels, Airbnb, and other rentals. They were buying jewelry in plain sight, not trying to hide. We'll have something shortly," Giroud said.

"Of course," Brochard nodded.

"The robbers wore hoods?" Brochard asked. Giroud nodded. "So why did the girl go with them?"

"Maybe she was afraid of him. Wanted to get away," Marie-Laure said, indicating the corpse.

"Why? He wasn't buying her a big enough diamond?" said Dr. Lemoine.

"Maybe she's illegal. Maybe it's us she's afraid of," Giroud said.

"The thumb, the woman, the whole thing is strange," Marie-Laure said.

"I still don't see why – " Brochard said impatiently.

"The thumb's not the only reason I called you, Jean-Pierre. The dead American had two mobiles in his pockets. This one," Giroud said, showing Brochard in a plastic evidence bag, "is a pre-paid. One can buy it anywhere. We'll be looking at all the calls on it. But this one is something I've never seen," holding up a cell phone in his latex-gloved hand. "It has no apps, no contact numbers, nothing although we're checking for anything that might have been deleted, even though getting at it may be difficult. All it has on it is a single text message that came in exactly thirteen minutes after midnight. See," showing Brochard. The text on the screen read in English: 'Weather today in Cannes, partial sun with light rain, possible disturbance, temperature 17.' "Except as you know," Giroud continued. "It's been warm and sunny for the past several weeks. The temperature in Cannes today was 28. *Ah*, but here's the truly interesting part: when we tried to contact the number this text was sent from – the call appears to have originated from Riga in Latvia – we got a recorded message that the number was no longer in service and we were disconnected. Curious, no?"

"You're checking with the Latvian police authorities?"

"We've begun with the State Police in Riga. Still waiting to hear back, but their bureaucracy, *pouf.*" Giroud made a face.

"Like ours?"

"Worse"

"Curious message. What do you make of it?" Brochard asked.

"A code of some kind. The robbers may have accidently killed someone involved in a more serious criminal enterprise. A man of mystery, our dead American," Giroud said, placing the cell phone in a separate evidence bag.

"What are you going to do with it?" Brochard asked, indicating the cell phone.

"Keep it plugged in at the Prefecture, in case there's another text or call." Giroud lit a cigarette. "One never knows. Meanwhile, we'll check all the hotels and rentals, find out who this American was."

"Good. We want to wrap this up," Brochard said, glancing at his watch. Nearly 5:40. *Merde.* He had to get to Juliette's party. As it was, his wife Gabi would have his head. "It's my daughter's birthday," he said by way of explanation, heading for the door. "Call me as soon as you get anything."

CHAPTER THREE

ZAMORA, MEXICO

THE SLIM YOUNG woman named Casey Ramirez sat in a sawdust cantina, listening to a mariachi with a hand-painted guitar crooning an off-key version of "Adelita". The air was thick with the smells of *cerveza* and tortillas baking in the kitchen. If she managed to live through this day, she thought, that's what she would remember: the mariachi and the smell of tortillas. Then he walked in.

He was a small man in a rumpled plaid shirt, jeans, no tie, high-heeled cowboy boots, with short arms whose only purpose seemed to be to feed his mouth. But the instant he entered the cantina, the mariachi stopped. Everyone went silent. It seemed to Casey she could hear the dust motes in the sunbeams that came through cracks above the door as they settled to the floor.

A chair scraped as one man started to get up, thought better of it and sat back down. A half-dozen bodyguards, red bandanas over the lower parts of their faces, cradling M4 carbines, took up positions by the front door and around the room. The people in the cantina, mostly local workmen stopping in out of the heat from the *Zocalo*, the town square, for a cerveza, were still as statues, the coppery scent of fear as real in the room as the smell of tortillas.

The small man in the plaid shirt came over to Casey's table. He sat, so close she could smell his aftershave. Armani, she thought. Having him that close, made her suddenly nauseous. She had to squeeze her legs together not to pee herself.

"You do this, Casey, you're on your own," her boss, Kent Ferguson, had told her back in the HSI office in Long Beach, California. *"Your connection might get you in, but there's no backup. No way we can get you out. You do this, you're solo all the way."*

"Coronita – and bring limes," the small man said in Spanish to the waiter who materialized at the table like magic and then to Casey: "Bad for my stomach – but I have to drink something. A matter of image. It captures us all, you understand?"

She understood all right. So did everyone in the room. And in the city and all of Mexico – and along the Rio Grande and in Washington, D.C. too.

He was *El Pintor*, the Painter. The head of the Black Knights drug cartel. A psychopathic killer whose cruelty was legend. It was said he once had a rival skinned alive and then had the skin tanned for a chair for his study. Once when a police chief in Zitacuaro arrested two of his men, he had the police chief, the chief's wife, and every member of his family, thirteen of them children, cousins, grandmothers, down to a three-month-old baby, killed, their bodies hung from a road overpass.

He got the nickname, *the Painter* because he once painted a room of his villa with the blood of the leader of a rival cartel. He, more than the Mexican federal government, ruled over a sizeable portion of Michoacan province. Now he was sitting next to her.

He waited. And when she didn't answer, he half-smiled, his teeth yellow from tobacco.

"It's good you know to keep your mouth shut," he said. "Most people, their mouths only get them in trouble. They talk too much, eat too much, some people maybe breathe too much."

The waiter brought the beer and limes. The waiter's hand trembled as he set the glass down, poured the beer and left. She and *el Pintor* sat in silence.

"So why does Don Ernesto send a skinny *concha* like you?" Using the insult word for a female. "to see me over something so trivial?" he said. His brown eyes scanned her, her body. Button eyes like a shark, she thought. Nothing human behind them.

"He wouldn't like you calling me that. A matter of family," she said, trying to keep it business or it would spiral out of control in a second.

"Would he not?" he said in Spanish. "Maybe I should give you to my men? You know what they would do before they gutted you like a fish and threw what was left to rot on the side of the highway? Why shouldn't I?"

Jesus, right to it, she thought, barely breathing. What if she'd miscalculated? Whatever you do, she told herself, don't show him how scared you are. When she was a kid and they were separated by the Los Angeles foster care system, her big sister Jessica had given her a set of rules to memorize in case Jessie wouldn't be there to protect her. Jessica's Rule Six was: *Never show fear. What you feel is yours; what you show belongs to others.*

"Why start a problem with Don Ernesto when there's no

reason? And you would force Washington, to do something." She was banking on him knowing she was an HSI Special Agent – the Homeland Security Investigations Directorate was the federal agency responsible for investigating the illegal trafficking or movement of people or goods across U.S. borders – and that he wouldn't want to poke a stick at the American bear if he didn't have to. "For what? For nothing? And perhaps we can help each other."

He reached over and pushed his hand between her legs. She thought of closing her legs, but didn't dare move or say anything, not sure if he was doing it to make sure she was a woman or just to show her he could do anything he wanted with her. She kept her hands on the table. By habit, she curled the fingers of her left hand to make them less noticeable. He pressed harder with his thumb, so painful so she nearly gasped, then let her go.

"So, a *panocha*, after all." Confirming she was a woman. "There have been attempts by those who want me dead," he explained with an expression she couldn't read until she realized it was his attempt at a foxhole camaraderie. "Don Ernesto was right about you. Most men would be pissing themselves. This girl, this *chinita*, what do you want?"

"A girl from Thailand. Her mother asked me to find her, get her back," Casey said.

"The mother, she's rich? A person of importance?"

"Not even. She works in a restaurant in Long Beach, smaller than this cantina. They took her daughter and now, she can't breathe. So for the first time in a long time, I went to Don Ernesto. Now, like a crazy woman, I'm here, talking to you." She stopped.

He tasted his cerveza. "You'll owe me a favor," he said.

She knew he would ask for something. The only question was how much and could she do it? What's a life worth, remembering how she sat over iced tea with the Thai woman in a strip mall restaurant in Long Beach's Eastside neighborhood. The woman showed her an image on her cell phone of a teenage girl standing on a flower-draped deck beside a canal that she assumed was in Bangkok.

"I can't promise. You know who I am; what I do. Either help me or," she said, "we finish our *cervezas* and you'll do what you were going to do anyway."

"Like a *habanera*," he nodded, comparing her to a fiery chili pepper. Coming from him, almost an accolade. "How did you come to Don Ernesto? I don't think you're of his blood." Give him that. A sociopath, but he did his homework, she thought.

"He took me in when I was a kid. I had nowhere to go, no one, nothing." She put her business card on the table. He didn't pick it up. His men would do it for him. "I'm at the Hotel Casa Grande in Morelia."

"By the Plaza de Armas?"

She nodded. "The same. I'm there tonight. Tomorrow, I'm back in California."

"The men you want, I know them. They are not men of honor, you understand?" Coming from el Pintor that was something. "*Chavalas* like you they kill for nothing, for pleasure. *Estupido*. To kill a *puta* you own is bad business, but *pendejos* like these . . . you're looking for trouble." He touched her cheek with his damp finger that smelled of cerveza and lime, leaving a scent that lingered.

"I need to know who they are and where I can find them."

He wrinkled his brow at her as if she were a foreign object, something from another world. "Why are you doing this? To do for strangers is surely strange, but for a *chinita*, a woman without money is beyond comprehension. My brother, when he was young, wanted to become a priest. He was like you. I used to think, how is it possible, such purity? But then with time, life intrudes. Even my brother, the almost-priest, became realistic."

"What happened?"

"He died. A competitor killed him. A common thing," El Pintor glanced at the ceiling, where a wooden fan turned slowly. "No matter the path, the end is the same."

"If these men are an inconvenience for you, I can make them go away."

"If that were to happen, and I say, *if*, this meeting never happened. You understand, woman? Me, you must never disappoint," El Pintor said, getting up. His men tensed, got ready. One of them picked up her card from the table and put it in his pocket.

"It is understood. That can never happen," she said.

CHAPTER FOUR

MARSEILLES, FRANCE

WITH EVERYTHING in his life going to hell, trouble with the Americans was the last thing Brochard needed. At first, the investigation of the Avenue de Verdun case had gone routinely. Based on the jewelry store's security camera videos and the gang's *modus operandi*, Kurt Giroud's team determined that the robbery was the work of the "Blue Panthers," a gang of jewel thieves named after the famous Pink Panther gang, called "Blue" because on several occasions they'd worn blue balaclavas on a job. To get tips from the public, Brochard had his office leak that information to the media, who ran with it.

Giroud's people located the BMW SUV, stolen of course, in a garage on Rue Barla near the Place Garibaldi. From descriptions from the store employees, security camera footage, dents and scratches on the vehicle, they had no doubt that it was the SUV used in the robbery.

The garage attendant, a Corsican, confirmed that the young woman from a security camera image from the jewelry store was with the gang of four men, one of whom may have been a North African. Their leader was a Frenchman with a mustache. He wore sunglasses and no observable scars or tattoos. The Corsican's descriptions were too general to be of much use, as were the descriptions he provided to the police sketch artist.

"He's lying, the little turd. They paid him off," Detective Marie-Laure told Giroud. They continued to sweat the Corsican, though despite going through hundreds of criminal photos, he was unable to identify any of the gang. He did better on the cars. The gang had left the garage in two cars: the leader and one other left in a late model blue Peugeot 308, the two other men and the young woman in a white Renault Megane.

The next day, the white Renault, also stolen, was discovered abandoned in the Nice Airport parking lot. Airport security camera footage was too far away to be able to identify their faces. It showed two men and the young woman getting into a Renault Clio and driving away. Police bulletins on the blue Peugeot and the Clio were broadcast across France, Monaco, and Italy.

Meanwhile, they got a hit on the dead man. According to a copy of a passport page attached to a rental agreement of a villa in Cap d'Antibes, the victim was Layton Gary McCord, an American from Chevy Chase, Maryland.

With the murder victim identified, once Giroud's team got their hands on the Blue Panthers and with luck, a line on the stolen jewels, Brochard could take the case to Mazeaud for prosecution. When Mazeaud asked how it was going, Brochard was able to reply, "We're close, Guy. We should have something shortly." Words like birds flying away he would come to regret.

The problem with the Americans began shortly after

Marie Laure notified the U.S. consulate in Marseilles, standard procedure for a foreign national involved in a criminal investigation. She also requested additional information about the dead American that might help explain the odd sequence in the video of what had happened. The way the girl abandoned the American even before he was shot, grabbed the diamonds and went off with the gang suggested that maybe she was in on it or that they all knew each other. Perhaps the killing was a result of a dispute within the gang.

Two days later, instead of a normal response, Giroud received a message saying there was a problem about the dead American. Instead of sending the usual paperwork, the U.S. consul, Martha Ravich requested a confidential meeting at the American consulate in Marseilles. Brochard didn't like the sound of that. Neither did Giroud.

"*La vache!*" Damn it! "This is a murder on French territory during the commission of a crime in Nice," Giroud protested, bursting in Brochard's office. "The Americans are holding back. Smells like old fish," he said, tapping his nose.

"We have to be careful," Brochard said. When it came to the Americans, their superiors would only back them up so far.

"What do I tell her?"

"We shouldn't meet on their territory. Tell Madame Ravich we'll meet her at the Marseilles police headquarters in the Old Port. This is still France," Brochard said.

Driving with Giroud on the boring stretches of the A8 autoroute to Marseilles, gave Brochard time to contemplate the disasters piling up. Career-wise, he was stuck. With Mazeaud staying on, he was like a piece in a chess game when one's opponent says, "that piece cannot be moved." Worse.

Gabi was talking about going back to Paris and taking Juliette with her.

They'd fought before, his *petite affaire* with that movie actress, Elodie and all the *oh-la-la* that came with her at Cannes that in the end amounted to a sour taste in the mouth and a feeling you've fallen among a circus of fools. But this time, coming so late to Juliette's birthday party, after everyone, even his mother, had left, and even though he'd bought Juliette a new dress, a Lego Disney Princess set, and the green *Lulu Vroumette* doll, the one from her favorite TV show, Gabi told him what he'd done, Papa not being at his own daughter's birthday, was "*impardonnable.*" Unforgivable.

Gabi, slender, dark-haired, stood there, her eyes like weapons. Brochard knew this time he had crossed a line. She'd had enough, she said. For a long time now, she'd been wanting to go back to Paris, back to her career as an industrial product designer that she'd put on hold to follow him to Nice; to keep them together as a family and to help run the family's furniture store business that his *Maman*, because of her dementia could no longer manage.

He'd sensed her nostalgia. How not? She'd been a rising talent as a product designer and even before they'd left, people had begun to take notice. For months she'd been reminiscing about their old flat in the ninth *arrondissement*, their local café, but he thought once he got his promotion, she'd let it go. There was also the problem of the family business. The two Brochard stores of *Provençal*-style furniture had been an institution in Nice for nearly half a century. One couldn't just walk away, especially with *Maman* losing a piece of herself day by day.

But if Gabi had been willing to give up her dream for his, to keep the business thriving and build a life of their own in a sleek high-rise on the Côte d'Azur, she wasn't willing to do it alone, with just her and Juliette.

She pulled down the birthday decorations with sharp, angry movements. If Jean-Pierre's job was going to be his mistress, she and Juliette were better off back in Paris where she had her *Maman* and interesting friends and could work at something she cared about. And if she were to make the move, now was the time, "before Juliette starts her *Grande*, the most important years of *Maternelle* grade school," she declared, face flushed, Her tone of finality, the angry way she said it was a knife in the heart.

The worst of it was the thought of how much they'd both changed. Now riding on the A8, he couldn't help thinking of the way she was the night they met; the exquisite girl with the *gamine*-style haircut at that corporate reception where she was being honored for her design of a new computer tablet. He went up to her and assuming she must have a boyfriend, asked her what her *copain* was doing and she'd replied, "Does a woman ever know what men are really up to?"

Later that night, they walked to the Pont Neuf. She'd made a joke about Camus – "*C'est vrai, it is essential to know the night*, but sometimes it helps to see too," she'd said, riffing on a famous quote. As if it were possible – to be so beautiful and so intelligent – looking at him with those incredible blue eyes. A *bateau-mouche*, strung with lights like a Christmas tree, slid down the Seine beneath them. She said, "Love's the only game worth playing, because it isn't a game. To lose is a little death." And that first kiss, the two of them, the Seine and the lights of *tout* Paris. No, it was impossible that she could leave.

"Don't go, please," Brochard said. "Let me finish this case and I'll fix things, I promise. We'll go back to Paris."

But she had already gone into the bedroom and closed the door. He wasn't sure she'd even heard him.

"Anything from the Latvians on that mobile number?" Brochard asked. They had turned south on the autoroute through Plan de Compagne.

"It seems all inquiries for Latvia have to go through a certain Colonel Seibelis."

"And?"

"He hasn't returned any of our calls or emails. Marie Laure says she's beginning to wonder if he exists," Giroud said.

So, going nowhere. For Brochard his life, the case, Gabi, the family business, the ground he stood on had turned to shifting sand. The atoms that make up our bodies, everything around us is mostly empty space. The world only seems solid. Even France wasn't the same France, he thought as they drove past a stream of Arabic graffiti spray-painted on the concrete side walls along the A51.

Madame Ravich was a woman of what the French call, *a certain age.* She wore a woman's gray business suit as though it were body armor. They met in the borrowed office of Marseilles' Director of Police, the window overlooking the cathedral. Her deputy handed Giroud's original paperwork back to him.

"I want to assure you we expedited your inquiry marked 'Urgent' directly to our embassy in Paris. Unfortunately, *monsieur,*" she said in passable French. "The request cannot be completed."

"What's the problem? Our request was standard procedure in cases where foreign nationals are involved," Brochard replied in English. No more nonsense, thinking of Gabi. Time to get to the bottom of this.

"You are the Prosecutor for this case, Monsieur Brochard?" she asked. Brochard nodded. "Unfortunately, *monsieur*, we can't complete the request because the victim, this presumed American, Layton Gary McCord is already dead. According to our records, he died more than thirty years ago at age six in Charlotte, North Carolina. The passport this dead man, whoever he was, was using, is a fake. To be more precise, a legitimate U.S. passport was issued, but it was based on false information. A birth certificate and the Social Security number of the dead Layton Gary McCord was provided to obtain it. Unfortunately, the passport was issued before we fully implemented computer matching against death records from every state," she said.

"So who is he?" Brochard asked.

"We haven't a clue," she said, her posture suggesting this meeting was a waste of her valuable time.

"We also sent his fingerprints and DNA, Madame. Surely that could be used by the FBI for identification," Giroud said, tapping his fingers on the table.

"Not the thumb or other transplanted prints," the deputy, Chris Johnson remarked.

"This individual appears to have had fingerprint transplants which suggests criminal activity," Giroud said. "But surely, the remaining fingers and DNA should be sufficient for an identification."

"I'm afraid unlike France, America doesn't have a National Identity Card system. We don't fingerprint or have a DNA registry on all our citizens."

"You should," Giroud murmured.

"Well, if anyone ever asks me, I'll be sure to let the United

States Congress know your opinion," she said. "Unfortunately, there's little more I can do."

"The real fingerprints and DNA must belong to someone. You could run them against your criminal database. Surely one doesn't need Congress's permission for that, Madame," Brochard countered.

"No, we do not and in fact we requested that. Show him the FBI report," she said to Johnson.

The deputy took out his laptop, pulled a file up on the screen and showed them a report that said the results were "Negative; no matches."

Madame Ravich and her deputy stood to go.

"We want to be cooperative, truly," she said. "It's possible your crime victim is an American, but we honestly don't know who he is any more than you."

Giroud also stood, blocking their way. "Pardon, Madame, but it was more than fingerprints and DNA. We also sent photos of the dead man's face. We're convinced this man is an American," he said in French, Brochard translating. "His clothes, his dental work, the type of English he spoke according to the store employees, the man's passport, faked or not. Everything about him tells us he's an American. He changed his fingerprints, which is not something normal citizens do, but not his face. He was buying diamonds, so he had money. Someone in America knows who he is. We require your assistance."

"We sent the photos, but so far we've received nothing further from the FBI," she said. "We'll do what we can, but for now . . . I'm afraid that's it. If you get anything new, forward it to me and I'll get it straight to Washington. For now, we're at a dead end."

. . .

The drive back to Nice on the A8. Giroud lit a Gauloise Blue, cracking the window open to suck out the smoke. He drove fast, now and then glancing at Brochard. On one side the autoroute was screened by a line of trees; on the other the slopes of the Alpes Maritimes, studded with white rocks poking out of the ground like the bones of the continent.

"She's lying, that American *pimbêche*," Giroud grumbled, calling her a stuck-up.

"Of course, but which part?" Brochard said.

"They got back to us in two days. Normally, the FBI's queued up for weeks – and that's for their own American police departments, much less a jewelry robbery in France. They checked it all: fingerprints, DNA, photos, everything in the FBI database and got back to us poor stupid *policiers* in France almost before we finished tapping 'Send'. *Formidable!*"

"Agreed. They put on a cabaret for us. The question is, why? Up till now this has been an ordinary, if somewhat bizarre case. Suddenly, not so ordinary."

"So what game are they playing?" Giroud exhaled a stream of blue Gauloise smoke.

"You know, I once had a law professor, Tricaud, who used to say, 'Sometimes when one is fishing for carp, you hook a whale.' So who was this American, this Layton Gary McCord? Suddenly, from the Americans we have a complete lack of cooperation under the guise of them tripping over themselves to help. It has the smell of bad fish."

"The robbery part is simple. We're convinced it's the same gang that hit the Cartier store in Lyon and the one in Cannes."

"The Blue Panthers," Brochard agreed as they zipped past other cars as though they were standing still, causing Brochard to reflect, not for the first time, that Giroud's driving was an exercise in fatalism.

"*Bien sur*, it's them. Their way of doing things. The planning, cutting the street parking posts the previous night, the SUV smashing through the front door. The American is an unexpected complication. Not their style. Something went wrong," Giroud said.

"How do you know?"

"They never killed anyone before."

Brochard frowned. "This business with the Americans, the phone number from Riga, a man who changes his thumbprints. What does that say to you?"

"Mafia, or a secret intelligence agency perhaps," Giroud said.

"You think the American was a spy?"

"I'm just a simple policeman," Giroud shrugged.

"So you keep telling me," Brochard said.

"Do we bring in the DGSE?" The French secret intelligence service. "Could make things messy," Giroud said. A disaster, Brochard reflected. Once called in, they might take the case over, drag in the CIA, probably also the Quai des Orfèvres, as the National Police Judiciaire headquarters in Paris was called. They would tie him up for months – and Gabi would be gone, back to Paris, Juliette with her.

"Not yet," he said. "For now, we just focus on the crime, the robbery, the murder and the 'Blue Panthers.' With luck we'll get a lead on the dead man before the Americans do."

"We'll check for any purchases he made. People he dealt with in Cap d'Antibes where he rented the villa. His mobile, perhaps?"

"Push harder on the Latvians. This code business with the mobile makes no sense. One can't tell if it's the lard or the pig," quoting the old proverb. "Think we'll get any more messages on it?" Brochard asked.

"Probably not," Giroud said.

But he was wrong. A text came in late that night on the dead man's cell phone at four minutes twenty seven seconds after midnight from the supposedly out-of-service number in Riga. It read: "Weather today in Cannes, heavy rain, flooding on Boulevard Alexandre III, temperature 21.4." More code, Giroud thought. The weather in Cannes that day had been sunny and warm, temperature 30 Celsius. Giroud told Marie Laure to forward the Latvian texts to the national Police Judiciaire headquarters in Paris for analysis. Though they kept the mobile plugged in and checked it several times a day, there were no more messages.

CHAPTER FIVE

MORELIA, MEXICO

CASEY MET Father Miguel in the dining room of her hotel, the Casa Grande. Despite the dinner hour and the lit lamps on the tables, she and the priest were the only customers. Like her, he sat alone. He had a beak nose that reminded her of a bird. After glancing at her a number of times, he suddenly stood before her, a crow in a stained black cassock, smelling of sweat and cerveza. A bad omen, reminding her of the Chicana women when she was a little girl and still lived with Erica and Jessie in that roach-infested apartment on Loma Vista in Central L.A. All the women of that neighborhood were superstitious. They believed if you walked near the L.A. river at night, the Llorona would get you, or if a child crawled between their legs, she had to crawl back again or she wouldn't grow.

"With permission, senorita. You're North American?" he said in English, swaying slightly, leaning his weight on the back of a chair, waiting for her to invite him to sit. His eyes were not normal, the pupils pinpoints. Christ, he's a user, she thought.

When the priest sat, she said: "*Si desea, podemos hablar en español.*" Offering to speak Spanish.

"English, please; for the practice. The CYO sometimes sends us volunteers from the States. I'm Father Miguel." He tucked his napkin in his neck over his priest's collar. "And you are . . . ?"

"Casey," she said.

"Are you Catholic?" The price of admission for talking to priests, she thought. Something off about him though, more than drugs, her antenna crackling.

"No."

"You were in the church," he said. It wasn't a question. He'd either spotted her – or she was being watched, she thought. In the rental car coming back from Zamora on the Guadalajara-Atlacomulco highway, she'd been followed by a black sedan through miles of empty farm land. They could've pulled her over and killed her at any time. Even after the sedan turned off at San Agustin, the feeling of being watched wouldn't go away. If *El Pintor* wanted to get rid of her, she was as good as dead.

Coming into Morelia, after checking into the hotel, she'd walked across the plaza and sat by herself in the cathedral, its interior white and empty and full of light. Until the priest sat at her table, she thought she'd been alone.

"Just visiting." She took a sip of Tecate beer, a slice of lime on the rim of the glass.

"Not a believer."

"Not anything." What do you want, priest, she almost said aloud.

"Your family perhaps?" he asked. My mother went to the same church as you, she thought: the Church of Heroin, but kept it to herself. When she didn't answer, Father Miguel nodded. "The people here believe with much force. Many times I think their faith is bigger than mine. I say the words, but with them is the music."

Maybe you should find another line of work. Maybe we both should, she thought, not answering.

"If one may ask, what brought you here?"

She was tempted to shock him by telling him she was waiting for *El Pintor*'s men. Or did he already know?

"Just visiting," she said again. The waiter brought fresh tortillas. Casey ordered a *tomatillo*, a salad; Father Miguel, *flautas* and tequila.

"Once a month I treat myself to a meal here and try to find someone to practice my English," he said, glancing around the room. "Not so many people come these days."

"No?" she said.

"The cartels. People are afraid." He made a face. "Why did you come to the church today, senorita? Truly?" So he hadn't come over to practice his English, she thought.

"Something to do. Does it really matter?"

"This is a good place. I don't want to see bodies hanging from the overpasses." A practice of the Black Knights and the Zetas cartels.

"You think that's who I am?" In her head, red lights were flashing. He wasn't selling Jesus. *El Pintor* had sent him and she was on her own, she reminded herself. No cavalry to the rescue.

"After you left the church, two men came. They wanted to know if you met anyone. Do you have trouble?" he said. Casey looked around. Was she being watched this second? Or was the priest their spy?

"Doesn't everyone? Did you know these men?" she said.

He shook his head. "I know the type. *Narcotraficantes.* Cartel men."

So, maybe not a spy. Treat him like a witness, she thought. "What makes you so sure?"

"They had the look. You know this look?" She knew it. She'd grown up with it in Central L.A. "These men, they kill anyone."

"Even priests?"

"Even babies," he said. The waiter brought the food. Father Miguel gulped his tequila like a sailor on a three-day bender. His eyes were swimming when he looked at her. He's scared to death, she thought. Well, who wouldn't be? "God watches, senorita. Even when we don't see. Even when we don't want Him, especially when we don't want Him," he whispered, glancing over his shoulder as if God was standing behind him.

Get away from me. I'm not a character in your God's TV show, priest, Casey thought. Maybe she should leave this second, make a run for the airport. Except if they were coming for her, she'd never make it. Don't make it easy for them, she thought.

"I went to the church because it's quiet. I wanted to think," she lied. Why *had* she gone into the church? Not to pray to empty air, but because there was a real chance today was her last day on earth. She wanted a place of silence, where she could think about her sister, Jessie and her Rules; to steady herself; along with her ever-present ridiculous fantasy that someday she'd be somewhere, a bar, a church, a crowded street, and look up and Jessie would just be there.

"What will you do?" Father Miguel said.

"Are you asking for yourself, Father, or for them?" She pulled her SIG Sauer 9mm from the holster at the small of her back and placed it on the table, her hand resting on the gun. "Tell them I'll be waiting," she said.

Casey stood in her hotel room balcony doorway, looking out at the night and the trees in shadow and the streetlights in the Plaza de Armas. They have to come soon, she thought. Finally as she was about to undress for bed, there was a knock on the door. She picked up the pistol.

The second I open it, they'll shoot. I won't stand a chance, she thought. Another part of her tried to reason, if they were going to break in and kill her, why bother to knock?

All this for a girl she didn't know who might already be dead. She walked to the door, the pistol in her hand behind her back. If they were there to kill her, she wouldn't even get a chance to fire back, remembering her training at the Federal Law Enforcement Training Center in Brunswick, Georgia. Oh God, she thought. Not breathing, she opened the door.

Two young Mexican men, the bulges of guns under their jackets unmistakable, stood in the hallway. One of them, pointy gel-shiny hair like a hedgehog, handed her a computer plug-in drive. They politely wished her "*Buenas noches*" and left. No rape, no shots.

Casey locked the door and leaned against it. Relief flooded her, knees nearly giving way. She'd survived this time, but what would her sister have said? She could almost hear her voice: *If you dance with the devil, sooner or later you dance to the devil's tune.* But she had the file!

She rushed to her laptop and plugged in the drive. On it was a single file with a list of names, dates, locations, and cell phone numbers of nearly a dozen Latin American and Asian trafficking rings. She recognized some of them. They ran Thai, Cambodian and Central American women through Mexico into California and Texas. One of the names was of a trafficker in Texas named Johnny Ha. A comment in the file indicated that his group was of greatest interest for finding the Thai girl. She Googled the address shown for Johnny Ha; a house off Highway 12 in northwest Dallas. Instead of flying back to L.A., she could change her flight and be in Dallas in the morning. Excited, she thought if she moved fast enough, she might be able to save the girl before they moved her.

Taking a deep breath, she pocketed the plug-in drive and stepped out onto the balcony. The night was alive with stars and the smell of *tacos* and the lights of the Plaza de Armas.

CHAPTER SIX

THE RUSSIAN'S shop was on Via San Lorenzo, a side street near the port. It was late afternoon, the shadows of the buildings lengthening over the piazza. Vincent the Cat and Lucas ignored the weathered sign above the steel front door that read: "San Lorenzo Oro;" it was always locked. Instead, they entered a narrow corridor through the side door from the *Tabacchi* shop. Glancing at the mounted CCTV camera, they waited till the Russian buzzed them in.

The Russian's back room, used for both a workshop and a meeting room, was dim by contrast with the bright daylight outside, lit only by a goose-necked high precision lamp. Neatly lined on the workbench were the tools of his trade: a high-precision scale, a laser diamond cutter, a bruting grinder and a horizontal diamond polishing wheel.

The Russian was a bearded man with wire-rimmed glasses, his fingers stained yellow by the R1 Red cigarettes he chain-smoked. Sipping tea from a glass, he looked like a conspirator from a nineteenth century novel. Clearly not thrilled to see them, he motioned for them to sit.

"You're on the *televisione*," the Russian said in accented English.

Vincent frowned. He could feel the price dropping. On the drive to Genoa, they'd kept the car radio tuned to Radio Azur for the news. The robbery in Nice was the lead story. According to the radio announcer, the police weren't talking, despite the fact that a bystander, a customer in the store had been killed. A police insider revealed that the authorities suspected the robbery "was the work of the notorious gang known as the 'Blue Panthers.'" *Eh bien*, they got that part right; that was them, though their balaclavas were black now, Vincent thought. The announcer said the manhunt for the Blue Panthers extended all across France.

"Just a name for the media. They know nothing," Vincent said, setting the plastic bag containing the diamonds on the table.

"Murder. I don't need you bring this to my door," the Russian said, not making a move to touch the bag. A bad sign. We're too hot, Vincent thought.

"The killing was an accident. But the diamonds are first class," Vincent said, opening the bag and spilling a handful of rings, earrings, pendants, and loose diamonds on the black velvet display cloth. "Also these good ones," he added, picking out from his pocket the fifteen loose diamonds that were D or E flawless and bigger than two and a half carats, six of them more than three carats and placing them separately on the velvet.

The Russian flicked the loose diamond rings and smaller stone jewelry dismissively with his finger. He picked up one of the three-carat stones with a pair of tweezers and using his loupe, examined it under the lamp light. He did the same with a second three carat stone, then looked quickly at the others.

"E's, two F's, no D's," he said. "Sixty."

Vincent felt the blood rushing to his head. Sixty thousand euros. Wholesale, the three-carat stones alone were worth at least four hundred thousand. Black market value with fences who'd cheat their own mother, a hundred easy.

"You're talking just the three-carats?" he asked.

"The lot," the Russian said, putting the loupe down. "It's too hot. Every one of these stones, even the one-carats, will have to be re-cut, re-numbered, re-bruted and polished. A mountain of work – You're all over TV, Internet. Famous. *Congratulazioni*! Congratulations! The Carabinieri have already been here to check. Even in Surat or Hong Kong I'll be lucky to find a buyer. "

"Piss on this. The small ones alone are worth more than sixty," Lucas said.

"Sell to someone else. This kind of trouble, I don't need," the Russian said, folding his arms. Lucas reached for the stones. Vincent stopped him.

"We'll take the sixty," he said. If they were this hot, if the Russian thought they were this hot, they needed to clean up their mess and move fast.

The Russian reached into a drawer and pulled out bound stacks of hundred-euro notes, each stack ten thousand euros. Lucas stared at the money and the drawer. Vincent almost smiled to himself. It wasn't hard to read Lucas' mind. Just grab the money from the drawer and run. But the Russian was connected to both the Russian Mafia and the Camorra, the Italian Mafia syndicate, who used his diamonds as a way to quickly launder and move money. Only a candidate for a straitjacket would've contemplated robbing him. The Russian counted out six stacks.

"This isn't what we planned," Lucas said.

"Nothing is what we planned," Vincent said and to the Russian, "Not a good price, *mon ami*."

"You shouldn't be so famous, Vincent the Cat. In our business, that's expensive," the Russian said. "The loose ends, the killing? All cleaned up?" So that was it, Vincent thought. If Nabil or the girl talked, if the flics didn't get them, the Russians or the Camorra would.

"Don't worry. No one's going to come knocking on your door, Russian," Vincent growled, putting the stacks of money in the plastic bag he'd kept the diamonds in. He and Lucas got up to leave.

"Let's hope the man you killed didn't have friends," the Russian said as they left the shop.

Night settled around them as they drove back to France on the E80, the lights ahead on the *autostrada* like yellow stars in the darkness. Something had gone wrong. Nabil wasn't answering his cell phone. Using a different mobile, Vincent called Patrice and told him to meet them outside Nabil's place.

"It's like that, is it?" Patrice commented.

"We'll see you there," Victor said.

It was almost midnight by the time they reached Nice. At this hour, there was little traffic in this part of Nice. The street off the *autoroute* was dimly-lit and silent. A concrete wall blocked the lights from buildings on the opposite side of the railroad tracks bordering the river bed. They turned onto an overpass over the tracks and the river.

Lucas drove cautiously through the narrow streets of the *banlieu* as though they were mined. L'Ariane was a *Maghrebi* North African neighborhood; a precinct of graffitied apartment buildings, battered older-model cars and clusters of Muslim teenagers still out despite the late hour. French hip-hop blared from a corner café. Lucas nudged Vincent. Nabil's white Clio was parked in front of a Coiffure Mod hair salon.

The little *salaud* bastard Vincent thought. Was he here all the time and didn't pick up my call? Him and the girl? They'd soon see about that. Time to finish this, he thought as Lucas maneuvered into a parking space. Patrice was waiting, leaning against a lamp-post next to the pizza place on the corner, cigarette dangling from his lips.

"There's a light on," Patrice said, coming over.

They glanced up at the balcony of Nabil's apartment. Light showed from behind closed shades. Lucas went to the front door and pushed the buzzer for Nabil's apartment.

No answer. He rang again. Nothing. Vincent told Patrice to watch the street and shielded by Lucas, opened the door with a pick. They rode up in the elevator, none of them saying what they thought, or perhaps, Vincent decided, they were all thinking the same thing. The little *salaud*.

Patrice pressed the light button on Nabil's floor. Arabic music came from one of the apartments down the hallway. Outside Nabil's apartment door, they took out their guns and snapped on sound suppressors. Vincent knocked on the door.

"Nabil, it's me. Open up," Vincent called. No answer. He knocked harder. "Don't play games, Nabil. We saw the light. Open up," Vincent said. He took Nabil's key out of his pocket and nodding to Lucas and Patrice to be ready, clicked the lock open. They charged into the apartment, ready to fire.

The apartment was empty. A light was on in the kitchenette, dirty dishes piled in the sink, along with the remains of old pizza, but Nabil and the girl from the jewelry store were gone.

"Where the *merde* is he? His car's still downstairs," Lucas said, looking around the living room. Patrice checked the kitchen. Vincent went to the bedroom and searched the closet. It was empty except for a few hangers and a torn OGC Nice football tee-shirt.

"They're gone," Vincent said. "Wait." He went to the chest of drawers. The top drawer was empty. He pulled it out and threw it on the bed. The second drawer had a few socks, underwear, condoms. He dumped it on the floor, turning the drawer upside down. Patrice came in and watched. The third drawer was full of clothes, jeans, shirts, a couple of cigarette cartons. Vincent felt each one of the pieces of clothing before tossing it away. He opened his Laguiole folding knife and used it to pry up one section of the bottom of the drawer.

"False bottom," he explained. "I made Nabil show me where he kept his *caisse*," his stash. The compartment was empty. Vincent sat cross-legged on the floor amid the over-turned drawers and crumpled clothes. "He's left us no choice," he said.

"He's crazy," Patrice said. "With all the heat on us, he knew we'd be back. He chose her over us."

"Nabil was always an idiot. She'll dump him faster than that old fool she was with," Vincent said.

"So where are they?" Lucas said, lighting a cigarette and sitting on the edge of the bed.

"They'll need cash. Nabil didn't have much left from the last job," Patrice said.

"What about the woman? Maybe she had money from her *papa-gâteau*?" Her sugar daddy, Lucas said.

"You think they planned this?" he said, getting up. "The whole thing happened in a second."

"Maybe *she* did," Lucas said, flicking his cigarette ash on the floor. "Maybe she wanted to dump that old *papa-gâteau*. She grabbed some diamonds. I saw her."

Vincent thought about the *flics* after them – and the Russ-ian. "Nabil knows who we are. Who knows what he'll say?"

"How do we find them?" Lucas said.

"They'll need money. You say she grabbed some diamonds. They'll have to fence them."

"The Russian?" Lucas asked.

Vincent shook his head. "Nabil's small-time. I never let him know about the Russian." He opened the apartment door, peered out to the hallway to make sure it was empty, then motioned them to follow.

"So how do we find them?" Patrice said as they headed down the stairway.

"If you want to find a rat, you look for rat holes – and rat shit," Vincent said.

CHAPTER SEVEN

SEVEN MINUTES before three in the morning; the night cool, silent; the only light from a single streetlight and a misty half-moon shining through a halo of cloud. Crouching behind a police car, Casey Ramirez had the bizarre thought that if she lived in a fairy tale, it would be a night for wolves to howl. She watched as the SWAT team in Kevlar helmets and armor vests moved into position at the entrance to a two-story apartment complex. The building was set back behind an iron fence and there were bars on many of the windows; that kind of neighborhood.

The SWAT team leader Sgt. Jimmy Lee Wright pointed at a sophisticated surveillance camera above the building's front door. One of his men aimed a .22 caliber pistol with a sound suppressor and fired a single shot, taking out the camera with a soft crack of glass. Everyone froze, listening. Sgt. Wright signaled for the team to move. Using a police master key, they unlocked the front door and went inside.

Patty Dunlop, the Dallas PD officer assigned as Casey's

liaison, took out her service pistol and steadied it on the car, aiming it at the building entrance. Although this was supposed to be a Dallas PD operation and Casey was there strictly as an observer, she pulled out her 9 mm and did the same. Suddenly, there was noise and two flashes of light in a second floor window. They heard the gun shots, then more shots. Shit, shit, shit. Don't, please don't, she thought. Don't kill any of the girls.

They heard loud shouts and screams and more shots from another apartment. Casey started to move, but Patty's hand on her arm restrained her as more Dallas cops ran to the building, using patrol car headlights to light the entrance.

A dog barked. Windows along the dark street lit up as SWAT officers marched four Vietnamese and Thai men in underwear, their hands cuffed behind them, out of the building. Behind them, two SWAT officers brought out more than a dozen young women clad in panties and bras, some barely teenagers, their hands raised. Some were crying, others looked around in terror, as if something worse than jail was about to happen to them.

Casey reached into the police car for blankets, then headed toward where the girls were being lined up. She went from girl to girl, wrapping each in a blanket and trying to calm them in English; also using the one or two phrases she'd memorized in Mandarin, not knowing if they understood her or not. The girls' faces flickered red and blue in the flashing lights from the police cars. All were Asian, but none of them was the Thai girl who'd had a photo taken once on a balcony beside a canal.

No, she thought, please no. Sgt. Wright came down the stairs and out the entrance way. Casey went up to him.

"The Thai girl . . ." she began. The look on his face stopped her cold.

"They used the girls for shields. I'm sorry," Sgt. Wright said. She walked past him into the building and up the stairs.

The hallway smelled of stale garbage and the burnt plastic scent of crack cocaine. The police had smashed the apartment door open. Casey went inside. A pair of Dallas PD investigators were working the scene.

The SWAT team's bullets had made a mess of two Asian men in undershirts in the front room that had been set up like a small reception room for the brothel with a couch, red lights, plants, and a flat-screen TV. Bullet holes perforated the walls and floor, splashed with blood. The Dallas crime scene guys made measurements and took photos. Casey walked down a narrow hallway past curtained "massage" rooms, each of which had room for a bed and little else.

She found the dead Thai girl in the last curtained room at the end of the hall. The girl's eyes were wide open as if she was looking at something. She wore a nightie top, the rest of her naked but for a bullet hole in her chest and another that had torn through her cheek. Her body lay partly on top of a Vietnamese man, his eyes and mouth open as if he was about to say something if only the back of his head hadn't been blown into a dark liquid on the floor. Two crime scene guys came in with a plastic body bag. They pulled the girl's body away from the man and began to put her legs in the bag.

"Wait," Casey said. Kneeling, she took a cell phone face photo, for confirmation comparing it to the one of the girl on the balcony given to her by the mother. It was the same girl, though now the pretty eyes were empty. The Thai mother Casey had sat with in that restaurant in Long Beach would never catch her breath again, she thought, getting up. The crime scene cops zipped the dead girl into the bag. Casey walked back down the stairs, the staircase so dark she had to feel her way till she saw the lights from the police car headlights.

She went over it in her mind, knowing as she stepped outside to question the other girls who had been trafficked, that she'd left a jagged piece of herself behind in that Dallas apartment.

CHAPTER EIGHT

"HOW LONG HAVE you been in Panama?" Casey asked. They were on the Corredor Sur toll road, driving in from Tocumen Airport. On one side were modern white apartment towers, on the other, a flat green sea.

"A long time, nearly six months," Roberto "Bobby" Marquez said. He was small, wiry, bronze-skinned with jet-black hair, aftershave hinting of lemon and oak. She found him easy to be with for a DEA agent despite the once-over he gave her when he picked her up at the baggage claim. A surprise to even think about a man or sex because part of her was still mourning the Thai girl, a dark well she really didn't want to fall back into.

"Six months is a long time?" she asked.

"Panama's like dog years. You have to multiply by seven," he grinned. "How'd you get hooked in?" As though the Isthmus wasn't a place, but an addiction.

"The Dallas PD turned a sex-trafficker we helped bust. He

was forwarding money to a numbered bank account here," she said. Johnny Ha had started cooperating once he figured that what was waiting for him in Huntsville Unit prison wasn't hard time, but a shank in the throat. "We thought that was interesting. Not just trafficking, but money laundering. My boss found it interesting too." After two days working the case in Dallas and a Facetime with Kent Ferguson, instead of coming back to L.A. she caught a red-eye flight through Miami to Panama City. "We figured if we started pulling the string, we'd see what might unravel? First, we went through official channels on the bank, got nowhere."

"Decree 238," Bobby said with a Latin sigh at the inevitable, like death or corruption. "The Panamanian Banking Secrecy Act. You're right about the money laundering. And *mucho mas*. This place is the real Sin City. Makes Vegas look like Des Moines."

"How do we find out who owns that numbered account?" she said.

"Luis Domingo Avila," Bobby pronounced as though announcing a soccer star.

"Who?"

"He's Balboa Bank's man. The one on Calle 50, Panama's banking street. You'll meet him tonight."

"How'd you arrange that?"

"He's having people over at the Waldorf."

"What's the occasion?"

"The usual. Bankers, middle-men, drug dealers, loads of arm-candy. That's the excuse," he said as they exited the toll road onto Avenida Balboa, its modern skyscrapers and palm trees making it look like a tropical Manhattan.

"The excuse? What's the real reason?" she said.

"You," Bobby said, glancing at her with frank curiosity. "You're the woman who met *el Pintor* – and lived to tell the tale. I booked you at a hotel in the Old Town. Better than the big fancy ones in Campo Alegre. They're all tourists and hookers."

He dropped her off at the hotel, a white colonial chic building on a square with a statue of someone on a horse and barefoot boys playing soccer in the street. It felt good to go from the air-conditioned car to the air-conditioned lobby. The few moments she'd spent outside were oppressive; the heat and humidity pressed down by a cloudy tropical sky as if with a steam iron.

Hard to decide what to wear tonight, Casey thought once she got up to her hotel room. For one thing, she wasn't a cocktail party kind of girl. She didn't even own an LBD. Not something they taught in the L.A. foster-care system. Luckily, she had a decent white silk blouse and black slacks. She could keep her small Sig Sauer P238 pistol in her ankle holster under the slacks. As for her hair, the humidity was going to frizz it whatever she did. For the billionth time in her life she wished she had her sister Jessica's hair: straight, dark, smooth. And her sister Jessica's beauty. How would Jessie handle tonight? *Smile at your enemies. Never let them know you know who they really are.*

Bobby brought his car around front to pick her up 9:30 that evening. Lights were on in buildings around the square, insects dive-bombing the streetlights.

"You look good," he said as they got into the car. He didn't look so bad himself in a tropical tan jacket and slacks, she thought. They drove through the cluttered streets of Casco Antiguo, where traffic was stop and go till they reached the fashionable boulevards of the downtown district. The Waldorf was hard to miss: a rectangular black tower dominating the buildings around it.

The party was at a pool-side restaurant on an upper floor

with an open-air view of the city lights. The pool was lit with blue light and only a glass railing to keep a drunken guest from stepping into infinity. There was a full bar and a DJ blasting hip-hop. White-jacketed waiters circulated among sexy young women in barely-there dresses and men dressed in everything from Ralph Lauren to mesh T-shirts.

Bobby nudged her to indicate Luis Domingo Avila, a heavyset man in a white Guayabera shirt draped like a tent over his bulging belly. He was standing by the pool with a pretty blonde, talking to a man wearing wraparound sunglasses despite it being nighttime. The two men smoked Havana cigars.

"*Hola*, Louie," Bobby called. "Serrano, Juarez Cartel," he whispered out of the side of his mouth to Casey as they walked over. Serrano glanced at Casey for a second as if photographing her with his sunglasses, then walked away. Bobby checked out the blonde. "Nice party. This one's a pretty one, *pelao*!" Winking at Avila. "Last time you had two."

A waiter with a tray stopped by. Avila grabbed a drink, handed it to Casey. Bobby took one.

"What's this?" Casey asked.

"It's called a *paloma*. A little dove. Tequila, grapefruit juice and Sprite. Everything in Panama comes with Sprite. If it was up to Panamanians, they'd float the ships in the Canal in Sprite," Avila said. And to Bobby: "So this is she? The very one?"

"This is her," Bobby said.

"*Mucho gusto*," he said to her.

"But don't get ideas," Bobby told him. "The part of Homeland Security she comes from, they'll have your *cojones* for breakfast and then say, now they want breakfast."

"Listen Linda, get me a black mojito," Avila said to the blonde. "The Abuelo rum makes it black," Avila explained to

Casey as they watched the blonde wiggle away. The three of them walked over to the rail. Casey got vertigo looking down at the street far below. She steadied herself on the glass railing, thinking it's too frail; it'll never hold.

"You still doing these young *chicas*, *pelao*? Your wife is very understanding," Bobby said.

"Window dressing, for business," Avila made a face. "Even with the blue pills, I can barely salute anymore. The other night with those two girls, we ended playing dominoes. That's my new game: dominoes and boobies. My wife doesn't care about the girls. All she cares about is that she and the kids don't have to leave Isla Contadora and come into the city."

"So what does interest you?" Casey asked.

"Birds," Avila said.

"Really?"

"There are more species of birds here in our little isthmus of Panama than in all of North America? Have you ever seen a yellow-crowned euphonia? It's hard to believe God created something so exquisite. Trust me, you've never seen the color blue till you've seen a red-legged honeycreeper. Beyond words. Or the sweep of a frigate bird or the fierceness of a white harpy eagle. People say the dinosaurs died out, that it's too bad you can't see a living dinosaur. They're wrong. They see them every day. They're called birds."

"This numbered account, Senor Avila. I need to know who it belongs to, all transactions, everything," she said.

The fat man looked around uneasily. "You understand, if it were discovered I broke Decree 238, my life would be over. Not in some legal way, or even jail, *Dios me libre*, heaven forbid, but in a Columbian necktie way," he shuddered, the reference to Cartel-style murder with the victim's throat slit, the severed tongue placed to stick out of the wound.

"There's one thing worse than the Cartels, Louie," Bobby

said. "The people who can shut you down tomorrow. No more Waldorf parties. No more pretty *chicas*. No house in Isla Contadora. The U.S. government. We're the badasses. We've always been the badasses and this one," tilting his head toward Casey, "she's the girl who can do it.".

Avila stared at the lights of the city as if stepping over the glass rail was an option. Behind them, a young woman in a see-through dress shrieked as someone threw her into the pool. Casey stepped back to avoid being splashed. A man jumped into the water after her. Lady Gaga blasted from the sound system and there were shouts and laughter as a second woman stripped off her skirt, top and bra and leaped into the pool. That time of the party.

"You'll be fine, Luis," Casey said, touching his shoulder. "Know why? Because in a day or two I'll be gone and my boss will be happy and you can go on playing dominoes with pretty birds to your heart's content."

"There's something I have to tell you," Avila said, looking around. "The account has a safety deposit box."

"We need to open it," she said.

"Impossible."

"What if we could prove criminal activity? Could we open it then?"

"Not even," Avila shook his head. "Only if the owner was dead and in the presence and with the permission of the executor."

"One thing at a time. For the moment, all I need is the name on the account," Casey said.

Avila licked his lip. "I've never done this before," he said, as if sensing doom, the dark birdcage of Latin fatalism.

"C'mon, Louie, you're a banker," Bobby winked. "You really want to try and convince us you still have some virtue left?"

Avila leaned so close to Casey his lips touched her ear. "The account belongs to a North American," he whispered. "The name is McCord. Layton Gary McCord."

CHAPTER NINE

BOULEVARD CARNOT, NICE

THE SETTING SUN spread a sheen of violet over the sea and the white houses on the shorefront as Brochard pulled into the driveway of his condo parking garage. For once, he wasn't home late. He'd bought Gabi a bottle of her favorite white Burgundy, a Domaine Raveneau Chablis. He had to do something. These days, she was more distant than ever. After dinner and taking care of Juliette, they were left with silences and television. Like water, she was slipping between his fingers and he didn't know how to stop it.

As if that wasn't disaster enough, they were going in circles on the Blue Panther case. No signs of any of the diamonds or other jewelry from the robbery. As for the gang members, they had dropped off the face of the earth. Giroud and his team were getting nothing from their usual snitches, nor had they turned up anything new on the non-existent American Layton Gary McCord. The Quai des Orfèvres in Paris' investigation into the mysterious Latvian phone number had run into a dead end. The Latvian phone turned out to be an end-point on a VoIP (Voice Over Internet Proto-col) network through which calls were sent by an unknown recipient via an encrypted virtual private network or VPN, effectively a private pipe through the Internet. The Paris tech-nicians traced the pipe through dozens of servers around the world from Riga to Moscow to Lagos to Rio de Janeiro to Tianjin, China to Skopje, Macedonia and so on. The VPN account was owned by a private holding company in Luxem-bourg whose ownership according to Luxembourg law could not be divulged, even to the police.

Brochard brainstormed with Giroud and Marie-Laure. Perhaps they were going about it the wrong way. Instead of concentrating on the Blue Panthers and the unknown dead American whom no one wanted to talk about, maybe it was time to take a harder look at the young woman who'd been with him. She was still alive and presumably with the Blue Panthers. She could be the key.

Giroud put Marie-Laure on it full-time. Marie-Laure suspected that the girl might've applied for a residence card, a *carte de séjour* at some point in order to stay in France. She was working that angle, Brochard was thinking as he got out of the car. He barely had time to register a sound of someone behind him when someone tremendously strong grabbed him around the throat and twisted his arm behind his back. Brochard tried to shout. A hand clapped over his mouth and a hard punch to his solar plexus knocked the wind out of him, doubling him over.

Two men hauled him towards a black SUV that pulled up with a screech of tires. They shoved him into a back seat and pulled a hood over his head. He tried to struggle and a man on his left twisted his wrist in a way that made him gasp in pain.

"Not a good idea, Jean-Pierre. Don't move even your little

finger," a man's voice said, in an unmistakably Parisian accent by the way he pronounced "*petit*" for "little," *p'tit* dropping the "*e*". The SUV began to move, pausing for the garage gate to open and then out onto Boulevard Carnot. He felt them turn right, back into Nice.

"Who are you? What do you want?" he asked into the hood. He could smell his own breath and sweat.

"Just a little chat," the man on his right answered. Also Parisian by his accent.

"If you know who I am, you know that kidnapping me is not a good idea," Brochard said, hoping it sounded braver, tougher than he felt.

"We're not going to hurt you, Jean-Pierre. It's just best for everyone that you don't see our faces and we wanted to talk to you in private. After we finish, we'll take you anywhere you want to go," the man on his right said.

"I want to go home," Brochard said.

"Of course, after we talk, but you may not want to."

"What? What are you saying?"

"Your wife, Gabrielle is gone, Jean-Pierre. Your daughter too. There's a note," the man said.

For a second, Brochard couldn't breathe. Gabi, Juliette gone. He couldn't believe it. What was worse? That they were gone, or that a complete stranger knew about it even before he did? This *merde* case was a cancer. It'd barely begun and already, it was wrecking his life.

"*Alors*, what do you want?" he said, a metallic taste in his mouth.

"The dead American . . ."

"This Layton Gary McCord, although we know that's not his real name. The Americans won't tell us anything," Brochard said. He could feel the SUV turning, going uphill. Towards the Mont Boron district, perhaps?

"We're very interested in anything you can find out about him. Especially anything he may have left behind."

"You're looking for something this Layton Gary McCord left behind? Is that it?"

"Yes. Anything you discover."

"Why?"

"It's essential that we recover it before others do. It's also important you understand the implications," the man said.

Suddenly, the pieces clicked into place for Brochard. "You're the Swimming Pool," he said, referring to the DGSE, the French CIA, also called "the Swimming Pool" because their headquarters in Paris' nineteenth *arrondissement* was located across the street from the French Swimming Federation with its big Olympic-sized pool. *Merde*. This thing was political. He had stumbled into something way over his head and the instant he found something, they would take it over. He should've turned it over to the Quai des Orfèvres and let them deal with it. Although, the men who'd taken him could also be from the *Milieu*, Corsos, the Corsican mafia or from who knew where?

"The girl who was with the American? Have you found her yet?" the man asked. So she was a key to this, Brochard thought.

"Why should I tell you? If you are who I think, why the *Milieu* tactics?" Brochard demanded.

"Relax, Jean-Pierre," the man's voice said. "It's we who have to remain anonymous, not you. We'll have you home shortly. Tell us about the girl? Any leads?"

"Not yet. We don't know who she is. If you know something, tell me," Brochard said.

"No, but she was with him. She knows something. Do you have anything?"

"Only the really odd thing, which is that she went with

these *malfrats*, the Blue Panthers, almost as if she was in on the robbery. Yet so far as we know, she was never part of their jobs before. You can see it on the security camera video. She joins them as if it was part of a plan. Very curious," Brochard said.

"If she's connected to the Blue Panthers, that might be a big lead."

"We don't know. Our people are investigating. So far, nothing," he said.

"The instant you find the girl, or anything about her, you'll let us know," the man on his right said. Although said in an ordinary tone, there was no mistaking the threat.

"Do I have a choice?" Brochard asked, the taste of metal back in his mouth. He felt the car turning, heading downhill, sensed traffic around them. It must be dark by now. In his mind he saw the headlights of evening traffic on the Côte d'Azur. And nothing waiting for him but an empty apartment.

"We'd like to help, Jean-Pierre. You're an ambitious man, intelligent. You belong in Paris – with your wife and child," the man said.

Brochard slumped in his seat. "Do you know where they've gone?" he asked.

"Your wife's mother has a big apartment in the 8th *arrondissement*. There's a top *Maternelle* school not far, perfect for your little Juliette. But a long waiting list. A phone call could be made."

Brochard felt the car turning again. For a few minutes, they rode in silence.

"How do I get in touch … ?" he began.

"We'll call you," the man's voice said.

Brochard felt the car slow, turn and stop. He heard the

sound of the electric garage door gate opening. Door locks popped open and he was pushed out of the car.

"Don't remove the hood till ten seconds after we drive away," the man said.

Brochard heard the car, counted to ten, pulled off the hood and found himself standing on the street outside his building. He saw the red tail lights of a dark SUV recede, lost in a caravan of lights on the Boulevard Carnot. Before the electric gate could close, he walked into the garage and up the elevator to his apartment.

For once, the sweeping view of the bay, the palms, and the string of lights along the shore and beyond to the running lights of a freighter in the darkness did nothing for him. One thing was clear: the key was to find the young woman from the robbery. His career, his life depended on it.

He found Gabi's note on the dining room table, in a white envelope propped against a vase filled with tulips he'd brought home just yesterday. The flowers were like something from years ago. He picked the envelope up, but couldn't bring himself to open it. Instead, he poured himself a glass of cognac and drank it all. Gabi, he thought. Juliette.

Brochard stared at his own reflection in the living room window against the darkness of the night and sea as if looking at a stranger.

CHAPTER TEN

PANAMA CITY

THE BALBOA BANK was a streamlined structure in the downtown Obarrio district that screamed private money and no questions asked. Casey and Bobby Marquez met Luis Domingo Avila in his office, its tinted one-way glass window providing a view of the traffic on Calle 50. Avila typed an access code on his computer and brought up the Layton Gary McCord numbered account on the screen.

"*Hmm, es extrano.* Most curious," Avila muttered.

"What is?" Casey said, peering at the screen.

"See there," Avila pointed. "Deposits in large amounts from various places. Note they are always under ten thousand dollars, the American IRS and bank scrutiny limit. Three or four times a day for several years back. Each time, the same amount is transferred to other accounts in the Caymans, Luxembourg, Switzerland, even other accounts here in our bank. Nothing retained. This account is a pass-through, a cover."

"We'll need to know who each one of those other

accounts belong to. This is good," she said, plugging a thumb drive into his computer. "But why strange?" she asked.

"Look," he pointed. "All these transactions for many months and then a week ago nothing. Everything stopped. No activity."

"I think I know why," Casey said. They looked at her. She thought for a moment. "I'm not sure I should tell you, but in order to go forward . . . According to the FBI, this Layton Gary McCord – or someone purporting to be him – is dead; killed in France six days ago. Apparently as a bystander in a jewel robbery." She opened her laptop and brought up the file. "Here's the FBI translation of the official French death certificate and autopsy report as well as the French request to the U.S. Consulate for information about this McCord's identity and passport, which according to the FBI turned out to be a fake. I'm showing you this to prove we have legal authority to open that safety deposit box. The man is dead."

A few minutes later, in the privacy of a windowless room, they opened the safety deposit box. It was empty except for a small brown envelope. Casey pulled on latex gloves and opened the envelope. It contained a safety deposit box key with no bank name, a slip of paper with a handwritten 12-digit number and an unevenly-torn half of a yellow "*Narodna Banka Jugoslavije*" bank note. Yugoslavia? Casey wondered. The country no longer existed. She tried the key into the safety deposit box they were looking at. It didn't fit, so it had to be for another bank box, though God only knew where. She put the three items back into the envelope which she placed into a plastic baggie that she put into her handbag, signing a receipt for Avila.

"What does it mean?" Avila asked.

She shrugged. "A code of some kind. For a person who doesn't exist. We may never know," she said.

"Where to?" Bobby asked as they left the bank and got back into the car.

"The American embassy. I have to work on my report and send it over a secure channel," she said. They drove across the city, past the greenery of the Metropolitan Nature Park to the U.S. embassy gate.

"We found something. We should celebrate before you leave," Bobby said.

She studied him for a moment. He was charming enough, worked and traded it because it was the currency he had and as for her, neither of them was in the business of forever. "I'm in room 608. Be there at eight," she said.

She thought about Bobby while she worked on her laptop in a borrowed embassy office. It'd been a while since she'd been with someone and with Bobby there'd be no strings and no regrets. He didn't wear a ring, only a narrowing of the ring finger on his left hand which meant either he was divorced or married and had taken it off so he could screw around while in Panama and the only thing real beyond the sex was that in the morning she'd be on a flight to L.A.

Her report filed, she was being driven back to her hotel in an embassy car when Bobby called. "Casey, you okay?" His voice was tense, businesslike; the agent side of him.

"Yeah, why?"

"Luis is missing. He left for lunch at the Mar de Grau but never got there. He hasn't returned to his office either. His assistant doesn't know where he is. He wasn't at his condo at the Yoo Tower. No one's seen him and his phone's not answering."

"You think it's this McCord thing?" They'd stepped on a land mine, she thought. The hairs stood at the back of her neck. All they'd done was open a bank box – and the reaction was so fast? Her sister Jessica's Rule Number One flashed like a neon sign in her brain: *Chance happens, but evil is a hunter. You can either be prepared or prey.*

"I don't know, but be careful, okay? I booked a room in your hotel. Room 907. We need to talk about this."

"Oh," she said. So he'd booked a room. Sex had definitely been on the menu. Only what now?

"I shouldn't compromise your location. Don't leave your hotel – and don't open the door to anyone except me. I'll see you in my room at eight," he ended.

When she got back to her hotel room, she double-checked her precautions. It wasn't just her sister's Rules or her HSI Training; her apprenticeship with Don Ernesto had taught her never to walk into any place without knowing where the exits were and how to avoid being taken by surprise. That evening as she was finishing her report and getting ready for Bobby there was a knock at the door.

"Room service," a voice called. She started toward the door, then remembered Luis Avila.

"Leave it outside," she replied.

"It's champagne, Miss. From the management," the voice said. Something's wrong, she thought. Why would they do that? This wasn't from Bobby. She pulled the Sig Sauer out of her handbag and aimed it with both hands at the door.

"Leave it, *por favor*," she said, standing beside the door.

"It'll get warm, senorita."

"Leave it."

A pause. "I'll come back later," the voice said.

No good, she thought. They could be waiting outside the door – or they might be impatient and break in. She had to warn Bobby. She tried his cell. No answer. Oh shit, she thought, her heart beating faster. She slipped on her jacket, grabbed her laptop, put it into her carry-on which she threw over her shoulder. The connecting door to the next room was locked, of course, except she'd already experimented with her lock pick to make sure she could open it. She picked the lock and flung open the door, gun ready.

The room was empty. Placing her jacket over her arm to conceal the pistol, she listened, ear pressed against the door to the hallway. She heard nothing and saw only an empty hallway through the peephole – and if they were waiting, they'd be paying attention to her room door, not this one. She stepped out to the corridor ready to shoot. The hallway was empty.

Don't risk the elevator, she thought and checking landings, climbed the stairs to the sixth floor. The door to Bobby's room was slightly ajar. Oh no, she thought. Now, she was really afraid. Possibly he did that because he was expecting her, but Bobby was too smart to have done that. She nudged his room door open with her foot and burst in, police-style, hands locked in a shooter's stance.

There was a bottle of champagne in a silver ice bucket and a tray of hors d'oeuvres on a table, but no Bobby. Her eyes raked the room. Moving fast, she checked the bathroom and closet. Empty. Where was he? The door to the balcony was slightly open. With a terrible sinking feeling she opened it and stepped out to the balcony. The lights of the buildings around the square shimmered in the humid night. Please, no, she thought. Peering over the railing she saw Bobby's body sprawled awkwardly on the sidewalk below like a broken doll.

CHAPTER ELEVEN

MARSEILLES

THE AFTERNOON SUN was still warm as Vincent the Cat wearing sunglasses, Lucas and Patrice, walked down the narrow Rue des Trois Mages. The street was in shadow, the walls of the buildings spray-painted with colorful graffiti. They passed an African in a green and gold dashiki. Loud Algerian *raï* pop music came from a hookah café. Two women in *hijabs* with babies in strollers had stopped to chat.

"France is over, *mec*," Lucas said, nodding towards the women. "It's all *Afrique* now. Soon instead of the *Marseillaisse*, for the national anthem they'll play an *Afriquenaisse*," Vincent didn't entirely agree with Lucas about the North Africans. He liked their energy, their food, but he understood where Lucas' sentiments were coming from.

They turned the corner and as they approached the restaurant, a warning whistle sounded from a rooftop. The three men glanced at each other. Doing anything in the La Castellane territory was always dangerous. In Lucas' words: "Like juggling balls filled with nitroglycerin." Even outside, they could smell the aroma of *harissa* and lamb *couscous* from the restaurant.

They had barely taken two steps into the restaurant when two Algerians levelled AK-47s at them. A third North African in a blue Marseilles Olympique tee-shirt frisked them, taking their pistols. He motioned that only Vincent was to go in; Lucas and Patrice were to sit near the front door.

Despite white stone walls, the restaurant was dark, the windows screened with blood-red curtains. The stone floors and walls were decorated with red Berber carpets. Vincent spotted Sammi at a rear table. Sammi Muhammed Bouhouche was head of the La Castellane drug cartel. They were based in the high-rise Tower K, off the A55 in one of the *cités* of North Marseilles, districts where gangs patrolled and the police never entered. With Sammi was his uncle, the once-notorious Djamel Malik Bouhouche, a man in a wheel-chair, twisted as a tree in winter with Charcot's disease (ALS). Also with Sammi was his right-hand man, Faouzi, a tattooed killer wearing a knitted green-and-red cap. The two men, Sammi and Faouzi, both still in their twenties had the same lidded look in their eyes. Both had publicly declared that neither expected to live to see his thirtieth birthday and neither cared enough for it to matter.

Vincent slumped in a chair and removed his Oakleys. The waiter, a bearded Moroccan, brought Vincent a glass of mint tea and sugared almonds, the kind he hated. Sunlight streamed through panes of colored glass in the front door as though they were in a church. The restaurant was empty, except for two tables occupied by more of Sammi's men, idling over *couscous* and 1664 beer, guns in waistlines. Their eyes darted between Vincent and a soccer match on the TV over the bar.

"Vincent the Cat, one hears you're looking for a *mec* and his little girlfriend," Sammi said.

"Even in Marseilles, people hear things. That's nice," Vincent said, lighting a Marlboro.

"In Marseilles, the *flics* want to know where to find the ass-faces who killed some *merde* foreigner in a jewel robbery in Nice. You'd be surprised what they'd let come through the port unopened for a word in the right ear," Faouzi said.

"You wouldn't do that, Sammi," Vincent said.

"*Non?* Why wouldn't I?"

"Because you hate the *flics* almost as much as we do," Vincent said, putting a pre-paid cell phone with a photo of Nabil on the screen on the table. "And we both have bigger problems," reminding Sammi that he was in a killing turf war with other Marseilles gangs, all of them with automatic weapons and GPS tracking devices and two could play that game as well as one. "I need to find Nabil," tapping Nabil's face on the screen.

"I thought he was your *copain*." Your pal.

"He was," Vincent said.

"So how badly do you want him?"

"Ten thousand for him – and the woman with him."

"You have a picture for her?" Faouzi said.

"You won't need one. She's a looker. Exceptional," Vincent said.

"They say you've been talking to fences in the First *arrondissement*, Vincent the Cat. You should've come to me first."

"You're right. It was a waste of breath," Vincent said. He'd seen it in their eyes. Small-time North African jewelry fences who didn't trust anyone not speaking their version of Arabic, especially a Frenchman.

"They don't like you *François*. Maybe they think you're a *narc*," Faouzi said.

"They're your people, Sammi," Vincent said. "Ten thousand."

"Twenty. Ten each, Monsieur the Cat."

"You and me aren't worth that, much less Nabil and that *nana* of his. Besides, the story on that job in Nice was all over the news. They can't move the jewels, too hot. Ten, Sammi," Vincent said.

"Fifteen or you and your *mecs* will need more than nine lives, Vincent the Cat."

"Fifteen, then. And you know better than to muscle me, Sammi," Vincent said, putting on his Oakleys. "Everyone needs friends."

"Half now," Sammi said, making a sign for money with his thumb and fingers.

Vincent counted out the seventy-five hundred euros, laid them on the table and got up. He looked at the old man in the wheelchair, a single yellowish eye staring into space. "Your uncle, does he still talk?"

"You're lucky he can't move or you'd already be dead, Vincent the Cat. Back in the day, my uncle wouldn't even let anybody say *bonjour* to him," Sammi said, scooping the money from the table. He nudged his uncle with his elbow. "Isn't that right, Uncle Djamel?" The old man didn't move.

"They say he once shot the eyes out of some *mec* because the guy said hello to the sister of a girl he fancied," Faouzi said.

"That so?" Vincent shrugged, giving nothing away. This was prison yard talk. He couldn't remember how many times he'd had to deal with *merde* like this. He leaned over the table. "It's good how you take care of him, Sammi. Family is above anything. Nabil was one of us. If he and that *chatte* were to betray us . . . " He left it hanging.

"One more thing," Sammi said. "Do you want them back or do you want them dead?"

"Either is okay," Vincent said.

They waited all evening in a *brasserie* on the Canebière. It was a lively place, smelling of *bouillabaisse*, with soccer and tennis on flat-screen TVs and locals stopping in for *kir* or a *pastis*, served with olives and peanuts for a free *amuse geule*. After eleven, the prostitutes in their skin-tight bright-colored minis and short-shorts showed up at the bar. A majority of the prostitutes were young African women, white teeth in smiling black faces. There was noise and laughing and at intervals, a male patron would leave with one of the women. As the night wore on, Patrice argued that the seventy-five hundred was money flushed down the toilet, when Vincent got a call from Faouzi with the name of the fence, Mohammed Besloub, and an address.

The fence's apartment was above a shuttered jewelry shop, "Bijoux Anaïs," on the Rue Longue des Capuchins in the First *arrondissement*. They cased the entrance to the building, deep in shadow, the nearest streetlight broken. The apartment was on the third floor. The windows were shuttered, but the shutters were old and light gleamed from inside.

Patrice jimmied the lock in seconds. They crept up the stairs in silence, using their cell phone flashlight apps instead of the hall lights. When they got to the apartment door, they took out their guns. Through the door they could hear a TV. It sounded like they were watching an *Actuality* replay. Vincent knocked.

"*Oui*, who's there?" An older man's voice asked in *Maghrebi* North African French.

"Monsieur Besloub, *s'il vous plaît*. I'm a friend of Sammi's."

"Who?"

"Sammi Muhammed Bouhouche. Open or else," Vincent said.

An elderly North African man in pajamas and robe, his wife behind him, opened the door chain. "La Castellane! What do you – " he started, but never got to finish as Vincent, Lucas and Patrice shoved past them and into the apartment. They led the old couple to the kitchen table and made them sit.

"Don't kill us! We'll give what money we have. Please don't kill us or our son, *je vous en prie*, monsieur," the old man, Besloub said in a tremulous voice.

"Your son? What are you talking about?" Lucas said.

"We know you have him. We've been waiting, *Y'Allah*, monsieur," Besloub said, staring at them.

"We don't know anything about your son. This man," Vincent said, taking out his cell phone and showing them a screen photo of Nabil. "He fenced some jewels, diamonds with you, yes?"

Besloub looked at the cell phone as if it were a mine about to explode and nodded.

"There was a woman. Very pretty," his wife said. "Too pretty," as if her looks were a crime, as if by being pretty she had somehow offended all other women.

"How much did you pay them?" Vincent asked, thinking it would help to know how much disposable cash Nabil and the girl had. Besloub glanced at his wife and Vincent knew he was about to lie. "The truth or I'll cut your heart out," Vincent added, giving Besloub a prison yard stare.

"Eleven hundred," Besloub said.

"More than they were worth," the wife put in. She was lying, Vincent smiled to himself. Even the handful of diamonds the girl had grabbed from the last case had to be worth at least four or five times that to any fence on the Côte d'Azur.

"Any idea where they are? What did they say?" Lucas put in. Besloub and his wife didn't respond.

"We could be more persuasive." It wasn't them with their guns frightening them, Vincent realized. He tapped the table with his finger. "What's this about your son?"

"She bewitched him! She's a demon!" the wife hissed, eyes darting at the door as if afraid demons were lurking to curse her if she said another word.

"What are you talking about? What happened? You better tell us. I'll blow your head off," Vincent said, grabbing the scrawny North African by his pajama front and showing him the pistol.

"Our son, Rachid. When those two came, all the time they were here, he couldn't keep his eyes off her. As if he was bewitched." Lucas scratched his chin, like he was trying to figure something out.

"When they were here, who did the talking?" Lucas asked. "The man or the woman?"

"The whore," the wife spat out. "She did all the talking. These young men are like poodles. She pulls them on a leash to go as she pleases."

"What happened?" Vincent asked, cutting her off; her fixation on the woman was getting in the way.

"After they left, Rachid followed them on his motor scooter. He insisted she was in trouble. He wanted to save her," Besloub said.

"Did he call you? Do you have any idea where they went?

You're his parents," Vincent said, his hand tightening on the pistol grip.

"Only for a minute. He said he followed them to a flat on the rue Loubon. It's in the Third *arrondissement*."

"Did he give you an address? Could be anywhere on that street," Patrice said.

"He said after they went in, a light went on in a top floor apartment. It was on a corner, across from a Superette, up the hill from a cinema. But he had to go. He thought someone else might be watching them. He had to warn her."

"When was this?" Vincent asked.

"Last night. We still haven't heard. We're terrified something bad has happened to him," Besloub said. "When you broke in, we thought you were the ones after them, that you had come for us."

"It wasn't the police? The *flics*?" Patrice asked. Besloub looked from him to Vincent.

"*Non*. Rachid was born to our business. He knows the difference and to watch out for the *flics*. A man was watching that apartment. Only one, he said. He thought they were in danger. So it couldn't've been the *flics*," the old man said, looking first at Vincent, then at Patrice and Lucas.

La vache! The hell! Vincent thought. Made no sense. Who else would be after Nabil and the girl except either them or the *flics*? Whoever it was, they better get to them first. He motioned to Lucas and Patrice and stood up.

"If what you're saying isn't right," he told the old couple, "we'll come back and kill you both."

Lucas parked the Peugeot under the overpass and the three men walked to the corner by the Superette. Vincent checked his watch; after midnight. The windows in the building were dark. Cars were parked partly on the sidewalk. Streetlamps cast the shadows of the trash bins and the bus stop far across the street. Vincent couldn't tell if there was anyone awake in the top floor apartment.

At the building's entrance. Patrice held a cell phone app flashlight for Lucas to pick the lock. Within seconds they were inside. They climbed the creaking stairs in the dark to the top floor. On the way over, they'd figured what must've happened. Nabil was originally from the Belle de Mai neighborhood in Marseilles' Third *arrondissement* before he joined up with them. Patrice suggested he must've had some family, a cousin, a *copain*, someone, he'd called for a place to hide out and to help find a fence for the jewels.

As to who else was after Nabil and the girl, maybe someone who wanted to do a deal with the *flics* or maybe thought there was a reward, Lucas suggested. That didn't sound right to Vincent. He kept thinking, there's something about that *imbecile* dead American. Even dead, he makes problems.

"Once we're in, don't hesitate," he'd warned them in the car. Now, at the apartment door, they all had their guns drawn. Lucas picked the lock and opened the door slowly and quietly as he could.

They stepped inside. The room dark, except for the light in the window from the streetlights outside. Time seemed to stop, then Vincent saw shapes on the floor. Two bodies. Patrice aimed his app flashlight on the faces. Nabil was dead; his face covered in blood. He'd been shot in the back of the head, professional style. Vincent rifled through his pockets. No diamonds, just the dead American's wallet. Vincent took it. He glanced at the other body. Another North African; possibly the old couple's son, Rachid.

Lucas hissed, pointed. Legs in the kitchen doorway;

another body. Suddenly Lucas crumpled to the floor though there was no sound of a shot. Vincent dropped to the floor, panicked. Where'd it come from? The darkened bathroom door started to open. Before Vincent could call to warn him, Patrice was down, the light from his flashlight app making a wild arc before hitting the floor. Also without the sound of a shot. Impossible! What was happening? A trap. He had to get out of there. Vincent fired his pistol one-two-three-four-five times at the bathroom doorway and without waiting to see if he hit anything, ran out of the apartment like crazy.

He leaped down the stairs, nearly tripping, catching himself, on the landing, turning to fire three more shots without looking into the darkness up the stairs in case the gunman had followed him. He ran down as fast as he could, again nearly falling, , not sure if anyone was behind him or not. Reaching the ground floor, he paused for an instant to listen, his breath so ragged, he had to strain to hear.

He heard a creak on the stairs. *Salaud!* He thought, fired twice at the sound and ran out into the street and pounded toward the car, trying to remember – had he fired ten or eleven shots – fifteen in the magazine. Suddenly, he had the terrible sensation of someone running behind him. He whirled to kill whoever it was, but it was a woman about ten meters behind him. The *chatte* from the robbery! He was so stunned, for an instant he couldn't decide whether to shoot her or keep running. All he could think was to get to the Peugeot and away. He was opening the car door when she came up beside him. He put the gun to her head.

"Get away!" he said. Down the street, lights had come on in several windows. In one of them, he saw the shape of someone looking out.

"Help me. They're trying to kill me too," she begged.

"I ought to kill you!" Vincent snapped. "You killed my *gars*." My pals.

"It wasn't me, I swear! They almost killed me too. I'll make it worth your while. There's a lot of money." Grabbing his arm, pressing in the car doorway so he couldn't slam it shut.

"What money?" She was lying. She got eleven hundred from the fence; nothing, he thought. "Get out of the way or I'll kill you," he said, leveling the pistol at her.

"There's more money than you can imagine. Why do you think they're after me? For the love of God, don't leave me," she begged, her fingernails digging into his arm.

La vache! The hell! He thought. If ever a woman was trouble, it was this one. She wasn't pretty now; she was scared. Whoever had massacred everyone in the apartment was a pro. Had to be. And how could they do that without the sound of a shot? Luckily, he'd thought of a way to get away. It wasn't far to the Gare de Marseille Saint-Charles train station. Time for him to find out if what she said about the money was real. He could always get rid of her later.

"Get in," he told her, motioning for her to get in on the other side, checking the side mirror to make sure no one was running after them in the street yet. "You do everything I say, understood? Lie to me once and I'll cut your lying throat."

CHAPTER TWELVE

LONG BEACH, CALIFORNIA

LANDING AT LAX FROM PANAMA, Casey picked up her car from Wally Park. Stuck in traffic on the 405, she called her office in Long Beach and told them she'd be in by eleven. Janine got on the line and told her she didn't have to come in today. Perfect, Casey thought. Stuck on the 405. Stuck in life. She was on a treadmill going nowhere. I shouldn't even be here, she thought. I should be in Panama, finding the son-of-a-bitch who killed Bobby Marquez.

"Kent said you're to be in his office first thing tomorrow morning, eight sharp," Janine said.

"Why? Is something up?" Casey asked. Something didn't feel right. She'd requested that she be allowed to stay in Panama to follow up on Bobby's death. Instead, Janine told her to return ASAP. Worse, while waiting for her flight at Tocumen Airport, she called the DEA desk at the U.S. embassy in Cardenas. One of Bobby's guys, Dave told her Luis Domingo Avila's body had been found by the roadside of the Autopista Colon on the outskirts of the city. The body showed burn marks and other signs he'd been tortured before death.

So instead of coming back to the HSI Long Beach field office with kudos for big wins in Dallas and Panama, there was that queasy feeling of vertigo as when she'd stood at the Waldorf glass railing looking all the way down at the street below. Two people dead and now she was the only person with knowledge of the bank account and safety deposit box in Panama. And what could be going on at her office? She'd broken a trafficking ring in Texas and was returning from Panama with important evidence, so her boss, Kent Ferguson, should be thrilled with her. Why the cold shoulder?

It's not like he was against her. Ferguson was a big guy, an ex-Marine who had seen something in her and encouraged it from the time she had first arrived at the Long Beach office despite her being different from the typical agent. If anything, what she'd accomplished in Mexico, Dallas and Panama was a win. As for what happened to Bobby, she was going to ask Kent to let her go back to Panama and find out who killed Bobby.

"I honestly don't know anything. All I know is to see Kent, Casey," Janine said in her whiny *It's your shit, I don't want to get near it* office voice.

"Come on, Janine? What's going on?"

Was Kent trying to reward her with time off? Casey wondered. What happened to Bobby was on the DEA. Maybe it was one of Bobby's old cases, like that Serrano guy from the Juarez Cartel. Dallas alone should be a feather in Kent's cap. One of his people pulling that off. He'd backed her on a long shot – and she'd delivered. It would up the Long Beach office's tally on international sex and human trafficking, felony arrests and likely convictions. Plus she was bringing back the money laundering leads from Panama.

"I don't know anything. Relax, we'll see you in the morning," Janine said and hung up.

The hell, she thought, taking the 110 to her rented apartment in San Pedro. Kent wasn't blaming her for Bobby, was he? Was it some kind of interagency thing? Kent Ferguson was the Special Agent in Charge of the L.A. HSI office, actually located in Long Beach because of its proximity to the Port of Los Angeles. While the HSI office cooperated with the FBI, the DEA, and other law enforcement agencies, it was no secret that all those offices, especially on the West Coast dealing with the Mexican border, competed with each other on busts and stats in order to get resources out of an increasingly tight Homeland Security budget.

Except – it didn't matter that she had graduated near the top of her class at UC Irvine and again on the Special Agent Test Battery, that she'd been recommended by her instructors in Brunswick, or that Kent had recognized her ability and till now had pushed her along. It was always hanging there; where she came from; who she was.

Because Kent had done that too, at the beginning, when she first interviewed for Long Beach. Told her he didn't care about the grades or the recommendations. If she was going to work for him, he wanted more. Dug deeper. Got her story; all of it. The foster homes, the sexual abuse, her life on the streets in Central L.A., her peculiar guardian-ward relationship with one Jorge Morales aka Don Ernesto, leader of the powerful Florencia 13 L.A. street gang, now in San Quentin. He even got her to tell him about her older half-sister, Jessica, separated from her by the L.A. DCFS (Los Angeles Department of Children and Family Services) when Casey was six.

No matter what, Jessie never gave up. Through Casey's thirteen foster homes, where Erica never once showed up for custody in court because she was either locked up in Lynwood jail or strung-out, crack-house wasted. Sometimes it was worse when Erica was around. "I never shoulda had you, pain in zhopa *ass. You'll never be smart, pretty like your sister."*

Beautiful smart-as-a-whip Jessica. Dark hair, blue eyes. When she turned twenty-one, Jessie swore to Casey, she'd come and adopt her legally. All those years Jessie going to school, the public library to study every chance she got, cleaning houses, toilets, scrubbing floors to earn money for the two of them, saving every penny, acing her SATs, getting into UCLA on a scholarship, sneaking over by bus to see Casey every chance she got. Almost there.

Until a golden autumn day in Westwood. Norman Rockwell-like Westwood! Million-dollar hi-rise condos on Wilshire and the gorgeous campus: U-C-L-A-Fight-fight-fight! Trees. Grass. Asian girls in shorts. California Pizza Kitchen in the Village. Jessica went on an early morning run around the campus, jogging up Veteran past white houses with green lawns and picket fences onto Sunset Boulevard . . . suddenly, gone. Vanished.

Even her name, "Casey" came from Jessica who began calling her "K.C." when she was still an infant, after her first and middle names, Katharine (after Erica's late mother, *Katarina*) Charlotte; Jessica, the one who took her to school, so her kindergarten teacher put it down as "Casey," and she was "Casey" ever after.

But Kent pressed further, the tough investigator with a new employee whose past might've left her too iffy to handle the job. When he started to dig into the foster physical and sexual abuse, Casey wouldn't look at him. She sat in the chair in his office, her hands in her lap, always self-conscious about her three crooked fingers – why she never wore nail polish, not wanting to draw attention to them – till Ferguson, a big, sandy-haired man in a gray suit, came around, sat on the edge of his desk next to her and said, "That's why you joined HSI, isn't it?" He nodded, reached over and shook her hand. "Good motivation, Special Agent Ramirez. I know you'll work hard. Solid background," tapping her recommendation letters. "You'll make a good investigator. But if you work for me, you'll spend 110 percent of your time on the assignments I give you and nothing else. No moonlighting on lost causes, understood?" Not stupid, Kent Ferguson. Clearly he'd sensed that if it killed her, she'd spend the rest of her life looking for her missing sister Jessica.

"Yessir," she'd said and they'd kept it that way till now. So was it Panama? The FBI and the Dallas PD had seemed pleased with the Johnny Ha bust. Before they parted, Sgt. Jimmy Lee Wright had said, "Hey Ramirez, if you ever want to leave the Feds and come work with real cops, Dallas is a good place." And she'd uncovered a lead in Panama that might enable them and Treasury to nail down other money launderers and sex traffickers. So where was the heartburn? Or was she reading too much into it?

Of course Janine was a miserable bitch, whom she knew couldn't stand her. The feeling was mutual. Being professional women in an office, their dislike manifested itself in excessive politeness. "No please, after you, Janine."

Her condo in San Pedro had that musty unlived-in smell when she walked in. She dumped the mail, mostly junk mail, flyers, bills, and some of her puzzles - a Rubik's cube, a new curled cast-metal Enigma assembly puzzle, a NY Times Super crossword book – on the small kitchenette table and opened a window to let in fresh air. From that one window she had a partial view between townhouses of the ocean, but a September haze made it impossible to see Catalina.

The apartment was empty, quiet. Just her and the TV. She didn't know what to do with herself, picking up the Rubik's cube, mixing it up and solving it in a little over three minutes, then picking up the Enigma and putting it down. It wasn't like she had a personal life. No man, no close friends – male or female – no family except for Don Ernesto, remembering the last time she had seen him in the visitor's room in San Quentin before she went to Mexico. She watched him shuffle in with shackles until he was inside the visiting room. They had to talk through the window with phones because he was a high security/non-contact prisoner.

"*Hola, Papi*," she said into the phone. The bags under his eyes made him look older, sadder.

"You know what you're doing, *nena*? Even Florencia Thirteen is nothing to these *pendejos*. They kill for nothing. With a man like *El Pintor*," he made a cutting motion to his neck, "there is no trust."

In the morning, she was at her desk early. Other agents came in, said "You're back," sat at their desk with their coffee, but oddly there was none of the usual morning chit-chat. Casey assumed they'd heard about Panama, about Bobby, but no one asked or said anything. She'd never been the belle of the ball, but suddenly she felt like a leper. It was creepy.

The minutes on the digital wall clock barely seemed to move. Once she caught Janine glancing at her and when she did, Janine immediately looked away. *What is your problem, bitch?* Casey thought. Finally, exactly at eight, she got up, refused to look at Janine, knocked on Kent's door and walked into his office.

Ferguson was behind his desk. Looking up, he gave her the kind of frozen stare she had previously seen him reserve only for perps. She placed the plastic baggie containing the safety deposit key, the slip of paper and the torn Yugoslav banknote from the Panamanian safety deposit box on the desk along with the thumb drive with the files from *El Pintor* and from Layton Gary McCord's Balboa Bank account.

Ferguson nodded. "DEA Agent Robert Marquez? You were both in the same hotel?" She nodded. So it was about Bobby. "He had champagne in his room?" he asked.

"We were going to celebrate," she said. The maybe-sex part, no one's business.

Ferguson stared at her for a second like she was the whore of Babylon. "I see," he said. Screw you, Kent, she thought. I'm not a nun.

"Why'd you pull me from Panama? Bobby Marquez was a good guy, good agent. He deserves somebody finding out who killed him," she said.

"We're not cops, Casey. Leave that to the Panamanian police and the DEA. In any case, I didn't order you back. Your new boss did," Ferguson snapped.

"What? What are you talking about?"

"I'm disappointed in you, Casey. If you wanted a promotion to go to Washington, you could've at least had the decency to talk to me first instead of going over my head," Ferguson said. "This is not what I expected from you. A certain amount of ambition is good in an agent – I always thought you had the potential. And God knows, I gave you plenty of leeway, even though you really stretched the rules in Mexico and Panama."

She tried to say something, but he shook his finger in her face, not to interrupt.

"I supported you, Casey. Backed you all the way. But did you ever think about us? The people in this office? Poor underpaid bastards trying to protect this country, working their asses off without anybody ever noticing?"

"But Kent – " she started to say.

"I'm not done," he said angrily. "You couldn't wait, could

you? Well, that's fine. I've got my orders. You've been transferred."

"I don't understand. Transferred where?"

"You're to report to Room 604, 500 12th Street SW in Washington, D.C., tomorrow at 9 AM sharp. And bring the evidence with you," handing her back the plug-in drive and the plastic baggie from Panama.

"Kent, please, I didn't do anything. I swear," she said, feeling abandoned, as if she'd been sent to the principal's office for cheating when she hadn't.

"I don't believe you, Casey. That's not how things work. Someone has to initiate them. Anyway, what I think doesn't matter. You don't work here anymore." He stared at her, his mouth a tight line. "When you first came here, that story you told me about the foster homes, the abuse, living on the streets. Was any of that true? Were you playing me or is this some other connection you're using?" Ferguson said.

He was tearing her heart out. She had exposed her soul to him. "I swear I told you the truth. I'm telling you the truth now. In Panama they tried to kill me too," she said, as if that mattered to him, almost in tears. No, she must never do that; pulling it inside. She never allowed herself to cry. Not since that foster care placement they put her in when she was six. *Supposed to be a good one, a husband and wife, Mark and Susan, in the San Fernando Valley, Sherman Oaks. The first time the DCFS had split up Jessica and her. Only anytime she did anything wrong – and she was always doing something wrong because Mark kept making up rules, like you only chewed your peas three times, but you're supposed to chew four times, or you had to leave the bathroom door open when you peed to make sure you didn't get a single drop on the toilet seat and he was always finding a drop even if it wasn't there – he'd start bending her fingers back till they were on the verge of breaking. "How do you like it?" he'd say. "You gonna do what I tell you now?" But when he hurt her and she screamed, she'd hear Jessie's voice whispering in her ear, "Say yes, agree with the bastard, but don't let him see you cry. Never cry." Till finally, after the third time he broke one of her fingers, the DCFS put her in another placement till Erica finished that particular turn on her merry-go-round in and out of Lynwood.* "I didn't request a transfer. I don't know what's happened," she told Ferguson.

"What's happened is we're done," he said.

CHAPTER THIRTEEN

LOS ANGELES

CASEY SAT STUNNED in her car in the building's parking structure, staring at the concrete wall, hardly knowing who she was. Because if she wasn't an HSI Special Agent, who was she? What happened just now made no sense. She felt like she'd been hit with a wrecking ball. She hadn't put in for a transfer or promotion. She had no "influential" contact in Homeland Security or anywhere else. Could it be Don Ernesto pulling the strings from his cell in San Quentin? Impossible. Besides, he hated HSI or anything to do with the government or the cops, only accepting that she had chosen to join because he understood the truth about her. It wasn't about cops or stopping bad guys; it was about Jessica. Always Jessie. Staring at the parking garage concrete wall it came. The memory, no way to stop it.

You and me, Kimmy. Their secret names for each other. Kimber was the name of Jerrica's little sister on Jem and the Holograms, the TV show that she and Jessie would sneak-watch

*when they lived in that apartment in Westmont in Central L.A.
Jessie was Jerrica-Jem; Casey was Kimber.*

*Jessie would tell her come out if there were no men in the
front room and Ma, who wouldn't let them call her that – said
they had to call her Erica after her favorite soap character on* All
My Children, *'cause nobody fucks with Erica Kane – would be
out cold as a dead fish, if a dead fish snored like a passed-out
sailor on a mattress on the floor. She would lay there in her pink
nightdress, legs akimbo, whacked out on black cherry Cisco and
Mex' Mud, which was what they called the brown-colored crack
from Mexico.*

*You're not some brat no one gives a crap about, Jessie would
say. You're not a throwaway kid. We're Jem and Kimmy. Sisters.
We can take care of ourselves; and someday we're both going to get
the hell away from here. Just the two of us, sisters.* That's what
she'd say, Casey remembered; the wound that never healed.

She'd just come back to the Long Beach office bearing
goodies from Dallas and Panama, so whatever happened,
despite the loss of a DEA agent, hadn't just caught her by
surprise, it had caught Kent too. And whoever pulled the
strings on this was well above his pay grade or he would've
dealt with it, argued against it, or at least given her some idea
of what the hell was going down; not treated her like she'd
violated the Marine Corps oath. What would Jessie do?
Whatever just happened, she realized, starting the car, the
answer was in Washington, not Long Beach.

She drove back to San Pedro, packed a suitcase and carry-
on because she had no idea how long she might have to stay
in D.C. By noon, she was waiting at a boarding gate at LAX,
when she heard her name being called on the loudspeaker.
Feeling conspicuous because as an HSI agent her name had
never been called out, she walked up to the United counter.
The agent told her she'd been upgraded to first class.

"How'd that happen?" she asked.

"Can't say, Miss. Frequent flyer miles maybe." He checked his computer for a second. "No, no change in your mileage status." He smiled showing beautiful teeth. "But you've been upgraded to first. No extra charge. Enjoy the flight."

She sat back down, waiting for them to start boarding. That was the second time today she'd felt like a piece on a chess board that someone else was moving; her life suddenly out of her control. What would Jessie do?

Erica got into trouble with Rico. He told her if she didn't pay him the money for the crack she stole he'd cut her throat. Sent her out on the street in the middle of the night to earn it. When she left, he told Casey to put her hand on the front of his jeans. No, don't put it, rub it, he said, his breath coming faster till Jessica walked in and screamed "She's only six, you bastard!"

"Cabrona!" Rico shouted. He jumped up and hit Jessie in the face. "You don't like I do it to her, I do it to you!" Rico punched Jessie in the stomach. She doubled over on the floor. Casey heard the snick of a switchblade. Rico put the point to Jessie's throat. "What you say now, puta? Maybe I cut your face. Not so pretty anymore," Rico said. Casey grabbed and bit his arm. Rico smacked her away. Jessie screamed, "Run!" Casey ran and hid in the closet.

She squatted, listening at the keyhole, but all she heard was Rico grunting. She waited and finally fell asleep. It was late, everyone asleep, when Jessie, finger to her lips, her face red and bruised, came and got her. Together they tiptoed down the stairs and ran away down the empty streets.

All that day, they hid inside a hot smelly dumpster behind a mariachi joint on Lorena Street. They knew Rico and his vatos must be looking for them. A couple of times, somebody from the restaurant raised the top of the dumpster and tossed chicken bones and scraps on them. The stink was so bad Casey threw up. She started to claw her way out, but Jessie held her back, whispering "They'll get us. We have to wait."

Finally after what seemed like years, Jessie lifted the lid just enough to peek out. It was late, the sun going down. The street was empty, a lone drooping palm tree and gang graffiti on the sides of the buildings growing indistinct in the shadows of the buildings. At the far end of the block, Casey could see the underside of the freeway silhouetted against a neon-red sunset. Now that it was finally time to climb out of the dumpster, Casey was scared. Jessie jumped first and pulled her out. "I've got you," she said.

Casey boarded the plane and belted herself into her seat in the first class cabin. A man in his sixties in an expensive sports jacket and jeans, no tie, gold-rimmed sunglasses, clean-shaven with a prominent widow's peak and Adam's apple, took the seat next to hers. He nodded once but didn't speak, spending the time before take-off reading his tablet. She pegged him for someone in the entertainment biz. When the flight attendant came, he ordered a vodka kamikaze. She asked for iced tea.

"You don't drink?" he said.

"I do," she replied, pulling out a John Le Carré paperback she'd barely had time to start, hopefully signaling she didn't want to start a cross-country conversation.

"But not on airplanes?"

"But not when I don't feel like it," she said, opening her book.

"Even when you're in a shitty mood."

"Who said I was in a shitty mood?" she said, closing the book. He wasn't going to let her off so easily.

"You mean this is how you are normally?"

She had to half-smile at that. "Define normal," she said.

"Or maybe you don't like meeting men on planes?" Looking at her invitingly.

"The problem is, the men I meet are usually men I've already met," she said, thinking he was too old, not attractive enough and if he thought being in First Class was enough for him to be able to jump her body, then despite his age he didn't know a thing about women, she thought, pivoting back to her book.

"Is the book really that interesting – or is it maybe you're only like this on days when you've been ordered to report to a certain building on 12th Street after being removed from where you were without explanation?" he said. The words hitting her like a sledgehammer. She sat up straight and was about to respond when the flight attendant brought their drinks. "Sure you won't have a cocktail?" he asked. "It's First class, no extra charge."

"No, thanks," she said to the flight attendant and waited till she left. "But if you're the person behind this upgrade, tell me who you are and what this is all about?"

"Wouldn't say I'm behind it. Cheers," he said, raising his drink to her and taking a long sip. "Not bad. Jerry Matthews, by the way."

"I'm . . ." she hesitated.

"Katharine Ramirez. Only everyone calls you Casey," he said, pulling out his mobile, tapping and reading from it: "Height five six, weight, one twenty-five." Squinted at her. " – ish. Black hair, medium length; green eyes. Quite nice actually. No distinguishing marks or tattoos. Born Los Angeles; father, Fernando Ramirez. Little known about him; just a name on a birth certificate apparently. Mother, Anastasia Makarenko; naturalized U.S. citizen. A piece of work, Mommy, but we won't go into that now."

"Let's not."

"As for you, recently an HSI Special Agent by way of the L.A. foster care system – you'll have to tell me how you survived that one – Central Juvy on Eastlake, so you almost didn't. Aced your math SATs. You like puzzles, near the tippy-top of your class at U.C. Irvine, ditto HSI training in Brunswick, Georgia, bullshit, bullshit, bullshit; usual Mexican border assignments, where they loved you because you spoke Mex' Spanish like a native – so Juvy and foster care was apparently of some use – also learned Russian from Mommy, Anastasia – which nobody gave a shit about along the San Ysidro drug corridor, then posted to the HSI Long Beach office, and now you're having a drink with me," he smiled.

"Is that supposed to impress me? That you know all about me?" she said.

"Yeah, kind of," he said. "Psychologically, it's supposed to put you at a disadvantage. There's all kinds of data."

"Well, it doesn't, Mr. Matthews, if that's your real name?" she said.

"Oops, you got me." He raised his hands in mock surrender. "I'm supposed to be undercover."

"Well, Mister Make-believe Matthews, here's another data point for you. Either you tell me what this is about or whatever it is you're supposed to tell me, or this conversation's over."

"Look, Casey, that's what they call you, isn't it? The truth is, I don't know. I have no idea what's happened to you or why, or even what you're doing on this flight."

"Then why are we talking? And how do you know all this about me?"

He turned in his seat towards her. "In a way, we're in a similar situation. I'm simply a babysitter. My job was to make sure you were on this flight and that you are who the people who employed me think you are. I'm also supposed to ask you a question."

"Before you ask me anything, who are these people who

employed you? And what do they have to do with HSI?" she asked.

"I'm not supposed to answer that," he frowned, "But they do want to know how you got to meet with '*El Pintor*', whoever that is – and how you got out alive? I suspect it impressed the hell out of them," he added and slugged down the rest of his drink.

"Does this have anything to do with Panama?"

"I have no idea. I didn't even know you were in Panama? Did you see the Canal?"

"I wasn't a tourist. And frankly, Jerry, since it's just us girls dishing between ourselves here," she said, opening her book. "Until I get some answers, there's no way I'm going to tell you anything."

"I told you. I'm just here to babysit and do a little vetting," he started.

"Which you'll report to somebody else who's anonymous," she said.

"And get paid," he said. "Look, I'll tell you this much. Consider what you're going to in Washington to be a job interview. An opportunity. Something that's very much right up your alley, otherwise you wouldn't have been selected," leaning close enough for her to smell the vodka and triple sec on his breath.

She turned in her seat and looked at him.

"You mean there are other candidates for whatever this is?"

"I have no idea," he shrugged: "For all I know, you're the only one. You must have impressed them. I suspect you've got balls."

"For a woman that's not exactly a compliment,"

"Trust me, it is. Because if they decide to go forward with

you, Princess, something tells me you're going to need *cojones* of steel."

"Because it's dangerous?"

"Don't ask me. I'm just the babysitter," he said with a smile that might've been painted on a doll's face. "Very likely," he added and leaned back in his seat. He closed his eyes, then opened them. "In Vietnam, the Viet Cong used to have these *punji* stick traps in the jungle. They'd sharpen bamboo sticks to needle-sharp points and smear 'em with human feces or snake poison, then stick 'em in a hole in the ground pointing up and camouflage it with dirt and leaves. Walking in the jungle, you'd never see it in a million years. When an American grunt stepped on it, the spikes would go right through his combat boot and be sure to infect or kill him."

"Were you in Vietnam?"

"I been in lots of places," Jerry Matthews said.

"Are you saying I walked into something in Panama?" she said. Of course. Why else would they've wanted her to bring what she'd found in that safety deposit box with her?

"I'd watch my step if I were you," he said. Jeez, Jessie, what was she flying into, she wondered. A dead American in France. Two dead in Panama and they'd knocked on her door too. An icicle chill rippled down her spine. When she was a little girl, the Chicana women in the neighborhood would say, a black moth had fluttered across her soul. They believed if a *polilla negra* flew into a house, unless it was swept out immediately and a prayer said to the Virgin of Guadalupe, someone in that house would die.

"I always have," she said.

CHAPTER FOURTEEN

QUAI DES ORFÈVRES, PARIS

"WHAT MADE you suspect it wasn't just another Marseilles gang killing?" said Guy Varane, Director of "*la Crim*," the Criminal Brigade of the *Police Judiciaire*. He was a stocky man in a gray suit that matched his salt-and-pepper goatee.

"At first, that's what the Marseilles *flics* thought," Brochard said. They were in Director Varane's office in the Paris police headquarters, the legendary 36 Quai des Orfèvres, with a view of the Seine. "But the parents of one of the victims kept talking about a very pretty woman trying to fence diamonds. One of our detectives, Marie-Laure suspected she might be the woman from the Nice robbery."

"And *alors* . . . ?" Director Varane prompted, popping a *mini-calisson* into his mouth, chewing the candy like a thoughtful cow.

"The victim's mother insisted the young woman was responsible for her son's death. She sat there, hissing, 'She's a demon! She bewitched him!' It was positively medieval. I thought she would spit on a dead bat or something. But if her son," Brochard consulted his notes, "Rashid Besloub followed the young woman to the apartment where the massacre occurred, then it's the second time that this woman got men to drop everything *comme ça*," he snapped his fingers, "to be with her."

"A seductress," Director Varane nodded, thoughtfully tapping his finger on his goateed chin. "So the son of this North African fence follows our seductress to the apartment, where there are two more *Maghrebins*," the slang term for Arab immigrants from North Africa. "All three executed by a professional. Was there a *C.J.* on the third *Maghrebin*? The one who might be one of the Blue Panthers?" Director Varane asked, using the abbreviation for a *Casier Judiciaire* or rap sheet.

"Indeed. The third North African," Brochard consulted his laptop, "Nabil Touil's *C.J.*, included stretches at Fleury-Mérogis and La Santé." Two of the toughest French prisons.

"What about the other two victims? Not North Africans? Killed in a gunfight?"

Brochard shook his head. "French – they were ambushed, caught by surprise. There were no burnt tissues or gunpowder tattooing on their wounds as with the North Africans, so they were shot at greater range, three or four meters. Both were ex-cons: Lucas Mathieu and Patrice Gignac. And here finally, we were able to make the connection. All three were in La Santé prison at the same time."

"So it seems three of the four Blue Panthers are dead? Were you able to recover the stolen jewels?"

"Nothing on the jewels," Brochard said. "We think the jewels were likely fenced by the fourth member of the gang. We expect he must've also been in La Santé at the same time as the others. I expect to track him down shortly, together with the woman. That's why I'm here."

"You think they're in Paris?"

"The day after the massacre in Marseilles, we found a stolen Peugeot in the Gare de Marseille-Saint-Charles parking lot. Security cameras showed a man and a woman who might be our seductress boarding the early-morning TGV to Paris."

"Astonishing how she hops so quickly from one man to the next, like a little flea. Perhaps we should warn our detectives when we finally arrest her; she might seduce the entire squad," Director Varane raised his eyebrows as if to suggest he was only partially joking.

"The sooner we get our hands on her, the better. Anything from the Latvians?"

"After talking to their Colonel Seibelis I felt like the turkey stuffing." The French idiom meant they were being played for fools.

"So we're stuck?" Brochard asked, staring blankly at the window view of the booksellers on the bank of the Seine.

"Not entirely. Our cyber experts were able to back-track the network. The mysterious calls made to the dead American came from an account belonging to a Luxembourg corporation."

"Do we know who owns the company?"

"We're still trying to find out. Luxembourg laws." Director Varane made a face.

Brochard uncrossed his legs. Time to get to it. "Naturally, we appreciate your assistance, but none of this explains why the Quai des Orfèvres is so interested in a jewel robbery in Nice or why I'm sitting here with the Director of *la Crim*." He'd come to Paris for answers and was getting the kind of information they could've emailed to him in Nice.

Director Varane straightened. He studied the young prosecutor sitting there, handsome, yet concerned he might be out of his depth, caught mid-expression like one of Rodin's statues. He remembered Laporte, the veteran detective from the 12th *arrondissement*, who when he was first starting out, told him, "There comes a moment, when the only way forward is the truth."

Director Varane took out the key to a locked desk drawer and opened it. He withdrew a silver-colored audio device and placed it on the desk between them. "Admiral Deschamps of the DGSE has authorized me to allow you to hear this. You are not to reveal it to anyone, not even the police detectives on the case in Nice or your chief. The call you're about to hear was picked up by one of the DGSE's Strategic Directorate satellite listening points. It originated shortly after midnight from a burner cell phone in Belgrade, Serbia. No doubt it was also picked up by the listening services of all the major powers, possibly others as well. We are not alone in our interest."

He pressed the playback. An electronically-altered voice spoke in good, but not native English, from the device: "*We believe that the French police have notified American officials of the death of a U.S. citizen they have identified as Layton Gary McCord. By now, the American authorities will have discovered that Layton Gary McCord is not the dead man's true identity. The dead man was in possession of certain information whose authenticity is indisputable. Those who know the dead man's true identity will understand the implications. They are profound. You do not want a repeat or much worse of Blue Madagascar. Unless a hundred million euros are deposited to the corporate account name X@G4$H9Y17t&*2#! at the BGL BNP Paribas Bank in Luxembourg, with no further action, investigation or interference by any police, intelligence or other agency or entity, within exactly two weeks to the second from the moment this call ends, the information will be provided in full to the New York Times, the Washington Post, Reuters, the AP, CNN, MSNBC, the BBC,*

AFP, France 24, WikiLeaks, GitHub, Sputnik and Milw0rm for immediate worldwide publication. The clock begins now." A click ended the call.

For a moment, they sat in silence. Brochard glanced at the window. October in Paris, the sun sparkling on the water of the Seine. The days could be golden like today, or cold and rainy. Both came with a touch of melancholy. Paris, he thought, is a city haunted by its past.

"Do we know to whom the call was sent?" he asked.

"The call was made to the private mobile phone of Ames Bergman, the Director of National Intelligence of the United States," Director Varane said, leaning forward.

"Why is it of concern to the Swimming Pool?"

"Blue Madagascar, in the message."

"I don't understand."

"I don't know either; but for whatever reason, it scares the DGSE to death. Their assessment is that whatever it is these people are threatening to go public with is dangerous to the security not only of the United States, but also NATO. They want us to" Director Varane's hands massaged the air as if trying to conjure the right word, *"coordinate* with the Americans."

"They're passing us this plate? How high up does the stink go?" Brochard said. So this was why they'd insisted he come to Paris? He'd stepped in deep *merde.*

"They'll assist, but you're the striker, Jean-Pierre." Using the soccer metaphor to imply they were all good pals in this. "You know the case better than anyone. You'll have to lead the attack. Although it may turn out to your benefit," Director Varane said too casually. Watch yourself. Here comes the honey bait for the trap, Brochard cautioned himself. "I've spoken with Madame Lecomte, President of the Paris Court of Assizes. Someone like you, a graduate of ENS, the

Pantheon-Assas. There's an opening of some importance here in Paris for a *Juge d'Instruction* of your caliber."

Brochard's thoughts raced. They must be desperate to dangle a carrot like that. It was a giant career jump. And he'd be in Paris, close to Gabi and Juliette. They must know that too.

"Can I count on you personally to fully support my efforts, Monsieur le Directeur?" Brochard asked.

Director Varane flashed his teeth like a car salesman. "My dear Jean-Pierre, this is our Number One priority. You have my complete support," he said.

CHAPTER FIFTEEN

WASHINGTON, D.C.

CASEY GOT off the Metro at the Smithsonian during the morning rush hour. The day was bright and clear, a chill wind blowing down Independence Avenue. She sheltered by a bus stop in front of the Department of Agriculture building, glancing casually to see if she could spot anyone following her, unable to shake the feeling she was being watched.

The fact that she didn't spot anyone didn't make her feel any better, because nothing that had happened since she'd walked into Kent Ferguson's office yesterday morning made sense. Certainly not the bizarre Jerry Matthews from the flight, who when he found out she'd made reservations at the affordable Embassy Suites on Tenth Street, immediately insisted on changing it to the way more expensive Willard Hotel, within spitting distance of the White House. Using his mobile, he booked her a room with a view of the Washington Monument, telling her not to worry about the cost; he had an "expense account fatter than the national debt" for just such purposes.

"Is my room bugged?" she'd asked Jerry Matthews.

"The Willard? Be serious," Jerry Matthews replied.

Still, she couldn't escape the nagging feeling as she undressed and got into the shower that every move she made was being choreographed.

"Enjoy the show, you pricks," she muttered under her breath, stepping into the hot shower and letting it waterfall over her. Why her? What did they want? Was this about Dallas? Panama? The 12-digit number and the torn banknote? She let the water pound at her, draining the questions away. Stepping out of the shower onto the white marble floor, slipping into the lush hotel terry robe, she had to admit, if they were fattening her up for the slaughter, at least they were doing it in style.

She turned down 12th Street SW, the wind blowing her hair as if pushing her towards HSI headquarters. She'd been there only once, when she was still a trainee. Looking at it now, the massive building with its square pillars was like a fortress. Whoever had wanted her here was well above Kent Ferguson's paygrade, the thought giving her little comfort. She checked her watch; seven minutes early. She took a deep breath and went inside.

The guard at the front counter checked her name on his computer. He gave her an electronic visitor's badge to pin on her suit jacket and motioned to a uniformed guard with a sidearm to escort her. She surrendered her pistol, passed through the metal detector, and waited as they inspected her handbag and laptop computer again by hand, then she and the uniformed guard went up the elevator together to Room 604.

"Do you take a lot of people to this office?" she asked.

The guard didn't answer; just stood there waiting as if he

expected her to know what to do. She knocked. There was no answer. She opened the door and went inside.

There was a small reception area with a single couch, a small magazine rack featuring news and men's outdoor magazines and bottles of water on a console. The couch faced an opaque greenish glass door. Looking at the door more closely, she realized that the "glass" was a multi-layered laminated polycarbonate composite that could easily stop a bullet. In every corner of the ceiling, she spotted micro-security camera lenses. Toto, I believe we're not in Kansas anymore, she thought, sitting up straight on the couch.

All at once she heard the click of the door automatically unlatching and a voice came from the direction of the console, saying: "Come in, please, Miss Ramirez."

She entered a room that looked more like an English library than an office. In the center were two comfortable chairs and a mahogany table. A small balding older man in a pin-stripe suit and club tie with bushy eyebrows behind gold-rimmed glasses was pouring tea. On a mahogany desk was a photo of the man pouring tea having a breakfast meeting in the Oval Office with a recent U.S. president.

"*Sadityes, pazhalusta,*" he said in Russian, politely gesturing, asking her please to sit. "I believe you prefer Earl Grey black with two sugars, but indulge me and try this Numi jasmine with nothing added. I think you'll like it. You do speak Russian?" he continued in Russian, placing the cup in front of her.

"My mother was from Russia. So what?" Casey answered back in Russian. Another test, or is this some different game we're playing, she wondered.

"She taught you the language. A gift," he said.

"The only one she ever gave me," Casey said, switching to English and not touching the tea.

"*Y tu apellido es Ramirez.*" And your last name is Ramirez, he said switching to Spanish. "But the Spanish you learned, you didn't learn at home. In fact, you don't know who your biological father was, do you?" He continued in Spanish and waited and when she didn't answer, continued. "For that matter, it's possible even your mother may not have known."

"*No te metas en mis asuntos.*" Don't stick your nose in my business, she replied in Spanish, not touching the tea, her arms crossed across her chest.

"Actually, everything about you is my business, Casey. My name is Dalton, by the way. Arthur Dalton," the small man switched into English, sipping his tea. "Try the tea before it gets cold. It's very good."

She hesitated a moment, wondering if the tea too was a test, part of the interview. She took a sip. He was right; it was good even without sugar. They sat in silence. She wondered which of them would speak first. Another test? Mazes within mazes.

"Look, Mr. Dalton," she started. "I was on an important assignment in Panama. A DEA agent I was working with, a good guy, got killed, and suddenly I'm yanked back here. I have no idea why and – "

"Do you have the things you found in the safety deposit box in Panama with you?" he said.

She put her laptop case on the table and pulled out the plastic baggie containing the paper slip with the 12-digit number: 208998628034, and the torn Yugoslav banknote and handed it to him.

"Fascinating. Old school," he said, shaking his head.

"Do you know what they're for?" Casey asked.

"I can guess. The number is either code, or more likely a password, probably for a bank account somewhere in the world. The torn banknote is to be matched when meeting with someone."

"With whom?" she asked.

"We have no idea. Could you memorize the number? Know it cold?"

"On the paper? I suppose."

"Go ahead," he said, handing her the paper. She studied it for more than a minute, then handed it back. "Recite it." She did. "Again," he said. She repeated it. Satisfied, he got up, pressed a hidden button in the bookcase that opened a section to a combination keypad and biometric wall safe and put the paper in. He locked it, closed the bookcase and handed her back the plastic bag with the bank note and key. "Outside this office, the only place that number now exists is in your head."

What's this about? Is this why Bobby – " she corrected herself – "DEA agent Roberto Marquez was murdered? Besides me, he and the Panamanian, Luis Avila, were the only ones to know what was in the safety deposit box." She hesitated. "I've stepped into something, a different operation, haven't I?"

Mr. Dalton reached for the teapot and poured himself a fresh cup, watching the leaf fragments swirl before taking a sip.

"There's no shortage of nasty people in this world, Casey. Of course you know that. But there is also evil on a scale you can't imagine. It's possible Agent Marquez and the Panamanian Avila were killed because someone wanted what's in this plastic bag," he tapped it with his finger. "But at this point, we cross a line, a Rubicon, if you like. Because everything I tell you from this moment on is 'Top Secret,' a matter of national security. You're right. You've stumbled into something. But before we go any further, you need to decide. Do we proceed?"

She took a deep breath. Maybe it would give her a chance

to find out who was behind Bobby's death? And a tug on the most private thread in the secret tapestry of her brain: *The chance to find what she'd been looking for her whole life.* She nodded.

Mr. Dalton smiled, though his eyes, she noticed, didn't smile.

"You know, the CIA doesn't always screw up the way people think," he began. "For example, they warned Jimmy Carter that if he allowed the Shah to come into the U.S. for medical treatment, it would put the life of every American in Iran, especially the U.S. embassy at risk. Carter did it anyway and Ronald Reagan won the election with ninety percent of the Electoral College. Or the so-called 'weapons of mass destruction' in Iraq; there was a critical dissenting CIA report that President George W. Bush never saw. But there have also been screw-ups the public knows nothing about. The worst disaster in U.S. intelligence history was something called 'Blue Madagascar.' Five of the black stars on the CIA wall and the loss of U.S. intel that left us blind for more than a decade was because of it." Mr. Dalton leaned back in his chair. "I've just told you something only eleven other people in the world know. You're the twelfth."

Mr. Dalton frowned. "Clearly we've been compromised – and by we, I mean a large segment of the security apparatus of the United States: The CIA, Homeland Security, the DIA, NSA, and FBI, as well as a number of key corporations. We're not sure how far the breach goes. The Russians and Chinese are already in the hunt."

"Were the Russians behind the killings in Panama?"

"Possibly. Might've been a drug cartel. The DEA fishes in a lot of muddy water down there, but the Russians and the Chinese are definitely interested. So are a lot of people, as are we, of course."

"Where do I fit?"

"The thing that triggered our concern was a message sent a few days ago to the personal phone of the Director of National Intelligence. It contained a reference to 'Blue Madagascar' and to a person: Layton Gary McCord. Now do you understand? The moment you opened that safety deposit box belonging to this McCord, you, and the others with you were involved – and now they're dead. Whoever sent that message knew something only someone at the very highest level could have known. Trust me when I tell you our national security, the safety of the United States is at stake. Whatever the dead American, Layton Gary McCord left behind, we have to find it before our enemies. Certainly before Moscow or Beijing," he said.

"Why me?" she said, eyes darting around the office to the bookshelves, wondering for a second if he'd really read all those books or like the ones in front of the safe, were they just for show.

"You're already up to your neck in this, Casey, especially after Panama. Also, we need someone clean. Someone from outside the Beltway, the usual circles. Someone smart as hell, trained, with a security clearance and who speaks at least one or more European languages, preferably Russian. Someone with high test scores in math, good at solving puzzles and who can keep their mouth shut. We need a unicorn; in short, you. Most of all, we need someone with the stainless-steel balls to walk into a situation and come out with the goods the way you did with *el Pintor*."

"I got lucky," she said.

"Neither of us really believes that, do we?"

"The dead guy, this Layton Gary McCord? Do we know who he was? What this is about?"

"The FBI's working it. We should know something shortly."

"You want me to find something this Layton Gary McCord left behind? Something so explosive it could start a war or topple governments, maybe even our own?"

"Exactly."

"Something that someone deliberately hid, that might be anywhere in the world and we're in a race against people, including foreign intelligence agencies, who have no problem murdering anyone who gets in their way?"

"A treasure hunt. The stakes are . . . " He looked at her with shrewd pale blue eyes. "Sometimes the world shrinks to a single person; a lead pilot on a mission in World War Two, a spy in a dark alley, and the fate of humanity hangs in the balance."

She felt a stab of panic. What had she gotten herself into? "How long have I got?"

"Two or three weeks at most. As of now, you're assigned as staff to my office with a permanent jump in grade from your previous GS-10 to a 14 with a nice salary bump. You'll report directly to me. No one else – or via Jerry Matthews."

She didn't know whether to thank him or to run. Her whole life had just turned upside-down – or maybe it had been upside-down all along. For Alice, which side of the Looking Glass held the truth? "This thing we're looking for, do we have any clue what it is or where it might be?"

"Information probably. Files or a video on a computer, a disk, a removable drive, a microdot, paper. The man's last location was France and you'll coordinate with the French police, but it could be anywhere. The only clue we have is that this man, Layton Gary McCord received a number of curiously coded cell phone messages," he said.

"What kind of messages?"

"Weather reports about cities in the south of France, once each day sent from another country, except the weather in the calls didn't match what the weather actually was."

"A code of some kind?"

He nodded. "Clearly. According to Orange Mobile, the phone service in the south of France, McCord called back right away each time. His calls were short, lasting just a few seconds. The French police reported that the incoming messages have stopped."

"McCord called back each time he got a call?" Casey asked.

"Except the last time."

"Because he was dead?"

"Yes."

She thought for a moment. "Perhaps this code didn't mean anything, or very little," she said. "Maybe it was a trigger, something to confirm he was alive or not being held under duress. So long as he responded, everything was okay, but if he didn't, say because he had died, it triggered . . . "

"Blue Madagascar." The little man put down his tea cup. "The same conclusion we came to."

"So that's it?"

He glanced at his watch. "You better get going. Your flight to Paris leaves in three hours."

PART TWO

FOUR WEEKS EARLIER

"When it's time to act, go all the way, like jumping off a cliff."

JESSICA "JESSIE" MAKARENKO

CHAPTER SIXTEEN

LA VILLETTE, PARIS

THE HIGH-SPEED TGV train from Marseilles arrived in Paris at 9:42 AM. Vincent the Cat and the woman – she said her name was Milena, though the *carte de séjour*, the foreign resident's identification card she showed him, was likely a fake – debarked onto the platform at the Gare de Lyon. Two *gendarmes* near the gate watched passengers with rollaways flow towards them. Vincent's blood froze as one of the gendarmes eyed him. Vincent's grip tightened on Milena's arm.

"Kiss me," he said, pulling her to him. She didn't hesitate, kissing him passionately, pressing the length of her body into him.

"*Pas mal*," not bad, she whispered as they walked by the smirking *gendarmes*.

"Shut up," he whispered back, not looking at the gendarme openly grinning at them as they entered the station hall, bright light streaming from the skylights and out to the street, where they got into a taxi. The morning was sunny, cool, the air so clear the edges of the buildings might've been sculpted with a scalpel, the light with that faint tint of blue unique to Paris. Vincent told the driver to take them to Boulevard de Sérurier in the 19th *arrondissement*.

They were on Boulevard Richard Lenoir when a siren and the loud blast of a horn sounded behind them. Vincent's hand instinctively went to his pistol before he recognized the fire truck siren. Every *flic* in France must be after him, he thought. They might not know his real identity yet, but once they identified Lucas' and Patrice's bodies from their fingerprints, it was only a matter of time. The sooner he got a new identity card, the better.

Following in the wake of the fire truck, the taxi turned onto La République. In the outdoor café in the center promenade, people barely glanced up at the sound of the fire truck siren. Life or death was happening elsewhere.

Vincent glanced at the woman trying to decide what to do with her. In spite of the murders and the long TGV ride from Marseilles, she looked like a fashion model, her hair tousled in a Jane Birkin-like way that stirred him. Even her perfume. *Joy* by Patou, unsettled him.

On the TGV she'd told him in excellent, but accented-French she'd gone with Nabil in the jewelry store because she was in France illegally. "I can't afford to be questioned by the *flics* any more than you," she'd said. He questioned her about what had happened in Marseilles. She said two men broke in and killed the others execution style, showing him a bruise on the side of her forehead. They kept her alive to rape her but then he and his gang showed up. Vincent didn't believe her. The bruise didn't look bad enough to knock out a kitten.

So what was he supposed to do with her? She might hold a clue about who killed his *gars*, his guys in Marseilles. It couldn't go unanswered. Also, he needed to know if they were still after him. When the time was right, he'd settle the score. Even so, looking at her in the taxi, she was an extra complication. He wondered if he'd made a mistake not leaving her in Marseilles.

"Where are we going?" she asked. She watched him constantly. There was a stillness the opposite of calm about him, something terrible and inevitable like a raised guillotine blade.

"To see *Tante* Rosine," Aunt Rosine, Vincent said.

"Who?"

"You know, you and me will get along better if you don't ask questions," he said.

The taxi dropped them in front of an apartment building. They waited till it left then walked several blocks, Vincent with his backpack slung over one shoulder, Milena with her handbag, all she'd escaped with from the apartment.

A sound of traffic came from the nearby Périphérique road. The constant hum reminded Vincent of the TGV. He pressed the intercom button at the entrance to an apartment building, said "Vincent" into the speaker and was buzzed in.

They took an elevator spray-painted with graffiti up to a darkened hallway, smelling of cooked fish and cassava. Vincent knocked on an apartment door. A tiny white-haired black woman let them in.

"Vincent the Cat," the black woman said. "Are the *flics* after you?"

"You know me, *Tante* Rosine," Vincent said. "Where's Manu?"

"In Nantes. You'll have *chai*," *Tante* Rosine said, ushering them into the kitchen with a window looking out at another building. "Can you stay? I'm making *saka-saka*," gesturing toward the stove. A Congolese *ragout* of cassava leaves, fish, peanuts, and palm oil simmered in the pan.

"We can't, except for the tea. What's Manu doing in Nantes?"

"A plumbing job. A real one, legit. They're refitting a building." *Tante* Rosine eyed the woman "You'll want the apartment?. And the van?" Vincent nodded. *Tante* Rosine boiled the water for tea. "What kind of trouble are you in this time?"

"No trouble, *Tante*. We just came for a visit." The black woman looked at him. "*Bien*, maybe it's better if you didn't tell anyone about us," Vincent added, motioning Milena to join him at the kitchen table. The kettle's whistle sounded. *Tante* Rosine brewed the tea and served it in bowls, stirring in cardamom, milk, and sugar.

"They've known each other since they were kids. Always in trouble, those two," *Tante* Rosine explained to Milena.

"Me, not Manu. He only made a little here-and-there trouble," Vincent winked, sipping the tea.

"The two of you boys, climbing over the fence onto the train tracks at the Gare du Nord. We lived in the 10th *arrondissement* then. It's a miracle you both weren't killed," *Tante* Rosine shook her head. "When Manu was little, his first year in *École*," she said to Milena. "The French boys beat him up, called him a '*sale africain*,' dirty African. Before then Vincent and Manu didn't know each other, but the next day, Vincent brought a brick with him to school. Went up to the biggest boy in the school, the one who'd been the leader and smashed him in the head with the brick. Dropped him like a sack of beans. They threw Vincent out of *École*, but after that, no one touched Manu."

"Manu and me were both from La Chapelle. We *potes* had to stick together," Vincent said, finishing his tea and getting up. "Listen, *Tante*, you'll let Manu know I'm back? No one else, *bien*?"

"A moment. I'd like to know more about Vincent and Manu," Milena said.

"No she doesn't," Vincent said, giving her a look.

"Don't tell me what I want," she said. "Did they do jobs together?"

"At first. You know young men. Big talk, always about '*le gros coup*,' the big score, those two, but then Vincent wanted a team for bigger jobs. Manu was content with the plumbing and little apartment robberies. Vincent's *Maman*, Lisabetta, was a strong woman. She pushed him," *Tante* Rosine said. "When she died, it was a bad time for Vincent. He was in prison and couldn't go to the funeral. The *mouchard*, the snitch who talked, Vincent took care of him. Manu helped."

"Vincent doesn't let things go, does he?" Milena said.

"Never. And you, you're Vincent's *petite amie*?" Girlfriend, *Tante* Rosine said.

Milena shrugged. "With men, who can say?"

"*Mais non*, he likes you. I can tell," *Tante* Rosine said. "Are you staying on in Paris?"

"I don't know, Vincent. Are we?" Milena asked. Vincent gave her one of his La Santé looks.

"We better get going. Tell Manu, *Tante*, *bien*?" Vincent said, getting up and giving *Tante* Rosine a *bise* goodbye kisses on each cheek.

"Always running, Vincent. Someday you'll run yourself into a place you can't get out of," *Tante* Rosine said. She got up, poked around in a jar and handed him a set of keys.

That night, Vincent decided to kill the woman. For two days they'd hid in Manu's flat in the 19th *arrondissement*, not far from the Buttes-Chaumont Park. Those first minutes in the flat, he'd shoved her down on the bed to take her. But instead of resisting, she came back at him, their bodies crashing together like speeding cars. The sex was that spectacular. They kept at it for hours. Each time he was ready to fall asleep, she reached again for him.

Around the corner from the flat was a decent café, *Le Bariolé*, where at night they would venture out sometimes. They went out in daylight just once to Galeries Lafayette to buy clothes, having fled Marseilles in only what they wore. Most of the time, they stayed inside. Until he got new identification Vincent didn't want to risk being stopped by a *flic*. During the day they watched TV and each other like tigers and at night, the bed was their battlefield.

Vincent glanced at his wristwatch dial glowing in the dark. Nearly one in the morning. Sleeping naked on her side, her dark hair partly over her face, Milena was a Greek statue, something exquisite created in a time long past. He had to decide what to do with her. The Russian's sixty thousand wouldn't last forever. If he was smart, he'd get rid of her now. The sex, the intelligence in her eyes she couldn't hide, was spectacular. But he always came back to the same place. Like the Russian said, she was a loose thread who could identify him. It was her or thirty years in La Santé.

He imagined his hands on her neck, squeezing the life out of her. Naked as she was, he could carry the body to Manu's car and drop it into the Bassin de la Villette canal. No, first smash her face to make identification impossible for the *flics*. A dead foreign girl, naked, no face, nobody looking for her, no way to identify her. She'd be forgotten in a day or two.

Except there was strength in her eyes that she tried to conceal, almost like a female copy of himself, calculating everything, giving nothing away. Sure she lied and used her body to control men, but didn't most women? If he was honest with himself, he felt something. And that, he couldn't allow. He straddled her body with his knees, hands at her throat. As he was about to squeeze, her eyes opened. They gleamed like sapphires in the dim light.

"Why haven't you asked me? I've been waiting," she said.

"Ask what?"

"What a woman like me was doing with such an old man? You think he was so handsome? Such a great lover?" she said.

"You're a whore. He had money," Vincent said, not moving his hands from her neck.

"We're all whores; the only question is price. What if I said a hundred million?"

"What lie are you telling this time?"

"It was about to happen when your robbery knocked everything sideways," she said.

"You'd say anything to save your life," he growled.

"When Nabil shot him, I had to move fast. I couldn't afford to be questioned by the *flics*. But it opened the door for the two of us – if you're not stupid. Or you can kill me. It's what you were going to do anyway."

"I don't believe you, but for the moment we'll pretend. Where is it? This *fric*?" The cash, Vincent said, hands still on her throat, undecided. He'd never met a female like her.

"Layton, the American I was with was clever. He told me the key to a secret worth a hundred million was in a safety deposit box in Panama. He said if anything happened to him, to see a friend, an Irishman, in Paris. We could go together," she said.

"Panama? A hundred million? I'm supposed to believe these fantasies?" Vincent said.

He stared down at her. A thousand to one she was lying to save her neck, but on the other hand, it was just crazy enough to be true. Why would a woman like her stay with some old American unless there was a pay-day? The hundred million were for sure *conneries,* bullshit, but what about the killings in Marseilles? A gun that makes no sound; done by a pro. There was something more than diamonds going on here.

He grabbed her by the hair and slapped her face.

"If you're lying, you know what will happen," he said, leaving the red imprint of his fingers on her cheek.

"I'll prove it."

"How?"

She got out of bed and went to her handbag on the chest of drawers. She dug for a minute, then pulled something out. "This, from the wallet Nabil took from Layton. Why do you think he wouldn't let it go? For the safety deposit box in Panama. The key to millions," she said, holding up the key.

Vincent took it away from her, thinking she'd played Nabil, now she was trying to play him. Except now he had the key. Was it possible? Could the hundred million be real?

"I ought to cut your throat now," he said.

"I'll do anything you say, *chéri.* Anything," she said, turning onto her belly, provocatively raising her bottom.

CHAPTER SEVENTEEN

LA MADELEINE, PARIS

"HAVE they found a comfortable place for you?"

"Yes. The hotel's close by. It's very nice," Casey said, looking across the table at what had to be the handsomest man she'd ever met.

It seemed incredible she was in Paris, sipping wine in a red-awninged café, the sun shining, a woman selling flowers in the square. Whatever else, this new job had its perks. There was an old colonnaded stone church in the middle of the square with a cluster of motorbikes parked nearby. The cobblestones were wet from being hosed down, giving the street a just-washed smell.

Distinguished-looking in a navy-blue suit and tie, Jean-Pierre Brochard was a movie idea of a Frenchman. She wasn't sure about his title, since he was some kind of judge *and* a prosecutor. The French system was so different from America it was hard to keep straight, except that it seemed in France the lines between judge, district attorney and police inspector were blurred.

She wasn't sure how she must appear to him. Although she'd only been in Paris one day, she'd already noticed how well put-together French women were. Even in jeans, they looked stylish. Make-up, hair, an Hermès scarf that seemed thrown on casually, yet all just so. Though she was wearing her best business suit, compared to them Casey felt like a scullery maid. She stole a sideways glance at Brochard.

They'd met that morning at the central Paris police office on the Ile de la Cité. Her first sight of Prosecutor Brochard, his looks, the sheer physicality of him almost took her breath away. He introduced her to the Paris Director of Police Varane and Commandant Claire Pinault, a no-nonsense Frenchwoman who showed her the Nice robbery reports, including crime scene photos and a store CCTV video. They went over the robbery, the Layton Gary McCord autopsy, the report from the FBI and the massacre in the apartment in Marseilles. Listening to them chatter between themselves, she realized she was way out of her depth, surprised they didn't see it. Or worse, maybe they saw it and would do their best to keep her out of the loop.

"Did you check again with your office about the American McCord's identity?" Brochard asked her. At the police office, when she'd told them she'd brought nothing new from Washington about Layton Gary McCord, except for the information from Panama, which so far had led nowhere, they'd asked if she would check again with the FBI, their disapproval clear.

"I did. Still nothing. I'm sorry," she said to Brochard at the café. He didn't look happy.

"What is 'Blue Madagascar'?" Brochard asked.

"I'm not sure how much I'm authorized to tell you," she said. "I don't know that much about it myself. It was classified Special Access in the CIA, which is an even higher level than

Top Secret. I was told it was something very bad that led to the deaths of a number of CIA case officers and field agents. It supposedly decimated American intelligence in Europe and the Middle East for years, even today. Pretty catastrophic," she said.

"Can you tell me what's going on? It isn't good this lack of cooperation on the dead American. In French we say, 'the end of not receiving.' It means no response. This isn't normal."

"I honestly don't know. I got pulled from Panama after a DEA agent, a good guy, was killed to come here and I still don't know why they picked me, or what we are and aren't allowed to give you. There's a lot about this case I still don't understand. Sorry," she said, thinking she must look like a complete idiot to him. Suddenly, Paris wasn't so beautiful.

Brochard said, "Are you saying, Mademoiselle Ramirez, not a single American law enforcement agency has any idea who the dead man is? We sent a copy of a passport, morgue photographs, fingerprints, DNA."

"Not everyone in America's been fingerprinted – and as you know, there were false prints. If the FBI or CIA knows anything they haven't shared it with my office. Our agencies don't always cooperate as well as we should. The one thing I do know is people are getting murdered. Two in Panama, your five in Marseilles; so whatever we're looking for is worth killing for. My boss indicated we may be targets too," she said, glancing at the columns of the classically-styled church in the square. "That church. Is it very old?"

"The Madeleine; it was built by Napoleon. So it's possible there are U.S. agencies who know the real identity, but who refuse to share it with an important police investigation?" he asked.

Ouch! She thought. "They're taking this seriously. That's why I'm here. But it's not just us. I get the feeling you're also holding back – look, what's the correct way to address you? You're a judge and a prosecutor, nothing like our system, and I'm sure to get it wrong," she said.

"Prosecutor Brochard. Or if you like, Jean-Pierre. And do I call you, Katharine?" he said, doing a quick inventory of her. Athletic body, a hint of *café au lait* color skin, dark brown hair parted on the side in a casual wave to her neck. Not pretty, but a woman you'd notice, her looks made disconcerting by sea-green eyes – what was that stunning line from Baudelaire? – *De tes yeux, de tes yeux verts. From your eyes, from your green eyes, lakes where my soul trembles and sees its hell . . . Sees its hell*, he thought, like a warning shot across the bow.

"Casey. No one calls me Katharine. Ever," she said. He really was attractive. She was glad she'd been forewarned he was married, because her girl hormones were shooting off sparklers like the Fourth of July.

"Exotic name, Casey Ramirez."

"I'm half-Mexican. Not very exotic in California. And you haven't answered my question, Pros– Jean-Pierre," trying his name on her tongue. "You're holding back too. You've talked about the jewel robbers, the Blue Panthers, but nothing about the girl who went with them. Who is she?"

"The others were easier. We had bodies, forensics, fingerprints to work with. With the girl, all we have are descriptions by witnesses who were frightened half out of their wits and a black-and-white security camera video from the jewelry robbery."

"But you've investigated her identity. Is she French? If anything, she should be the main focus," Casey said, thinking please don't be one of those asshole male investigators who can't stand anything that smacks of criticism from a woman.

"Why should she be the focus?" Brochard asked, taking out a cigarette and lighting it. She straightened, almost an unconscious reaction, he noticed. Americans weren't used to people smoking.

"Let's get serious," she said. "This Layton Gary McCord, whoever he was, is dead. Those daily coded calls were probably a trigger, a mechanism probably set up by McCord himself because he knew he had a good chance of dying. We've got a safety deposit key, so it's in a bank box somewhere, but the only lead we have to whatever it is he hid or where it might be is something he told his girlfriend. She's the only person we know about who knew him at the end. She's the key. Find her and we'll find what we're looking for."

"I agree," he nodded. "Monsieur McCord rented a villa in Cap d'Antibes, not far from Nice where he was killed. We assumed the woman was either a French citizen or if she was a foreigner, she applied for a *carte de séjour*, a French resident's card. One of the store employees thought she had an accent."

"She wasn't French?"

"No, but it's not as helpful as you might think. Five months earlier, a young woman applied for a *carte de séjour*. See for yourself," he said, turning on his electronic tablet, tapping till he found it and showed her. It was a French identity card with the photo of a dark-haired woman in her twenties named Milena Kolavitch.

"Is that her?" she asked.

"Unfortunately, no. When we showed this identity photo to the old couple in Marseilles who met her when she and her accomplice fenced some diamonds from the robbery, they insisted that the young woman in the photo wasn't her. They were certain of it. Also, this Milena Kolavitch was supposedly from Serbia. When we sent the photo to police headquarters in Belgrade, we got the same response as we did about Monsieur Layton. The identity of the young woman Milena Kolavitch was fake. She didn't exist. But there's a connection, another twist in the case," he said.

"And that is?"

"The call to Ames Bergman that set everything off and even brought you here to Paris, was also made from Belgrade. That can't be a coincidence."

"No it can't be. So where do we go from here?" she said, finishing her wine.

He smiled. "La Santé Prison, one of the worst. And the prisoner you're about to meet, one of the very worst."

CHAPTER EIGHTEEN

LA SANTÉ, PARIS

BROCHARD DROVE under a train trestle and parked across the street from La Santé prison, a brooding edifice surrounded by a high brown stone wall. The prison was in the middle of a working class neighborhood in Paris' 14th *arrondissement*. They crossed to the entrance, a solid steel door with a plexiglass-enclosed phone bolted next to it on the wall.

"So the prisoner we're here to talk to knew the three dead Blue Panthers, so hopefully he'll help us identify the fourth?" Casey said.

"Also possibly a lead to the woman, the key as you said," Brochard nodded. "Security camera video from the train station in Marseilles, showed a tall man who could be the fourth Panther boarding the train to Paris with a woman."

"You think it's her?"

"She wasn't found dead with the others in that Marseilles apartment. It's possible they both escaped whatever happened and linked up. They could even be in it together," he said.

"And this convict? He'll talk because . . .?"

"I've arranged to reduce his sentence eight years. If he cooperates," Brochard added.

Brochard picked up the phone inside the plexiglass enclosure and spoke in rapid French. The steel door opened and they stepped inside. A guard in a cage behind bulletproof glass electronically scanned their IDs and opened an interior steel door.

They went inside to a small reception room where they passed through metal detectors and were intimately, too damn intimately, Casey thought, patted down by guards for weapons or contraband. To simplify things, she'd left her Sig Sauer P238 pistol and ankle holster in the car.

Two guards led them through another steel door to a hallway painted in an institutional cream color. She was surprised by the amount of natural light that filtered from soaring barred windows. Through one of the windows, she caught a glimpse of the prison yard, its high walls topped with concertina wire. The cells in the hallway had heavy steel doors painted the same cream color as the walls. Except for their footsteps, the silence was deadening. The minutes in this place must creep like eternity, Casey thought with a shiver.

A sign on a wall read: "*Problème de Drogue? Nous pouvons vous aider.*" Under it, a hand-scribbled graffiti: "*J'ai besoin de 10 Kg de coca.*"

"What's it say?" Casey asked, pointing at the sign.

"Drug problem? We can help," Brochard translated.

"And the graffiti?"

"I need ten kilos of cocaine. A joke," he half-grinned as the guards led them to a windowless room, empty except for three plastic chairs.

"I'm not sure why you want me along? I don't speak French," she'd asked Brochard on the drive over.

"It's good to give him a woman to look at. A reminder of the world. An incentive," Brochard said.

They waited. A guard brought in a man with a shaved head in gray sweats. Brochard had briefed her on him: Julien Lacaze, sentenced to thirty years for a string of armed robberies and two murders.

Lacaze sat legs crossed, eyes devouring Casey, who tried to act as if she understood every word. She assumed he was undressing her with his eyes. Go to it, she thought. If we get something, pretend all you like, creep.

Brochard asked him something and Lacaze said something directly to her. She caught only that he'd been talking about someone named "Vincent *le Chat*." Vincent the Cat. Colorful names these perps had, she thought.

"Who's 'Vincent the Cat'?" she asked Brochard in English.

"He says two of the dead Panthers, Patrice Gignac and Lucas Mathieu were close pals with a third, Vincent Grumier, also known as 'Vincent the Cat'. Apparently, this Vincent was the leader of the gang. He said he doesn't know anything about the dead North African," Brochard said.

The prisoner looked at her. "You want find Vincent *le Chat, cherie*? Visit me in private, I tell you," he said in heavily-accented English. "

"Tell me now or forget it," Casey said, standing up. "The deal with the French is no good unless my office agrees as well."

Lacaze stared at the two of them. His face showed nothing, but Casey could hear the gears working. Start easy, she thought.

"Is he tall, this Vincent?" she said, holding up her hand to indicate height.

"One meter eighty-five, *peut être* more," he said. She

mentally did the math: Six foot one. It could help confirm if this Vincent was the man in the train station video.

"Where would he go in Paris?" she asked.

"Vincent *le Chat*, how you say, not *stupide*. He never stay any place more than one day. Maybe two. Still . . . " he ran his eyes over her body. She reminded herself he was a murderer.

"Ask him what does he want? He's not getting out of here. He's not having sex with me. So ask him to tell us something he wants that we can do?" she said to Brochard, who repeated it in French to Lacaze.

"More books. Mysteries. Pierre Lemaitre, Varenne, Brigitte Aubert. I like to read," he said.

"If it's allowed, I promise," she said.

"*Alors*, is it a deal? Eight years off your sentence . . . ? How do I find Vincent the Cat?" Brochard said in French, then translated for Casey. Lacaze licked his lips, the tip of his tongue darting out for a second like a little fish.

"There's a little *Vietnamien* restaurant, *Chez* Nguyen, rue de Belleville near the Place des Fêtes. That's his *quartier*. If Vincent *le Chat*'s in Paris, you'll find him in the 19th," Lacaze said.

As they stood to leave, Lacaze stared at Casey again and smiled. If thoughts were actions, I'd be spread-eagled naked, she thought.

"The books, you won't forget?" Lacaze said in his awkward English.

"I won't forget," she said.

CHAPTER NINETEEN

BOULEVARD DE COURCELLES, PARIS

THE WEATHER TURNED COOL, rainy that morning as if the summer had never been. Paris could be like that, Brochard thought. A breeze rustled the trees, yellow leaves soggy underfoot on the Boulevard de Courcelles.

He sat alone at a table, watching drops of rain slide down the steamed window. The brasserie was warm and smelled of *café au lait* and tobacco, a place he and Gabi used to frequent because it was close to her mother's apartment in the 8th *arrondissement*.

His thoughts kept circling back to the HSI agent, Casey. She'd handled herself well questioning the prisoner at La Santé, but there was something solitary, locked-up about her, a fortress on a hill. Since then there had been no progress. If Kurt Giroud was here he'd say it was *baisée*, a screw-up.

They'd set up undercover surveillance in a commercial van across the street from the Vietnamese restaurant, but so far neither Vincent the Cat nor the girl in the video had showed. We're like bicycle racers, chasing ourselves, he thought, then forgot everything as Gabi came into the brasserie, collapsing her umbrella.

She greeted him with her usual *bise*, cheek-kisses and allowed him to help her off with her trench coat. She was *chic* as always in a floral top and black slacks, her *gamine*-cut black hair damp from the rain and the old feeling came back in his throat. True, it'd be interesting to take that exotic Casey to bed, but there was only one Gabi. She affected him as if she were the only woman in Paris.

"Sorry I'm late. A conference with the counselor at Juliette's school," she said and to the waiter, "A *pichet* of chablis. Burgundy, not the house wine."

"A problem?" Brochard asked. Gabi had enrolled Juliette in an exclusive private elementary school near the Gare Saint-Lazare train station. Its graduates included President Hollande, Jean-Paul Sartre, and Brigitte Bardot.

"She doesn't want to go to school. The other kids talk about their fathers. She misses you, Jean-Pierre." Her words like a knife in his chest. He remembered the day Juliette was born, holding her in his arms for the first time in the hospital, looking down at her tiny face, still red from the birth, thinking, she's mine. Part of me. Feeling a surge of love like nothing he had ever felt before, thinking he would give up his life in a second to protect her. Now he was failing her.

"It's my fault. All of it, my stupid career," he said. She didn't respond. "They're dangling an important Deputy Chief Prosecutor position for me here in Paris. I'll sell the business. I know you hate it. We can keep the condo in Nice and my mother's *bastide* in Provence for the August vacation," he went on. She didn't respond. "If you want, we can sell those too."

She pulled her hand away. "I'm having an affair, Jean-Pierre. His name is Henri Belanger."

It sucked the air out of him. He felt like he'd been kicked

in the solar plexus by a horse. How could he not have known this was coming? And yet, he could barely breathe.

"Who is he? I don't think I know him." His voice sounded odd to him, like it was someone else's voice.

"He's Deputy CEO of Canal Plus, in charge of their TV programming. We've been seeing each other for eleven months."

Eleven months meant while they were in Nice, while she was snapping at him for coming home late, for missing Juliette's birthday party. All that time she'd had her legs in the air with this Henri.

"Eleven months. Where'd you meet?"

"A party. Madame Boulloré," she said. Lilliane Boulloré was a billionaire's widow, an older woman whose primary activity consisted of throwing lavish parties to troll for handsome young men whom she went through at an astonishing rate. Brochard noted that Gabi didn't say the obvious, that as usual he'd been too busy working to come to that party, too busy to keep his wife from jumping into bed with Henri.

"All that time in Nice – how did you manage?" he asked. His voice really was different, as if the molecules in his throat had rearranged themselves.

"He had a condo in Monte Carlo. I would drive over. You never suspected?"

No, he hadn't. Had he really been that self-preoccupied? Eleven months. What a fool he was, he thought. Her and Henri of Canal Plus in Monte Carlo, just far enough away so they were unlikely to be seen. It made a horrible kind of sense.

"He's here, in Paris?"

She nodded. "We're together now," she said.

The waiter brought the wine and poured it for her. She

took a sip. Neither of them spoke. Brochard felt the world had tilted sideways and he had fallen into someone else's life.

"Do you want a divorce?" he asked. It felt bizarre talking as though it were a normal conversation. His ears rang as if a bomb had detonated and yet they were talking as though life was going on normally. Around them in the brasserie, even mid-morning, people were eating, talking, meeting as though the world was a rational place, though Brochard understood now in a way he never had before there was no such thing. Everything he had ever thought or done before was an illusion, except Gabi, more desirable than ever, talking about an affair with someone else as casually as if they were deciding what to have for dinner.

She shook her head. "For the moment, I want things as they are. Juliette needs you. I don't hate you, Jean-Pierre. There's something else."

"*Merde*. Am I going to need another *pastis*?" he asked, signaling the waiter.

"Probably," she said, her smile showing a dimple he loved. "Thank you for that, Jean-Pierre. I'd forgotten you could be funny."

He glanced at the window. It was raining harder. He watched the drops slide down the glass and when he turned back to Gabi, the waiter had brought the *pastis*. He drank it down.

"I'm pregnant," she said. "Third month."

Another punch to the solar plexus. There was a carafe of water on the table and he poured it into a glass, spilling some of it on the table and his hand. His throat was bone dry. He drank the water; it tasted like bile.

"Is it mine?"

"I don't know," she said. "I don't want to risk amniocentesis now. We'll have to wait for the DNA."

"What are you going to do?" he asked in his stranger's voice.

"I'm going to do a TV reality show, for Canal Plus. Contestants vying for best new design innovations in fashion, products, web, commercials. Henri's helping me. I'll have my own design boutique too. It's very exciting." She'd entered a new country, he thought. They spoke a different language there. They were different people now, strangers to themselves and each other. From the moment he'd started this case, life as he knew it had ended.

"When I came to Paris, I imagined . . . " He left it unsaid.

"*Ah*, Jean-Pierre," Gabi said, touching his hand. "Love's a fairy-tale that we sometimes fall into in the middle of ordinary life. But life is love's enemy. Like gravity, it pulls us down." This can't be happening, he thought with a stab of panic.

"Do you remember that night? The Pont Neuf, the two of us?"

"If I saw that girl on the street today, I wouldn't know her." Gabi frowned. "Sometimes, love is cruel."

"Funny, I always thought it was easy," he said. A young couple came into the brasserie, shaking water off their coats. The girl was pretty, with light brown hair that she wore swept to one side. The young man touched her hand, obviously smitten. Brochard felt like shouting a warning to them, but they were both busy tapping on their smart phones. A different generation, he thought, feeling suddenly old. They're like a different species. "You and Henri, are you going to live together?" The words stuck in his throat; they came out on their own.

She shook her head. "He wants to, but no. I don't want that and for now it wouldn't be good for Juliette. *Maman* has plenty of room. If you're in Paris, you can see Juliette two times a week and have her all day Saturday, if that's agreeable?"

Brochard nodded. He didn't trust himself to talk. Gabi stood, put on her trench coat, picked up her umbrella. Brochard also stood. She leaned towards him as if to give him a goodbye kiss on the cheek, then stopped herself.

"I'm sorry," he said, conscious of what an odd thing to say it was, given that she was the one having the affair and leaving.

"I know," she said.

CHAPTER TWENTY

BOULEVARD DE CLICHY, PARIS

CANDY-COLORED neon signs from the strip shows and porn shops along the Boulevard de Clichy illuminated the night like a carnival. Prostitutes prowled the boulevard's center divider for customers. Pigalle, Vincent thought.

The camera shop was on the rue Pierre-Fontaine, sandwiched between Le Thai Massage Sexy and Le Zanzibar Club. To Vincent's practiced eye, every shop on the street had a state-of-the-art burglar alarm. The woman Milena sensed his unease.

"Can we risk being out like this?" she asked.

"We need new identity documents now," Vincent said, as they crossed the street to the shop. "The *flics* are after both of us. Not to mention whoever's behind the hit men in Marseilles."

"How do you know this camera guy?"

"The *milieu*," Vincent said, the catch-all word that encompassed the entire criminal universe.

A buzzer sounded as they opened the shop door. A bulky

black man wearing a loose-knit red-yellow-green cap, the colors of Senegal, came out of a back room.

"*Hé*, Mamadou, everything ready?" Vincent said.

"Who's the woman?" the black man demanded.

I wish I knew, Vincent thought. "Never mind her. You deal with me," Vincent said. "How good are they?" Meaning the new IDs.

"The best," Mamadou said, kissing his fingers to show how good they were. He motioned them to the workroom in back. "These identities are genuine. Hacked from Assisted-living *residences* for Alzheimer patients. The real patients are too far gone to even know who they are, much less that their identities have been stolen *and*," Mamadou winked, "even if they did, they can't do anything."

Mamadou motioned Vincent to a stool to take his photograph, then Milena took her turn. A half-hour later, they had new passports, national identity cards and *Carte Bancaire* credit cards. Vincent was now Louis Canet from Villeneuve-d'Ascq. Milena was Isabelle Dusollier from Roubaix, both cities in northern France.

"And the chips?" Vincent asked, referring to the RFID chips in the passports and cards.

"Perfect, don't worry. Where's Lucas?" Mamadou said.

"He went to see his mother," Vincent said. In a way it was true. The old girl was dead. "Twelve hundred?"

"Each," Mamadou said. Seeing Vincent's sharp expression at the price, what the French call putting mustard on your nose, added, "You get what you pay for. You're safe with these."

"They better be," Vincent grumbled, counting out the money. "And the special item?"

Mamadou went to a safe, opened it and handed Vincent

something that he placed into a messenger bag slung diagonally over his shoulder.

"You know how to use it?" Mamadou asked.

"I was a *parachutiste*. First Regiment," Vincent said, not saying he'd been court-martialed for selling FAMAS F1 assault rifles to a German in Stuttgart. The Army had swept the problem under the rug by cancelling his enlistment contract.

Mamadou motioned Vincent aside. "My mother was a *sandoma*, you understand?"

"No. What are you saying?"

"She had the gift. Your woman has a dark shadow. You need a *gris-gris*," he said, pulling Vincent a small canvas sack from a cord around his neck.

Vincent pushed it away. "You just be sure what you sold me works, *mec*," Vincent said. Mamadou kept his eyes on the woman. Not a sexy I-want-to-screw-you look, but a this-woman-is-trouble-get-her-out-of-here look.

"Be careful you don't run out of lives, Vincent the Cat," Mamadou said.

Vincent and Milena walked back to the Metro, the street crowded with tourists, prostitutes and African immigrants selling Eiffel Tower trinkets along the Boulevard de Clichy.

"This Irishman, why would he do business with us?"

"Because we have the key – and no one knows all the pieces but me. I spent months with the American," she said.

"And he's just going to hand it to us? I don't like this," Vincent said, stopping. It's a trap, he thought. Except why would she have stayed with that old man unless there was real money in it? Except everyone who got near her, the American, Nabil, the North Africans, Patrice, Lucas, ended up dead. Having sex with her was like making love with Death, he thought. He looked at her. Who knew Death was a woman and so beautiful? "We should just walk away from each other right now," he said. "I'll stand here. You keep walking."

"Don't," she said, coming close, looking up at him, her breasts grazing his arm, traffic and people buzzing by. "The money's real. Why do you think I stayed with him? We're so close," she whispered, pressing against him. For a second, he thought she was going to go down on him right there in the street.

"You better be telling the truth," he said. They crossed to the Place Blanche Metro.

"That African, can we trust him?" Milena said, as they waited on the Metro platform. The sound of the oncoming train and the rush of air filled the tunnel.

"More than I trust you," Vincent said.

CHAPTER TWENTY-ONE

BARBIZON, FRANCE

CASEY MET the man from the CIA at a restaurant on the narrow Rue du Mont Thabor near the Tuileries. His name was Nick Farrell and when the waiter came, he helped her order the asparagus soufflé from the French menu and the duck with peach for himself. He appeared to be in his late fifties and his suit had a loose sleeve button, no woman taking care of him, and his eyes, behind black-rimmed glasses were brown and intelligent.

"You're late," she said.

"Wanted to make sure you were clean. What's this about?" Farrell said after they exchanged introductions and she showed him her HSI badge and ID. Before she'd left Washington, Jerry Matthews told her if she ever got stuck or really in a jam to call the American embassy and ask for a "Mister Harrington." When asked who was calling, she was to say, "Stanley Boyle" and hang up. One minute later, she got a call-back on her cell phone. A machine-like voice stated a meeting location and time, after which the call abruptly ended. At first they chatted about nothing – the rain, Paris "Yes, a beautiful city even on days like today," checking nearby tables to make sure no one was paying attention. Casey took out her tablet computer, brought up the Layton Gary McCord autopsy face photo and showed him. Farrell reacted like he'd been electroshocked.

"Put it away!" he said, pushing the tablet away like it carried the Covid virus.

"Did you know him, Layton Gary McCord? I mean his real identity," she said.

Farrell shook his head. "Langley's got their panties in a twist over this," he said, looking around to make sure they weren't overheard. "Why are you here? Who sent you?" The waiter brought the food; she waited till he left.

"My boss, Arthur Dalton, HSI Chief of Staff," she said.

"He said to contact me?" Farrell asked.

"Not exactly," she said, biting into the best soufflé she'd ever tasted. Impossible that it was just asparagus, she thought.

"Then what, *exactly*?" Farrell said, putting down his fork.

Casey leaned forward. "Blue Madagascar," she whispered.

"Jesus," Farrell breathed, looking as if he'd just lost his appetite.

"I need information."

"Don't we all?" he said, looking at the restaurant window as if there was an answer in the rain. The day was gray and wet, the pavement shiny. Before she'd left her hotel, Casey borrowed one of their umbrellas.

"The dead guy, McCord. We think he might've been an old Company hand," she said, using the inside term for the CIA.

"I can't help you," he said, making a face. "I didn't know him. All I know is after, you know," avoiding saying 'Blue Madagascar' out loud again, "supposedly there was a major housecleaning. We're not even supposed to talk about it."

"Look, this guy's passport was fake and he'd had thumbprint transplants and yet, both the FBI and you guys claim you don't have anything. I'm just trying to find someone who knew him so we can identify him. You say you can't help, fair enough. But do you know anyone who might? Maybe someone from the old days"

Farrell sipped his wine, thought for a moment. Suddenly, Casey felt a surge of optimism. She could tell he had someone in mind.

"Swear you'll tell no one where you got it. I mean it," he said.

"Of course. Absolutely," she said.

"This person is no longer," he paused to find the right word, "active."

"Great. Anything."

"Don't be so sure. He's pretty paranoid. The story goes that he used to jury-rig the door handle of any room he was in with batteries and wire, so anyone trying to open it while he was sleeping would get an electric shock and set off an alarm. He always slept with a .50 caliber handgun. For all I know, still does. He's retired, never receives visitors. I doubt he'll talk to you – or anyone."

"But you think he might know?" Casey persisted.

He motioned her closer. "His name is Todd Brighton. Haven't spoken to him in a dog's age. Has a house on the Grande Rue in Barbizon outside Paris. Something of an artsy type now he's retired. Even exhibited paintings here in Paris. Every once in a while I'll spot him in town at some la-di-da art show or a café. If you can get him to talk . . . " Farrell shrugged.

"I appreciate this," Casey said.

"Don't tell him you got the name from me," Farrell said. "Todd doesn't have much use for the new people and methods in the CIA."

"Does that include you?"

"It includes everyone," Farrell said, returning with interest to his duck.

Casey drove a rental on the A6 south out of Paris in the rain; the sky a slab of gray, the Renault's wipers slapping back-and-forth on the windshield.

Brochard and Commandant Claire Pinault had ordered a plain-clothes watch on the Vietnamese restaurant on the rue de Belleville that Vincent "the Cat" Grumier was believed to frequent in Paris. Meanwhile, she was at a dead-end, unless she could find someone like this Todd Brighton to help her identify who Layton Gary McCord really was and maybe get a clue why what he was hiding had kicked up such a firestorm.

She turned off the *autoroute* onto a two-lane toward Fontainebleau. According to a guide book it was an historic place; the chateau where Napoleon abdicated. Driving into Barbizon, it was easy to see why an ex-CIA type like Brighton might've retired here. It was a stunningly picturesque town with 19th century stone buildings, trees flaming autumn red and gold, quaint little inns, narrow cobblestone streets. Each house was surrounded by a vine-covered stone wall; probably attractive to someone like Todd Brighton who wanted privacy.

She parked in front of Brighton's address and got out. It was raining harder now. A high stone wall topped by barbed wire surrounded the house. The only entrance was via a spike-topped wrought-iron gate with a security camera mounted on the gatepost. A sign read: "*Propriété Privée, Défense d'Entrer*", which Casey even with her next-to-zero French understood to mean "Keep out." Nick Farrell was right. It was a house for someone who didn't want visitors.

She pressed the doorbell on the stone gatepost and heard a distant buzz like a beehive. Two large Doberman Pinscher dogs bounded towards her, snarling and barking. They hurled themselves at the wrought-iron gate as if they wanted to tear her apart. Casey flinched back as they barked and growled inches away behind the gate. *Instantly in her mind she was back in Central when she was a little girl, terrified of Rico's pit bull, Tigre, who would snarl and try to bite her every chance he could. The only one who could save her was Jessica, who would jump between them to protect Casey. Once when Rico wasn't around, Jessie took a broomstick and when Tigre lunged for her, rapped him hard on the nose. "You touch her, I'll kill you," she hissed at the dog. Tigre gathered himself into a ball, then hurled himself back at Casey. This time Jessica rapped his nose even harder, causing him to yipe. Four times he lunged at her and four times, she smacked his nose with the broomstick. After that, he growled every time he saw Casey, but wouldn't come near her. Even so, Casey tried to hide behind Jessie whenever the dog was around.* She pressed the doorbell again, letting the buzzer ring through the dogs' snarling for at least ten seconds. She kept pressing it.

"*Allez-vous en!*" Someone shouted from inside the house, setting the dogs barking and howling insanely. Casey leaned even harder on the doorbell.

"*Va te faire foutre!*" The same voice shouted and Casey had the sense whatever it was, it wasn't polite. The dogs howled and clawed against the iron gate to get at her.

"Mister Brighton, I'm Casey Ramirez! I need to ask you

one question! Please!" she shouted in English. She pressed the doorbell again and held it.

"I've got a gun pointed at the door. I'll shoot," the voice shouted back in English.

"Arthur Dalton said to see you. Just one question, sir!" she shouted.

"I don't know who that is – and I don't care! Go away!"

"No, dammit!" she shouted back and pushed the doorbell harder and longer.

"Angelique!" the voice shouted. After a minute, a young African woman in a raincoat came out of the house. She shouted at the dogs, grabbing hold of their collars and opened the gate, motioning to Casey to follow.

Casey stepped into the house. The African woman shoved the dogs outside and closed the door. An older man in paint-stained jeans and tee shirt, lean, in his late seventies, she guessed, stood in a doorway pointing an AR-15 assault rifle straight at her. The African woman took off her raincoat. She was completely naked.

"Who are you and what do you want?" the man said in American English.

Casey took out her tablet and brought up the morgue photo of the dead American, Layton Gary McCord. "One question, sir. Do you know this man?" she asked. Brighton barely glanced at the tablet.

"Never seen him. Get out," Brighton said. Casey's heart fell, but she'd spotted a flicker in Brighton's eyes.

"You recognized him. And I know you were once CIA," she said.

He looked again at the tablet, then at Casey. She was sure he recognized the man in the photo. "Who sent you? Bergman? Fitzgerald? Any of those clowns?" he said. She shook her head.

"I don't know any of those people. The man in the picture, Layton Gary McCord, not his real name," she said.

"What makes you think I know who or what you're talking about?"

"Because you do."

"Who gave you my name? Paris station? Was it Farrell?" he asked.

"I'm with the Homeland Security Investigations Directorate. I work directly for Arthur Dalton," she said.

"Don't know him. You better leave," he said, motioning with the rifle.

"It's about Blue Madagascar," she said desperately.

For a long minute he didn't say anything. Finally, he lowered the AR-15. "I've heard of Dalton," Brighton said. "They're all assholes. What kind is he?"

"I'm not sure," Casey said.

What does that mean?"

"I only just met him. Tell the truth, I can't tell if he's a super-brain professorial type or a double-dealing son-of-a-bitch – or both."

"Both. Definitely both," Brighton said. He looked again at the computer tablet image and shook his head. "Christ, so Fleetwood's really dead, huh?" Casey's heart skipped a beat. A name. A real name! "No wonder Langley's running around like their pants are on fire. You better come in, but only for a minute. Angelique, *ma minette*, could you bring some wine?" he said to the African woman. "You better come in. You're like a drowned cat," he said to Casey, glancing at her hair, soaked from the rain. He led her into a living room filled with modern paintings, a fire crackling in a stone fireplace.

"Fleetwood, is that his real name?" she asked, after she took off her coat and they were seated.

"Dale Fleetwood. You really didn't know?" he asked. She

shook her head. "Unbelievable. Bunch of clowns. Who killed him?"

She noted that it never occurred to him that Dale Fleetwood aka Layton Gary McCord might've died of natural causes.

"Accidently, as a bystander in a robbery in Nice," she said.

"An accident? Fleetwood? And now the wheels are turning. Well, well," he smirked as Angelique, still naked, padded in with a bottle of red Bordeaux on a tray with olives, slices of baguette and different cheeses. Casey watched her walk away, graceful as a black panther.

"She's working on her Masters in Ecotechnologies at Ecole Polytechnique in Paris," Brighton said.

"I didn't say anything," Casey said.

"No, but you thought it," Brighton said.

"Doesn't she get cold?" Casey asked, grateful for the fire that warmed the room on a wet gray day.

"You'd have to ask her. She also likes art and sex," Brighton said, sipping the wine.

"So do I."

"Really?" Brighton said, giving her a wicked smile.

"I lied," Casey said, giving it back to him. "I don't know anything about art. You're a painter? Is that the attraction?"

"I dabble. This is an artist's village. Millet, Rousseau, Corot, Renoir; they all found something here. Half the town pretends to paint or sculpt, some more than others. As to what's the attraction, women seem to love men for reasons I've never understood. Between you and me, we don't deserve it, but I'm profoundly grateful. So, Dale Fleetwood's dead and now they're all running around like chickens with their heads cut off looking for whatever ticking bomb he might've left behind. Is that it?"

Wow, right on the money, Casey thought. "Sounds about

right. Do you have any idea what it might be or where he might've left it?" Casey said.

"Not a clue," Brighton said, putting a piece of brie into his mouth. "Wouldn't tell you if I did. Hope the whole damn thing blows up in their faces." Shook his head. "Dale Fleetwood," he repeated.

"What did you mean when you said Fleetwood's 'ticking bomb'?"

"I didn't mean anything. Forget it," he shrugged.

"Ah, but you did. You really shouldn't drop little hand grenades and then pretend you have nothing to do with the explosion. Whatever Fleetwood left behind might hurt the wrong people. It often does," she said.

"That wasn't half-bad, what you said," he said, holding up one hand. "Alright, I'll play."

"Fleetwood's ticking bomb. What'd you mean?"

"Just guessing," Brighton grimaced. "Dale was always finagling something. He even got sent to prison. ADX, the Fed Supermax, no less."

"Prison, why?"

Brighton shrugged. "Dale was a character. He was always up to his ears in shady shit. He finally got nailed."

"If he was in a Supermax prison, how'd he end up on the French Riviera buying jewelry for a much younger woman when he was killed?"

"Is that what happened?" Brighton said. "It doesn't surprise me. Like I said, Dale always had an angle."

"Did you know him in the CIA?"

Brighton inhaled, let it out. "Back in the day, Dale and I did stuff together when he was first in the CIA. Anti-Commie stuff in Europe, arms to insurgents in Africa. Dale went on to bigger and better things. For a while, he flew pretty high, right up to the sun."

"Burnt his wings like Icarus?"

"In those days it was easier to tell the good guys from the bad guys. Cold War, James Bond spy stuff. I was even part of Fleetwood's most famous stunt, the one that made his reputation."

"What happened?"

"This was back in the '60's. The Italian Communist Party and the Communist Trade Union, the CGIL, had tight ties to the KGB. The Russians nearly took over the Italian government; it was that close. This one time, the Soviets were staging a giant CGIL Union meeting in Milan to gear up for elections.

"Dale had this crazy-ass idea. The two of us commandeered a gang of young toughs, teenage kids really, just starting to scratch their way up in the Camora and Ndrangheta Mafia clans. We paid 'em to catch rats," he grinned. "Those kids must've scoured every cellar in Milan. Before you knew it, we had two giant crates crammed with live rats. Must've been a million of 'em.

"The Commies had gathered hundreds of delegates for this big shindig at the Grand Hotel. Just before the first meeting started, Dale and me, along with a bunch of these kids snuck the crates up in the freight elevator. We released the rats in the meeting halls and delegate suites. Just let 'em run and took off. Freaking unbelievable!" Brighton said, eyes sparkling. "You never saw such pandemonium. People were screaming and running around like nuns with the devil on their heels. Pretty soon all the papers in Italy were doing cartoons about 'Reds' and 'rats'. Made Fleetwood a name within certain precincts of the CIA."

"And after that?"

"Dale and I went in different directions, lost touch,"

Brighton said, drinking his wine. "You should try the wine. It's a Saint Emilion."

"It's wonderful," she said after a sip. "Did you know about Blue Madagascar?"

Brighton shook his head. "Just a whisper. Not the details. Heads rolled. Decimated the Company, including a lot of dedicated people who had nothing to do with it."

"Including you?" Casey said. Brighton nodded. "And Fleetwood?"

"By then, he was outside, doing his own thing." He said vaguely and she could see he wasn't going to tell her anything more. "I'm not the person to ask. I'm retired in the most artsy-fartsy touristy village in France – and in a country that majors in 'touristy', that's saying something," Brighton said. "There's one of mine," he gestured at a painting mounted on a stand, an abstract that almost suggested a cubistic figure in metallic moonlight. "The nice thing about living here is that you're out of the hassle, the insane prices and traffic of Paris, but you're only an hour's drive away when you want to get back to civilization." He stood and picked up the AR-15. "So, you've dried off, had a decent wine, seen my *copine's* ass, Mademoiselle Ramirez, I think it's time to leave."

Casey took another swallow of the wine – it really was very good – and put on her coat. Brighton walked her to the door.

"You said you weren't the person to ask about Dale Fleetwood. Who is?" Casey said.

He looked at her with what in another person might've been compassion, a doctor hesitant to tell a patient her real diagnosis. "I don't think you have a clue what you're involved in. You're walking blindfolded in a minefield. You'd better go."

"About Fleetwood, there must be someone," she said

desperately. "Whatever this is, it's probably not good for the wrong people to get their hands on it."

He studied her as if she were a painting. "Have you ever been to Budapest?' She shook her head. "Go to the Lion House Gösser in the Castle District. It's on the Buda side – and whatever happens, don't mention my name, this house to anyone," opening the door. He swore at the dogs, holding them by their collars till Casey scooted down the path and out the gate in the rain.

As she drove away, a black Citroen pulled out from where it was parked down the street and followed her car.

CHAPTER TWENTY-TWO

AT NIGHT, Boulevard Mortier was a street of shadow and light and tall brick walls topped by barbed wire and security cameras. It didn't feel like Paris. Getting out of Brochard's car, Casey found herself squinting in the glare of streetlights on the facility wall.

They held their IDs against a scanner recessed in the wall beside a heavy steel door. After a minute's wait, the door clicked open. They filed one at a time into a room where two tough-looking agents frisked them. One of them put her Sig Sauer pistol into a black plastic bag and gave her a receipt, telling her something in French. Brochard translated that she could have it back when she left.

A third agent accompanied them in an elevator to a third floor office. He knocked and the door clicked open. The moment they entered, Casey could smell the brandy. A bearded man in a three-piece suit gestured for them to sit.

"I'm Jacques Marchand," the bearded man said in good English. He uncorked a bottle· of Napoleon cognac and poured three glasses. "Admiral Deschamps has cleared you both to be briefed. *Santé*," he toasted.

Brochard gulped his down. Something had changed with him, Casey thought. She'd noticed it the minute he picked her up from her hotel. He was distracted; his suit not as fresh, not as put-together.

Brochard gestured at the cognac bottle. Marchand nodded and Brochard refilled his glass and drank again. He's flying on one wing already, Casey thought. wondering what had happened and if she would have to carry him out to wherever the hell this was going.

"I believe you have new information for us, Mademoiselle," Marchand said.

"We now know the true identity of the American killed in the robbery: Dale Fleetwood, an ex-CIA agent who was living in France." She turned to Brochard. "At this point, you should be able to close that part of the Blue Panther case."

"The pieces are beginning to come together," Marchand said. "The American NSA picked up some Latvian cell phone communications. The head of the Latvian Special Police, SIRENE, Colonel Seibelis appears to have been in communication with a company in Belgrade, called Srxbyx Transport, S.A. And, surprise! It turns out, this same company owns the VPN in Riga through which the coded calls were made to the mysterious dead American, Dale Fleetwood, whom we now know was a former CIA agent.

"Another interesting *entrefilet*, there was a bank transfer from a Belgrade bank to this Srxbyx company's bank account in Luxembourg. Also, the woman from the robbery, Milena Kolavitch, although her identification is false that's probably not her real name, appears to have come from Serbia. *Finalement*, the mobile phone call to the American DNI, Ames Bergman, demanding the hundred million euros originated from Belgrade. In short, Belgrade is at the center of this conspiracy."

"Something more," Brochard added. He'd been on the phone with Giroud. "We've done ballistic analysis on the bullets that killed the victims in Marseilles. They were all from a very rare pistol: an OTs-38 Stechkin 7.62x42mm. It's a special revolver, a weapon that's completely silent when fired, used exclusively by the Russian SVR."

"A Russian operation. The water gets deeper," Marchand frowned. "So what were they after in Marseilles?"

"The same thing we are. What Fleetwood left behind. It's a treasure hunt – and after the events in Marseilles, they're ahead of us," Casey said.

"What about this Serbian company, this Srxbyx Transport?" Brochard put in, tapping the ash from his cigarette into an ashtray on the desk. The way he did it, nearly missing the ashtray, made Casey nervous. Great, a lush for a partner, she thought.

"The Luxembourg authorities refuse to divulge anything."

"That leaves Belgrade," Casey said.

Marchand looked at her approvingly. "We were hoping you and Monsieur Brochard would go to Belgrade to investigate," Marchand said. "Neither of you are from the intelligence community, so that shouldn't make the Serbs paranoid. The Quai des Orfèvres and your CIA, Mademoiselle, agree you should go." Belgrade! Casey's mind screamed. She was already miles over her head in Paris. Not to mention, the French were missing the point.

"I'll talk to my superiors in Washington about Belgrade, but for me this Serbian company is a sideshow. We're missing the main point," she said.

"And that is, Mademoiselle . . . ?" Marchand said, leaving

it dangling. Brochard wasn't looking at her. I'm not part of his world, she thought.

"The woman. The one that got away – and by the way, how is it she always gets away?" she said. "She disappears from the robbery without the security cameras getting a good image of her. Prosecutor Brochard's people discover her residence card, only the name and the photo on the card aren't hers, so no one knows who she is. Don't you think that's curious? And yet, if there's anyone who knows what Fleetwood left behind or where it might be, it's her."

"Clearly, she's clever. Possibly a criminal," Marchand said, with an impeccable Gallic raising of the eyebrows.

"I suppose it's possible she's just a girl caught in the wrong place at the wrong time, but look what happened," she said. "Her American boyfriend is murdered and literally within seconds she's off with the Blue Panthers. She walks away from a mass killing by a pro in Marseilles and the next morning she and the surviving Blue Panther are boarding a train together to Paris."

"You think she's behind the hundred million demand?" Marchand said, leaning forward.

"Look, odds are Fleetwood set up this whole elaborate Luxembourg-to-Latvia trigger mechanism in case he died because he knew his life was in danger. He must've also planned a way to complete the hundred million deal – and the only person who was close to him and would know is the girl without a face."

"I agree," Brochard nodded, looking at her with the pleased expression of a teacher with a prize pupil.

"So do we," Marchand said, refilling their cognac glasses. "For that reason, *Procureur* Brochard must remain in Paris to direct the police search for the woman and Vincent the Cat."

"What about me?" Casey asked.

"If you and your superiors agree, Mademoiselle, we need you to go to Belgrade. It may be the only way to find out about this company and who the woman really is."

"I'm not the right person for Belgrade. I don't know the area, the language," she said. She was falling deeper and deeper down the rabbit hole. What was it Brighton had said, that she was walking blindfolded in a minefield. She had a bad feeling about this.

"You're an American official. You'll do better there than we would," Marchand said. "We have to get to this woman before any of the other players, especially the Russians. They have very nasty ways of eliminating evidence *and people.*"

CHAPTER TWENTY-THREE

BOULOGNE-BILLANCOURT

THE PUB WAS in Boulogne-Billancourt outside Paris, on Quai Georges Gorse, facing the Seine River. It had a nautical-Irish theme as though it were a 19th century sailing ship manned by jolly leprechauns. The majority of customers were after-work British and American expats, the hub-bub of conversation drowning out Irish music on the speakers. When the waiter recommended O'Hara on tap, Vincent the Cat gave him the kind of look only a Frenchman can manage and ordered a Stella; Milena chose apple cider.

"This is a cheery place. *Très* Irish. We could pretend to be Irish," she said.

"You pretend. You're good at it," Vincent said. In her red mini at night, he thought she looked like a whore. He wasn't sure why that irritated him, but it did. Every minute he was liking this meeting less; and her for talking him into it.

"That doesn't mean I like it."

"You like it fine. Where's your Irishman?"

"I don't know." Milena brightened. "Let's talk about something else."

"Like what?"

"If we got the money, what would you do?"

"What business of yours is it?"

Her face reddened as if she'd been slapped. "You're right, how could a *putain* like me have feelings? You know Vincent, you don't have to play the *gangster* with me."

He lit a cigarette. "*Non,* how should I act, like a lover?"

"You think what we do is love?"

"I think we both do what we have to. The rest is *conneries,* bullshits," he said.

She stared at the window. Through it she could see the evening traffic and the outlines of trees bare of leaves along the bank of the river.

"You can see the Seine from here," she said.

"I've seen it."

"You know, you don't have to be a shit all the time. I'm not your enemy. I don't want to be." She bit her lip. "Tell me something true. Something you never told anyone. Something *Tante* Rosine doesn't know."

"You want true, *cherie?* You haven't said one true thing since the second I laid eyes on you. I don't even know your real name, except with that fake *carte de séjour* I know it's not Milena. The only true thing I know about you is you're a liar."

At another table, some American ex-pats were singing "Happy Birthday" to someone named Craig, who looked like an IT guy. One of them shouted in English: "Watch out, girls! He's a killer!"

"I'm Russian," she said.

"Russian," he repeated. "And your Irishman, McBride. Is he Russian too? A happy Irish-Russian? What game are you playing?"

"No game," she said straightening. "I'm not . . . It's not what you think."

"You have no idea what I think."

"I do now. You want to know what the game is," she said.

"You tell me, *cherie*."

"I told you, but you don't believe me. The money is real. It could be for the two of us," she said, looking at him with those incredible blue eyes.

"Answer me one thing," he said. "Why didn't your American boyfriend just give Nabil the wallet? What was so important, the safety deposit key?"

She nodded. "There were two reasons I went with Nabil. One, like I told you, I'm not here legally. I can't talk to the *flics*. The other was the bank key. It was in the wallet and I knew the password. With the key, I could get what was in the box in Panama. Nabil killing him opened a door. All you and I have to do is walk through it."

"And if you're lying?"

"If I'm lying we part. You'll never see me again."

For you for sure, he thought. At the bottom of a canal. Still, what if she was telling the truth, just this once? "You're a strange one." He plucked a shred of tobacco from the tip of his tongue. "The dead American. How'd you two connect?"

"He spotted me stealing something at the *supermarché*. Said I could do better. I thought he wanted sex, told him I wasn't a *putain*."

"What'd he say?"

"He laughed. Said he wasn't much good for the bed anymore, but if I wanted to change my life, I should let him buy me a glass of wine at a café."

"You liked him?"

"*Like's* a strong word. Our interests coincided. People thought I was just the *petite amie* of a sugar-daddy, but it wasn't true. I was a partner in his quest. Also, sometimes it was useful for him to have me along as arm candy.

"Quest for what? The mythical hundred million?"

"Maybe. Layton could be secretive, but I had the sense it was more than money. Can anyone ever know what's in someone else's heart?"

Vincent thought about La Santé, about his best *gars*, Remy, who'd been the optimist con, the *mec* who always saw the bright side no matter what *merde* happened, who kept you going when you were ready to pound your skull to mush against the cell wall; Remy, who killed himself seven months before his release by drinking a half-liter of rat poison.

"With Layton," she continued. "Something was driving him. It was an obsession, biblical almost. Like Samson, he wanted to pull down the pillars of the temple."

"So we're part of a dead man's quest, is that it?" Vincent asked.

"No, I'm like you. All I care about is the money. I'm alone. All I've got are my wits and looks – and as every woman knows, there's a shelf life on that. But the money's real. You saw in Marseilles; people are willing to kill for it." Her cell phone rang. She listened for a few seconds. "We're to go upstairs. Third floor. Apartment 16."

"I thought we were to meet him here," he said, slipping his hand into his jacket.

"We were. How do you want to play it?"

"Your Russian Irishman is upstairs?" She nodded. After a second, he said, "*Bien*, let's go meet him."

They left the pub, walked outside, and were buzzed into the building through another entrance. She hesitated in the hallway.

"Maybe we shouldn't do this," she whispered.

He grabbed her. "To hell with your Irishman. Just one

question – and for once in your life tell the truth – the *fric*, the money, it's real?" She nodded.

They started up the stairs. Halfway up, he stopped and did something behind her back she didn't see.

"What is it?" she whispered.

"Nothing. Go on," Vincent said, nudging her ahead. She knocked on an apartment door. A giant man, broad as a house and a good two meters tall, opened the door. The giant pointed a 9mm pistol, tiny in his hand, at Vincent's chest.

CHAPTER TWENTY-FOUR

BUDAPEST, HUNGARY

PHALANXES OF MEN in black uniforms marched stiff as toys, their boots echoing on the cobblestones. They chanted slogans and held aloft black banners with white lettering and Hungarian crosses.

"What are they saying?" Casey asked a man in the crowd next to her.

"The truth. 'Death to Soros the Jew.' 'Fidesz sells the nation to the E.U.' You're a foreigner," he said, staring at her. "Where are you from?"

"Canada," she said, a safer answer than America in situations like this. Conscious of his eyes on her, she edged away from the crowd. Her sense of unease grew with every step; the look of the Castle District on this, the Buda side of the Danube, only adding to the unreality. It looked more like the Hollywood set for a historical movie – she wouldn't've been surprised to see sword-fights and Musketeers – than a real city.

Luckily, it wasn't far from the square to the Lion House

Gösser pub. She went inside and found a table. After the cold outside, the place was warm, almost steamy. The walls were covered with framed photographs, but of no one she recognized. The customers were mostly locals; well-fed Hungarians with half-liters of beer and plates of sausages in front of them. She was waiting for someone from the embassy, not sure they would show. Since Paris, she wasn't sure of anything, as if the earth had tilted off its axis.

She sipped an apple-beer and tried to refocus on the case, on Dale Fleetwood, but what had happened between her and Brochard in Paris wouldn't go away, like a song you can't get out of your head – or maybe, she told herself – she didn't want it to.

After their meeting with Jacques Marchand at the Swimming Pool, Brochard was in no shape to be by himself. They wound up in her hotel room, though she wasn't sure even to herself whether sex was on the agenda, or if it was, whether he'd be able to manage it.

"My wife left me," Brochard told her, his tongue thick. "She's been having an affair."

So now she had permission, she thought. She'd seen he was wounded; now she knew why. Was that what she wanted? To be the rebound female? The revenge fuck?

"Did you know?" she asked.

"No, I didn't. The truth is, I can't blame her."

"Why not?"

"I took her away," jamming a cigarette in his mouth, but not lighting it, fumbling around for his lighter.

"From what?"

"From Paris, from work she loved, to run our family's business, something she hated. And I was busy working. My stupid career. I even missed my daughter's birthday party."

"You missed your daughter's party so it's okay for your

wife to screw someone else? You French have a funny defini-
tion of marriage," Casey said.

"It's not that simple," he said.

"No," she said, coming close. She took the unlit cigarette
from his lips. "Were you thinking about sex? Is that why you
came up here?"

He looked at her. "I don't know," he said. "It's
complicated."

"No, it isn't," she said, unbuttoning her blouse.

That night was the most intense sex of her life. It began
gently, with him pulling her to him, his hands tight on her
buttocks. Kissing her lips, neck, breasts, nipples, his lips soft
as down on a bird's breast. It'd been too long. She'd forgotten
how sexy kissing could be. They took their time, lying facing
each other, tongues darting like fish, at last taking him in her
hand, guiding him into her, Then he was on top of her, inside
her, a feeling so intense it frightened her. And as it was
happening, she knew he needed it. She wanted him to need
her that way. They began a rhythm that was theirs alone,
feeling him so much inside her she didn't know where he
ended and she began.

"Don't stop!" She urged him. She could feel him along the
entire length of her body, skin tingling, lips, tongues seeking,
and in the midst of moving, there was gentleness and an electric thrill and she felt herself soaring somewhere between the
Pleiades and the Moon in the night sky.

Afterwards, they lay beside each other, catching their
breath, saying nothing. Just before he turned over, he touched
her cheek with his finger and closed his eyes. When she
looked over, he was asleep.

She watched him sleep, breathing the smell of him, a
mingling of sex and sweat and cognac, his hair tousled, a little
spot at the top thinning. She trailed her fingers along his thigh,

hoping he wouldn't wake and see their ugliness, the ones broken in her childhood. She liked watching him while he slept, looking at his solid male nakedness, thinking it wouldn't be hard to go overboard on him. Then she took a breath. What idiocy are you imagining, she asked herself. He's married and in love with the woman who's cheating on him. That's not your life, reminding herself of Jessie's rule: *Lying to others is what everyone does. Lying to yourself is suicide.* Brochard was broken – and she herself was only half a person, wreckage left on a beach from the storm that cut her life into before and after the day they told her Jessica was gone.

In the morning, sunlight streaming through the hotel window, she and Brochard were awkward with each other. She said, "What happened last night wasn't a future."

""It won't happen again," he said.

"No," she'd said, thinking it was obvious neither of them believed it. Now, sitting in the Lion House Gösser in Budapest, she understood that as Marchand back in Paris had suggested, the ocean she was swimming in was getting very deep. She might never see him again; her Paris one-night-stand; Brochard, her fantasy *married* French boyfriend.

A white-haired man in a peacoat and a newsie cap came into the pub and without asking, sat at her table. Deep bags under ancient brown eyes gave him the look of a disillusioned Basset hound.

"You contacted the embassy blind. Any port in a shit-storm, right?" he said. "Bence, *Dreher*," he called out to the barman, who nodded at him from behind the bar.

"You are . . . ?" she hesitated. She'd done the "Mister Harrington - Stanley Boyle" call to the embassy and received a call-back; a man's voice stating a time and click. She needed no location since Brighton had already tipped her to the Lion House Gösser.

"Tench," he finished for her. "Wiley Tench, the last of the Mohicans. *Kosci*," he said to the barman, who placed an enormous glass of beer the color of Coca Cola in front of him. "Who knows you're here?" he asked her.

"No one knows I'm in Budapest. Not even my office," she said. From the instant she saw him she was certain he was someone senior from Budapest Station, the CIA's office for this part of Eastern Europe.

"Actually, that's not true, Casey. That's what they call you, isn't it?" She nodded. "You were followed from the Hilton. Small guy, blue jacket with a hood. Don't worry. He's been taken care of. But from now on, you're going to have to be a lot more careful," he frowned.

"You know why I'm here?" she said.

He took a swallow of beer and wiped a foam mustache off his upper lip with his hand. "Dale Fleetwood." When she nodded back, he murmured: "The chickens have finally come home to roost."

"Why does everyone keep saying shit like that? Revenge, chickens home to roost, Blue Madagascar. Only nobody ever says what it means," she said. "You knew him?"

"Too bloody well," he looked around. "Not here."

"Where?" she said.

"Finish your beer. We'll walk. First time in Budapest?"

She nodded. "I saw a parade earlier. It was eerie, like the Nazis."

"Jobbik," he grimaced. "They're an extreme-right party. A lot of Europe's tilting that way. We're living in the Thirties Redux. All we need is a little guy with a mustache. Mind you, it's not like America's immune. We're half-way there ourselves. Let's walk," he said, finishing his beer and waving at the barman, so Casey assumed he had a tab. She drank a bit more of her beer, left money on the table, grabbed her coat and bag.

Bence the barman let them out a backdoor. It led to an outside patio with tables and chairs where no one was sitting because of the cold, but which had a gate to another street. Wiley walked them up one side of a long block and down the other to confirm no one was following, then ducked through a side alley to another street. He took her arm and together they walked at a fast pace to an open area that he told her was Holy Trinity Square.

A column with figures on top holding a cross stood in the center of the square, faced by a high-spired church. Both the column and the church were white as bone in the sun. Catty-corner to the church was a small park, screened by trees from the street. They found an empty bench in the park. Casey buttoned the top button of her coat and wrapped her scarf around her neck against the cold. The sun gave no warmth; it was a winter sun.

"You knew Dale Fleetwood?" she asked. He nodded. "Why was he sent to prison?"

"That came later. Dale was always into all kinds of shit," Wiley said, looking around. Except for a woman with a child in a stroller walking on the path, there was no one around to overhear them.

"He stepped over the boundary?"

"Blasted through like a bat out of hell," Wiley said. "I first knew him in the '70's. By then, Dale had left the CIA and set up on his own. It's not like anybody in the States paid attention to Africa. The war in Angola was . . . " he exhaled.

"Bad?"

"There was this one area along the Angola-Namibia border they called 'the Castro Corridor.' The MPLA, backed by the Cubans and Russians, killed every single male over the age of ten to keep them from joining the UNITA rebels. I saw thousands of bodies of men and boys, little kids, children by the side of the road. It was sickening. We –"

"The CIA was involved?" she interjected.

He nodded. "The killing was done by the MPLA and Castro's troops. We were providing secret support to the UNITA and FNLA rebels. All under the table, because we were up to our eyeballs in Vietnam, not to mention it was a violation of the Clark Amendment, so it had to be done privately. Dale made a fortune shipping arms to UNITA, the FNLA, anyone who'd pay, no questions asked."

"He was an arms dealer for the CIA?"

"More than that. You know Readers Digest used to have this feature they called 'The Most Unforgettable Character I've Ever Met.' Well, that would've been Dale Fleetwood. This one time," Wiley grinned, "he sold heavy-duty weapons to Congolese rebels, the FNLC. Somehow these idiots got it into their heads that because he'd once been a U.S. Marine, Dale was a military genius. So here was Fleetwood, riding in a Jeep mounted with a .50 caliber machine gun, followed by a truck packed to the roof with cases of beer, leading an invasion of guys on bicycles from Angola, like a New Jersey Lawrence of Africa, riding into Shaba province in what was then Zaire, to overthrow Joe Mobuto. You had to see it to believe it."

"Beer, why?"

"That's how he paid 'em. The Angolan economy was in free-fall. Money was no good. Cans of beer was the currency. I'm not kidding. In the 'Keep Your Mouth Shut Market,' which was what they called the main market in Luanda, a can of Cuca beer was worth two or three thousand *kwanzas*. That's if you could get anybody to take *kwanzas*.

"Dale had dreams of getting hold of the copper and cobalt mines in Kolwezi. You want to know the crazy part?

They actually beat the Zaire army, the FAZ, most of whom ran away at the first shots. I think Dale fancied himself King of the Congo – and you know, those mines would've given him a big percentage of the entire world cobalt and copper market. Would've made Fleetwood one of the richest men on earth. Of course, the whole scheme collapsed like a house of cards when the French sent in real soldiers: the French Foreign Legion and some Moroccan troops. There were massacres; it was a godawful mess.

"So maybe you'd think Dale was screwed, a war criminal, right?" Casey nodded. Wiley shook his head. "You didn't know him. This French Lieutenant-Colonel comes to take him prisoner. Cool as a cucumber, Dale explains how he was stopping the Soviets from grabbing the copper mines. He offers the Lieutenant-Colonel not some crappy Cuca beer, but cases of Stella Artois on ice for the Lieutenant-Colonel and his men. In the middle of the Congo jungle! Dale walks out of it with a concession dealing weapons, booze, and women to the French. He was selling to both sides," he said, grinning.

"You knew him pretty well?"

"Too damn well," he said. Something there, Casey thought. Same as Brighton.

"How'd Fleetwood get into it, all this?"

"I got to know him pretty well. There were times between actions in-country, we'd go to this pub, Kitchener's in Jo-burg. South Africa. I guess you could say Dale Fleetwood was the American Dream. He came from nothing – or New Jersey, same thing," Wiley shrugged. "Parents were Polish immigrants. His old man Americanized the name from something unpronounceable to 'Fleetwood'. Little Danek – he changed that to 'Dale' in like the second grade – began his career rolling drunks in Trenton's North Ward. The day he graduated high school, he joined the Marines.

"The Corps sent him to Okinawa. But the thing to understand about Dale is, he always had an angle. He discovered there was money to be made trading Marine Mart liquor to the local Japanese Yakuza. The Corps nearly court-martialed him for supplying booze, drugs, and prostitutes to Soap Land 'massage' parlors outside the base, but he somehow managed to finagle his way out with a clean discharge.

"He told me his life changed forever on the flight back from Japan. Some guy sitting next to him suggested somebody with his unique set of talents ought to think about the CIA. Gave him a number to call. Next thing Dale knew, he was standing guard over U2 spy planes in Turkey. Soon the CIA had him sabotaging Left-wing political parties in Europe and on the side, trading arms in Angola, Mozambique, the Congo. He left the CIA and set up his own company to act as a middle man. Made him rich. Living the good life; villas, private jets, beautiful women."

"He was a con man," Casey said. Wiley looked at her with a pitying half-smile, like a math professor looking at a student trying to understand advanced calculus.

"You don't get it," he said. "Dale was a sociopath. He'd tell you whatever you wanted to hear, pretend to be the best buddy you ever had, but inside, he could give a shit. If you got blown to bits next to him, he wouldn't let it interrupt his conversation.

"One time we were in Kitchener's, these three raggedy-ass black guys from the townships broke in. They were wild-eyed, crazy high on *dagga*. They had machetes and this rusty old pistol and I'm thinking I've been through Angola, the Congo, and a million bloody scrapes and I'm going to get killed in Kitchener's next to goddamn Dale Fleetwood.

"They herded us and the waitress into the back, waving their machetes, screaming for money and they're going to kill us and Dale calmly says to the guy with the gun, 'You gonna shoot me with that piece of *kak*, mate? That *kaka* Tokarev pistol from World War Two? It's defective, Jocko. It'll explode your damn hand off. Now you want, I'll get you all good guns: brand new Colts, Berettas. No money. A present from me. Here, let me look at that thing before you hurt yourself.'

"And so help me, the idiot hands Dale the pistol. Dale checks the magazine, slams it home and shoots all three of them: *Bam, bam, bam.* The waitress grabs his arm, says, 'Thank you, thank you. You saved us!' Dale shoots her in the head too. *Bam.* 'What'd you do that for?' I said. I was stunned. He puts the gun in one of the dead guys' hands and says, 'When the cops come, we can show they killed her. Justifies what we did. No blowback on us, no riots in Soweto.'

"He invited me to his place in Ibiza once. Fancy villa. We were sitting out on this white terrace sipping Sangria on a cliff overlooking the sea. He wanted me to come in with him in Bosnia.

"'There's fortunes gonna be made in this war, Wiley. Shit, the booze and food into Sarajevo alone's worth millions,' he said with that patented Dale Fleetwood grin. I was married at the time. My wife was pregnant and I didn't want her to be another CIA widow. I turned him down. 'Time and tide, Wiley. Don't be a Schmuckatelli' – one of his favorite Marine Corps expressions – 'If there's one universal truth of business, *amigo*, it's 'Never waste a good war,' he said."

"You didn't do it?" Casey said.

"Look, I suppose I knew him well as anyone and I think he regarded me as a pal. But I also knew that in a jam, Dale would kill me without turning a hair. He was a charmer till the second he betrayed you. He wouldn't feel a thing.

"He was right about one thing though. The Balkans in the '90's was where he hit the jackpot. Everybody killing each other and everybody needing everything: guns, food, drugs, women, booze, you name it. And sitting like a pasha in the middle was Dale Fleetwood, the man with his fingers in every pie."

"Were you two still connected?" she asked.

Wiley shook his head. "After Ibiza. Dale was on his own. Off in the wild blue yonder. You'd hear stories though."

"What kind of stories?"

"Look, the spy game isn't for nice little boys and girls, okay? I mean who do you think you're dealing with, the Dalai Lama and Martin Luther King? But some of the people Dale was dealing with, I wanted no part of."

"What about Blue Madagascar?"

"Grandmother of a disaster. There was a leak, a double. Someone sold the store. Five U.S. case officers dead, agents disappeared or executed, networks we'd spent years building completely blown. Intel wiped out for years. The United States was blind – so the politico types ran the show. It was like watching drunks drive bumper cars. That's how America got no warning on 9/11, bullshit about weapons of mass destruction in Iraq, the garbage."

"Was it Fleetwood? Is that how he wound up in prison?"

"Can't say. We'd lost touch. But what I can tell you is Dale Fleetwood was on the inside for a long time. He knew where a lot of bodies were buried. Whatever he left behind is explosive. People will kill to get it and to stop it," Wiley said, standing up. "We better get going. Remember, you don't know me. If anyone asks, I'll call you a liar."

"People in that pub saw us together," Casey said.

"They'll assume you're some young cutie I'm screwing," Wiley said, putting on his sunglasses.

"Thanks, women love to be thought of that way," she said.

"It works. It stops people thinking because they assume

they know what's happening. The best place to hide a body is a battlefield. Where do you go next?"

"Belgrade," she said.

He made a face. "Be very careful there. Trust no one."

"I know," Casey said, also getting up.

"No, you don't. You're living on borrowed time," he said.

"Story of my life," she said as they parted.

CHAPTER TWENTY-FIVE

PLACE LOUIS LÉPINE, PARIS

BROCHARD AND COMMANDANT Claire Pinault entered the interrogation room hoping they might have finally gotten a break in the hunt for Vincent the Cat. One of *la Crim*'s network of informants, an Algerian drug dealer named Mehdi from Bondy – a notorious *banlieue* known to everyone in Paris as "the 93" – claimed to have spotted Vincent with a young woman like the one the *flics* were looking for, going into a camera shop in Pigalle. The shop on the rue Pierre-Fontaine was suspected by the local *gendarmes* to be a front for fake documents. The police had brought the shop's owner, a Senegalese named Mamadou N'Diaye, in for questioning.

A pair of *la Crim* detectives had been sweating the Senegalese for several hours when Commandant Pinault and Brochard walked in.

"Monsieur N'Diaye says he's never heard of Vincent the Cat," one of the detectives said, getting up. "As for the woman, he says if he'd seen a beautiful woman he'd remember," the detective added as he and his partner left the room.

Pinault and Brochard introduced themselves and sat opposite the Senegalese, who stared at them as if over a rifle sight.

"You pretend to cooperate, but you really intend to tell us nothing like a good *copain*, *n'est-ce pas*, Mamadou?" Commandant Pinault said, lighting a cigarette.

Mamadou looked at her, bored.

"Bad for business if you talk about your customers. We understand," she continued.

"We have enough to send you to La Santé for five years on counterfeiting," Brochard put in. "You lose your business. Your nephew, Salif. We know he's here going to the *lycée technique*. He'll be deported back to Senegal. Pity, such an intelligent boy."

Mamadou looked like he wanted to spit. He told Brochard what he could go do to himself.

"Do you know how many *malfrats* have sat in that chair cursing me and ended up crying like girls, Mamadou?" Pinault said. "Perhaps you think these stupid *flics* don't know *merde*. But maybe we know more than you think. You won't get another chance." She waited. Mamadou stared at them. Commandant Pinault sighed. "*Non*? Perhaps you should listen to what Judge Brochard has to say."

"We know about your *Maman*, Mbayang, back in Dakar. You send money for her every week, don't you, Mamadou?" Brochard said. "Also your sister, Fatou Yally and her family, you support them too. It would be terrible if something were to happen to stop that. But unless you give us everything we want right now on Vincent *the Cat* Grumier and the woman who was with him, it won't be just you going to prison and us deporting your nephew, Salif. Bad things will happen. The

National Gendarmes in Dakar will move your *Maman*, your sister, all of them to the Commance region. They won't be allowed to return to Dakar. You wouldn't like that, would you?"

Mamadou stared at Brochard, fists clenched as if he could kill him. For a moment, neither spoke. Brochard continued: "My understanding is you and your family are Wolof; the people in the Commance are Jola, under control of the MFDC. Bad business. Plenty of killing. The Jola people don't like the Wolof," Brochard continued. Mamadou's eyes widened. "They say the Jola are good Muslims during the day, but at night, they burn people. Without money, how long do you think your family will last? Or you can tell Commandant Pinault and me about Vincent the Cat and the woman and be back doing business in your camera store in thirty minutes." Brochard leaned forward. "With no more problems from the police. Your choice, Mamadou."

Brochard waited. Mamadou stared at both of them, but his hand clutched at a thing on a leather thong around his neck; a *gris-gris* charm, Brochard thought. Still Mamadou said nothing. Brochard motioned to Pinault. He stood and feeling like an actor in a play, headed for the door, wondering if they'd done all this opera for nothing.

"Louis Canet from Villeneuve-d'Ascq," Mamadou said.

"What's that?" Brochard said.

"Vincent the Cat's new identity. The woman's is Isabelle, Isabelle Dusollier. I have digital copies," Mamadou said. "A safeguard in my business."

"We searched your shop and found nothing like that," Pinault said.

"If I hid something and you found it, I wouldn't have hidden it well, would I?" Mamadou said.

"Show us. We'll take my car, not to draw attention," Brochard said.

Forty minutes later, they were in the camera shop on the rue Pierre-Fontaine. A plain-clothes detective waited outside while Commandant Pinault and Brochard watched Mamadou go to an electrical outlet behind the counter and unscrew it to reveal a hidden compartment packed with computer plug-in drives. Mamadou sorted through them, picked one and handed it to Brochard, who inserted it into his laptop. A file of images came up on the screen.

Mamadou paged through passports and National Identity Cards till he found the ones he'd done for Vincent the Cat as Louis Canet and the woman. The card said her name was Isabelle Dusollier from Roubaix.

"Is that her?" Brochard asked, his excitement quickening. Their first good look at her.

"That's her," Mamadou said.

"Pretty," Brochard said, thinking, we've got you, Milena or whatever your name is.

"Even more so in person. But she has a black shadow inside her. I tried to warn Vincent the Cat, but he ignored me."

"What are you saying?"

"That woman is a night-cannibal," Mamadou said.

"We'll get her. Don't worry," Pinault said.

Mamadou ignored her and turned to Brochard. "Be warned, Monsieur Judge, that she doesn't eat your soul too," he said.

CHAPTER TWENTY-SIX

CIMETIÈRE PIERRE-GRENIER, BOULOGNE-BILLANCOURT

THE OLDER MAN with graying hair, stylish as a fashion model in a black shirt and slacks, sat on a couch, his legs crossed. A bottle of Beluga vodka and glasses were on the coffee table before him. Another man watched from a stool near a dining counter. This was no *merde*-faced Irishman, Vincent thought, eyes darting a dagger at Milena. These were Russian mafia. She'd set him up!

"Vincent the Cat, *bienvenue*," the man on the couch welcomed him in accented French, gesturing for them to sit. Milena perched on a settee, crossing her long legs, the red mini giving them all plenty to look at. Vincent sat in an armchair facing the older man.

"My name's McBride, but you can call me Maksim. We need proof you knew the American," the older man said.

Milena took her cell phone from her handbag, opened it to a photo of her and Layton Gary McCord by a beach and showed it to him.

"We should drink to our future success," Maksim said, pouring vodka for the three of them. "*Santé*," he toasted.

"*Santé*," Vincent said and drank. He put down the glass. "If we're done with these *conneries*, these bullshits, where's the *fric*?" The money.

"Good question, Vincent," Maksim said in French. "But your involvement is over." Sensing what was coming, Vincent started to get up, but he was too late. The big man had the 9mm pistol to his head.

"Do you think I'd walk into a meeting with people I don't know unprepared? That I trusted this whore?" Vincent said, pulling out the hand grenade he'd kept under his armpit, the pressure keeping the lever depressed. "The pin's pulled." With his left hand he plucked the pin from his shirt pocket and let it dangle from his index finger so they'd understand that it was only his hand holding the grenade that kept it from exploding. "The kill radius is six meters. Shoot me, even touch me, say something I don't like, everyone in this room dies," he added.

Maksim stared at the grenade, his welcoming mask gone. "So now what, Vincent the Cat?" he said. "You want to kill all of us, the woman, you want to die too? Even before you hear what I have to say?"

"I don't know you, *mec*. Sing me an Irish song, you *foutu* Russian," Vincent said, emphasizing the curse word.

"What's she told you about the dead American?" Maksim said.

"That he had something worth a hundred million. You know what, *mec*? You keep it. But I've got the key to the American's safety deposit box in Panama. Pay me one percent. One million euros and it's all yours. I walk away. You never see me again," Vincent said.

"What about her?" Maksim indicated Milena.

"Keep her. All I want is the money."

Maksim frowned. "There's a problem, Vincent the Cat. The safety deposit box in Panama's already been opened."

Milena said something in rapid Russian. Maksim answered her back sharply. So she was definitely Russian, Vincent thought. She'd been with them from the beginning.

"How? Who opened it?" Milena asked in French.

"American government agents. Whatever was in that box the Americans have it," Maksim said.

"Do we know what was in it?" Milena asked.

Maksim nodded. "We persuaded a Panamanian banker to tell us – before he died. And you. You should've kept your mouth shut. Get her out of here," Maksim said to the giant Russian. "We'll deal with her later,"

"She stays," Vincent said.

Maksim's finger wagged toward both of them. "*Ah*, true love. You have feelings for her?"

"I have feelings for me," Vincent said. "Give me the money. Do what you want with her."

"Your key is of no use to us," Maksim said.

Vincent's eyes narrowed. La Santé yard time. "You're the one being stupid. She knows all the American's secrets, which you need because the Americans already have what was in the safety deposit box. One million or I let go. Only you better decide now. My hand's getting tired," he said, holding up the grenade.

"I don't have that kind of money here. Besides, if we pay you now, it's nothing to how much you'd get later. Become our partner. Think about it," Maksim said, lighting a cigarette.

"You think about it. I want the money now. I don't like foreigners, especially Russians," Vincent said.

"If you want the *fric* now, I can only give you ten percent.

A hundred thousand," Maksim said. "But I don't have the money here. We'll have to go get it."

"And have you come back with reinforcements. *Non, Monsieur,*" Vincent stood, his eyes lasering at the Russian. "We go together – or we end it now. I'm ready."

"What about her?" Maksim said, indicating Milena, who stared at Vincent, her eyes wide with something he couldn't read. Was it fear, or one of her games?

"Her too. She's more dangerous than you," Vincent said.

The smaller man drove the Mercedes in traffic on the street along the Seine. The night had begun to mist, the lights from cars and shops glowing hazy in the darkness. Barges with necklaces of electric lights glided on the river. Milena was wedged in the back seat, between Maksim and Vincent, who kept the grenade gripped tightly. The big man sat up front, his head barely clearing the roof.

Every instinct in Vincent screamed for him to get out of the car now. The Russian Mafia *mec* had given in too easily. Milena had played him, the same way she'd played the dead American and Nabil. Unless Vincent could figure something out and fast, he'd be dead as Patrice and Lucas. The Russians must have killed them. Only he could see no way to do it in the car without getting himself killed too.

The Mercedes drove into a quieter, less-trafficked neighborhood. There were apartment houses across from a walled park on a silent street. Vincent didn't like the look of it. *Forget the money. Get out now,* he warned himself. Meanwhile, he had to keep the two of them, Maksim and the giant in his line of sight every second. His hand gripping the grenade was beginning to cramp. The Mercedes slowed and found a parking space near the entrance to the park.

"We're here," Maksim said and got out. Vincent opened his door with his free hand, but as he got out of the Mercedes, he grabbed Milena and pulled her with him to use as a shield. He kept one arm around her neck as they stepped away from the car. The others were quickly out of the car, the giant the closest.

The giant made his move with speed that surprised Vincent. He wrapped his hand around Vincent's holding the grenade so Vincent couldn't let it go. The giant squeezed, crushing Vincent's fingers like a vise. The pain was excruciating. The giant twisted Vincent's hand, making it hurt that much more. Vincent couldn't hold on. If he couldn't find a way to let go, his hand would be pulverized – except as soon he let go, he'd have only a second or two to live.

He let Milena go, freeing that hand to grab for the stiletto knife in his pocket. He opened it against his leg and stabbed wildly at the giant's hand. The knife caught for a split-second on the giant's jacket cuff and cut through. The giant barely grunted, loosening his grip on Vincent's hand for a split-second, the two of them still hanging onto the grenade. Vincent stabbed the giant's hand as the giant ripped the grenade from his grasp and stepped away. Maksim in a shooter's stance, fired.

The shot was close enough to Vincent's face for him to feel the bullet pass by. Milena headed to the opposite side of the Mercedes. Vincent ran like a mad man, anticipating a bullet in his spine. He dived through the open park gate as Maksim fired again. The bullet cracked into the stone wall centimeters from Vincent's head, splintering stone chips, one of which cut his hand. He scrambled down a path, suddenly realizing it wasn't a park; it was a cemetery. A sign read: "*Cimetière Pierre-Grenier.*" The Russians had brought him here to bury him. Where better to hide a body than a cemetery?

Vincent ran among the headstones. He dodged around a stone mausoleum, nearly slipping on the wet grass. Recovering his balance, he ducked sideways through an opening in a hedge and getting low, crept on all fours behind a row of headstones and trees into a mausoleum's shadow. Suddenly, the force of an explosion knocked him to the ground, leaves from the tree spattering him. The hand grenade. The giant must've thrown it in his direction. It was a miracle it hadn't got him.

He hugged the ground, telling himself that the only way to survive was to be silent, to not even breathe. All that talk about her and the American, asking him about himself like she cared – and then she led him into this trap. He should've killed her when he had the chance, swearing to himself if it was the last thing he did, he'd cut her lying throat. The sounds of voices speaking Russian grew louder. They were on the other side of the hedge.

Vincent lay on his side, head down on a grave. It smelled of wet earth. What we all come to, he thought. The beams of flashlights moved closer in the darkness.

CHAPTER TWENTY-SEVEN

BELGRADE, SERBIA

THAT NIGHT CASEY caught a taxi from Belgrade's Nikola Tesla Airport that took her across a bridge over the Sava River. Driving on a highway into the main part of the city, they passed a closed-in area of shacks and tents surrounded by a chain-link fence guarded by Serb Army trucks and soldiers. Inside the fence, people huddled around steel-barrel fires for warmth, ignored by the soldiers smoking cigarettes and drinking beer. After the jack-booted Jobbik Fascists in Hungary, the scene of soldiers in the light of the streetlamps and barrel fires reminded Casey of those black-and-white images of World War Two concentration camps.

"What place is that?" she asked the driver in English and when he raised his hand indicating he didn't understand, she repeated the question in Russian.

"A camp for refugees. People from the Middle East, *Gospoja*," the taxi driver said, addressing her as *Miss*.

"Why do they keep them there?"

"Nowhere else to put them," the driver said. He drove her

to the Metropol Palace, a luxury hotel on a broad boulevard in the heart of the city. She had dinner at the hotel. Over a dish of a *pljeskavica*, spiced hamburger patty and fries – clearly no one in Serbia had ever heard of a salad – she tried to focus on the case, but her mind kept returning to the disturbing images of the refugees around the barrel fires and the Jobbik Fascists in Budapest, their boots stomping in unison on the cobblestones. She shuddered; an evil people thought gone from the world was rising again.

In the morning, before she left her hotel room she set a series of little traps, like old keys arranged in a specific random-looking pattern in a drawer with her clothes or a hair over her suitcase lid, as a way to see if anyone searched her things. She was taking Wiley's warning seriously. The hotel concierge called for a taxi. Jacques Marchand of the Swimming Pool had arranged a meeting for her with someone named Rade Vuković, supposedly the head of the BIA, the Serbian Security Intelligence Service. She wanted his help in tracking down information about the mysterious Srxbyx Transport Company.

They met in his office in the Serbian Defense Ministry building on Kneza Miloša Avenue, a broad thoroughfare with traffic and red electric trams in Belgrade's downtown Savamala district. The day was cold and crisp, the sky a perfect blue.

"You ask from Srxbyx Transport Company. No good," Director Vuković, a man with sleeked-back hair in a pin-striped suit, said in bad English when she asked about Srxbyx Transport.

"What's the problem?" she asked.

"Zemun Clan is owning Srxbyx."

"And they are?"

"Zemun Clan is the one mafia group we never penetrating. Their leader two brothers: Srđan and Darko Razanović. Darko is brain. Srđan is crazy man," Vuković said, tapping his head with his finger.

"You seem to know a lot about them," Casey said.

"We spending two years infiltrate our best guy undercover in Zemun. But Razanović brothers, they find out. They sending our guy home to wife, kids in mail, one piece at time. One finger. One lip. One ear. Every other day one piece. Tongue. Strip of skin. Each week for half-year. Younger brother Srđan is devil." He tapped a Drina cigarette on his desk and lit it, adding, "You seeing problem."

She saw all right. She was in deep shit. If she wanted to find out about Srxbyx, she'd have to take on this Zemun mafia clan.

"How were they involved with an ex-CIA agent named Dale Fleetwood?" she asked.

"Razanović brothers having hands in many pots. Someone ask . . . " Vuković shook his head. "Someone disappearing." In effect telling her he wasn't about to risk any more of his own men. He went back behind his desk.

"What about the Srxbyx company itself? Who handles their business affairs? Their banking? There must be something?" She asked.

He held up a finger. "I tell you this, you must being careful. A lawyer doing for Darko. Name lawyer Jovan Bulatović. More finding is you, lady person," Vuković said. Things were getting out of control, she thought, panicking. She was on her own in a foreign city dealing with very dangerous people.

When Casey got back to her hotel room after her meeting with Vuković, she discovered that the little traps she'd set had been moved. Someone had gone through her things. She could no longer trust her hotel room, if she ever could. She wasn't sure what to do. She was flying blind. Maybe it was time to pull the ripcord. What would Jessie say? *Action without a plan equals failure.*

Everything changed at lunch. She was at a place recommended by the hotel concierge, the Dva Jelena, an airy wood-paneled restaurant with mounted rifles on the walls. It came in the form of a text from an unknown number that began with the code word "Honolulu," which Arthur Dalton had told her would only be used in case of extreme emergency. It read: "*From Honolulu rdv jm hoy sqrt 49 81 kneginje ljubice luv dad.*"

For Casey, a practiced puzzle solver, the message wasn't that hard to decipher. "Honolulu" was the emergency alert, so all hell must've broken loose. RDV meant *rendez-vous*. She was to meet with *JM*, Jerry Matthews. Dalton would send someone she knew by sight; *hoy* was Spanish for now or today. Arthur Dalton also knew she'd been good in Math. The time for the RDV was the *sqrt* or square root of 49, so 7 pm. Then the address for the meet: reverse the number 81 to 18 Kneginje Ljubice Street, which when she GPS'd it turned out to be a restaurant in the Skadarlija section of Belgrade.

She was getting seriously scared. Marching Fascists, a vicious Zemun Clan Mafia mob that even the BIA, the Serbian Security Services didn't want to touch, and now Honolulu! Back at the hotel, she discovered the little traps she had reset had been moved again. Time to go.

She packed her essentials into the carry-on, leaving her suitcase and any clothes she didn't absolutely need in the room and not checking out, so someone looking for her would think she was coming back. She took a taxi to the Central Train Station, then another one to a park, not far from her hotel. A sign in Cyrillic and English read "Pioniski Park." A quick walk into the park, then back across the street to a movie theater, where the latest Marvel movie was showing. She bought a ticket and still lugging the carry-on, went inside to wait out the time to the RDV. She kept looking at her watch, barely paying attention to the superhero antics on the screen. God, Jessie, she thought. I have no idea what I'm doing.

Jerry Matthews was late. Casey had been waiting nearly a half-hour in the outdoor restaurant on Kneginje Ljubice, filled with students and faculty from the nearby university. Despite an outdoor heater, the night was growing cold. She was getting a very bad feeling. Sitting alone at the table felt like inviting a bullet.

The waiter came over. She ordered a waffle with strawberry *slatko* and a bottle of Miloš water and tried to decide what to do. Every fiber of her being was telling her to forget Jerry Matthews and get out of Belgrade now. She kept looking around for anyone suspicious. Was that man with the newspaper at the bar watching her? How long had he been there – or was she becoming paranoid? And then there was the Honolulu emergency. What was that about? Why was Jerry Matthews late? Why hadn't he called? If they'd gotten to him, would she even make it to the airport?

The waiter brought the bottled water and a waffle. She nibbled, but couldn't swallow, checking her watch again. There was no point waiting, she decided. Jerry wasn't coming. She was about to call the Beogradski Taxi number when a blue VW screeched to a stop in the street. A window rolled down. She flinched. This is it, she thought, expecting a gun barrel.

"Get in!" Jerry Matthews shouted through the open car window. She dropped a couple of 500-dinar notes on the table, grabbed the carry-on and jumped into the VW. Jerry

Matthews gunned it down the street, his gaze bouncing around like Pachinko balls, checking the mirrors for tails.

"Todd Brighton's dead," he said, driving fast. "Also that piece of African pastry he was shacked up with. Both of them, plus four Syrian refugee kids they were sheltering. All dead." Casey stared at him, stunned. "Oh, you didn't know about the refugee kiddies, Princess? Me neither. Kept lots of secrets, our Toddy. Here's yesterday's *Le Figaro*," Jerry Matthews said, handing her a French newspaper. "They've got a photo of Todd at some artsy-fartsy Paris gallery. Clever how you got onto him, Princess."

"Why didn't you put me onto him?"

"Didn't know he could identify Fleetwood. Didn't put two and two together. You did. Good work," he said. Yeah, terrific. I killed six more people, she thought grimly.

"Something tells me there's a lot I don't know about you," she said, holding on as he swerved in front of a car ahead of him.

"You could say that about everybody," he said. "Me, I always figured Todd for just a weekend painter. Guess someone took his paint-splashing seriously."

"When did this happen?" Casey asked, staring at a photo of Todd Brighton in the paper under the headline: "*Todd Brighton, artiste moderne remarqué assassinée à Barbizon.*" I did this. I killed them, she thought, feeling nauseous. This happened because I went to see him, like Bobby and Luis Avila.

"As soon as we heard, Dalton put me on the next flight," Jerry Matthews said, stopping at a red light. They waited, cars and red electric trams crossing in front of them.

"Where are we going?" she said, feeling sicker. I'm Typhoid Mary. Everyone she came near died. And in Panama they'd knocked on her door too. They'd followed her in

Budapest and in Belgrade, they'd searched her room. The space between her shoulder blades prickled like someone was about to stick a knife there.

The light changed and Jerry turned onto the boulevard, the lights of traffic and streetlamps gleaming on overhead tram lines, shop windows brightly lit in the darkness.

"Seatbelt tight?" he asked, glancing over. She checked, tightened it a fraction.

"Why? What's happening?"

"Gray Skoda. Been following us since the café. Hang on," he said and cut into the left lane, forcing a red sedan to slam the brakes, horn blasting, fishtailing, missing them by barely an inch. Jerry Matthews didn't pause for a second. Tires skidding, he made an illegal U-turn right across on-coming traffic, cutting in front of an electric tram coming straight at them, bell clanging.

The VW slid into the space between two cars, nearly clipping the rear bumper of a Dacia in front of them. Honking his horn, Jerry Matthews forced his way over to the far right lane. Now going in the opposite direction from which they'd come, they almost went past a side street, when Jerry Matthews suddenly turned into it. A car was stopped on the narrow street, blocking his way, Jerry Matthews drove up on the sidewalk around the car and back into the street. They went around several blocks, reversing directions.

"Now that you've taken ten years off my life, where're we going?" she said.

"First, nowhere," Jerry Matthews said, speeding up and taking a tight corner turn onto a dark street. "Want to make sure we're not being followed. Then, get you to a safe house, at least for the night. Mister Dalton's thinking of pulling you, Princess. You've been holding out on us."

She felt a chill. "What do you mean?"

"Didn't tell us about your little excursion to Budapest. Who'd you see?"

Casey thought about Wiley Tench's Basset hound eyes as he told her: *You weren't here. We've never met.* Todd Brighton had said the same and now he was dead. She didn't want to kill Wiley too.

"No one. It was a bust," she said. "Brighton thought someone in the CIA's Budapest Station might know something about Fleetwood or that Srxbyx company, but when I went to the meet, no one showed. Given what happened to Brighton, probably just as well," she said as Jerry Matthews made a turn onto another brightly lit street, cutting a driver off. The driver honked at him.

Jerry Matthews ignored him and circling the same block twice, pulled into a space in a red *Zona 1* parking zone and looked at her.

"Nobody's pulling me out of anything, Jerry," she said, hardly believing the words coming out of her mouth.

"What'd you get from Vuković?" he asked.

"The Zemun clan, some Serbian mafia bunch, owns Srxbyx. He gave me the name of a lawyer who handles their business: Jovan Bulatović; office at 7 Boulevard Milentija Popovića in New Belgrade." She texted it to him. "I just sent it to you."

"A lawyer. We won't get much," Jerry Matthews mumbled. He put the VW in gear and let the GPS guide him through the narrow city streets. They were in a different part of the city. The streets were dark, not well lit and lined with older buildings, the facades spray-painted with graffiti. He stopped in front of a two-story building, a yellow Renault parked in front. Casey looked around. The street was empty, shadows cast by a single streetlamp.

"Listen, from now on, when you meet someone, it's in a

public place," Jerry Matthews said. "A train station, movie theater, a department store, a place with multiple exits. And take these burner phones," he said, handing her four mobile phones. "Keep 'em off, use once, then toss 'em, pulling the SIM and throwing it down a sewer or toilet or something. Keep your own turned off. It's a shame about Todd. He was one of the good ones," he said, shaking his head.

"You're holding back, Jerry. Everybody's getting killed and I'm next. What've I gotten into?"

His eyes scanned the street. "You tell me, Princess. You're the one with the magic password. What'd Toddy tell you?"

"He gave me Fleetwood's name. I don't want to stay here, Belgrade," she said.

He shook his head. "Sorry, Princess. We have to close the circle with Srxbyx." She looked at him oddly. "Why was Dale Fleetwood sent to prison? The Fed Supermax, ADX, no less. I mean, Jeez," she said.

"All I know is what the FBI told us," Jerry Matthews said. "Fleetwood was charged with selling several tons of C-4 explosive, labelled 'drilling mud,' to Saddam Hussein in Iraq. In his defense, Fleetwood claimed it was a CIA operation. Unfortunately for him, then-Deputy Director of the CIA testified under oath that Fleetwood hadn't been connected with the CIA for years. He was sentenced to forty-two years in ADX, in Florence, Colorado. They say he was carried out of the courtroom screaming he'd been framed and that those who did it would pay."

"So how'd he wind up at that jewelry store in Nice?"

"Seems he caught a break. After fourteen years in prison, his sentence was overturned. His attorney got evidence under the Freedom of Information Act and they were able to show an Appeals court there'd actually been hundreds of contacts between Fleetwood and the CIA. Fleetwood was free, but broke. The government had confiscated all his companies, properties, everything. He wound up in Europe."

"Fourteen years in Supermax. What does that do to a person?" she murmured.

"It's basically being in Solitary. Some go crazy," Jerry Matthews said.

"Long time to plot revenge," she said.

"You think that's what we're dealing with? The Count of Monte Cristo? I hope to God you find something fast, because between you 'n me, Princess, I got a feeling we're running out of time," he said. He fished in his jacket pocket, handed her a pair of keys. "The apartment's on the second floor. You'll be safe here tonight. When you go, leave the keys on the yellow Renault's left rear tire."

"What about you?"

"I'm grabbing a night flight out of this godforsaken city."

"Okay," she said, opening the car door.

"Princess . . . " he hesitated, "You need to understand something. From now on, there's no cavalry to rescue you."

She exhaled. "Tell Arthur Dalton I'll find whatever it was Fleetwood left behind and then I'm out of here," she said, getting out of the car. Now she could smell the river. It had to be somewhere close by.

"I'll say this, Princess, you're a tough little cookie," he said.

"Thanks for the lift," she said and closed the VW door, wondering if she would ever see him again.

She waited in the shadow of the streetlamp till he drove away, then walked alone to the building, her footsteps echoing in the night.

CHAPTER TWENTY-EIGHT

PORTE MAILLOT, PARIS

ELEVEN FIFTEEN AT night in Porte Maillot, the Hip Hop group "Le Overdose" blasting like a rocket launch. Roving spotlights slid across the faces of densely packed Parisian Bobos gyrating to the beat. Young women held their arms high and undulating as if undersea in the light of flashing strobes as Vincent the Cat snaked his way through the crowd to a side door. A beefy man wearing a fur Cossack hat and a suit jacket that made it impossible to miss the bulge of his gun holster, guarded the door. The Cossack frisked Vincent, looked disgusted as he brushed off dirt from the cemetery and opened the door.

The sound of the music and the crowd went away as the heavily-padded door shut behind Vincent. Unlike the space-ship-like décor of the club, the office was decorated in a pre-Revolutionary Russian style, complete with icon art, Oriental rugs, and red wallpaper.

A heavily tattooed middle-aged man smoking a hookah water pipe sat on a couch. He wore biker black leather and boots and around his neck was a heavy gold chain. A large gold cross hung from the chain, a Russian Mafia emblem. Two men slouched in armchairs. One was a muscled man in a Paris Saint-Germain soccer T-shirt and gold chain, a 9mm pistol tucked in his belt. The other wore black leather like his boss.

"Vincent *le Chat*, you've been making big farts," said the biker on the couch, exhaling smoke smelling of peach blossoms. The slang *péter* for fart implied Vincent was attracting too much attention to himself.

"Look who's talking Egor. You look like a fugitive from the Village People," Vincent said, settling into an armchair.

"What are you doing here? The *flics* put the word out. Every *mouchard* snitch in Paris's got his eyes peeled for you," Egor said. He snapped his fingers. The muscle man in the soccer T-shirt went to a wall cabinet bar and brought over a bottle of vodka and glasses. Egor poured drinks. Vincent picked his Jean-Marc up and drained it, turning his empty glass open side down on the table.

"I'm looking for Russians," Vincent said.

"Go to Russia," the muscle man in the Saint-Germain soccer T-shirt said.

"One particular Russian named Maksim. Fancy clothes, Moscow type. His bodyguard is a giant with a bullet-head. Can't miss him, got to be two meters," Vincent said, indicating height with his hand. "Also a third *mec* and a woman sometimes called Milena. She's *canon*, super sexy. Very hard to miss."

"What do you want with them?" Egor said, glancing at his men. It was obvious they knew who Vincent was talking about.

"That's my business," Vincent said.

"So why make it mine? *Santé*," Egor said and drank. He

motioned Vincent closer. "These guys you mention, are Moscow *bratva*. You don't play games with Moscow *bratva*."

Vincent put a thousand, then another thousand euros on the table. "Where do I find these Moscow *types*?" he said.

"You're not listening, Monsieur the Cat. These *types*, I heard they took some tough *mec*, cooked him in a *ragout* and forced his whole crew to eat it," Egor said. "What do you think they'd do to me if I told you where to find them?"

"Three thousand," Vincent said, putting another thousand down on the table and standing up. Egor stood to confront him. The other two Russians also stood. The one with the pistol took it out of his belt. Vincent slid the Italian stiletto knife he had concealed in his sleeve into his hand. Egor looked at him.

"Five," he said. After a moment, Vincent counted out another three thousand.

"You're in big trouble, Vincent the Cat," Egor said. "You think no one in Marseilles has smart phones? First the *flics*, now Moscow *bratva*." Egor shook his head. He wrote something on a piece of paper, held it up for Vincent to read: *Mme. Fedorovna, 21, Bd. Barbès, 18ème.* "Memorize it," Egor said and when Vincent nodded, Egor lit the paper with a match, letting the flame lick his fingers to show how tough Russians were before he finally blew it out. With his other hand, Egor picked up the money on the table, gave it to the muscle-bound man, who swung open a gold-icon painting and put the money into a wall safe. The man in the biker black leather opened the door. Blasting music hit the room like a wall of water.

"Don't come back, Vincent" Egor said, raising his voice to be heard over the music.

. . .

Vincent came up the stairs from the Château Rouge Metro station. A chill breeze rustled the trees along Boulevard Barbès. At this time of night, there were few cars in this part of Montmartre. Store windows covered with steel shutters made the street look like a city at war.

A homeless *clochard* slept on the sidewalk beside a parked motorbike, one arm flung out as if in death. Vincent felt a superstitious trickle run down his spine. It occurred to him that since Lucas and Patrice had been killed in Marseilles, maybe he hadn't outrun death, only put him off for a little.

The address from Egor was a small fortune-teller's shop with a blue-neon outline around a window sign that read: "*Cabinet Mme. Fedorovna, Medium, Voyante, Tarologue.*" Vincent pushed the button, the loudness of the buzzer startling him in the silence. No one answered. He rang again, waited, and finally heard someone stir inside. A tiny old woman in a housedress and disheveled white hair opened the door. She looked suspiciously up at him through blue eyes set deep in wrinkles, like sapphires in white mud.

"One hundred fifty," she said, in Russian-accented French and without waiting for him to respond, turned and thumped her way with a cane to a round table. The room was lit with a dim red lamp and there was a samovar on a side console. They sat facing each other at the table. He put a hundred and fifty euros on the table.

"I'm looking for – " he started, but she waved him dismissively to silence.

"Everyone is either looking for someone or running from someone. Sometimes both," she said, squinting at him. "In your case, both, Monsieur. I am a hundred and two years old, Monsieur, so there's little you can tell me, I haven't heard. The human heart is a black pit whose bottom no one can see. Even from the innocence of children, such evil may grow as would frighten God. I've seen it." She took his hand, held it, studied his palm, then looked at him shrewdly.

"Do you know the Blue Krait snake of Southeast Asia, Monsieur?" Vincent stared at her wondering what mumbo-jumbo *merde* she was peddling. "It's very beautiful," she continued. "With exquisite blue and white stripes; but so deadly that a single bite kills, even if the victim uses anti-venom. Its venom is thirty times more deadly than that of a cobra. And vicious. They eat other snakes, even other Blue Kraits. And yet, is not even the Blue Krait a prisoner inside herself, Monsieur?"

"What are you babbling on about?" he said, wondering if she was Egor's idea of a joke. If it was, he'd skin him alive.

The old woman smiled. "You seek a woman. She is very beautiful, yes?" Vincent nodded. "Do you understand? You are two Blue Kraits, Monsieur, both prisoners inside your-selves," she said. Sitting there, the tiny old woman in her shapeless housedress and wild white hair looked like a fairy tale witch. This is nonsense, Vincent thought.

"I have some questions. I'll pay you more for answers," he said, reaching for money. She stopped him with a trembling hand.

"The price is one-fifty, Monsieur. You have already paid – and will pay more. Much more" She looked up at him, her eyes nearly concealed in wrinkles. "You're looking for men from Moscow. A man named Maksim, yes? So elegant, Maksim Nikolayevich. Also a very large man, Big Yury. And another, Kolya the Blade, yes?"

Vincent slid the stiletto from his sleeve into his hand. "How do you know this?" he said softly. She waved her hand dismissively, her fingers trembling.

"Paris is a village. I know every Russian, but do you?"

"Just tell me where I can find them," Vincent growled.

Her wrinkles grew even deeper. Was it possible this ancient creature was smiling? Vincent wondered. "They are all servants of the Tsar of all the Russias. Ah, but who is the Tsar?"

Vincent was getting angry. Old fool! "What the devil are you talking about?"

"In the old days of the KGB, Monsieur, you would see an important man, a Russian ambassador say, being driven by a chauffeur. So who was the *nachalstvo*, the truly important person, and who the servant? Not the man in the suit sitting in the back."

"What are you saying? Are you suggesting it's the woman, Milena? She's the boss? Forget all that. Just tell me where they are."

"We must see what the cards say, Monsieur," she said, taking out a deck of Tarot cards. She spread the cards face down on the table.

"Choose three," she said. As he reached over, she said, "Be careful. Much depends on which you choose." He selected three cards. She turned the first card over. "The Tower," she said, looking at the card, then at him. "What you do next is very dangerous. Your actions will impact many. For good or evil I cannot say, but what you do next is of great importance. But beware, Monsieur." She tapped the Tarot card. "There are moments when the whole world holds its breath, balanced on a razor's edge. This is that moment." She turned the second card over. "The Chariot. You will travel very soon, but this you already know. The woman is gone."

"What does that mean *gone*? Where is she?"

"Not in Paris, Monsieur," she said, looking away.

"I'm tired of riddles, witch. Speak plain," Vincent said, feeling for his stiletto.

"You chase the wind, Monsieur. That's not how you catch her."

"Really?" Vincent said sarcastically. This is *fou*! Crazy, he thought. "So how do I catch her?" he said, playing along.

"Ah Monsieur, you chase the wolf; the wolf chases the rabbit; the rabbit seeks the cabbage. Find the cabbage, you find the rabbit and the wolf."

"You're saying find the American's secret and I'll find what I'm looking for? How do I manage that?"

"There's still another card," she said and turned it over. The card showed animals looking up at a white crescent moon with a face in it. "The Moon. It is as I said, Monsieur. You will be severely tested. There are high risks, but the moon has two sides. There are rewards too; great riches, even love."

"What are you talking about?"

"Blue Kraits don't only eat each other, they also mate." The old woman closed her eyes. For a moment, Vincent wondered if she'd fallen asleep – or died. She looked dead. Her eyes opened.

"Are you truly a hundred and two years old?" Vincent asked.

"T-t-t," she sounded, waving a disapproving index finger back and forth like a metronome, "one should never ask a woman her age, Monsieur," she said.

"You still haven't told me where she is. But I think you know who they are, these Moscow *types*, don't you?"

She moved the three Tarot cards together so they balanced against each other, like a little mountain. "Three worlds: government, business, the criminal *milieu*. They overlap, always. Someone must watch."

"What are you saying? You were – are KGB? At your age?"

"What do you know?" she snapped. "When those Nazi *salauds* were marching in Paris, who do you think formed the heart of the Resistance? We Communists! There are two professions that never retire: actors and spies. Perhaps because they're the same. We pretend to be someone else." She looked at his hand where the stone chip had cut it. "You're bleeding."

"Leave it," he said.

"In that cabinet there are bandages, antibiotic cream and tape. Second drawer," she pointed.

"It's nothing," Vincent said.

"You think this is the first wound I've bandaged? Get them." Vincent got up, found the bandages and she bandaged his hand.

"You still haven't told me how to find her, Milena," he said.

"Find someone who knew the American. It's the game, Monsieur. It's all about the game."

"Except the game is life and death."

"For Blue Kraits, what else is there?" she said.

CHAPTER TWENTY-NINE

NEW BELGRADE, SERBIA

CASEY WOKE that morning and for a terrible moment, she didn't know where she was. A bedroom. Daylight filtering through white-curtained windows, the light pale as if winter had already set in. Belgrade, the safe house, she remembered, taking a breath. Only she was far from safe and still dazed from the end of a nightmare. She could remember only a fragment of her dream.

The night of the orange moon. That steamy L.A. summer when Jessie disappeared. The worst time of her life. Dashanique telling her "Po-lice? You ain't goin' to no po-lice, girl? 'Sides, po-lice don't know nuthin', don't care nuthin' neither. You ain't never gonna see that girl again. You best forget that sistuh shit." *I'll come for you, Kimmy. I have the lawyer and the papers ready. The day I turn twenty-one, swear to God.* But after Jessica disappeared in Westwood, vanished into thin air, there was no God; no sister; no air. Nothing and no one till the night the orange moon hung over the water tower on Slauson Avenue.

After Jessica disappeared, Casey ran away from the latest foster shit-hole the DCFS had dumped her into, Erica inside again, twenty-two months in Lynwood. Her latest foster mother was a big-ass black woman named Dashanique who wore her hair in a style she called "criss-cross goddess braids," that made her look like she was wearing snakes on her head. The first day, the minute Ms. Gibson, the DCFS social worker left, Dashanique slapped Casey so hard across the face, she saw stars. "We got some rules, girl," Dashanique told her and Casey thought, oh shit, Mark and Susan again. Only worse.

Every day, as soon as she came home from school, she'd have to clean the house, the dishes left on the table, in the sink, floors, cigarette butts, toilets. Nothing in that house was ever cleaned up by anyone else. No time for homework. If she found even a single spot, Dashanique would whack her with a sawed-off broomstick and send her to bed without food. Jafaris-Malik, Dashanique's crack-smoking old man was always grabbing at Casey's boobs or ass whenever Dashanique wasn't looking.

At night, Jafaris-Malik would slide into her tiny bed and try to put his fingers inside her, saying "What you fightin' for, lil' boo? You know you want it." She did what Jessie taught her; kneed him hard as she could between his legs. He grunted, was going to smack her silly and she told him, "You put it inside me, the second you fall asleep, I'll get Dashanique's big scissors and cut it off. Swear to God, I'll do it."

"Bet you would, you lil' bitch," he said, pushing himself off her.

The next afternoon after school, she ran away and never went back to that house again. She took a chance they wouldn't report it to the DCFS because it would stop the checks from the state. She slept in freeway underpasses or the parking lot behind the Express Coin Laundry on Corona Ave, living on machine snacks from quarters she swiped from the Laundry or left-overs from the dumpster behind the KFC on Slauson.

Until one day she was hanging with Santiago, corner of Fishburn and 60th. *Santiago was selling rocks for dime- and nickel-buys and then she saw it: a Caddy Escalade gunning down Fishburn, rap blasting from the speakers and in her head, following Jessie's Rules, she'd practiced for drive-bys, thinking "What could you do?" She decided that unless you're the primary target, it's safer to be closer than far.*

Some vato *inside the Escalade shouted: "Kansas Street, pendejos!" She dived to the ground, towards the edge of the curb, so anyone inside the Escalade would've had to shoot almost straight down and the shots were loud they were so close. Pop! Pop! Pop! Pop!*

A screech of tires, a smell of gasoline and the Escalade roared back up Fishburn trailing a wake of shouts and rap. Santiago lay on the sidewalk, red flowers blooming on his chest, blood pooling on the sidewalk and down to the gutter and Santiago's eyes stared up the sun, seeing nothing.

Casey looked around. No one on the street. Everyone too scared to come out of their houses. She rifled through Santiago's pockets. Took money, baggies of crack rocks she could sell and from his belt, his Hi-Point 9mm pistol and from that instant she understood that if she had the cojones, *she'd never have to eat out of a KFC dumpster again. She decided then and there to go where the money was: The base house of the Florencia 13 gang on Pine.*

The night of the orange moon in steamy Central L.A., the early evening brown haze tinting purple against the silhouettes of downtown buildings. Casey had worked it out per Jessica's Rule Thirteen: Action without a plan equals failure. *She paid Angel with three baggies of rocks to be her decoy with a pack of Chinese firecrackers from Chavelita's party store. In exactly five minutes from go, Angel would set them off on the sidewalk in front of the Florencia 13 house and take off like a* bandito *outta hell while she went in the back way.*

Her plan was to be inside two minutes max, then she'd zig-zag through the backyards, a way only she knew to the stolen bike she'd hidden behind the Oaxacan-Mex restaurant on Pine. Twelve minutes on the bike and she'd be on the other side of the 710 through the Freeway underpass and into Commerce, out of Florencia 13 territory. They wouldn't dare cross over and from there, anywhere in East L.A.

Angel's firecrackers exploded like gunshots in the street in front of the house. Casey slipped in through the back window she'd spotted earlier and tiptoed to the hallway and a room where three Chicana women worked with crack rocks and weight scales, packing plastic baggies. At another table, two Chicano men ran money-counting machines, creating bound stacks of twenty and hundred-dollar-bills.

*"*Mira,*" Casey said. They looked up, saw the gun.*

"You loca, chica?" One of the men said in Spanish. "This is Florencia Thirteen. You don't walk out of here alive."

"Put the hundreds and twenties in here," she said in Spanish, handing him her backpack. He shook his head.

"I do, I'm a dead man," he said.

"I'll kill you if you don't," she said, aiming the gun at him with two hands, the way she'd seen on TV. He put in stacks of hundreds and a couple of twenties and handed it to her. At that moment, four heavily-tattooed vatos pointed their weapons. One of them Mateo, known for the big .50 caliber handgun he carried aimed it at her, the muzzle hole the size of a tunnel.

"Put down the biscuit, chica,*" Mateo said in Spanish.*

She pointed her Hi-Point at his head, said in Spanish, "Let me go or you die."

"You crazy?"

"You're the crazy one," she said. *"I'm nobody. You kill me, who cares — only you'll be dead too. Someone else'll get your big gun. Besides, the way you do business is stupid. You're losing money."*

"We're Florencia Thirteen! You know what we're going to do to you, puta?" Mateo said. *Everyone in the room tensed, ready to shoot or duck. She sensed someone behind her.*

At that moment, the dream changed from what had really happened, because instead of Don Ernesto standing behind her with two of his bodyguards, saying "Espere!" Wait! Don Ernesto who saved her life, the closest thing she'd ever had to a father. Instead, behind her were Jobbik fascists, and three Serb thugs with no faces from the Zemun Clan. They grabbed her, tore her clothes off, hit and kicked her and pinned her naked, screaming, on the floor. The three Mexican women watched from their weight scales, their faces indifferent as the Fates.

One of the Serbs put his hand over her mouth. She couldn't breathe — and that's when she woke up, not knowing where she was; then it came back. The white-curtained windows. The safe house. Belgrade. Jerry Matthews. Todd Brighton dead. Fleetwood's secret. Srxbyx.

In the shower, Casey felt the weight of the dream and a lurking fear as if someone was standing outside the shower curtain. Why were the most terrible days of her life surfacing now? Was Jessie trying to warn her of something? Wrapped in a towel after the shower, she snuck a peek from behind the curtain. The street was busy with cars and people going about their business as though the world was a normal place.

She had breakfast, yoghurt and a minced-meat *burek* pastry that was very good at a restaurant on the corner. Looking at the window, the day was overcast, chilly, the wind whipping at people in winter coats and her fear was real as the wind. She had an espresso, and tried to decide whether it was worth the risk to see the lawyer mentioned by Director Vuković or should she leave Belgrade now on the next plane back to Paris? Her odds were getting worse by the minute. Except for what was in Arthur Dalton's office safe, she was the only one in the world who knew the number password to Fleetwood's secret. Todd Brighton had been watchful as hell with his dogs and his AR-15 and they'd killed him and his mistress and the kids they were sheltering and the dogs. And whoever they were, they'd followed her in Budapest and here in Belgrade. She was the next target. Time to pull the ripcord.

On the other hand, the lawyer's office was in New Belgrade, a business district and she was going in broad daylight. No one knew she was coming – she had both her Sig Sauers with her – and Jerry Matthews was the only one who knew her location at the Savamala safe house or where she was planning to go next. She could just check out the lawyer to tell Dalton and the French she'd done what she could and get the hell back to Paris. Her dream and what she was feeling now was just fear. What would Jessie have said? *Fear is a liar. Remember, we are the most dangerous creatures on the planet.*

She called Beograd Taxi using one of the throwaway cell phones. Getting into the taxi, she noticed it was the same driver who'd brought her in from the airport. Coincidence or danger? The driver spoke Russian, not English, she remembered.

"What's your name?" she asked him in Russian.

"I am Duško, *Gospoja,*" *Miss,* he said.

"Do you have a wife? Children?"

"I'm married. I had a son," the taxi driver said.

"Had a son?"

"My son, Radomir was in Kosovo. A bomb fell on him."

Bloody hell, she thought. You think people are one thing and without realizing, you rip away the adhesive. "Who dropped the bomb?" she asked, immediately regretting asking, but it was too late.

"America. Bill Clinton," Duško said.

Serves me right for asking, she told herself. They drove over the Sava River. The wind ruffled the white-caps on the gray water. Glancing towards the place where the Sava flowed into the Danube, the city built on the confluence of the two rivers, she felt a superstitious chill at the back of her spine as if someone just blew out a candle. *Tell the driver to forget New Belgrade and go to the airport*, a voice whispered. She shook her head as if to rattle it out, but the fear got bigger and wouldn't go away.

New Belgrade, on the other side of the river, was a different city: a place of blocks of tall concrete apartment structures, yellow buses on wide boulevards, brand name hotels and red trams on tracks. The taxi pulled into the curved driveway of a futuristic-looking green glass office building.

"Do I wait?" Duško asked. He seemed worried about her and she was touched.

"I'm not sure how long I'll be," she said.

"Here's my number. Put it in your cell phone. You need, I'll come back," he said.

She walked into the lobby. The light filtering through the green windows created an underwater feeling. It affected her balance, like walking inside an aquarium.

A concierge in a gray uniform stood behind a green marble counter. She asked in English about the attorney, Jovan Bulatović and he said something in Serbian she didn't understand. Not sure what to do, she put a twenty-euro note on the green marble. Slick as ice, he peeled the money into his pocket and pointed toward the elevators, flashing ten fingers then six. She took the elevator to the sixteenth floor and stepped out to the hallway.

She wasn't sure which office was the lawyer's so she paused at every door, laboriously translating the Cyrillic lettering on the name plaques till she found the name *Jovan Bulatović* on expensive-looking wooden double-doors and went in. A blond receptionist sat behind a desk in a glassed-in reception area.

"*Izvolte?*" the receptionist asked.

"I'm here to see Mr. Bulatović," Casey said.

"You have appointment, *Madam*?" the blond responded in English.

"It's a police matter," Casey said, showing the receptionist her HSI badge. "Which is his office?"

"He don't allow in office without appointment, *Madam*. You cannot go."

"Don't worry. He'll see me," Casey said, stepping around the desk. The receptionist tried to stop her until Casey showed her the Sig Sauer. Wide-eyed, the blond pointed to a closed oak door at the far end of an open area where people were working at desks next to the outer green glass wall.

Casey walked to the door and knocked and when there was no answer, knocked again. He had to be in there or the receptionist would've said something, she thought. She tried the door, but it was locked. Pulling a pick from her handbag, her back shielding what she was doing from the people watching her from their desks, she picked the lock and opened the oak door.

Bulatović – she assumed it was the lawyer – lay face down in a pool of blood on the desk. Instantly, the reptile part of her brain told her to run. Go! The enemy had gotten here first. Then the prefrontal cortex kicked in. Whatever they were looking for might still be here, she thought, shutting the door behind her.

Coming closer, she saw the bullet hole in the side of the lawyer's head. She saw no gun, so they weren't even trying to make it look like suicide. But if the door was locked from the inside, how did they get in? There was a second door to the office that opened to the hallway, but how was it possible no one heard the shot? Unless, of course! The special silent gun: the OTs-38 Stechkin. The same assassin as in Marseilles had been here.

The blood was still pooling. It must've just happened. She'd barely escaped getting killed herself. And she was at a dead end, unless . . . wait! What about the Srxbyx account in the Vojvodjanska Banka bank?

Forget it! Run! The reptile brain screamed inside her. But if she could find it before the police came, it might be just enough for Arthur Dalton, she thought. *Don't do it*, said the reptile brain. Or she could risk another three or four minutes that she could maybe leverage with Arthur Dalton to help her in her lifelong quest to find what happened to Jessica – only the clock was ticking. She fumbled in her handbag and pulled out latex gloves.

She tried Bulatović's computer, knowing that was a long shot. Of course it required a password to login. Someone else would have to crack that unless she could find a password scribbled on a slip of paper in a drawer or something. She looked through the lawyer's desk drawers, but found nothing. No password on a piece of paper, no hidden file or drawer. She looked at the file cabinets against the wall, but they were locked.

What else? She checked his pants pockets, found a set of

keys and trying each of them, found one that opened the file cabinets. She searched in the files under "C", the Cyrillic "S," but couldn't find a file for Srxbyx. What about the bank? Looking under "B" for Vojvodjanska, she found the bank folder. In it were about ten accounts associated with the bank, but none were Srxbyx. Casey checked her watch. She'd been there four minutes. The receptionist had probably already called security. She was running out of time.

What about a safe? She looked behind a landscape painting on the wall, but there was nothing behind it. That just left the bookshelves, filled with law books, expensively leather-bound to impress clients. She went through them one at a time, picking up each in turn, riffling through the pages, placing them back as they'd been. On the sixth book she got lucky. Although it looked identical to the others, it wasn't a book, but a locked steel book-safe that couldn't be moved from the bookshelf.

She tried the keys she'd taken from the dead man's pocket, half-expecting the office door to be flung open any second. Her latex-clad fingers fumbled at the lock. C'mon, c'mon, she thought. She was close. She could feel it. One of the keys turned. She opened the safe, pulled out a folder and there it was: the Srxbyx Transport Company A.D. account papers, bank statements, everything.

She began taking photos of the pages with her cell phone, all the while skimming through to see who owned it. She expected to see the Zemun Clan's Darko Razanović's name, but was taken aback. One hundred percent ownership of the company belonged to another company called Pronova, OAO. Its address was 21 Ulitsa Usacheva, Moscow 119048, Russian Federation. The lawyer, Bulatović, and someone named Sergei Kulyakov, Director General of Pronova, had sole signature privileges on the account. The Russians were in this up to their necks. Next to Kulyakov's name was a hand-written notation with a line drawn under it: "*Jackdaw.*"

What the devil? she wondered. A codename? A 'jackdaw' was a kind of bird, like a crow, wasn't it? So who or what was 'the Jackdaw'? Was it this Kulyakov guy in Moscow? She didn't know why, but something about the notation, the underline, gave her the feeling this lawyer, Bulatović had written the notation and underlined it because he'd been afraid of the Jackdaw. If so, with good reason, because someone had sure as hell blown a hole in his head.

Casey straightened. Like Latvia, Belgrade was a red herring. Srxbyx, the blackmail, the hundred million euros, the missing data everyone was looking for: all coming from Russia. She had to get this to Arthur Dalton at once, she thought, putting the papers back into the book-safe and locking it. Pulling off her latex gloves, she was about to leave when she heard a sound outside in the hallway – and more sounds outside the office door. She reached for the Sig Sauer, but it was too late.

The doors burst open. A half-dozen policemen with auto-matic rifles and handguns charged in from each door, screaming in Serbian.

Casey barely had time to raise her hands to surrender before they slammed her to the floor and handcuffed her hands behind her back. Someone kicked her in the stomach. Two policemen hauled her to her feet. A plainclothes detec-tive with hippy-long blond hair that women would kill for opened her handbag. He pulled out the Sig Sauer and said something in Serbian to the other cops.

A bulky policeman with a buzz-cut handed the hippy a clear plastic bag for the Sig Sauer. It was clear to Casey that as far as the hippy detective was concerned, he had already solved the murder. In the doorway, the blond receptionist and at least ten workers watched. I'm a prisoner in the land of the blonds, Casey thought.

Another policeman ran his hands down her ass and legs, making sure to cop a feel before removing her ankle holster and Sig Sauer P238 pistol, making a big deal of showing it to the other cops. The hippy detective slapped her hard across the face and said something in Serbian.

"I don't speak Serbian," she said in English. "I'm an American Homeland Security Special Agent. If you look again in my handbag, you'll see my ID badge and a letter from your Minister of the Interior Dordević. Do you speak English?"

There was a gasp from one of the women workers watching from the doorway. At least someone understood what she'd just said.

"No English," the blond detective said. He poked in her handbag, lifted out the letter with the seal from the Serbian Ministry of the Interior and ripped it to pieces in front of her, dropping the pieces like snowflakes on the floor. Casey took a deep breath. One last chance.

"*Vy gavarítye pa ruski?*" Asking him if he spoke Russian.

"Shut up," he said in Russian and gave an order to his men, who marched her into a hallway filled with office workers in doorways and along the walls. They watched as the police led her to the elevator. The ride down was the longest of her life.

They took her through the sea-green lobby to a black police van outside. The blond detective opened the van's rear door. Three men in black leather jackets were waiting inside the van. As soon as Casey saw them, she screamed and fought wildly. They weren't police! It was Zemun Clan – a kidnapping – shot through her brain! They shoved her into the van and slammed the door shut.

The men inside strapped her to a horizontal bunk. A

heavyset man stuck a needle in her arm and hooked it up to an IV. Another held a hand over her mouth. The heavyset man adjusted the IV slide clamp. A milky-white fluid flowed into her arm. Her heart beat wildly like a trapped bird's as the van lurched forward. Within a second or two, she was unconscious.

PART THREE

TWO WEEKS EARLIER

"Revenge will keep you alive when nothing else will."

JESSICA "JESSIE" MAKARENKO

CHAPTER THIRTY

COMMANDANT CLAIRE PINAULT and Brochard watched the video for the fourth time. They were in the Charles de Gaulle airport security center, a room filled with security camera monitors and technicians at computers. Claire – by this time they were on a *Claire, Jean-Pierre* and *tu* basis – made a face.

"You don't like her," Brochard said.

"What's the game she's playing? Is she a dog on the Russians' leash, or is she the Alpha wolf of the pack?" Claire Pinault said, turning from the monitor to Brochard. The day-old security video showed the mystery woman from the Nice robbery aka Milena Kolavitch, parting from two men to board an Air France flight to Belgrade. She was travelling under the name Isabelle Dusollier.

"Belgrade again," Claire Pinault said.

"The men with her are Russian Mafia," Brochard said. One of the Paris police's snitches had spotted the woman, Milena, and Vincent the Cat in Boulogne-Billancourt with three men the Quai des Orfèvres identified as Russian Mafia gangsters. The descriptions matched the two men in the video, especially the big one.

"The Russians are deep in this. And according to the Swimming Pool, the American who was murdered, Brighton was ex-CIA. Murky waters, Jean-Pierre," Claire Pinault said.

"Very," Brochard agreed. "We have to assume the Russians are involved with or know about the Srxbyx company. As for this Milena woman . . ." he shrugged.

"She could be Mafia or a Russian agent," Claire Pinault said. "SVR, FSB, who knows?"

"What about Vincent the Cat? Where is he?" Brochard said. They'd been watching the Vietnamese restaurant on the rue de Belleville, but so far nothing. Vincent the Cat was either very careful or had lost his taste for Vietnamese food. They re-ran the video of the woman Milena boarding the Air France flight.

"Maybe the Russians got rid of him. Why aren't they together?" Claire Pinault said.

"Maybe she ran away from him. Maybe she was afraid," he suggested.

"Of what? She was with the Russians. That big man, the giant could kill anyone."

"You think Vincent's dead?"

"Maybe, although haven't you noticed? Vincent's not so easy to kill. Maybe he's infatuated with her like the others. Another man made a fool over a woman," cocking her eyebrow in a very Gallic way.

"That's a large fraternity; show me a man who's not a member," Brochard said. At that moment, his mobile phone rang. It was Gabi, near hysterics.

"Jean-Pierre, did you send anyone to the *Maternelle*? Someone tried to take Juliette!" she said, panic in her voice.

Brochard's blood ran cold. "I sent no one! Is she okay? Where is she?"

"She's with me. I'm with her teacher, Mademoiselle Laurent. She saved her! Jean-Pierre, what've you done?" Gabi cried.

"Stay there. I'm on my way. I'm sending police. Don't go home. Tell Mademoiselle Laurent to stay. It's very urgent!"

"What's going on? Why would someone do this?"

"Stay where you are! I'm coming!" Brochard shouted, grabbing his coat as he ran out of the security room. Claire Pinault hurried to catch up, both on their mobiles as they ran. In less than a minute, Paris police had been dispatched to Juliette's *Maternelle* school near the Gare Saint-Lazare. Once in Claire Pinault's car, magnetic flashing light on the car's roof, police siren blaring, horn blasting they cut through traffic on the A1.

When they pulled up at the school, four Paris police cars and gendarmes had already thrown a cordon around the area. Flashing their badges, Brochard and Claire Pinault passed through the protective line of *gendarmes* in SWAT gear and into the school.

Gabi, tightly clutching Juliette, sat at a table with a young dark-haired woman, whom Brochard recognized as Mademoiselle Laurent, one of Juliette's teachers. As soon as Juliette saw Brochard, she squirmed to go to him. After a moment's hesitation, Gabi let her go. Brochard knelt and as Juliette ran and jumped at him, cocooned his arms around her, holding her tightly to him. *Mon dieu*, what if he'd lost her, was all he could think.

He felt her quick breathing against his chest, the fear the child sensed in the grown-ups around her. She clutched at him as if clinging for dear life. Brochard breathed in the child smell of her, staggered by the thought that to lose her would be to die. How could he have gotten so deep in this case that it came to this? He looked over at Gabi, at the burning judgement in her eyes. A mother bear protecting her cub, he thought. She had every right; he'd brought evil into their lives. Carrying Juliette, he came over to Gabi and the teacher. A *policier* whom Brochard assumed was one of the first *flics* on the scene, and Commandant Claire Pinault stood by.

"Monsieur Prosecutor, Commandant, two men, foreigners – they may have been Russians," the *policier* began, "came to pick up little Juliette. They claimed you sent them, Monsieur Prosecutor. One was a very big man, with a tattoo on his neck; the other average-looking, but the witness said there was something *louche*, not quite right, in his manner. Fortunately, Mademoiselle Laurent here told them that only a parent or a person known to the school as designated in writing and with legal identification on file may pick up a child. She warned them they had alarm procedures in place. Mademoiselle Laurent feared they might use force."

"I said I'd set off the alarm if they tried to take the child. Fortunately, they didn't use their pistols," the young teacher said in a shaky voice.

"You're very brave, Mademoiselle. I'm grateful beyond words," Brochard told the young woman. "Did they say anything else?"

"*Oui*, Monsieur," the teacher said. "The smaller man – he had an accent and did all the talking; I did not like him – said 'You're right to be careful. One has to watch children all the time. You take your eyes off them for one second and they're gone and never found again.' The way he said it terrified me, Monsieur."

"Jean-Pierre, who are these gangsters?" Gabi demanded. Brochard glanced at Claire Pinault.

"I'm not sure. Russian Mafia, perhaps," he said, his mouth tightening. "They may be trying to frighten us."

"They succeeded. I'm terrified. What do they want with you – us?" Gabi demanded.

Brochard put Juliette down, kissing her hair, squeezed her hand. He motioned Gabi aside to talk. On the way over, he'd called Director Varane and they'd put a plan into motion.

"We're not sure, but I will never allow anything to happen to you or Juliette," he said.

"What've you gotten us into, Jean-Pierre?" Gabi demanded.

"It was an ordinary robbery case. It changed into something no one expected," Brochard said. "Everyone agrees, the most important thing is yours and Juliette's safety. Director Varane of the Quai des Orfèvres has arranged a safe apartment for you both in the Trocadéro. There'll be *policiers* outside the door and in the street, watching. You'll be under guard, you and Juliette, wherever you are twenty-four hours a day until this is over."

"This is insane. I'm not moving," Gabi said, folding her arms across her chest. "I could move into Henri's flat. He's asked me." Their marriage lay there between them like a dead body.

"We'll do it any way you want," Brochard said, voice barely a croak, his life hanging by a thread. "Stay with your *Maman*. Or if you feel it's safer, go back to Nice or even the *mas* – " they had a stone country house in Roquefort-les-Pins, in the hills above Mougins and the Riviera coast – "or if you prefer, stay with Henri, but believe me, the apartment arranged by Director Varane is safest."

"And you, Jean-Pierre? What about you?"

"I'm going to arrest these scum," he said.

She shook her head. "I meant, where will you stay?"

"If you allow me, I'd stay with you and Juliette at the safe apartment." He looked into her eyes. "I could sleep on a cot. It might make Juliette feel safer."

There are moments, Brochard realized watching her, when your entire life balances like a ballerina *en pointe*. "Fix this, Jean-Pierre. Then we'll talk," she said. Claire Pinault was with a police lieutenant. She came over to Gabi.

"Jean-Pierre and I are colleagues, Madame. I promise we won't let anything happen to you or Juliette. Lieutenant Clément is in charge of the squad assigned to protect you both. You can leave with him when you're ready to go to the safe house," Claire Pinault said.

Brochard kissed Juliette goodbye. After speaking again with Mademoiselle Laurent, he and Commandant Pinault headed back to the Quai des Orfèvres. On the way, he tried calling Casey Ramirez's cell phone. It went immediately to voice mail, suggesting the phone had been turned off. Not a good sign, Brochard thought, images of the dead bodies in Marseilles and the woman, Milena boarding the plane colliding in his mind. He had to warn Casey about the Russians.

When they got back to Claire Pinault's office, she tried connecting with Director Vuković of the Serbian BIA Intelligence Service. She couldn't understand a word of Vuković's fractured English and handed the phone to Brochard. Vuković told him that the American agent, Casey Ramirez, had been arrested, but no one knew where she was.

"What is it?" Claire Pinault asked when he finished the call.

"The American agent, Casey Ramirez. She's disappeared," he said, his voice thick.

"We'll have to tell Washington," she said.

CHAPTER THIRTY-ONE

SAVAMALA, BELGRADE

THE ROOM WAS vast and dark and icy cold. A warehouse, maybe, Casey thought. Small windows high above were dark, so she knew it was night. She was tied to a chair, her wrists strapped to a wooden block, unable to move. When she woke up after being arrested, she discovered she was locked with more than a dozen young women in the cellar of a strip club, the Blue Velvet. Speaking to the women, she learned they'd been trafficked from all over Eastern Europe. They told her harrowing stories of rape, beatings, murder, of being stripped of their passports, clothes, even their names, given new ones like "Natasha," "Ayvri," and "Okeana." They were there to provide sex for the customers to pay off their "debts." Casey thought that was what they'd planned for her, but sometime during the night, they'd thrown a hood over her head and brought her here, though she had no idea where she was. Once or twice she thought she heard the sound of a boat horn, so perhaps she was near the river.

Suddenly, a lamp hanging over her chair came on and

something told her things were about to get a lot worse. She was in a pool of light in a meat processing plant of some kind. Rows of metal racks held plastic bins filled with chops of meat. A line of hog carcasses hung from a rail suspended from the ceiling over grinding machines, chopping blocks and metal tables.

She heard footsteps and a man who looked like the devil stepped into the light. He had black eyes like chips of onyx, cropped hair coming to a widow's peak and was dressed in a stained all-white smock, a butcher's meat cleaver in his hand. Though she had never seen him before, she knew instantly who he was: Srdan, the younger Razanović brother of the Zemun Clan, who according to Director Vuković was the devil.

She understand that she was about to die in this room. With crazy people, the old women of the *barrio* in Central used to say, you must not look in their eyes. Casey stared at his eyes and saw death.

"I ask question, you answer, *bliad*," Srdan said in English, except for the word *whore* in Russian. "You don't answer, you lose finger, hand, foot, lips, eye. Understand?"

She heard more sounds. Although she was in a pool of light and the rest of the room was dark, she could make out the glowing red tip of a cigarette in the shadows. Also one of Srdan's men in a heavy coat and next to him, the blond hippy police detective, leaning against a metal counter piled high with a coil of pale pink sausages. No way out, she thought. She wasn't going anywhere.

"You American? CIA?" Srdan said, coming close enough for her to smell his garlic breath.

"Not CIA; HSI, U.S. Homeland Security," she said, thinking he would ask about the agency, but he only nodded.

"What you wanting in Belgrade?" he said. Her mind

exploded in a thousand different directions like fireworks. How much could she hold back without him chopping off pieces of her? She wasn't getting out of this alive unless she pulled a rabbit out of a hat. Jessie, what do I do? *Never show fear. What you feel is yours; what you show belongs to others.*

"What's your connection to the dead American, Dale Fleetwood?" she said, her words visible breaths in the cold air.

"I ask question! You make answer!" Srdan shouted at her, his face so close she saw the fillings in his teeth. He raised the cleaver and swung down, the blade embedding with a *thunk* deep into the wood barely a half-inch from her fingers. He wrenched the metal out of the wood.

"What you wanting with Lawyer Bulatović?" he demanded. The hell, she thought. The hell.

"My name is Casey Ramirez. I'm the one who opened the safety deposit box in Panama. If you want Dale Fleetwood's secret, I'm the only one who can get it. If you and Darko want the money with Pronova, I must talk to Darko," she said.

He grabbed her face in his hand, his fingers digging into her skin.

"Darko not so nice like me. You tell. What in bank box in Panama?"

Help me, Jessie, she prayed. *Never show fear.* "Stop this now or I'll tell you nothing. You'll never get the money! I'm no good to you like this," she said.

"No good answer." He raised the meat cleaver again and she closed her eyes, steeling for the pain. She opened them. He had lowered the cleaver and was looking closely at her fingers. "Ugly fingers for woman. Who do this?"

"When I was a child," Casey said. Susan and Mark. *You gonna do what I tell you?*

Srdan almost smiled, pointed at her. "Yessss," he hissed.

"One of damned, like us. We the children Jesus not love. Oh yessss," He nudged her fingertips. "Such ugly fingers. Better for you I cut off," he said and raised the meat cleaver.

The words tumbled out of her. She couldn't stop them. "Bulatović was a link to the Srxbyx company. We know it's connected to the Russians, Pronova. There was a long number in Panama. We think it was a password for another bank account."

"What bank?"

"We don't know. That's what I was trying to find out from Bulatović," she said.

"Where password?" Srdan shouted, slapping her hard across the face.

"In my head!" she shouted back. "Touch me again you bastard and I swear to God, no matter what you do to me, I'll lie. I'll make something up. I'll tell the wrong numbers. You'll never get it. You're going to kill me anyway. I've got nothing to lose." Stop it. Keep your voice cold, she told herself. You're dealing with Srdan, the devil, the deranged killer about to chop her to pieces. "But I'll tell it to you and your brother. Don't you get it? You don't win by killing me; you win by making a deal with me."

At that moment, a man's voice shouted, "*Stani*! Stop!" A balding muscular man in a business jacket over a blue "Partizan Vaterpolo Klub" sweatshirt stepped into the light. He gestured. A heavyset man came and unstrapped Casey's hands and feet. She tried to stand up, but was wobbly and the heavyset man had to steady her. She shoved his hand away and stood on her own. The man in the Partizan sweatshirt – she assumed it must be Srdan's older brother, Darko, the brains of the outfit – studied her.

"Like a tiger. '*Better to reign in hell than serve in heaven,*' *neh*? You could almost be a Serb," he said to her in good though accented English. "Upstairs," he gestured and walked to a narrow metal staircase. Casey and the others followed up the stairs to an office on the second floor.

Darko sat down at an ornately carved desk. TV monitors of interior and exterior security camera views and a large "BCC Water Polo Association of Serbia" sports organization flag were hung on the wall along with a cluster of sports trophies atop a credenza. A plate glass window reflected back the lit interior of the office against the night outside. From somewhere Casey heard music; it sounded like a kind of Russian rap. Darko gestured for her to sit.

"If you waste my time, I'll give you back to Srdan. He'll turn you into sausages. No one ever finds you, no one cares," Darko said. Srdan sat in an armchair; the others arranged themselves against the wall; the heavyset man positioned himself by the door. "What else did you find in the bank box in Panama?" he said, lighting a cigarette.

"A safety deposit key and the torn half of an old Yugoslav 100-dinar note. We assume it's to prove identity to someone," Casey said.

"You have these items?' he asked.

Casey shook her head. "Somewhere safe," she lied. The key and the banknote were both in a plastic sleeve under the innersole of her right shoe. "I memorized the password. It's in my head – I'm the only one who knows it. If I give you everything, your brother will turn me into hamburger. Not good for either of us."

Darko's eyebrows went up. "How not good for us?"

"I'm a Special Agent of U.S. Homeland Security. Do you really imagine no one's looking for me? They'll bring so much shit on your tiny Serb government, believe me, even Zemun Clan isn't immune. Why would you want that? We're talking a hundred million euros. You can't get at Fleetwood's secret without me; I can't do it without you. We have no choice. We have to work together," she said.

Darko took a drag on his cigarette and exhaled a stream of smoke. "Why did you kill our lawyer, Bulatović?"

"I didn't. Ask him." She glanced over at the blond hippy detective. "Go on, ask him! They must have done a firearm analysis. Neither of my guns had been fired. So if it wasn't my gun, where was the murder weapon and how is it workers only two or three meters away didn't hear it? In fact, I assumed you did it," she turned back to Darko. "So if neither of us did it, who did?"

Darko looked at the dark window, his face grim. "May a dog mount their mothers," he muttered. Srdan cursed in Serbian, his eyes darting around the room as if looking for someone to kill. He really is crazy, Casey thought. But if they didn't do it, who did? Who had a motive? Suddenly, the pieces came together.

"It's the Russians. You see it too, don't you?"

"You tell me, little American girl. What do you see?" he said.

"Pronova owns Srxbyx. Maybe they're shutting things down. That could create problems for both of us. If they killed Bulatović, you need me as leverage," Casey said, taking a shot in the dark that Darko might figure he was being double-crossed by his Russian partners. "So where does Pronova fit in all this?"

"Truly, the great and powerful CIA doesn't know?" She didn't bother to correct him that she wasn't CIA. Besides, no matter what she said, he wouldn't believe her anyway.

"Not all the pieces," she said, trying to reel him in. "I know it's a big company."

"Pronova is led by Sergei Mogilevich." Darko looked at her quizzically when the name didn't appear to impress her.

"Mogilevich is also of Solntsevskaya, the most powerful Russian *bratva* clan in Moscow."

"*Bratva?*" she said.

"Russian mafia. Americans will never understand. Russia is shells within shells, like a *matryoshka* doll. Mogilevich also has connections with the FSB. Some say he's a colonel in the FSB."

The revelation was a stunner. "Are you saying the Russian security service, the FSB, is in the drug and sex trafficking business?"

"You still don't understand. Everything is shells within shells. They call Sergei Mogilevich, 'the Octopus'. He has tentacles *everywhere.*"

"The Kremlin too?" She was dumbfounded. What had she fallen into?

"My brother and I have no interest in taking on the Russian government. Is that clear enough?"

"Because they're your partners," Casey said.

"For once, an intelligent female," Darko frowned. "So woman, where is Fleetwood's account where you use the password? Where do we find his secret?"

"I thought you knew."

Darko motioned to his men. One of them held Casey's arms. Srdan took out his knife and put it to her throat, trailing the tip down between her breasts. "You said you would be of use to us. Take her downstairs," Darko said. They stood and opened the office door. Casey's life dwindled to seconds. She could feel the cold from downstairs.

"All right! I know where!" she cried out. "Fleetwood set up the Srxbyx messaging through Latvia with you. You must've met him at least once."

Darko held his hand up to stop them. "Once."

"Where? It's important," she said, grasping at straws.

"A hotel room in Athens. Why?"

"Which hotel?"

He paused to remember. "The Grand Bretagne, why?"

"Didn't you find that strange? Fleetwood lived in Paris and the south of France. Why would he meet you in Athens?"

"That's where the account is? Athens?"

"One way to find out. I have the banknote, the key, and the password. I'm the only one who does. It's worth a hundred million euros if I find it. You need me to do it or you'll have the Russian Mafia, the FSB, *and* the CIA after you. Not a fight you want, even for Zemun Clan." She looked at the men holding her. "Tell these idiots to take their hands off me," she said.

Darko gestured. His men let go of her. "Alright, you go to Athens, but my brother Srdan and one of my men go with you. Anything you find, you bring to me," he said harshly.

"I have demands too," Casey said.

"You're in no position – " Darko began.

"You can't do this with a gun. The only place the password exists is in my head. If you torture me I'll lie. You want me to cooperate," she said.

"What do you want?"

"Pick someone else, not your brother."

Srdan gave her an evil smile, more the devil than anyone she'd ever seen. He's going to kill me, she thought. No matter what his brother says or does. It's who he is. Darko shook his head. The sound of the music from outside floated across the silence.

"What's that music?" she asked.

"Club 69, a *splav*, a floating barge nightclub on the river. We own it. We own many businesses," Darko said. So they were near the Sava River front, she thought.

"If I have to go with him," indicating Srdan, "I want something – or kill me now. Everyone loses."

Darko stared at her. "What?" he said gruffly.

"The girls in the Blue Velvet, the ones who've been trafficked, let them go."

"You crazy woman! You know how much moneys costing?" Srdan exploded.

"Impossible. You go to Athens. Your reward is you get to keep breathing," Darko said.

Casey shook her head. "Their cost is nothing compared to a hundred million euros, not to mention having a war with the Russians *and* the CIA, because they won't let it go. I'm an American agent. The girls for Fleetwood's secret or war. That's the deal."

Darko peered at her as if seeing her from a distance. "Why are you doing this? You don't know these women. Who are they to you?"

"It's a simple business choice. I'll go with your brother to Athens and you get the money or kill me," she said.

Darko studied her as though she came from another planet. "You were right," he said to his brother. "This one's a tiger; another child Jesus forgot." He raised a cautioning finger. "But remember, woman, no tricks or even God won't save you. Anything else?"

Relief flooded her. She realized she hadn't eaten anything since that little piece of *burek* and yoghurt yesterday. "Does anybody deliver pizza in this country? Domino's? Pizza Hut? Anything? I'm starving," she said.

The heavyset man laughed out loud. Srdan smirked at her in a way that Casey understood with blinding clarity. The instant she got her hands on whatever Fleetwood had left behind, Srdan would rape and kill her. The chopping block downstairs was prelude.

CHAPTER THIRTY-TWO

AJACCIO, CORSICA

THE BAR WAS on the Place De Gaulle, a block from the beach. Gaspar, a bearded man in Prada sunglasses beckoned Vincent from a rear table.

"Vincent the Cat, you're a blond now. So you can kiss the boys?" Gaspar said, taking off his sunglasses.

"Be careful I don't kiss you," Vincent said. He'd shaved his mustache and put on the blond wig in Paris to alter his image from the one the *flics* were after. The waiter came over. "Casanis," Gaspar ordered, "– and you?"

"Pietra," Vincent told the waiter, pulling out a cigarette pack and tapping one out. He preferred beer to the local pastis.

"Too bad about Lucas," Gaspar said, referring to the dead Blue Panther.

"Marseilles," Vincent said, as if the city's name was a metaphor for everything wrong in life. He lit his cigarette. "How goes the war?"

"They did Vittini last week. Someone left his head, minus

his eyes and tongue in a basket in the Place Foch market," Gaspar said.

"He always talked too much anyway."

"A woman was buying Zinzala olives. Gave her a hell of a scare."

"Who did it, Petit Bar?" Vincent asked, referring to a Corsican gang that was a rival to Gaspar's own Mafia clan, the Jean Jé.

"Antoine Squint-eye." The waiter arrived with drinks, the smell of *anise* discernable from across the table. "You saw your mother?" Gaspar asked. He and Vincent had become pals in La Santé, when Gaspar learned that Vincent's mother had come from the same Bastelicaccia section of Ajaccio where he grew up.

Vincent nodded. He'd made it to Marseilles with every *flic* in France looking for him by hitching rides from truckers on the autoroute. After the ferry crossing to Corsica, his first stop as always was the cemetery in the hills above Ajaccio, where his mother had insisted she be buried, even though she'd lived most of her life in Paris. The first time he'd been arrested – still a kid when he robbed a *tabac* in the Marais – she'd told him, "You have a brain, Vincent, not just a penis. If this is how you want to use it, do it for real money, not *centimes* at a *tabac*."

"So what do you need?" Gaspar said, filching one of Vincent's Marlboros and lighting it.

"A name," Vincent said. He told Gaspar about the dead American, Layton Gary McCord and his younger *petite amie*, showing Milena's photo on his cell phone screen to Gaspar. "Anyone who was a friend or business associate, close with either of them."

"A looker," Gaspar said about Milena. "She was good?" Implying sex.

"Very. She has Russian Mafia connections in Paris. The dead American, who knows?"

Gaspar made the sign for money with his fingers. "That kind of information is expensive. Two for me, the same for whoever can tell you about the girl and the American."

Vincent nodded. "Add another fifteen hundred. I need a new *Carte nationale*."

"One hears every *flic* in France wants a piece of you." Gaspar said. "Do you need a woman? We got some new ones at our club in Porto-Vecchio, from Eastern Europe. Afterwards, you won't be able to walk straight."

Vincent touched his cell phone. "I've unfinished business with this one."

"Vincent the Cat bested by a woman?"

"Just find me someone who knew the American."

"It's not just the *flics*. I heard Russians too. You're in big trouble."

Vincent turned and spat on the floor. "*La vie*," life, he said. "Marseilles is Marseilles."

"Lucky for you, Corsica is still Corsica," Gaspar said.

Vincent rang the doorbell of the private townhouse in Monte Carlo's Carré d'Or district, near the Casino. A butler answered the door, a Glock in a shoulder holster peeking out from his jacket. A second man in a vest and tie held tight to the collar of a growling bullmastiff. The butler escorted Vincent to a gold-plated elevator up to the top floor, the elevator door opening to a magnificent view of the harbor with thirty-plus-meter yachts lined up at the dock.

Vincent glanced around the salon. What appeared to be a vaguely familiar painting of two men playing cards – Cézanne? – hung on one of the walls. On the opposite wall was a portrait of a man in a black jacket leaning on his elbow that Vincent, who'd occasionally dabbled in art theft, was fairly certain was by Van Gogh.

A bald man in his seventies in a sports shirt and linen slacks gestured for Vincent to sit. The butler went to the bar, poured a bottle of Stella into a glass, brought it to Vincent and left.

"My name is Constantin," the bald man said in passable French. "You're here for two reasons: first, because I have dealings with the *Jean Jé* clan in Corsica and second, we both have interest in a certain dead American who went by the name McCord, but whose real name was Dale Fleetwood."

Already this was news, Vincent thought. Was it possible the hundred million Milena talked about wasn't fantasy after all? "You did business with him?" he said.

"Fleetwood amassed a large fortune because he had two useful traits," Constantin said. "He knew how to make himself agreeable and he had no moral qualms whatsoever."

"So the money for the secret Fleetwood's *petite amie* talked about is real?"

"There are certain persons who prefer that Fleetwood's secret not fall into either the Americans' or the Russians' hands."

"You want Lay . . . *pardon*, Fleetwood's material – and you're prepared to pay?" Vincent said. Constantin went to an ornate desk, pulled out a bank card and placed it in front of Vincent on the coffee table.

"Go to the EFG Bank here in Monte Carlo. You'll find a private account in your name with ten thousand euros, for expenses. Bring what Fleetwood left behind to me."

"What's in it for me?"

"Five million U.S. dollars. What you do to get it, how you do it, is no concern of mine."

"What about Fleetwood's *petite amie*, Milena?"

"Surely by now I'm sure you know her name isn't Milena."

"Do you know what it is, her real name?"

"What she was born with I'm not sure even she knows," Constantin said. "In the Russian FSB, the successor to the KGB, her name is Natalya."

"And you know this how?"

"In my business, as in yours Vincent the Cat, knowing who you're dealing with is everything," Constantin said.

"Did you know Lay– Dale Fleetwood personally?"

"There were times when he was of use," Constantin said carefully.

"Tell me. It might help," Vincent said. This was like planning a jewel job, he thought. You put the pieces together one at a time and it leads you to a plan.

"As I said, Dale was easy to get on with. Not that he tried to charm you. He could be direct, sometimes brutally so. But he was willing to get things done and didn't mind how – " Constantin paused. "Of course, that was before he went to prison."

"And after?" Vincent asked.

"He still played the game, but underneath one sensed an anger vast and frigid as Antarctica. Sooner or later you knew there'd be a reckoning. Once he disappeared for a month. No one knew where. I met Natalya for drinks at the Hotel de Paris here in Monte Carlo. She thought I might know where he was. Offered herself to me if I'd tell her."

Vincent felt a bee sting of jealousy. "Did you?"

"I told her I didn't know. But I found it interesting how desperate she was to find him," Constantin said.

"Fleetwood's secret was that important?" Vincent said.

Constantin nodded. "In all of human history, there've

only been four currencies: money, goods, sex and information. Which do you imagine is the most valuable?"

"So where did Fleetwood hide his secret?" Vincent asked.

"If I knew, we wouldn't be having this conversation."

Vincent put down his glass. "Why are we having this conversation?"

"Twice in the months before he died, Fleetwood left France. Once from Paris, once when he was here in Cap d'Antibes. I had some of your friend, Gaspar's Corsicans follow him. Both times he went to Greece," Constantin said.

"What's in Greece?"

"I'm not sure. Fleetwood hadn't recouped the money he had before prison, so he must have had a compelling reason. But Fleetwood was clever. In Athens, both times he lost the Corsicans," Constantin said.

"So whatever we're looking for is in Athens?" Vincent said. He picked up the EFG Bank card and put it in his pocket.

"Find Fleetwood's secret and bring it to me. You might even find that Russian girl as well. I suspect you have a reason to want that," Constantin said.

"Five million reasons," Vincent said.

CHAPTER THIRTY-THREE

MONTMARTRE, PARIS

THE MOLOTOV COCKTAIL arched high over the crowd, exploding in flames at the feet of a line of Paris police in riot gear. A woman screamed as a policeman, engulfed in fire, rolled on the pavement. The crowd of demonstrators, waving National Front banners that read "*Vive* Lemaire" and "Jews and Muslims Out of France!" surged forward. The Rue de Rivoli near the Louvre was completely blocked. Their best chance to catch the Russians who'd threatened Gabi and Juliette was fading fast.

"How do we get out of this?" Brochard said to Claire Pinault, who was driving.

"Boulevard de Sébastopol," she said, turning on her police siren as she made an illegal turn against traffic, two cars nearly plowing into them. Klaxon sounding, she sped through side streets away from the demonstration.

Brochard's thoughts raced. The tip about the Russians couldn't've come at a worse moment. The American woman Casey had gone missing in Belgrade. He'd been trying to organize an effort to rescue. In case of an emergency, she'd given him a contact phone number. She'd told him to identify himself as Alan Jenkins and ask for Walter Pettifer regarding a lost dog named Clarence.

The man who answered, said: "You the French prosecutor, the one the women all go crazy for?" Brochard told him they had to find Casey.

"It's being handled," the man at the other end said and hung up.

Brochard stared at the phone, then called the American embassy, but all he got was a recording telling callers to leave a message. He hung up in fury. The Americans had constructed a system perfect in its futility.

The tip, on the other hand, looked good. It was from the same police snitch as before. He told them the Russians had been spotted at a Russian restaurant on the rue d'Orsel in Montmartre.

Claire Pinault posted a *policier* in workman's clothes to watch the restaurant from the roof of a building across the street. For added support, Director Varane placed a *Police Judiciaire* response squad on standby. Brochard and Claire Pinault remained late at her Quai des Orfèvres office to wait. At 20:16, they got the call. Three men matching the descriptions of the Russians had entered the restaurant.

Only the *P.J.* response force wasn't available. Governor Jeffrey Smullen, the American candidate for President had arrived in Paris for two days of "fact-finding" intended to burnish Smullen's foreign affairs credentials. Earlier in the day, Smullen met with French President Deschamps at the Elysée Palace and toured the Arc de Triomphe and the Tomb of Marshal Foch. More controversially, Governor Smullen would be meeting that evening with Emmanuelle Lemaire, radical leader of the right-wing National Front, who'd called for the expulsion of Muslims and the registration of all Jews in France.

Tens of thousands of pro- and anti-Smullen demonstrators filled the streets of Paris. The Paris mayor's office issued a "*UA*" for *Urgence Attentat*, Attack Emergency, the highest terrorist alert level, in fear of potential Islamist terrorist attacks and National Front retaliations. Brochard was told a full response team couldn't be spared. Police resources had been stretched thin. Three RAID policemen was all that could be spared.

Claire Pinault, siren wailing, threaded her way through traffic up the Boulevard de Sebastopol, occasionally skidding into the bus lane and back. Brochard held tight and tried to focus on the Russians, but he was torn in three directions: Gabi and Juliette's safety, the Russians and the *femme fatale* Milena, and thoughts of Casey. He had a bad feeling about what was happening with her. She wouldn't've dropped out of sight on her own. Brochard didn't trust the Americans to save her. And what about Gabi and Juliette? They had to be his top priority, he thought, hanging on as Claire Pinault slipped through a red light, barely avoiding getting hit to make a tire-squealing left onto Boulevard Saint-Denis.

They found a parking space at the corner and walked down the narrow street. A Delaporte dry cleaning van was parked near the restaurant. The evening was cool, cloudy; a breeze whipped at the restaurant's awning. Inside the van, Lieutenant Cadart and his RAID squad were waiting.

"None of the Russians have come out," Lieutenant Cadart, a rugged man in black combat gear and cradling an HK assault rifle said by way of greeting.

"What about civilians? We don't want to turn this into a gangster movie shoot-out," Brochard said.

"We take them by surprise. It'll be over in seconds," Lieutenant Cadart assured them.

Brochard's heart was pounding. These were the men who'd threatened his daughter. Maybe Gabi would see him in a better light. If they could take them alive, they could lead him to Milena, the woman from the Nice robbery. The case might finally be over. He nodded the "go" signal.

Lieutenant Cadart and his men exited the van and approached the restaurant door from either side, weapons at the ready. Claire Pinault, gun drawn, and Brochard followed. Lieutenant Cadart and his men burst into the restaurant, shouting: "*Attention! Danger!* Everyone on the floor now!"

They motioned and shoved the patrons at tables down to the floor amid a clatter of plates, overturned chairs, and a man's shout. Brochard looked around. The Russians were gone. Claire Pinault grabbed a man in a waiter's apron.

"Where's the back exit?" she demanded. The waiter pointed towards the kitchen. Claire Pinault and Lieutenant Cadart crashed into the kitchen.

"Did you see three Russians, one very big?" Brochard asked the waiter.

"*Oui*, Monsieur. They were here, but left the back way in a hurry."

"How long ago?"

"Perhaps four or five minutes," the waiter said.

Merde, Brochard thought, a sick feeling in the pit of his stomach. Claire Pinault and Lieutenant Cadart returned from the kitchen with sour expressions. How is it these gangsters have been a step ahead of us at every turn, he wondered. Only eight or nine people knew about their raid on the restaurant. There could be only one explanation: a *mouchard*, a snitch within the Paris police. Brochard began to get a bad feeling about the botched restaurant action.

"My wife, my daughter," he said to Claire Pinault.

"Let's go," she said, touching the gun in her holster.

Brochard briefed Director Varane from Claire Pinault's car on the way to the apartment in the 8th *arrondissement* where they'd moved Gabi and Juliette. Though Claire sped through the streets, the lights of other cars and the city at night like a blur, the seconds ticked by like hours. All Brochard could think of was to get there before the Russians. Gabi and Juliette were in even greater danger, he told Varane, unable to keep the panic out of his voice.

"Go take care of your family, Jean-Pierre. We'll deal with the rest in the morning," Director Varane said, the sounds of a restaurant on his end. They'd caught him at dinner.

The apartment building where Gabi and Juliette were staying was on an upscale residential tree-shaded street, the Avenue George Mandel. The night had turned cold; the shadows of the trees in sharp contrast to the white building behind an iron fence. Claire Pinault pulled the car diagonally into a narrow parking space.

Brochard looked for the *policier* who was supposed to have been posted outside by Lieutenant Clément. He saw no one. Something tightened inside him like a violin string screwed tighter and tighter. If the Russians had advance word about the restaurant raid, that meant they also knew about this place. He pulled out his mobile and called Lieutenant Clément.

"Clément here," a voice responded.

"This is Brochard. Where's the outside *policier*?" Brochard said.

"There was an *Urgence Attentat*, Attack Emergency notice because of the riots. They needed every extra policeman. I'm in the apartment next to theirs. Do you expect trouble?" Lieutenant Clément said.

Brochard told him about the failed raid and the possible snitch within the Paris police. "Don't shoot. I'm coming in," Brochard said.

"Me too. This is Commandant Pinault," Claire said. She handed Brochard her police Sig Sauer pistol.

"What about you?" he said, feeling melodramatic holding the gun; something he couldn't imagine using.

"I have another," she said, taking a smaller Sig Sauer pistol out of her handbag. She touched Brochard's arm. "You should know, it wasn't a snitch who alerted the Russians. Someone hacked my computer at the office. The tech guy alerted me just before we left. It must've been the Russians. I wasn't sure until what happened at the restaurant. Anyway, I'm coming with you," she said, checking her gun.

Brochard got out of the car and went to the building's front door, Claire Pinault beside him. He was about to ring the concierge's bell but something told him not to. He tried the building front door, which was supposed to be kept locked at all times. It was open. "They're here," he mouthed to Claire Pinault. Holding the pistol, he turned on his cell phone's flashlight app and went inside. Claire followed.

The lobby was pitch black; the concierge's apartment was on the right. Brochard touched the concierge's door. It moved; not locked either. Inside, they found a fifty-ish woman with a surprised look on her face and a bullet hole in her forehead on the floor.

A floorboard squeaked in the next room. Claire urgently motioned to Brochard to leave and dropped into a kneeling shooting position.

"Go," she mouthed.

Brochard tiptoed his way out of the apartment. He was halfway up the stairs, when he heard a shot from what sounded like a gun with a silencer from the concierge's apartment.

He panicked. Should he go down to help Claire or up to protect Gabi and Juliette? No choice there, he thought, running up the stairs two at a time. When he reached the third floor where Gabi and Juliette were, he shut the flashlight app to let his eyes readjust to the darkness. When he was ready, he opened the door to the hallway.

One of Lieutenant Clément's men was supposed to be on duty outside the apartment door, but the hallway was empty. *Merde*, he swore to himself as he tiptoed to the door to Gabi's apartment. Locked, thank God. He knocked and stepped to the side, clumsily aiming the pistol at the door with both hands. A frightened voice came from the other side.

"Who's there?" Gabi's voice, he thought, flooding with relief.

"It's me, Jean-Pierre," he said. She opened and he stepped inside, closing the door behind him. The apartment was dark except for the lone light of a lamp in the living room. "What's going on?" he whispered.

"I don't know," she whispered back, locking the door and putting on the chain. "Lieutenant Clément came and said they couldn't keep all the *policiers* here. They're short-handed because of the terrorist riots. He's in the next apartment himself. I was putting Juliette to bed when I heard a noise. I got her down, but just before you came, I heard a shot. I'm scared to death, Jean-Pierre," she whispered.

"Where's Juliette," he said urgently. They tiptoed into the bedroom. Juliette was asleep, her *Lulu Vroumette* doll next to her. Brochard's heart flip-flopped at the sight of her. Thank God, he thought and motioned for Gabi to get into Juliette's bed with her. He positioned himself on the floor, his back against the bed frame to steady him, keeping his pistol aimed at the terrible empty space of the bedroom doorway open to the living room and called Director Varane.

"I'm at the safe apartment," he whispered. "The concierge's been shot. Pinault stayed because of a sound. The Russians are in the building."

"Don't move. I'm sending help. They'll be there in three minutes. Hang on, Jean-Pierre," Varane said and hung up.

The sound of a muffled shot came from next door, then a scuffle and two more shots. *Mon dieu!* They were next door. Brochard hadn't heard them break in or anything. Somehow they'd gotten in. He and Claire must've arrived at the same moment the Russians were in the concierge's apartment. He should call Lieutenant Clément, he thought, but was afraid to. It might alert them and if Clément was dead, it would make things worse. The help from Director Varane would be here any minute, but if they'd finished Clément, this apartment was next. Brochard could barely breathe. He tried to steady his hands as he aimed Claire's pistol at the empty doorway.

He expected them to break through the door, but he heard only the faintest scratching sound. No sound of breaking in or footsteps. Suddenly, the massive silhouette of the biggest man Brochard had ever seen filled the door space. Without thinking, he fired at the center of the giant shape, the shot deafening in the dark room. It appeared to have no effect. The giant came at him like a locomotive.

Brochard fired again at the center of the mass nearly on top of him. A powerful blow knocked him flying to one side, leaving him stunned. Gabi screamed. He heard others in the room. One of them grabbed Gabi and said, "*Ta gueule!*" Shut up!

His shoulder in pain, feeling woozy and barely able to breathe. Everything seemed to be happening in slow motion.

The giant was reaching for Juliette. All Brochard could think was *Not Juliette.* Somehow, impossibly, he'd managed to hang onto the gun. He raised himself from the floor and fired again at the giant.

The massive bulk tilted sideways and crashed to the floor. Brochard twisted and shot again, this time at an angular man with a knife holding Gabi. The man grunted. Pulling Gabi with him with one hand, the angular man lunged at him, slashing Brochard's arm. Brochard felt nothing. With his free hand he pulled the man close and fired into his side twice more.

Brochard staggered to the light switch and turned it on, at the same time peering into the living room. He saw the back of the third man in an overcoat run out of the apartment door. Feeling dizzy, his arm starting to really hurt, Brochard staggered back to the bed and clutched Juliette to him. She was crying "*Papa! Papa!*"

The giant man on the floor stirred. He grabbed at Brochard's foot and squeezed. Brochard cried out in agony. It felt like the bones in his foot were being crushed to powder. Leaning over, he fired almost point blank into the giant's head. Juliette screamed as glop burst out of the giant's head. The pain from the squeezing stopped; the giant lay motionless on the floor. "*Papa! Papa!*" Juliette sobbed.

Gabi got up from the floor, staring at Brochard as if she'd seen a ghost.

CHAPTER THIRTY-FOUR

ATHENS, GREECE

FROM HER AIRPLANE WINDOW SEAT, Casey saw the coast and then the city of Athens, with its ruins and mountain backdrop. Srdan and Miroslav, the heavyset man from the meat-cutting plant were wedged in the seats beside her. During the hour-and-a-half flight from Belgrade, Srdan had managed to touch her breast a half-dozen times, whispering in her ear the various ways he was going to have her the minute they got to a hotel room.

Slapping his hand away or jamming an elbow into his side barely slowed him down. Each time she told him to stop, his eyes glinted as if he was adding to the tally of things he had planned for her. She remembered Jessica's words: *If you dance with the devil, sooner or later you dance to the devil's tune.* The only thing that made it bearable was remembering watching from Darko's Mercedes on Tiršova Street in downtown Belgrade as the girls from the Blue Velvet were released to the Women's Shelter. It was the best moment of her life.

Darko had turned to her in the Mercedes. "You get what

you want?" he said. Casey nodded. "What'd you accomplish?" he said. "It cost me money, but we'll buy new girls. They come from all over Eastern Europe. Our business is old as the world."

"But these are free," she said, thinking *Did I do good, Jessie? Did someone do this to you? Is that what happened to you? I think about that every day. Maybe this time, we got a little back.*

But psycho-Srdan was proving more of a problem every second. Always next to her, never giving her a chance to contact Jerry Matthews or Brochard. The only way she would survive was to get away, the sooner the better.

She decided to take her chance at the airport car rental.

"I'm driving," she told the female clerk at the car rental counter, handing over her passport, driver's license, and credit card. While in the airport ladies' room before they'd boarded the plane, she'd Googled car routes to the main part of Athens from the airport. Her plan was desperate, but right now she couldn't see another way out. The moment the Serbs got their hands on whatever secret Fleetwood left, they'd rape and kill her.

"He drive," Srdan said, jerking his thumb at Miroslav.

"I've been to Greece before," she lied. "Athens is thousands of years old. There are weird one-way streets that double-back. Besides, these Greeks are crazy. If you think I'm risking my life with one of you driving, you're crazy as they are."

"You don't drive," Srdan said in a dangerous tone raising a sharp glance from the woman clerk.

"I drive or I start screaming right here. The police will come. You'll never get to the hotel," she said. The car rental clerk looked at them, alarmed.

Miroslav nudged Srdan. "Let her. What difference?" he said.

"No tricks," Srdan said. The female clerk looked at them like she felt she ought to call security, but didn't want to risk it with these men. Srdan smiled at the woman clerk as if he was going to ask her to dance at a club. The remark she'd made about "the hotel" had gotten to him, Casey thought. All he had in his little psycho brain was what he was planning to do to her.

They took the shuttle to the rental car park. The day was partly sunny, warmer than Belgrade. They found the car, a red Opel. Casey got behind the wheel, adjusted her seat belt and pulled it tight.

"Greek drivers," she said by way of explanation, shoving Srdan's hand from her thigh. "Stop. I can't drive like that," she said, starting the Opel.

She drove on the airport access road. The question was how long before Srdan got wise to what she was doing. Minutes probably. The Google map had indicated that the highway into Athens ran east–west. If she turned west, there was no way to get away. Heading east would take them to the beach at Artemida and hopefully, her one chance.

She came to a stop at the highway. Here we go, she thought and turned east, conscious of the seat belt, uncomfortably tight between her breasts. It was the only weapon she had, two of Jessie's rules leaping simultaneously into her mind as she pressed down on the accelerator: *There's always a weapon. Find it.* And: *Revenge will keep you alive when nothing else will.* Because she hated Srdan with every fiber of her being. One of them, either Srdan or her was going to die today.

Srdan poked her hard with his finger. "Sign say Athens other way," he said.

"We'll be stuck in traffic for an hour that way. I've been here before. Going by way of the beach is faster," she said, speeding up. The speedometer read eighty kilometers per hour. Ninety. A hundred. She passed a car. A hundred ten. Passed a truck and a mini-van. Hundred and twenty. All around were flat fields and houses along the road. It can't be here, she thought. A hundred and thirty, around eighty miles per hour. She pressed harder on the accelerator. A hundred and forty.

"Why so fast?" Srdan said. "No want police."

"We need to beat the traffic. What are you, a girl?" she said. Hundred and fifty. How fast could this stupid Opel go, she wondered. Not much faster.

"I say *slow*!" Srdan snapped.

She slowed at a round-about and sped up again. Now there were more houses and stores, the road a two-lane in a village. She whipped around an old SUV and swerved back into her lane to avoid colliding with an oncoming car.

"You crazy, whore? I say *slow*!" Srdan shouted. Casey smacked his face hard as she could with the back of her right hand.

"Don't you ever call me 'whore' again!" she said through gritted teeth. He raised his hand to hit her and she screamed: "Hit me, I swear we all die!" Srdan grabbed for the steering wheel. Casey fought him for it. The Opel careened into the opposite lane. An old truck came toward them.

The Opel skidded snakelike left and right, careening straight at the truck. Miroslav shouted something to Srdan in Serbian, grabbing Srdan's shoulder. The truck looming, Srdan let go of the wheel. Casey swerved back into their lane, missing the truck by inches and stepped on the accelerator, building speed up to one-thirty-five.

"Wait I get you hotel," Srdan hissed. His face had the same expression as when he was about to chop off her hand.

The road ahead was straight. She could do it anywhere now, Casey thought, heart pounding. She just had to watch for pedestrians, as a mother with a small boy ahead darted across the road. The last thing she wanted was to hurt any innocent bystanders. There were buildings and telephone poles along the road, but something told her the beach was close. They were on a straight-away; for the moment, no other cars.

She nudged the speed to one-forty; eighty-five miles per hour. A car was ahead. At the speed she was going, she would crash into the back of it. Srdan and Miroslav shouted. She swerved around the car, tires squealing. Ahead she saw a traffic light where the road ended at the beach road. A stone fence and a lamppost bordered the beach. Finally, a target. Better to die than be touched by Srdan, she thought.

She jammed the accelerator to the floor hard as she could, bracing herself, the men screaming as they sped through the red light. Casey aimed for the passenger side of the car, Srdan's side, to hit the lamppost. Her last thought: *If I die, at least I'll never have that bastard inside me*, as the Opel crashed into the lamppost, air bags exploding into their faces.

Casey's breastbone hit the seat belt so hard she thought she would burst through it. The force knocked the wind out of her. But the seat belt held. The air bag smacked hard against her face and chest. She glanced at Srdan. He was stunned, face bloody, the airbag against his face. Miroslav lay twisted against the back of Srdan's seat.

Casey tried to get out, but her door wouldn't open. The front of the car was a mass of metal. Incredibly, the power window button still worked. She opened the window, unhooked the seat belt and managed to wriggle out through the window opening.

The front of the Opel was crumpled like an accordion. People on the street had stopped to look. Feeling lightheaded, she staggered to her feet. Think, Casey, think, she told herself. Don't just run. Jessica's rule: *Emotion equals error. When a shooter wants to hit a target he holds his breath.* Her stuff – her handbag, carry-on – were in the trunk and she had the key in her hand. She walked zombie-like to the back of the Opel and popped the lid.

Srdan was trying to wriggle his way out of the other door window. The car on his side was crushed in, giving him little room to maneuver. At that moment, he wasn't looking at her. She grabbed her handbag and carry-on and looked for some-where to hide.

There was a *taverna* about forty meters down the beach. She ran to it, pain stabbing at her breastbone with every breath. Luckily, there were no customers in the *taverna*. An older man in an apron behind the bar looked up.

"Help me, please. Bad men kidnapped me. Hide me. Call the police," she said in English, hoping he understood. "Hurry, they're coming," she begged. Srdan might be there any second and he wouldn't care who he killed.

"Come," the man in the apron said in accented English, motioning for her to get behind the bar. She crouched low behind the bar, trying to make herself as small as possible. The man picked up a phone. He was speaking in rapid Greek when she heard Srdan's voice; his fury cut through every word like a machete.

"You see woman, hair black, this high?" Srdan's voice demanded. Casey held her breath. Would this *taverna* guy protect her? Srdan would kill them both in an eye-blink.

"No one here. I'm talking to the police," the man in the apron said and spoke into the phone in Greek.

"No one come?" Srdan said. His voice was just on the other side of the bar. If he leaned over he'd see her. She'd be dead.

"Come, look if you like," the man in the apron said to Srdan, his hand grabbing hold of a club below the bar, positioning himself so Casey would be harder to spot. "The police are on their way," the man in the apron added. Casey held her breath. Time stopped. She could hear time in the wind and the chirp of a bird outside. "You can come out. He's gone," the man in the apron said finally. She stood, clutching her top, ripped in the crash.

"Thank you," she said.

"I could see he was a bad man. Not the first to come into my place," the man in the apron said, setting the club on the top of the bar.

The office was on the fourth floor of a building on a busy street. Casey checked the building directory, using an online guide on her iPad to translate the Greek letters. About half-way down the list, she saw it: ΛΓΜ, AE (it stood for LGM, AE; AE being the Greek equivalent of *inc*). L – G – M. *Hello Layton Gary McCord*, she said to herself. Near the bottom of the directory she saw: *Srxbyx, AE*. Both companies in the same suite! She was getting close; she could feel it. Except she knew Srdan was hunting her; her time was running out.

She had taken a Kosmos taxi from the taverna into town. On the way, she booked an AirBnb room in the Koukaki district, near the Acropolis. Per a recommendation from her AirBnb hostess, she'd gone to Attica, a department store on Syntagma Square, to replace the clothes she'd left behind in her suitcase in the Opel. She also bought a burner phone and called Jerry Matthews.

"Good to hear you're back in business, Princess. We were about to send in the Marines," Jerry Matthews said.

"You have no idea what you got me into, Jerry. Some Serbian home-boy almost chopped me into hamburger," she said.

"I'll never eat at McDonald's again," he said.

"What about the girl?" she asked. Jerry Matthews filled her in. He'd forwarded to her photos of Dale Fleetwood from the time he'd gone to prison. Also one of Milena he got from Brochard. She was probably traveling under the alias Isabelle Dusollier, last seen boarding a flight to Belgrade, he told her.

"Is she following me?" Casey asked.

"Either that or she's on the same scent. Your Frenchy boyfriend seemed to think she might be a Russian spy. You better watch your cute little butt," Jerry Matthews said, putting a leer into his voice.

"You never fail me, Jerry. You're always a dick," she said and hung up.

That evening Casey went to the Grande Bretagne, the hotel where Dale Fleetwood had supposedly stayed in Athens. Dangling a pair of hundred-euro bills as bait, she tried to tempt first a front desk clerk and then the hotel concierge about Fleetwood, but both responded with a curt "Sorry, Madame, we never discuss our guests." Dead end.

Walking into the Grande Bretagne bar was like stepping into a 1930's movie. Successful-looking men in suits and ties and tanned slim women who looked like they'd never seen the inside of an office sipped cocktails against the backdrop of a tapestry of Alexander the Great behind the mahogany bar. Luckily, she'd dressed for the part in an LBD from the Attica Mall.

The Greek bartender poured her a single malt. Leaning forward, exposing her cleavage for all she was worth, she showed him photos of Fleetwood and Milena on her iPhone, passing him a hundred-euro note that he scooped up with practiced ease.

"You ever see him, them here?" she asked.

He nodded. "Him I saw a few times. Her once."

"But they stayed here?"

"No, he pretended," he said, wiping a glass. "He actually stayed at the Plaka, not far, cheaper. One of the waiters saw him."

"Did you ever hear him talk? Ever talk to him?" she asked.

He studied her. "What's your interest, Madame?"

"Personal," she said, watching him over the rim of her glass.

"Of course, an affair of the heart," he nodded. "He's too old for you."

"But you talked?"

"Once, after four or five martinis. It was late; he was in a mood. Said he had a business here. An office."

"Really?" Trying to not look too interested. "Did he mention where?"

"I don't remember. Omonoia, perhaps," the barman shrugged.

"What's that?"

"A business district. I don't recall what street, if he even mentioned it."

"Did he talk about his business?"

"He was in a mood. I remember him saying 'Everything ends.' Whatever was ending for him, I had the feeling it was soon," the barman said.

She left the bar and walked back to the hotel concierge. "I

don't read Greek. I need to look something up in the Athens business directory," she told him.

"What's the name of the business?" he said, tapping on his computer tablet.

"S-R-X-B-Y-X," she spelled it out for him. He found it in seconds.

"It's on Mpenaki Street in the Omonoia district, Madame," the concierge said, circling the street on a paper map. He wrote the address in the margin. "Would you be interested in our Roof Garden for dinner. You can see the Acropolis."

Maybe she should treat herself while she could, she thought. Shame to waste her Little Black Dress and if Srdan caught up to her, she'd be a long time dead. Besides, she'd probably never be in Athens again and she needed to touch base with Brochard. A quiet restaurant would be perfect.

The maître d' seated her at a rooftop table that looked out at the Acropolis, its ancient pillars lit in gold in the night. She took out her cell phone.

"Jean-Pierre," she said. "It's Casey Ramirez."

"Casey, *mon dieu*! You're okay? We notified Interpol about you," Brochard said. For some reason he was whispering.

"I was kidnapped, but managed to escape. I'm in Athens," she said.

"*Ça alors*, kidnapped! Why Athens?"

"Srxbyx has an office here," she said.

"Listen, Casey, I can't talk now. We'll talk in the morning," he said. As he ended the call, she heard a woman say something in French. Gabi, she thought. Or worse, not Gabi; some other woman. She looked at the ruins of the Parthenon, a luminous island floating in the darkness over the city. Once, it was the center of the world. Everything ends, she thought, something tightening in her throat.

The next day she took three separate taxis back and forth in opposite directions and walked around a block to make sure she wasn't followed, then walked into the LGM – Srxbyx office and asked for LGM, AE. The receptionist pointed her to a young dark-haired Greek woman at another desk.

"Ours is a service office. We handle calls, emails, correspondence for different companies," the dark-haired woman explained in English.

"Are LGM and Srxbyx companies you handle?" Casey asked.

"We handle many companies."

"Did Mister Layton Gary McCord come here to get messages, packages, personally?" Casey asked.

"He did, Madame, although I'm not sure I should discuss his business."

"What was his business?"

"I'm not allowed to answer that, Madame. In fact, I don't know. We're a service, nothing more," the woman shrugged. Casey tried another tack.

"Did you and he ever talk?" she asked.

"I can't discuss our clients," the young woman said, glancing over at the other woman in the office. "What's this about?"

This wasn't going to work. Casey thought about pulling out her Special Agent ID, then reached for something out of the blue.

"He was my father. He's dead. We can't find his will. Do you have anything here? Any papers, anything?"

"I'm sorry, Miss. He seemed like a nice man. I don't believe we have anything here for him, but I'll check," the woman said. She got up and went to a set of locked mailbox slots against a wall, unlocking one and coming back. "Sorry, nothing. But he only used our service to forward letters, emails, that sort of thing." She touched Casey's hand. "I'm sorry. You look a little like him,"

Yeah, right, Casey thought, but sensing she was close, almost there. "Please, you're my last hope. Where'd you forward his mail, emails to?" she asked, holding her breath.

The young woman nodded sympathetically. "Let me check," she said, working her computer. "Mmm, a moment, *parakalo*. To Samos. The island. He had a friend there. An Englishman, named, uh – what is it? – Cornwell, Peter Cornwell. Your father told me Cornwell was his oldest friend. He once said Peter was his only friend. He was a lonely man, your father. I felt sad, you know, because he seemed nice." She sighed at the loneliness of life. "I hope I've been helpful."

"More than you know," Casey said.

CHAPTER THIRTY-FIVE

SAMOS, GREECE

THE HOUSE WAS white with blue shutters and a red tile roof. It stood by itself on a rocky promontory overlooking a road winding down the steep hill to Karlovasi on the coast. There were trees on the hills and in deep green gullies and closer in, olive trees shaped by the wind. A stone fence enclosed the house and an adjacent orchard of lemon trees. Getting out of the rental car, the view was spectacular. From here, down the steep slope to the beach, the water was clear enough to see its pebbled bottom and out to the blue Aegean Sea.

Casey breathed the lemon-scented air and felt she'd never been so alive, her skin almost prickling with electricity. Her instincts told her she was at the doorstep of Fleetwood's secret, but Jerry Matthews' warning that the woman, Milena and the Russian FSB were hot on her heels, not to mention Darko and Srdan, had her looking behind as she approached the house. As far as she could tell, her car hadn't been followed out of the main town, Vathy. For the moment, she was clear.

A dog barked and a German Shepherd appeared at the top of the concrete steps, blocking her way to the house. An old fear raised its head, involuntarily remembering Rico's pit bull, Tigre. But the German Shepherd only watched her. It didn't move. Well-trained, she thought, or maybe that was a wish. As she walked up the steps, the dog barked again, watching her but not moving a muscle.

"Good puppy," she said as she approached, heart rate accelerating. The dog growled. She stopped.

"It's all right, Odysseus, I've been expecting someone," a male voice speaking BBC English leaked out of an open window. Its owner, a balding older man, stepped out of the house and patted the dog. He was so ex-pat Brit in his colored shirt, glasses, and sunburned skin, she was positive it was Cornwell.

"I call him Odysseus because he likes to wander. Do you like Muscat wine? Samos is famous for it," Peter Cornwell said, motioning her inside to a comfortable living room cluttered with books. Tall windows overlooked tree-covered hills to the sea. "They say Muscat is the oldest wine in the world. The island was famous for it back in Pythagoras's time – his island, you know; Pythagorean theorem, square of the hypotenuse of a triangle, all that – although you may find the taste a bit sweet. If you prefer retsina . . . ?" He left it dangling.

"How could you be expecting me? I didn't call. Until yesterday I didn't know you existed," Casey said.

"Ah," Cornwell puffed his cheeks, looking for a moment like a professorial chipmunk. "Ever since Dale Fleetwood died – or do you prefer the fiction of Layton Gary McCord? – I knew someone would be along. More than one, I suspect. The clock is ticking. But then, we all live on borrowed time, don't we?" he said, the words jarring because they reminded her of Budapest. He gestured for her to sit in the nearer of two armchairs, a small coffee table between them, angled so one could talk and enjoy the sea view.

"I can see why you settled here," she said, looking about for the German Shepherd before she realized with a catch of relief it hadn't come back into the house. "It's beautiful. Perfect, in fact."

"Interesting word that, *perfect*. Sometimes, at sunset, I watch the sun low over the sea, a perfect glowing red circle and imagine I'm Aristarchus, trying to see what he saw from these very hills. He was the first person, you know, to comprehend that the earth rotates, to realize that the earth went around the sun, to calculate the sun's diameter, the solar system, that the stars were suns just like ours. He did all that thousands of years ago. Of course, he was a genius. I'm just a retired spook," Cornwell said, pouring two glasses of wine, Muscat for her, Kourtaki for himself and raised his glass. "*Yeeah mas!*"

"Cheers," she toasted back and drank. The wine was sweet with a tang; a dessert wine. "You were MI6? Is that how you knew Dale Fleetwood?"

"Hm-mmm," he cleared his throat. "Before we start tripping down memory lane, I'll need to see some ID." She started to take out her passport and HSI Special Agent card, but he waved those away. "Not that silliness. I've seen a thousand fabricated IDs, often better than the originals. No, your real ID. Something that confirms you're the person I'm supposed to talk to. Otherwise, jolly as it is having an attractive young woman visit me, our conversation's going to be very brief."

Casey understood; she'd been carrying it with her all this

time. She slipped off her shoe, raised the inner sole and pulled out the plastic sleeve with the half of the Yugoslav bank note from Panama. She removed the Yugoslav note from the plastic and placed it like a roulette bet on the coffee table.

He nodded, got up. "Come," he said. She followed him to a flagstone patio facing the lemon orchard. He went over to a terra-cotta urn in the corner. Moving the urn aside, he raised the flagstone underneath and retrieved a leather pouch. He untied the pouch, pulled out another torn half-banknote and brought it back inside. He put the two halves together. They fit perfectly.

"What's your name?" he asked.

"Casey Ramirez. I've been carrying that around for weeks. Tell me about Fleetwood," she said, breathing again.

"Ah, Dale. The thing about Dale was that he was a pleaser. One of those curious people architected in a way that when it suits them, they know how to charm others. Did him no end of good with women. They love it in a man till they wake up one day bored to death with it. Mind you, he combined that almost feminine desire with a ruthlessness that made a KGB assassin seem like a choir boy. Made him wonderfully successful. At the end though, he was bitter, cynical. But then, the world disappoints most of us, one way or another." He gave a sad smile.

"You were his friend?"

"I'm not sure that's the word. Dale could charm the knickers off you, but there was a vacuum like outer space inside him. He had partners, not friends. Like most people, we bonded over a shared past. We'd both done nasty things in nasty places, more often than not to cover up the misdeeds of those higher up. That's the thing, isn't it?" Cornwell sighed. "One begins with adolescent notions of adventure or honor or country. Words really, not much more. Shakespeare. All of us little boys, playing at cowboys or soldiers or spies. Except, as that great American philosopher, the boxer Mike Tyson once said: 'Everyone's got a plan till they get punched in the mouth.' Because that's the thing about truth in a reality show world: it's unmistakable. The bullets are real. All your spring roses turn into a stench of rotting flowers."

"Where'd you meet Fleetwood?"

"In the Balkans, Dale was the middleman. He played both sides. One day, he'd be under siege in Sarajevo, dodging snipers like some comic book hero, next day he'd be hosting a *splav* party complete with sexy tarts for the Serb brass in Belgrade. They were a pair: him and his bloody doppelganger, 'Mastercard Fitz'. A worse bastard than Dale ever was."

"Mastercard Fitz?" The name hit her like crashing into a brick wall. "Is that Thomas Fitzpatrick, Deputy Director of the CIA?" Cornwell nodded. "Why Mastercard Fitz?"

"Because he always took credit for what other people did. Slimy bugger," Cornwell said.

"Blue Madagascar?" Casey said.

"So you know about that, do you?"

"Only that it was a disaster, that it led to deaths and a purge within the CIA."

"Not merely the CIA," Cornwell said. "It was the mother lode of all cock-ups. Inside Number 10 Downing, it became a synonym for *the worst possible outcome one could even imagine*. Dale and I met in Dresden, on the deck of one of those little paddle steamers on the Elbe. He said he wanted out. Only once you're in, it's like the Mafia; there is no out."

"Was he framed because he wanted out?"

"There were men – " Cornwell stopped. "What I'm going to tell you now is very dangerous. You remember that Saudi journalist?"

"The one that was murdered?"

He nodded. "He tumbled to it. These people are beyond vicious. They're relentless."

"What about you? You're alone here," she said.

"I have Odysseus. I've lived a long, occasionally interesting life. My death would be a loss to no one, except perhaps Dale – and now he's gone," Cornwell said, draining his wine. The curtain by the window stirred with a faint breeze like a premonition. Casey understood that Cornwell expected to die very soon, that he'd been waiting to tell someone.

"What was Blue Madagascar?" she asked.

"Not a what, who," Cornwell said.

"A person? Do you know who?"

Cornwell indicated no. "It happened because of the Oil Shock in 1990."

"Before I was even born," Casey murmured.

"According to Dale, a very senior American intelligence official from a rather wealthy family whose business was in dire trouble, got hold of a juicy piece of intel suggesting Saddam Hussein's threat to attack Kuwait was a bluff."

"The intel came from Blue Madagascar?"

Cornwell nodded. "Only it was a fake, what our KGB colleagues call '*Kompromat*'. But the American thought it was solid – and he was absolutely desperate. He sold oil futures short. He bet the bank, every last penny on it. Of course, Saddam did invade Kuwait. The price of oil sky-rocketed. Between July and October of 1990, the cost of crude nearly tripled, from $17 to $46. The American couldn't cover the short. He was facing complete ruin. Our Moscow friends offered him a lifeline and a chance for a good deal more."

"Money from Pronova? With Blue Madagascar as the go-between?" Casey said.

He responded with a little smile. "Jolly good. What you

Yanks call 'spot on'. The first President Bush responded to the Iraqi invasion with Operation Desert Storm. The Fed stepped in and by 1994, the price of oil was back under $16 a barrel. Except now the Russians had a mole deep inside the highest level of U.S. intelligence and decision making by the short and curlies."

"Did Fleetwood know who the American was, the one who betrayed the U.S.?"

"The last time I saw Dale was about three months ago. He sat right where you are now. 'We sold our country, Peter,' he told me. 'They sent me to ADX for the wrong crime, because I've done worse, way worse than what they sent me for, but they were a thousand times worse.' That wasn't all that bothered him. He told me: '*Blue Madagascar is still running.* And I helped,' he whispered. Guilt's a rot; a disease that day after day eats you up from the inside. In his own twisted way, for all his many sins, Dale was an American patriot. In the end, it wasn't about money, or even revenge, though that was a fire that never died down inside him."

"What then?"

"Redemption," Cornwell said. "The final illusion for us all."

"The CIA mole. Who was it?"

Cornwell put down his glass, stood. "If you don't mind, I'd prefer we don't discuss such things indoors, even here," he said. He motioned her to follow him outside. He poked about till he found a gardening trowel, which he took with him. They walked down the stairs and through the olive trees to a narrow path along the rim of the hill hemmed in by maquis brush and shaded with pine.

"Odysseus! Here, lad!" Cornwell called out, looking around as they walked. "Where the devil is that dog? Sorry, where were we?"

"The CIA agent," Casey said.

"'I've got the bastards nailed good, Pete. Not just Blue Madagascar. Just the tip of the iceberg,' he'd say. 'It's all in the bloody package.'"

"He didn't tell you who the double-agent was?" Casey said, unable to keep the disappointment out of her voice.

"No, but I can bloody guess. Remember, it was the testimony of someone high up in the CIA that sent Dale to that prison in Colorado," Cornwell said.

"Mastercard Fitz?"

"He's one of them," Cornwell nodded. They came to a bench on the side of the path and sat. She gazed out over the tree-covered hills to the sea. Cornwell dug with the trowel at the base of a tree that shaded the bench. After a minute, he worked a wedge-shaped piece of metal from the ground and sat down next to her.

"You've seen one of these?" She shook her head. "It's called a 'spike' in the trade, used for 'dead drops'. A way to leave information for agents so that they don't have to risk meeting in person," he explained, opening the latch. He pulled out a plastic-wrapped DVD. "Old fashioned technology, I'm afraid," handing the DVD to her.

"What's this?"

"My instructions from Dale. His last wish so to speak, was to get this into the hands of whomever had the other half of the banknote." He looked around uneasily and lowered his voice to a whisper. "Whatever Dale Fleetwood left behind is in a safe deposit box belonging to a numbered account in the Bank of Cyprus bank in Limassol, the one near the Cathedral. The account number and all the information you need to access the safety deposit box is on the DVD. Everything except the password," he explained.

"I've memorized a twelve-digit number from Panama,

where I got the torn Yugoslav bank note," Casey said, dying to put the DVD into her laptop and get the account number.

Cornwell stared at something on the path. "Oh bloody hell," he said, getting up and running to kneel over something. Inside, Casey felt the world crashing in on them. Cornwell stood and faced her, his face stricken, holding the body of the dead German Shepherd in his arms.

"Were you followed? Did you see anyone?" he said.

"No one. I was careful," she said.

"Not good enough. You have to leave. At once. Now!"

"Why? What's going on?"

"Go! Run!" he shouted.

Casey didn't hesitate. She ran back toward the house and the car, ducking low though she wasn't sure why. Looking back over her shoulder, she saw Cornwell following after her on the path, the dog in his arms. His face had the strangest expression, as if to say, life is a disappointment but no more than we deserve. All at once, he stumbled. A black circle appeared on the side of his forehead as he pitched forward to the ground.

No sound of a shot. No warning. The OTs-38 Stechkin, Casey thought, running for her life. Nearing the car, she did a quick scan for any sign that someone might've tampered with it, but there was no time to really check. She opened the door and jumped into the car.

If it's been booby-trapped, I'm dead, she thought and pressed the Start button.

CHAPTER THIRTY-SIX

THE PLAKA, ATHENS

"WE SMUGGLE in refugees from the Middle East and place them in hotels as maids, maintenance men, male and female prostitutes; a way for them to pay us back for their passage," Giorgios Kapelenis said in French. He was the boss of Lafkos, the most powerful of the Greek Mafia clans. An elegant gray-haired man, who favored expensive Montecristo cigars, his nickname in Athens' underworld was "the Godfather of the Night." Vincent the Cat's *copain*, Gaspar, had texted Kapelenis to set up the intro. Gaspar's Jean Jé Corsicans did business with Lafkos on drug routes in southern Europe.

Vincent met him at Kinky Prison, one of a half-dozen Lafkos-owned strip clubs in the Kolonaki district. Two young women, naked except for G-strings, gyrated to Dua Lipa's latest on small stages.

"And to have them keep watch on things," Vincent said.

"And to keep watch," Kapelenis acknowledged. "Very little happens in this city that we don't know about. This woman, what's her name?"

"She's using a French passport with the name, Isabelle Dusollier. Although she might also use the name Milena Kolavitch or possibly, Natalya," Vincent said, handing Kapelenis a copy of Milena's photo.

"Very pretty. She'd be good in one of my clubs," Kapelenis said, looking at the photo.

"You can't afford her," Vincent said.

"What about you?"

"I can't afford her either."

"We'll offer fifty euros to anyone who spots her. For these people, that's good money. If she's in Athens, we'll find her," Kapelenis said, blowing a cigar smoke cloud, eyes mechanically counting the crowd in the club.

"The sooner the better," Vincent said, handing him a rubber band-bound roll of fifty 100-euro notes.

Midnight in the Plaka district. Vincent stood across from the Elektra Palace, a boutique hotel around the corner from the line of souvenir shops and cafés on Adrianou Street, most of them shuttered at this hour. He kept in the shadows to hide his face from the hotel's exterior security cameras. There was an *Appel à témoins* out for him in France and the *flics* were sure to have passed it along to Interpol, so even the Greek *flics* would be looking for him. Fortunately, it had taken Kapelenis' refugee workers only two days to find Milena.

Vincent crossed the street into the hotel. The lobby was upscale, stylish; exactly the type of place he'd expect Milena to pick. He made sure not to glance at anyone as he headed for the elevator. He'd learned one of the secrets to not drawing attention to yourself was that if you don't look at people, they're less likely to look at you. One of the lessons his

Maman taught him when he first started out robbing hotel rooms in Paris.

She said: "The best thief in the world is not the famous one on the *télé*. The smart one is invisible. People see the uniform, not the person."

At this hour, the lobby was nearly empty, though there were still people in the bar, a murmur of voices and music spilling out over the checkerboard marble floor.

In the elevator, Vincent looked away from the security camera, his hand shielding his face. The room number from Kapelenis was near the end of the corridor; the more expensive side of the hotel; the side with the view of the Acropolis. She likes it *chic*, he thought putting his ear to the hotel door.

Hearing no sound, he took out a dry eraser marker, having long ago learned to use it to pick card-key locks. He removed the cap and stuck the marker tip into the small opening on the underside of the lock. The lock clicked open. He snicked his stiletto knife open, put a mini-flashlight into his mouth and tiptoed into the room, closing the door behind him.

The suite was dark except for the window spectacle of the flood-lit Parthenon. Moving on the balls of his feet to the bedroom, he shone the light on the bed.

With a click, the lights came on. Milena was sitting up in bed naked, holding a revolver aimed at his chest. Her beauty stunned him, like a Renaissance painting with blue eyes that looked out at eternity.

"You've been a busy girl, *chérie*," Vincent said.

"Did you come to kill me or were you going to have sex with me first?" she said.

"Is that what you want, your legs in the air?" he said.

"You think I'm just a whore, don't you? Except I'm the one with the gun. I know how to use it," she said.

"You set me up, *chérie*. You and your Russians."

"I'm Russian too. I didn't have a choice. I've never had a choice." The bitterness in her voice surprised him.

"You didn't have to lead me to them, *chérie*. Boulogne-Billancourt, the jolly Irish pub, that was you."

"Maksim and I, we're both FSB. Russian security. If I didn't do it, they would've killed us both. I didn't want to. Do you remember, just before we went in, I said, 'Maybe we shouldn't do this?' I almost disobeyed my orders because of you."

"So I should thank you? *Tiens*, there isn't a word for what you are. You better shoot. You'll have to," he said, taking a step towards her.

"Stop!" she said, aiming. "We don't have to play their game. The money's real. We could keep it," she said.

"*Mon dieu*, you are truly the best liar I've ever met. If they bottled you in beer, every man on the planet would walk around all day mumbling idiocies," he said.

"Vincent, don't make me shoot. I don't want to."

"Unbelievable! You can't stop, can you? You think I've forgotten the cemetery – or Marseilles," he added, taking another step.

"Vincent please! I don't want to kill you."

This is when she's at her most dangerous. We're both Blue Kraits, Vincent thought, flashing on the old woman on the Boulevard Barbès.

"Why not?" he said.

"I like you."

"I like you too, but . . . "

"But what?"

"When Blue Krait snakes mate, usually one of them dies," he said, coming closer.

CHAPTER THIRTY-SEVEN

LIMASSOL, CYPRUS

CASEY DROVE the coast road back to Vathy like a crazy woman, sliding on curves, glancing every other second in the rear-view mirror. She pulled into a parking space at Vathy Airport, grabbed her suitcase and carry-on and dashed into the terminal, ready to grab the next flight out no matter where it was going. After what happened with Peter Cornwell, she knew she had only minutes before they got her too.

Only there wasn't another plane off the island till an Olympia flight to Athens at 18:25 hours. A three hour wait! By that time, if she was still on Samos, she would be dead. She looked around the terminal, thinking there has to be a way off this island. At the far end of the check-in counter, she saw a sign: "Jet Samos. Private Plane Flights."

Twenty minutes later she was fastening her seatbelt in a single-engine Cessna piloted by a Greek wearing a New York Yankees baseball cap. His name was Costas. He'd told her he didn't have time for a roundtrip to Cyprus, but he could have her in Santorini in under an hour. Checking the Internet, she found an Aegean flight from Santorini to Limassol. It would be close, but she might be able to catch it if they took off at once.

Using the airport WiFi, she booked a seat on the Aegean Cyprus flight. Costas called his flight plan for Santorini into the tower in Greek as they taxied. Soon they were climbing over an impossibly blue sea, the sun reflecting a lake of diamonds on the surface of the water below.

"There's an extra two hundred if you don't tell anyone about me," she told Costas.

"The police after you, Missus?" Costas said, raising his voice to be heard over the engine. She shook her head. "Keep your money. Anyone asks, I'll say my passenger was a man, a Turk," he said.

"You don't like Turks?"

"I like their money," he said, pulling back on the wheel to climb, till they levelled off at ten thousand feet, a speck lost between blue infinities of sky and sea.

Fifty minutes later, they were on the ground in Santorini and Casey took her first real breath since Samos as she boarded the flight to Cyprus. For the moment at least, she had a head start over whoever was chasing her. Before buckling in, she texted Brochard: "Meet me Limassol. Urgent. C." And to Arthur Dalton just three letters. "LCA," the international airport code for Cyprus' Larnaca Airport. All she could do now was hope Dalton would provide some backup and that Brochard would come. Whoever was after her, the Serbs, the Russians, Pronova, the Jackdaw, the FSB, the Zemun Clan, she knew wherever she went, they wouldn't be far behind. The bank in Limassol was the center of the bulls-eye – and there was no way to get her hands on Fleetwood's secret without walking straight to where they would be waiting.

But she didn't have to make it easy for them to find her. On the way into town from Larnaca Airport she asked the taxi driver if he knew of a hotel where they wouldn't ask too many questions. He took her to a small hotel on a side street off Makarios Avenue, Limassol's main business drag. She registered as a Canadian, using the name Kendall Hart, a character from Erica's favorite soap, *All My Children*, telling the clerk she'd lost her passport.

"That's unfortunate, Miss. I'll need something," the clerk said, tongue peeking out of the corner of his mouth as if to say that whatever was on the menu, sex, money, drugs, he was willing to play.

"For the room," Casey said, counting out cash for three days in advance and putting it on the counter. He scooped it up. She then added an extra 100-euro note. The clerk took it without a word.

"Bring your passport tomorrow, Miss," he said, giving her an I'll-see-you-later wink.

"Of course," she said, thinking tomorrow it would be another hundred – or maybe more.

Now that she had a place to stay, she parked her suitcase in the room and keeping her carry-on with her, took a taxi to a luxury hotel on the beach This time she checked in using her real name. If they were looking for her, they would come here.

Judging by the clientele in the colonnaded lobby, the hotel was a mecca for Russian oligarchs who came to Cyprus to launder their money in the sun. Even the hotel employees spoke broken Russian. She went into the gift shop to buy a floppy straw beach hat and the biggest pair of sunglasses she could find to help conceal her face. It saved her life.

As she was about to come out of the gift shop, her face obscured by the beach hat and sunglasses, she spotted Srdan standing in the lobby not thirty feet away. With him were the blond cop and another of Darko's men, a bulky man with a five o'clock shadow whom Casey recognized from the meat plant.

She nearly panicked, not sure what to do. If one of them just looked up or came into the gift shop, she was done. She studied the racks in the store, pretending to shop, keeping an eye on the lobby.

She waited till they left the lobby, heading toward either the swimming pool or the beach. Looking straight ahead, she marched through the lobby to the front entrance and told the taxi driver to take her to the center of town.

She'd been lucky, very lucky, breathing a sigh of relief as the taxi pulled away. Jessie wouldn't approve, she thought later as she walked in the sun on Makarios Avenue in her beach hat and sunglasses pulling a carry-on, the perfect tourist, back to her hotel.

Except the one certainty she knew about luck is that sooner or later it's bound to turn.

An early-evening three-quarters' moon hung over the buildings around Heroes Square. Casey sat in a pub across from the Rialto movie theater while she waited for Brochard. She nursed a brandy sour, feeling for all the world like a girl on her first date. The pub had a hip vibe with *faux*-ancient stone walls and a wire sculpture over the bar. It was filled with tanned Euro twenty- and thirty-somethings, babbling in a dozen languages.

It'd been a week since she'd seen Brochard, but so much had happened it felt like years. The electric lights in the square blinked on. All at once there he was, shirt open at the collar, impossibly handsome, trying to find her in the crowd.

She gave a little wave and he spotted her. He limped over, grabbed her by the shoulders for a proper French *bise*, kissing her three times on alternate cheeks, then pulled back and studied her.

"Are you okay?" he asked.

"I'm good, fine," she said, faking a smile. "What happened to your leg?"

"Foot. The Russians tried to kidnap Juliette." He lowered his voice. "I had to kill two men. Felt like a coward and a brute. First time I ever fired a gun in my life," he said. "How are you?"

"I'm good," she said with more of a smile than she felt. Seeing him was like sunshine. She felt lighter, more like a woman.

"Truly?" he asked.

"Not really. You?"

"These past days, you can't imagine . . . " Brochard said, exhaling. He took her hand. She let him hold it, not knowing where they were in this thing, whatever it was, between them. "How'd you get away from the Serbs?"

"I'm not sure I did," she said and told him about seeing Srdan and the two thugs at the beach hotel and about checking into the small hotel under a fake name telling the clerk some story about a lost passport.

"Did he believe you?" he asked.

"He believed the extra hundred euros," she said. He looked at her as if to say, you've changed. "I got lucky," she breathed, trying to push away all that had happened: Brighton, Budapest, Belgrade, Athens, Cornwell, the dog, the flight from Samos.

"Lucky for all of us," he said.

"And you?"

"It's been *merde*, total shit," he said as the waitress, a

blonde in a blue bar T-shirt and tight shorts, came over. "What are you drinking?"

"Iced brandy sour. Someone said it's the local thing," she said. He ordered the same. "How's Juliette, and Gabi?" she asked.

He smiled in that wry French way she liked. "Trust a woman to get straight to the point."

"Gabi must've freaked when the Russians came after her and Juliette. I would've."

"I think she's doing better than me, though who can say?" He lit a cigarette, exhaled. "Everyone's very pleased you discovered Fleetwood's real name and secret account, but they think the bank's too dangerous. The minute you get Fleetwood's thing, whatever it is, you're a big target. That's why they sent me," he added.

She nodded, looked around. "Look, do you want to stay? Have another drink?" she asked. The pub was getting noisy. At a nearby table, they were doing iced vodka and brandy shots. A young woman in a tank top showing plenty of cleavage slammed hers on the table and shouted, "*Yamas*, my ass!"

"Let's get out of here," he said, dropping money on the table and getting up.

Her room had a partial view of the street and buildings. In an outdoor area below, a corporate party was going strong by the swimming pool. The party's DJ was trapped in the '90's: Nirvana, Whitney Houston, Pearl Jam, the Red Hot Chili Peppers. Casey turned on the table lamp and Brochard turned it off, leaving the room lit only by the city lights. He slid his arms around her waist. They danced, swaying in the darkness to the music.

"We shouldn't do this," Casey said, liking the smell of his after-shave and the feel of his hand at the small of her back.

"No, we shouldn't," he agreed.

"But we're going to, aren't we?" She didn't want to say, because we might die tomorrow. "It's our last chance, isn't it?"

"I don't know. It's a . . . " He left it unfinished.

They danced, feeling the closeness of each other's body. Down by the pool, Toni Braxton wanted to unbreak her heart. His hand slid down to her ass. He pulled her tight and kissed her, not moving, but she could feel the hunger. She stopped him.

He looked into her face, then pulled out a pack of cigarettes out of his satchel. He lit one and sat on the edge of the bed, looking at the three-quarters' moon in the window.

"I'm sorry," he said.

She sat beside him on the bed. "It's not you, Jean-Pierre.".

"We're all turtles, you know. We carry our shells with us wherever we go."

She started to shake. "They were going to chop my hands off, They . . . " she hesitated. "I'm a pretty screwed up girl," she said.

"Don't say that. You're better than that."

"Wow, that sounds like pity. Now I really am fucked," she said, staring at nothing.

"What do you want me to do? Tell me."

"I don't like a lot of people, Jean-Pierre, but I like you. You're a gorgeous man. Part of me wants to make you crazy with sex any way you want. Only I can't. I don't even know why. And there's Gabi. You love her. Way more than me. I know it."

"When we walk out of the bank tomorrow, I don't know what's waiting . . . " he hesitated. "I feel like a soldier in the World War, waiting to go over the top."

"I don't want to destroy a family. I don't want to be that girl," she said, touching his hair.

"Should I go?" Reaching for his satchel.

"I feel safer with you here," she said.

He put the satchel down. "We should probably get some sleep. Tomorrow's going to be tough," he said, stubbing out his cigarette. He started to take off his clothes for bed. Before he took off his trousers, he removed a compression support bandage from his foot. Russians, she thought. A U2 song about a beautiful day floated up from the pool.

Casey stared at the moon like a lamp in the window and listened to the music.

CHAPTER THIRTY-EIGHT

AYIA NAPA CATHEDRAL, LIMASSOL

THE BANK OF CYPRUS was across from the big Ayia Napa cathedral. On the opposite corner was a *taverna* with outside tables with blue and white-checked tablecloths. Srdan, the blond hippy detective and another of Darko's men, a bulky man with a five o'clock shadow were sitting at one of the tables. The three Serbs watched as she and Brochard got out of the taxi. By the time they made their way up the steps to the bank entrance, the Serbs were already there, standing in their way.

"You think I not find you?" Srdan, squinting in the sun, said to Casey.

"How's Miroslav?" she asked.

"In Athens hospital because you," Srdan said, raising his hand to slap her face. Brochard was quicker and grabbed his wrist.

"Don't," Brochard said, the two men staring at each other till the blond detective jammed a pistol into Brochard's side. The Serb with the five o'clock shadow grabbed Casey.

"He's a senior French police official, a judge! Darko will have your heads," Casey snapped at Srdan in Russian. "That's if the Cyprus cops don't get you first."

"Why did you run away?" Srdan said to her in Russian, motioning to the blond detective to put the gun away.

"Who wouldn't? Now either let us go inside or you face Darko and Pronova with empty hands because you wouldn't let me walk inside and get what we're all looking for," she said.

Srdan's brow furrowed with the effort of processing any choice that didn't involve violence. "I come with," he said in English for Brochard's benefit.

"Not with a pistol inside a bank, Monsieur," Brochard said, waggling his index finger in the French way of signaling something socially unacceptable, like murder or something truly appalling like poor table manners.

Srdan handed his pistol to the blond, then he, Casey and Brochard entered the bank. The blond detective and Five o'clock Shadow planted themselves like bookends on either side of the bank entrance.

Inside, Casey got in line for a teller. Not knowing what Fleetwood might've left, in addition to her handbag, she'd brought her laptop in a canvas beach bag. She asked the teller about the account. He looked it up and pointed her to a woman teller in a separate boxed-off window. Casey walked over and went through it again, this time entering the account number on a key pad. A digital screen prompted her for the password. Casey entered the twelve-digit number she'd memorized from Panama and held her breath.

"Is it your first time accessing this account, Madame?" the teller asked in English as she checked her computer screen.

"First time in Cyprus," Casey said, holding her breath.

She'd been asked to find an object that might be anywhere in the world and here she was, on the verge.

"Thank you, Madame. This way, please," the woman teller said. She led Casey to a safe deposit vault while Brochard and Srdan watched from the bank area.

Casey took out the key from Panama from her handbag, thinking this is for all the marbles. She and the teller both inserted their keys into the box and turned. The teller lifted out the safety deposit box and led Casey to a tiny room for privacy, pointing out a button on the wall to press when she was finished. Casey waited till the woman left and opened the box.

The first thing she saw was money. A roll of gold Krugerrands and stacks of 100-Swiss-franc banknotes, 100-euro banknotes, and a bundle of U.S. Benjamins. Fifty to a hundred thousand bucks worth, she guessed, feeling disappointed. It wasn't what she had come for. She stuffed the money into the beach bag and peered more closely, feeling with her hand on the bottom of the metal box. And there it was.

She picked up the DVD disk. She'd imagined Fleetwood left papers or a thumb drive, but the DVD made sense. It'd been done with older technology. Luckily, her laptop had a Blu-ray drive. She slipped the disk in, plugging in an earphone to keep the audio private.

She opened a video file. The screen showed an older man in a floral shirt looking straight into the camera. He was sitting on a couch in a living room, a bottle of wine and an ashtray in front of him on a coffee table. Hello Dale Fleetwood, she thought. Seeing him alive like that was like seeing a ghost.

Fleetwood said: "If you're watching this, it means I'm dead, which doesn't exactly make my day. And if you're looking for a coda, some final words of wisdom, some insightful end-of-life revelation from the Great Beyond, you've come to the wrong guy. Life is shit and as for death, all I know is that it's pretty common, Pilgrim. I love that. John Wayne, though most dumb-asses today don't even know who the Duke was. Anyway, if you're looking at this video and think you've hit the jackpot, well, don't start spending your money just yet."

He had a New York–New Jersey accent, but with the edges smoothed, Casey thought, expanding his image to fill the screen. As for the apartment where the video was shot, something made her think it was Paris. The French touches: the bottle of Bordeaux on the coffee table, the ashtray, the faint sound of traffic from the street. And Fleetwood had been living in France, an exile from the U.S., returning her focus to what he was saying.

"You think you know people? Trust me, you don't," Fleetwood said. "Everyone has a secret. Your husband. Your wife. Your mother. Everyone. You look at this place, this apartment, this *chi chi* neighborhood, you think, what's his problem? Looking at me, you probably think I'm some retired Schmuckatelli in a Tommy Bahama shirt. You wouldn't know I once owned over a hundred corporations. I had a two-story apartment in Knightsbridge in London and another on Park Avenue, along with a manor house in England, a villa in Ibiza, a townhouse in Georgetown, condos in Monte Carlo and Panama, houses in Malibu and Maine, another in Dubrovnik and a 2,400-acre estate in Northern Virginia where I entertained everyone from the Director of the CIA to two U.S. presidents. Lil ole me," he said with a sarcastic grin.

"I owned a private Gulfstream jet," he continued. "Knew the names of every flight attendant on the Concorde – back in the day when you could fly from New York to Paree in three and a half hours and flight attendants had to be good-looking broads, who you could grab their ass while they poured you a martini – and in those days nobody ever said that was sexist – and I personally screwed some of the most beautiful women on the planet. Women who were famous, who if I told you their names, trust me, you'd know. Me – this windy old fart sitting in front of you.

"But you're not watching this to listen to me talk about the bad old days, are you? Who gives a damn, right? That world's gone now; the champagne's gone flat. But you know, once it did sparkle. Of course, you didn't want to look under the hood. Not so pretty.

"So yeah, I screwed up. Paid for it. Paid for it a lot more than bastards who did a million times worse than I ever did. They skated free these great men, pillars of society, but I could tell you things about people you wouldn't believe. But that isn't what you came for either, is it, Pilgrim? You're a seeker, searching for the *emmes*, as people in Jersey used to say. The *truth*.

"But getting at the truth, that's not so simple. Ask old Pontius Pilate. He didn't get the answers he wanted either.

"And what you're after, it's not free, Pilgrim. No, no, no," Fleetwood shook his head. "Nothing's ever free in this dog-fight of a life, my friend. Also, there's a problem. I'm dead – so I have no way of knowing whether the person or persons looking at this is the person I intended it for. That leaves me with a problem. So here's the deal: I have information that is of incredible value in the right hands. The information is documented beyond dispute, visual in a way that is undeniable and damning. The people to whom my message is addressed should by this point know exactly who and what I'm talking about and understand the implications.

"I guess you assumed the hunt was over, that the information was sitting here in a bank deposit box. As if I would ever trust something so important and dangerous to a box that could be opened by some second- or third-world government official or for anyone who could fake an ID! Only an idiot would do that. So here's your first and most important clue: What you're looking for is hidden in one of the houses or properties that I used to own. Simple huh? Only don't have goons try to rip apart every one of them. First, you won't find it, and secondly, if you do something really bad will happen, I promise.

"Not enough of a clue? I'll help you out with my second and final clue, which I will read only once, then destroy. Here goes:" In the video, Fleetwood took a folded piece of paper out of his pocket. He put on reading glasses, and began to read out loud:

"All the king's horses and all the king's men,
  Never could put Humpty together again.
  Now we are engaged in a great civil war,
  A charter to commit the crime once more.
  Baa, baa, black sheep, have you any wool?
  E = mc² imagined by Einstein was their tool,
  Little Bo-peep has lost her three sheep, and can't tell
where to find them,
    Leave them alone, they're lost for good without their
mothers to mind 'em.
    Endless greed we carve in stone, goodness we write
in air,
    Evil that we do lives after us. Hell is empty; the devil
is here."

Fleetwood looked up with a smirk. He crumpled the paper, put it into the glass ashtray, took out a match, lit it and watched it burn.

"If you find what I've hidden, you'll understand everything and know what to do. As for me, I'm done," he said, making a dismissive hand gesture to the camera. The video went black.

She saved the video MP4 file on her laptop, removed the DVD, put it back into its sleeve and into the beach bag. Turning the safety deposit box upside-down to make sure there was nothing else inside, she closed it and pressed the green button. A few minutes later, she was back in the main part of the bank with Brochard and Srdan.

"What was in the box?" Brochard asked.

"Money," Casey said, showing them in the bag.

"Money ours," Srdan said, touching his chest.

"Half yours," Casey said.

"Ours," Srdan repeated.

"What about the information? Was it in there?" Brochard asked.

She nodded. "A DVD. I played it. Whatever we're looking, this isn't it. He left a poem, a puzzle with clues. The hunt's not over."

"What you saying?" Srdan said, his eyes like pin-points. He looked insane.

"It's a video of Fleetwood. He used to own properties all over the world. What we're looking for is hidden in one of them," she said.

"*Merde*. So it's going to be a race, with everyone going to all of the houses and tearing them apart to see who finds it first," Brochard says.

"He said don't do that. The poem's a clue, a puzzle. If we can figure it out, we'll know which property and where he's hidden it. The way he talked on the video, we won't find it unless we figure out the clue," she said.

"What kind of stupid poem is it?" Srdan asked her in Russian.

"I'm not sure. It's very dark. Sort of half Mother Goose, half a prediction of an apocalypse," she said as they walked to the main door.

They stepped out from the front portico into the sun. The two Serbs closed on them from either side. The blond detective grabbed Casey's arm, Five o'clock Shadow grabbed Brochard. The blond detective handed Srdan back his pistol and wrenched away Casey's beach bag. He found the DVD, showed it to Srdan.

Suddenly Srdan crumpled to the ground. The blond detective looked up toward the cathedral's white towers and he went down as well, blood exploding out of the back of his head. Five o'clock Shadow started to run. Before he took three steps, he went down.

Casey grabbed the beach bag from the dead detective and dashed across the street toward the cathedral. Behind her, she heard Brochard's footsteps and heavy breathing as he limped after her. Why hadn't they killed her too, she wondered as she ran into the cathedral courtyard. Whoever had done it was too good a shot to miss.

She opened the cathedral door and ran inside, her footsteps clattering on the marble floor. White light streamed from the high arched windows as she looked around, desperate for somewhere to hide. A row of peaked wooden confessionals like little houses ran along on one side of the nave; on the other side were three doors. She ran to one of the doors and opened it into a hallway. Brochard limped after her, a peculiar look on his face. She grabbed his arm and they rushed down the hallway to a small room with priestly robes hanging on pegs. The sacristy.

"Who was shooting?" she demanded. "You didn't arrange anything like that?"

"It wasn't me," Brochard said. "I spoke with the local Police Chief, Kyriakos. They were supposed to send squad cars to detain the Serbs. Who shot them? I think it came from the top of this building."

"From the roof, or the one of the towers," she nodded. They'd been saved, but by whom? And why? Why didn't they shoot her. The deeper she got into this, the more confusing it got. Brochard still had that odd look on his face.

"What is it?"

"When we ran in here, I saw a man in wrap-around sunglasses. For a second I thought it was Vincent the Cat," he said.

"Vincent the Cat! What would he be doing in Cyprus?"

"I must be mistaken. But whoever was shooting could have killed us. They still might."

From outside, they heard the *ee-you ee-you* of approaching police cars.

"I had the DVD. Why didn't they?" she said.

CHAPTER THIRTY-NINE

SAINT-GERMAIN-DES-PRÉS, PARIS

PARIS in late October was cold and gray. The trees on the boulevards and along the Seine were bare. A brisk wind had driven pedestrians off the streets.

The first thing Casey did after checking into her hotel was go to the Galeries Lafayette. She splurged on new jeans, blouses, a sweater, a stylish wool-blend navy suit and a Burberry trench coat to replace the clothes she'd lost in Greece. She'd never spent that much on herself before. Seeing her hesitate at the price, the French saleswoman, thin as they all were and intimidating in a red Hermès scarf, told her "It's a lot, but you'll have it the rest of your life, Mademoiselle." Except that might not be very long, thinking about Brighton and Cornwell and the Serbs. Everyone who touched Blue Madagascar died, she thought.

Her next stop was the American embassy. In a rear cubicle, part of the CIA's closed-off section on the fourth floor, she connected with Arthur Dalton in Washington via a highly secure Skype-type JWICS (Joint Worldwide Intelligence

Communications System, pronounced 'JAY-wicks') link. It was the first time she'd ever used anything beyond SIPRNET, the U.S. government's normal network for classified communications up to the Secret level.

Arthur Dalton's face filled the screen, his nose alarmingly larger than its normal size because of his closeness to the camera. He appeared to be not in his book-lined office, but in a room with computers and TV screens in the background.

"It's a hodge-podge," Arthur Dalton said, talking about the Fleetwood poem. "I took it personally to someone we can trust at the Black House," Beltway-speak for the headquarters of the NSA at Fort Meade.

"And?"

"Their analysis indicated Fleetwood's doggerel wasn't encrypted, that it was just random bits and lines, in many cases stolen from other poems: Mother Goose, Shakespeare, Lincoln's Gettysburg Address. They came up with nothing. Their best guess for wherever Fleetwood hid something is his former place in Malibu."

"Because of the house number?" she asked. Dalton had emailed her a list his team had compiled of every property around the world ever owned by Dale Fleetwood. On the video, Fleetwood hadn't exaggerated. There were fifteen in all; some quite large, like the estate in Virginia encompassing hundreds of acres, with a million places to hide something.

"Exactly. The line about the three sheep suggests the address number of the house in Malibu: 6333 Ocean Breeze Drive. Three threes and six is two times three. The rest just seemed to be some kind of vague warning of impending doom. As if we didn't already know the world's going to hell in a handbasket," Dalton said.

"Cornwell implied Blue Madagascar was still up and running."

Dalton leaned closer to the screen, his nose a bulbous Mount Everest. "Which is why we must find Fleetwood's secret. Focus all your energies on this – and connect with Jerry Matthews. He's in Paris."

Lucky me, she thought sarcastically. "What about the French? Should we coordinate with them?"

"No. Limit their access. This is for us. We'll have to solve this ourselves."

"I've been trying. The poem's a warning, but of what?" she said.

He watched her. "I didn't pick you at random, Casey. At this point, you know more about Fleetwood than any of us. You have a sense of him. We'll continue to work it at our end, but I think you have the best shot." She didn't say anything. "You're holding something back. What is it?"

God, am I that easy to read? she thought. "Look, I don't know whether it's good or bad poetry or plagiarized or anything else. It doesn't matter. Fleetwood was in that ADX prison for a long time. Maximum security, like solitary confinement, for a crime he didn't commit or at least, thought was part of a legitimate CIA operation. Nothing for him to do all those years but think. All that burning inside him. The NSA's wrong. The poem does mean something. I just can't put my finger on it," she said.

"What's stopping you?" Arthur Dalton said, filling his pipe with tobacco.

"For one thing, it's got all these literary references. I don't know anything about that stuff." She looked away. Arthur Dalton lit his pipe and puffed out a cloud of smoke. The way he held his pipe made her think of Sherlock Holmes. He looked down at a print-out. Fleetwood's poem, Casey assumed.

"The lines about "*All the king's horses*," are from Mother

Goose. Humpty Dumpty is an egg that falls from a height and gets broken," Dalton said.

"What does it mean?" she asked.

"A metaphor, one assumes. An important person about to fall."

"Like who?"

"Could be anyone. Perhaps someone who doesn't want Fleetwood's secret let out," Dalton said. "As for '*Now we are engaged in a great civil war*,' he copied that from Lincoln's Gettysburg Address."

"The Civil War. Is that another warning? The next line too: '*A charter to commit the crime once more.*' What crime?" she asked.

"A crime by the Humpty Dumpty person. Or perhaps some horrible crime from the past like the Holocaust, about to be repeated. Either that or stories around a campfire to scare children," he frowned.

"Blue Madagascar?" she said.

"I think you're onto something," Dalton murmured, looking at her on his screen as if she was right in the room with him.

"The one that bothers me the most is the last line: '*hell is empty; the devil is here.*' I mean, WTF?" she said.

"He pinched that one as well. From Shakespeare's *The Tempest*," Dalton said. "Only if I recall in Shakespeare, the word is '*devils*', plural, not '*devil*' singular. Let me look it up." She saw him type on a computer. "Mmm, here it is: "'*And all the devils are here.*'"

"That's something. Fleetwood deliberately made it singular: *the devil*. A specific person. But who?"

"If we solve the riddle, perhaps we'll solve that as well," Dalton said.

"But even if we knew who, so what? How does that get us to finding whatever it was he left behind?" she said.

"You're close; closer than you know, Casey. You're a good puzzle solver. Keep at it," he said.

"What about the Russians?" she asked. Still a target, everywhere she went she expected a stab in the back from one of those poison injections with umbrellas the Russians were so fond of.

"We're working on it," Dalton said, ending the connection.

Later that morning, Arthur Dalton's boss, HSI Director Tommy Cociarelli called him into his office. Cociarelli was an odd-looking man, hair-slicked back like a Fifties crooner, a small neck-less head mounted on a bulky torso above short legs that might've belonged to someone else. A former Congressman, he called everyone by a nickname.

"How's it going, Artie?" Cociarelli said. He did it deliberately knowing Arthur Dalton despised the familiarity.

"What's up?" Arthur Dalton said, sitting.

"The Fleetwood business. We close to wrapping it up?"

"We're in the final phase. Whatever Fleetwood left, we'll have it in a few days," Dalton said, poker-faced. This was way out of bounds. Since the day Cociarelli was appointed, Dalton's understanding with him, as with all his predecessors, was they kept their hands off his Dark Group activities. That way no one had to perjure themselves in front of a Congressional committee.

"We need to shut it down. In fact, all your 'special' activities. I want them all shut down immediately. And start shredding – and reformatting hard drives. Starting now till it's done. I don't want even a comma left," Cociarelli said, hands clenched in front of him on the desk as if he expected a fight.

"Where's this coming from?" Arthur Dalton said, keeping very still. This wasn't some bureaucratic flanking maneuver. It was the Beltway equivalent of a declaration of war.

"Oh for Chrissakes, Artie, can't you see what's happening? Smullen's gonna win this election. We may all be out on our collective ass the day after he's sworn in. You think your seniority will save you, that you're one of the pillars holding this place up? Because if you do, you're an idiot. Especially with Blue Madagascar hanging out there. Shut it down," Cociarelli said.

"Tom, we're about to crack this thing. It'll give us leverage," Arthur Dalton said quietly.

"We're not cracking anything. You're not seeing the big picture," Cociarelli said, his dislike of Dalton out in the open. "Don't mess with me, Artie. Not on this."

Arthur Dalton didn't hesitate. He hadn't been in Washington all these years without knowing a panic play when he saw one. The rats were deciding how to abandon ship; every man for himself.

"Of course, Tom. I'll get on it right away," Arthur Dalton said, getting up, feeling Cociarelli's eyes on his back as he left the office.

That afternoon, Arthur Dalton had a secret meeting in a wooded ravine in Battery Kemble Park in the Palisades. He seemed to recall that the park had played some part in the Civil War. There was a wind and Arthur Dalton held onto his Trilby to keep the wind from blowing it away. He waited, shielded from the wind by a cluster of trees.

All that day he'd gone over it in his mind, even at one point, going back and rereading Casey's HSI personnel file, though he'd already gone through it with a fine tooth comb before he'd ever brought her in. She can do it, he thought. She had to or they were all dead – and America as we knew it gone. At that moment, two fit-looking men with something unmistakably military about them materialized like shadows out of the trees.

"Mister Dalton, what do you need?" one of them, blue-eyed, broad-shouldered, with an air of quiet competence, said.

Arthur Dalton told them.

When they finished, he waited in the shadows of the trees till they were gone. It's all on her now. A girl from the L.A. streets, he thought grimly. A pit bull, Jerry Matthews called her. She damn well better be, God help us. This was war, Washington Judo style – using your opponent's own power to destroy him. He was damned if he was going to shut her down. The die was cast.

Casey looked at her print-out of Fleetwood's poem, trying to will the words into a meaningful pattern. She'd been at it for hours in the reading room at the Bibliothèque Mazarine in Saint-Germain-des-Prés that someone at the American embassy had suggested as a good place to work. The room was lined with floor-to-ceiling bookshelves and wooden tables crowded with students from the nearby Sorbonne, looking for a place out of the wind to study.

She was getting nowhere on 'the Blue Madagascar dossier,' as Dalton now called what she'd brought back from Cyprus. All her focus was concentrated on Fleetwood's poem. Maybe it was a hodge-podge of other poems' lines, but there was a message in there somewhere. She was sure of it.

She played with the words, the spelling; parsing every line dozens of different ways. Nothing. If only Jessica was here. Jessie's rules: *There's always a weapon. Find it.*

There must be a key. What is it? She tried counting letters, then stopped, realizing that was something the NSA computers had probably already done forwards and backwards. Besides, would Fleetwood have done that in his cell? In the middle of the night when he couldn't sleep? She was missing something. But what? It was right in front of her and she couldn't see it. None of them had. Not her, not Arthur Dalton, not HSI's computing gurus or the French DGSE, nor the NSA code-breaking geniuses. Why? How? What did you do, Dale Fleetwood? You hid it in plain sight right in front of us. A perfect puzzle.

Except it wasn't perfect. It couldn't be. He'd made mistakes on the quotes. Unless they weren't mistakes. He'd done it deliberately. Don't look for what's right, she thought excitedly. Look for what's wrong.

She read Fleetwood's poem again. And again. Something wasn't quite right. Some wording. She read it again.

"All the king's horses and all the king's men,
Never could put Humpty together again."

That wasn't right. How did the nursery rhyme go? Where had she first heard it? Then it came: Jessica and her, a little girl, in Rico's apartment in Westmont in South Central, Erica out cold every night on Mexican Mud and Cisco. Jessica had found a Mother Goose board book with a stained yellow cover that someone had tossed in the trash. Jessie read it to her in a whisper, the two of them huddled in a closet not to wake Rico. Only she remembered Jessie's Humpty Dumpty differently. It was:

"Humpty Dumpty sat on a wall,
Humpty Dumpty had a great fall;
All the king's horses and all the king's men
Couldn't put Humpty together again."

Like Arthur Dalton said, it was a metaphor. The fall of

someone important, but also something else. Fleetwood's line went, "*Never could put Humpty together again.*" Not "*Couldn't put Humpty together again.*" He'd changed it. Why? She looked at the page again. Something about the whole poem. Fleetwood had woven it like a tapestry to send a specific person a message. And then she had it.

CHAPTER FORTY

LA DÉFENSE, PARIS

THE HOTEL SUITE had a partial view of the towering Grand Arch of La Défense. Jerry Matthews had arranged a spread of pâtés, cheeses, and a bucket of champagne on ice. When Casey arrived, the TV was showing a riot in the street outside a campaign rally for the Democratic candidate, Senator Ferris in Pittsburgh. Supporters of Senator Ferris battled those of Governor Smullen, some of whom wore black shirts and caps and carried signs like "Diversity = White Genocide". Shots had been fired; four people had been killed, dozens injured. A jumpy cell phone video showed a bleeding woman being carried away.

"What's going on at home?" Casey said.

"Tweedledum versus Tweedledee. There's no cure for stupid." Jerry Matthews made a face. "So Princess, where's *le* French boyfriend? I'm dying to meet him."

"Don't start, Jerry. I'm not in the mood. In fact, with you, trust me, I'm never in the mood," she said.

"Listen, we know it's been tough," he said sympathetically.

He popped the champagne cork and poured a glass. "But hey, you're back alive in *Paree* and congrats. You said you have something for us. Have some bubbly. Cures anything."

"You know, Jerry, for a millisecond, you almost sounded sincere."

"Don't kid yourself, Princess, this is Bollinger. This champagne is very sincere." He handed her the glass and poured one for himself. "Here's to you, kid. You've done a helluva job," he toasted and drank, then shut the TV and gestured for her to sit. "There's a lot to unpack," Jerry Matthews said. "The riddle of Fleetwood's poem, for starters. Thanks for typing it out, by the way."

"Cyprus first. Who tried to kill us in Limassol?" she said.

"The short answer is, we don't know. The obvious choice is the Russians, but your report that Brochard thought he spotted Vincent the Cat threw us. Any thoughts?" he asked.

"There's no shortage of candidates. I considered Darko Razanović from Belgrade, but why would he shoot his own men, his own brother?" she said. "It could've been the Russians, Pronova. Plenty of Russians in Cyprus. But then there's Vincent the Cat showing up out of the blue, if it was him. What was he doing there, unless maybe he and that Milena or Natalya or whatever her name is did a deal? And what about her? If she's a Russian agent, maybe it was her or the FSB or the Jackdaw or for all I know, the CIA? Hell, Jerry, I even thought of you," she said.

"Me? That's nuts."

"Yeah, well when the Zemun Clan kidnapped me, I wasn't exactly overwhelmed with everyone charging to the rescue. I've done a lot of thinking, Jerry. I was the goat you and Arthur Dalton tethered to the stake in a tiger hunt."

"You got it wrong, Princess. Put on the old thinking cap," he said. "There's a very good reason why we wouldn't want anyone to hurt a hair on your pretty little head. Whether you believe it or not, Arthur, Mr. Dalton was convinced from Day One you were not just the right person, but the only person to find what we're looking for," he said.

"So why didn't you protect us in Cyprus? Whoever it was could've easily killed us and taken the DVD for themselves. Which raises another question: why didn't they? We were out in the open, right in their sights. I had the DVD."

"Good question. Look, none of this went down the way we planned. Your French boyfriend may've called the local Limassol police chief, but Arthur Dalton had the Secretary of State himself call the Cyprus Minister of Justice, Antoniades, the guy who oversees all the cops in Cyprus. Your Serbs or Russians were supposed to have been arrested before you and your boyfriend ever walked into the bank. Why would we need to shoot anyone? The Cyprus Keystone Cops were late," he said.

"So who killed the Serbs? The Jackdaw?"

"Your report said shots from the Cathedral killed them, but that there were no sounds of shots."

"I didn't hear any," she said, thinking back to the sun-drenched steps outside the bank. Srdan jerking violently as he went down, the back of his head exploding. The only sounds, her screaming "Run!" to Jean-Pierre, their breathing and the sounds of their footsteps on the pavement. No sounds of shots.

"Russian *Spetsnaz* snipers use a special rifle, a VSS Vintorez with a subsonic cartridge. Almost completely silent. The Jackdaw's kind of weapon," Jerry Matthews said.

She shook her head. "It still doesn't compute. If the Jackdaw is working for the Russians, why would he kill Serbs presumably working with Pronova in order to help me and a French prosecutor? Why didn't they kill us? And if Jean-Pierre did see him, how did Vincent the Cat wind up in the middle of this?"

Jerry Matthews got up, smeared a slab of pâté on a piece of baguette on a plate, refilled his champagne, poured a little more into her glass. "Maybe for the same reason as us, Princess. Everyone figures you're the one who's going to pin the tail on Fleetwood's donkey." He pointed his finger at her. "Do the math, kiddo. Of the properties Fleetwood owned at least half were in the good old U.S. of A, where you're not only a citizen, but a senior-level Homeland Security Special Agent. You can move around and investigate a lot easier than some Serb thug who barely speaks English. Not to mention how far you've come on this case in just a couple of weeks. Sure you won't have some? It's good. Duck, I think," he said, indicating the *pâté*.

"So you think the Jackdaw's stalking me, keeping me alive so I can lead him to the secret? Maybe he's been stalking me all along? Killing along the way."

"Entirely possible," he said, his mouth full.

There was a knock at the hotel suite door. Jerry Matthews put down the champagne, pulled out a 9mm pistol. He stood beside the door to surprise anyone coming in and motioned Casey to answer. It was Brochard. Back in Paris, he was once more in an expensive suit, black with a matching black-and-white tie and looking good enough to eat, she thought.

"Monsieur *le* Prosecutor, I believe. C'mon in. Have some Bollinger and *pâté*," Jerry Matthews said, gesturing with his pistol at the table.

"And you are, Monsieur?" Brochard asked, not moving from the hallway.

"Jerry Matthews, a colleague of Casey's. She and I work in the same department," Jerry Matthews said, his smile full of teeth like he wanted to sell them a timeshare. Brochard glanced at Casey for verification.

"Unfortunately," she said.

"She doesn't mean that," Jerry Matthews said.

"Actually I do," Casey said. Jerry Matthews poured Brochard a glass of champagne.

"How's the wife and little girl?" Jerry Matthews said, putting on a serious face to Brochard. They sat facing each other next to the window view of the towering La Defense arch.

"They're safe, though my superiors want me to take a leave because of the threat. French regulations are very strict. *Santé*," Brochard said and drank the champagne.

"Down the hatch," Jerry Matthews toasted back. "So you're going on leave? I know how important that is – for your wife and family," he added, glancing at Casey to see if she picked up on the sarcasm.

"Not quite. There are elements on our side who are demanding we finally get answers about the dead American, Dale Fleetwood," Brochard said.

"You have a print copy of the list of addresses for the properties Fleetwood owned?" Casey said to Jerry Matthews.

"Right here," Jerry Matthews tapped his pocket. "Only you don't need it, do you? You've already solved it, haven't you?" he said, gesturing at the *pâté*, cheese and champagne. "Help yourselves, guys. Hate to leave it for the hotel help."

"Show us the list," she said.

Jerry Matthews pulled the paper from his pocket and spread it on the coffee table in front of them. Casey looked for a moment, then straightened.

"You know, all right. I can tell," Jerry Matthews said.

"I want some guarantees, Jerry," she said. "I don't trust you as far as I can throw that big arch out there," pointing at the window. "Not to mention, there's a pretty good chance the Jackdaw or someone just as nasty is going to do their level best to kill me the second I find it. That's assuming I'm right, and whatever it is, is still there and Fleetwood's stuff is as explosive as everyone seems to think."

"Mister Dalton's given the okay. Your cards, you're dealing, Princess," Jerry Matthews said.

Casey looked at Brochard. "We need to talk, Jean-Pierre. You have an obligation to," she hesitated on their names, afraid he would think she was treading into areas she shouldn't, "Gabi and Juliette. I can't ask you to be in on this."

Brochard took out a cigarette, lit it. "Americans," he said, exhaling a breath of smoke with every word. "You always see things so simplistically. Gabi and I spoke last night. She wants me to go."

"Giving you the old heave-er-roo, is she?" Jerry Matthews said.

"Jesus, Jerry, do you have to be a dick all the time?" Casey snapped.

"My wife and Henri are no longer together. I'm coming – assuming you, Monsieur Matthews will arrange cooperation from the Americans," Brochard said.

"It's Casey's call." Jerry Matthews turned to her. "C'mon, I'm dying to know how you figured it out."

"I want some guarantees, Jerry. I mean it. You start pulling crap and I swear to God the whole thing winds up on the front page of the New York Times."

"Whatever you say, Princess. So, where is it? Personally, I think it's the place in Surrey. You ever seen one of those old English manor houses? There's like a million secret panels and places to hide stuff where you'd never think, like some Agatha Christie novel," Jerry Matthews said.

They bent over the paper listing Fleetwood's former properties:

"Properties owned at various times by Dale Fleetwood (mentioned by Fleetwood):
   7 Trevor Square, Knightsbridge SW7, London, U.K.
   740 Park Avenue, #38D, New York, NY 10021
   8 Granville Road, Weybridge, Surrey KT13, U.K.
   Villa Florina, Jesus 3, Ibiza, Ibiza 07800, Spain
   2703 P Street NW, Washington, D.C. 20007
   1, Avenue Henry Dunant, Monte Carlo 98000 Monaco
   6333 Ocean Breeze Drive, Malibu, CA 90265
   99 Beauchamp Lane, Rockport, Maine 04856
   Zagrabačka ul. 18, 20000, Dubrovnik, Croatia
   Long Creek Estate, Rogers Clark Boulevard, Colemans Mill Crossing, VA 22546
   Properties Dale Fleetwood had an ownership interest in, but didn't mention:
   55 Wythe Ave., 18th Floor, Brooklyn, NY 11211
   Aquilina Tower, #4204, Vía Punta Darién 0833-0032, Panama City, Panama
   Royal Cargo, Mill Street, Belville South, Cape Town, 7530, South Africa
   Road 18, Hoora, Block 319 Building 41, Manama 199, Bahrain
   Bahria Complex 1, MT Khan Rd, Lalazar, Karachi, Sindh, Karachi, Pakistan."

"It's not the UK, Jerry. It's not Europe; it's in the States," Casey said. "But before I simply tell you, you have to understand how I got there. Fleetwood was in prison for fourteen years. A long time to think. That poem of his doesn't just tell us the location, it's also something else."

"Yeah, what's that?" Jerry Matthews said.

"A warning," she said. "He wants us to take him very seriously. Something terrible is coming."

"As I discussed with Mister Dalton, these lines all have meaning," she told Jerry Matthews and Brochard. "The ones about "*All the king's horses,*" are from Mother Goose. Humpty Dumpty is an egg that gets broken. Some kind of metaphor about an important person about to fall. '*Now we are engaged in a great civil war*' is from Lincoln's Gettysburg Address. To dedicate a graveyard. The Civil War. Another warning. The next line: '*A charter to commit the crime once more.*' A threat that a crime from the past is about to be repeated: Blue Madagascar. The last line: '*hell is empty; the devil is here,*' from Shakespeare's *The Tempest*. Only in Shakespeare, the word is '*devils*', plural. Fleetwood made it singular. A specific person."

"Yeah, we all got the sense he was predicting something bad coming," Jerry Matthews nodded. "But that still doesn't tell us where. So enlighten us, Princess. Out of all of these, which?" Jerry Matthews said, tapping the paper.

"You need to understand how I got there. The location needs to literally be on the ocean. There were other clues that confirmed the location absolutely," she said.

"Why? I don't see anything like that in the poem. In fact, it doesn't have a single reference to the sea," Jerry Matthews said.

She said: "Fleetwood's poem is an acrostic. The first letter of each line spells out the real clue."

"How'd you get to that?" Jerry Matthews asked, squinting at the page to spell out the first letters.

"The second line about Humpty Dumpty was the tip-off.

It should have said: 'All the king's horses and all the king's men, *Couldn't* put Humpty together again.' But instead it reads: '*Never could* put Humpty together again.' For the acrostic to work, Fleetwood needed that line to start with the letter 'N'. If you go down the first letter of each line, it reads: ANNABELLEE or ANNABEL LEE. I Googled it. It's a famous poem by Edgar Allan Poe. I've read it so many times now I know it by heart." She recited:

> *"It was many and many a year ago,*
> *In a kingdom by the sea,*
> *That a maiden there lived whom you may know*
> *By the name of Annabel Lee;"*

"So it says, '*a kingdom by the sea.*' So what?" Jerry Matthews said.

"Everything in this poem is about '*a kingdom by the sea.*' Fleetwood's love, his lost kingdom. According to the poem, what we're looking for, Fleetwood's treasure, like the woman Edgar Allan Poe loved and lost, is shut up inside a vault, a tomb, a sepulchre by the sea: '*In her sepulchre there by the sea . . . In her tomb by the sounding sea.*'"

"I still don't see how that tells us which property it is. What about the Malibu place? That's on the coast," Jerry Matthews said.

"Not quite. I kept rereading it, putting myself in his place," she said. "Edgar Allan Poe's poem is a terrible fantasy. He wants to sleep in the grave with his beautiful wife who just died. Think about it. Fleetwood every single night in his prison cell went to sleep dreaming, thinking, obsessing about what he'd hidden in a secret vault, in a '*sepulchre there by the sea.'* "The thing we're looking for," she said, looking at both of them, "is waiting for us in a hidden place literally on the shore. I Google-mapped every one of these," tapping the list of addresses, "and studied the street views closely. The other properties, while some are perhaps near a shore, like Malibu, or even have a view of the water, weren't directly touching the sea itself."

"So which is it?" Brochard asked.

"This one," she said, pointing to the Maine address: *99 Beauchamp Lane, Rockport, Maine 04856.*

"You say that like you're sure," Jerry Matthews said.

"I am."

"I'm not convinced," Jerry Matthews shrugged. "What about the other stuff? Einstein and Bo-peep and all that other crap?"

"I'm coming to that," she said. But just to prove to you, let's Google Map the Maine address."

She opened her laptop, checked the WiFi, and Googled the address. The earth map showed an isolated house on the shore of Penobscot Bay in Maine.

"Okay, it's a possibility," Jerry Matthews conceded. "What did Mister Dalton say?"

"He agreed once I told him the clincher. The $E = mc^2$ and *three* sheep."

"Convince me," Jerry Matthews said.

"The letter '*c*' in the equation again evokes the '*sea*', what Poe's poem keeps pointing to the way a compass needle always points north. Also, the original Mother Goose rhyme never mentions how many sheep Bo Peep lost, but Fleetwood is very careful to specify a number: *three*."

"What's the significance?" Brochard asked.

"At first it threw me," Casey said. "But when I realized Fleetwood was pointing us to both the *sea* and the letter '*c*', I had to pay closer attention to Einstein. 'C' is squared. The number *three* squared is 9. Take 9 twice, you get 99."

"Why twice?" Jerry Matthews asked.

"Because squared in Einstein's or any other equation is represented by the number '2'. It's the only other number in the poem and the only thing that relates to any of the addresses. So now we have two 9's. The address of Fleetwood's house in Rockport is *99 Beauchamp Lane*," she said.

"Who owns the property now?" Brochard asked.

"Let me check," Jerry Matthews said, working on his laptop. It took a few moments. "Oh yeah, I remember. A U.S. company that's a shell for another company. We're still digging."

"Are you kidding me? You don't know?" Casey said.

"We only just started on this. Give us a couple of days," Jerry Matthews said

"We don't have a couple of days. You realize the minute we find this thing, the Jackdaw or someone else will try to kill me," Casey said.

"Pretty much guaranteed," Jerry Matthews agreed, smearing *pâté* on a slice of baguette.

PART FOUR

TWO DAYS EARLIER

"Boys don't matter – until they do. But sisters are forever."

JESSICA "JESSIE" MAKARENKO

CHAPTER FORTY-ONE

PORTLAND, MAINE

THE HOTEL BAR was decorated orange and black for Halloween with Jack o'Lanterns on the window ledges, a skeleton in a torn top hat and tuxedo, and mini-pumpkin cornucopias with candles on the tables. Casey and Brochard had arrived that afternoon from Paris and had driven a rental car up the I-95 from Boston. On the bar TV and later at the restaurant over oysters on ice, the talk around them was about the election.

A Twitter meme from a group called 'Americans for Freedom and Traditional Values' had accused Democratic candidate, Senator Jennifer Louise Ferris, of having had a series of lesbian shack-ups in San Francisco. Battling back, Senator Ferris charged that Republican candidate Governor Jeff Smullen's campaign promise to bring back jobs lost in the current Recessionary Spiral, was "snake oil that would lead to economic collapse for the American people."

For his part, Governor Smullen railed against recent anti-Wall Street riots in New York, Denver and Los Angeles and called for a "return to decency and law and order". In response to accusations his campaign encouraged violence, Governor Smullen declared he'd never encouraged violence of any kind, despite a video of him at a fundraiser telling wealthy donors that "given the present crisis when the American people are demanding action, it might be time for the President to govern by decree under the National Emergencies Act and Article II of the Constitution."

After dinner, they took a walk along Commercial Street. Traffic was sparse. The night was frigid and New England misty. Lonely cries of gulls echoed in the darkness and the lights along the wharfs were ghostly in the fog.

They passed an encampment of tents on the sidewalk. Homeless camps were becoming ever more numerous these days as the economic crisis deepened. A half dozen men huddled silently around a fire in a garbage can. It reminded Casey of Belgrade. What have we come to, she thought. A police patrol car slowed, the cops inside taking a good look at them before driving on.

"Maybe we should go back? This part of America is quite cold," Brochard said, his words visible as puffs of fog in the icy air.

They walked back to the hotel and took the elevator up to their suite. Someone on the staff had turned down the bed and lit the fireplace, making the room cozy. They opened a bottle of Glenlivet from the courtesy bar and sat on a rug on the floor in front of the fire, their whiskey glasses reflecting the firelight.

"I like this," she said, looking at the changing shapes and colors of the fire, her arm brushing his.

"So do I," he said.

"This election feels weird. There's something wrong about it."

"It seems so to me," he said, "but I'm not American."

"I keep thinking about that poem by Fleetwood. The last line: '*hell is empty; the devil is here.*' It's not just a warning; it's a prophecy. It feels like something really evil is coming closer."

"What we're doing, you think it's part of this?"

"I'm starting to think so. Blue Madagascar. Fleetwood. The CIA. All the pieces are there, we just haven't connected them yet." She turned to him. "Was it okay with Gabi, you coming here now, with me? How was it?"

He sipped the whiskey. "It was good. It was awful. I spent a whole evening with my daughter, Juliette, and as I put her to bed, she had her hand wrapped around my finger like when she was tiny and wouldn't let go. I wanted to die, that's how shaken I was.

"Afterwards, Gabi and me, we went to Le Vigny, a little brasserie nearby we used to go to. My mother-in-law stayed with Juliette. I told her how you were kidnapped and escaped from the Serbian gangsters. How we barely escaped assassination in Cyprus. I told her– " he hesitated. "I think you've had a hard time."

"What'd she say?"

"She admires you, said you were '*extraordinaire*', that it was no wonder there was an attraction between us. Gabi's decided Juliette is too important. Also, after what happened when those Russians broke in, she realized her feelings for me were still . . ." he stopped. "She was angry with me in Nice. She was in the right. I'd trapped her in a life she hadn't bargained for, had never agreed to. Worse, I didn't even bother to show up." He looked at Casey, losing himself for a moment in sea-green eyes reflecting the firelight. "She wants us to be together as a family again. But only if I truly love her and that I can leave you without regret."

Casey touched his cheek with her finger. "She's so French,

Gabi. Do you really like me?" she said. Even now, even knowing he wasn't hers, if he said the word she'd go with him. But could she?

He kissed her. She tasted the oysters and the fog and the whisky on his lips. He pulled away in a way that suggested if he didn't they'd be in bed in another minute.

"Very much. And you? You never say."

"After Belgrade with those trafficked women, knowing that I was almost one of them or worse, the thought of sex . . . I'm pretty screwed up, Jean-Pierre. My mother was an addict, in and out of jail a lot. I learned not to trust anyone."

"There must've been someone," Brochard said.

"My sister, Jessica," she shook her head, setting her hair swaying. "I can't talk about her. You should go back to Paris, Jean-Pierre. You could easily be killed. I don't want Juliette to be without her father. And this might sound strange, but I don't want Gabi to be without you either. She still loves you. I like to think of you being loved," she said.

"That sounds very French," he said.

"I must've caught it from you," she almost smiled. "So you're going back? It's settled?"

"No," he shook his head. "You're right, what we're doing is very dangerous. I can't let you do it alone." He looked at the window, wrapped in fog like white cotton. Nothing outside could be seen. "Is it me or has America gotten very strange recently?"

"You know, I hadn't noticed before. Maybe it's me being away in different countries, but yes, America seems different now," she said.

CHAPTER FORTY-TWO

CAMDEN, MAINE

IN THE MORNING, they took I-295 north, turning onto Route 1 at Brunswick. The day was cold, gray, dark clouds threatening rain, typical Fall weather in Maine, the waitress at breakfast said. Casey drove and now and then, Brochard fiddled with the car radio.

The radio news was about a terror attack in Birmingham, England, Islamic extremists suspected, the upcoming World Series game between the Boston Red Sox and the Los Angeles Dodgers, and the election. The polls showed Governor Smullen increasing his lead in Florida, Ohio, and Pennsylvania. A group of leading economists, including nearly all the U.S. Nobel Prize laureates, had taken out a full page ad in the New York Times stating that "Governor Smullen's proposed fiscal and monetary proposals to deal with the current Recessionary Spiral situation will plunge the U.S. economy from a serious crisis into an unprecedented crisis from which there might be no possible recovery." When the news began to repeat itself, Brochard turned the radio off.

Route 1 was a two-lane bordered by trees and white clap-
board houses, more than a few with "For Sale" signs. Others
advertised homemade pottery or firewood. The sky grew
darker. It began to rain, the windshield wipers swishing back
and forth. All at once, Casey turned into a private farm road
and U-turned the car so they could watch the road.

"What is it?" Brochard asked.

There was a blue Chrysler van behind us when we left
Portland and again when we got off I-295. I want to see if
they're still following us. After Belgrade, I learned to always
keep one eye on the rear view mirror," she said.

They waited, watching cars going by. Casey could smell
the sea in the air. It had to be close by, but she couldn't see it.
After a while, Brochard turned on music, interrupted with
news about the attack in England. A terrorist suspect had
been killed in Sparkbrook when police came to arrest him.
After fifteen minutes, no blue Chrysler van had gone by. She
started the car and drove into Rockland.

Driving through the town, they could see boats in the
harbor in the gaps between the buildings on Main Street. A
squatter's camp of homeless people's tents had been set up in
an empty lot next to a shuttered restaurant with an "Out of
Business" sign. The second such camp since Portland. A
policeman in a rain slicker, leaning against a telephone pole,
kept watch on the tents. Just like Belgrade, Casey thought.

They drove into Camden. Traffic was single lane, the rain
slowing them as they neared the harbor. The inn was on a hill
overlooking the harbor. They left their luggage in the car, and
scurried inside, sharing an umbrella. There was a welcoming
fire in the lobby fireplace and although it wasn't noon, people
were already crowding the restaurant. Casey spotted two fit-
looking men sitting at a table in the back of the bar, one of

whom glanced at her, then away. Jerry Matthews delivered, she thought.

"They're here. Our backup," she whispered to Brochard as they went up to the desk. "We left our bags in the car. The rain," she said to the woman behind the counter. "Thought we'd eat first." And with luck, we won't be staying the night, she thought. Hopefully we'll find what we're looking for and get the hell out of here before the Jackdaw or whoever else is hunting us can even find this place, she thought.

"We'll squeeze you in," the woman said, motioning to someone in the restaurant.

"Maybe a quick drink first, then the luggage," Casey said.

"Of course. Andre at the bar will take care of you," the woman said.

They found seats at the bar. Casey ordered an Old Fashioned, Brochard, Pernod. One of the men she'd spotted, dark haired, North Face jacket, got up and as he brushed by, she felt a note being slipped into her hand. She glanced down at it as she drank. "*Sumatra. 5 min.*"

Five minutes later, while Brochard got the luggage and checked in, she left the bar and went up to the second floor. All the rooms had distant locale names. When she found Sumatra, she knocked. The other man from the bar, heavily-muscled, light brown hair cut high-and-tight military-style, opened the door and motioned her in with a Glock.

"I'm Wyatt. He's Ryan. You must be Casey," the high-and-tight said. The room was small though the harbor view made it seem bigger. On the bed was an M4 carbine and two pairs of night view gear and binoculars.

"They gave you my description?" Casey said.

"Your photo. Also, Jerry said to watch for a cute Mexican-American chick who didn't take shit from anyone," Ryan, a square-jawed blue-eyed type who probably had to fight the women off with a club, said with a grin.

"It's almost noon. We'll get going as soon as my colleague – Brochard, Jean-Pierre Brochard, he's a senior French official, kind of like a district attorney – and I grab a quick bite. Say 12:30. Have you reconnoitered the property?" she asked.

"We did a drive-by, but didn't stop," Wyatt said. "Not much to see from the road. Mostly trees, hedges, private road. Didn't see anybody. Is anyone supposed to be there?"

"Unknown. In theory no, but we won't know till we're there," she said. The rain streamed down the window; the harbor as seen through it was an Impressionist painting. "I need to know who you guys are. What've they told you about this?"

Wyatt smiled. "With due respect, Casey, I'm not sure of your clearance, so let's just say this isn't our first rodeo. Ryan 'n me have both done clandestine ops in places you wouldn't believe. We're both ex-Green Berets, ex-JSOC Delta, both highly trained. Is that good enough for you?"

"I hope so," she said. "Because the opposition seems to know everything before we do. And they're *Spetsnaz*-trained, including the kind of *Spetsnaz* snipers who use a completely silent VSS Vintorez rifle and don't miss."

At that, the two men looked at each other. Ryan stood up.

"Ground rules; what's our assignment?" he asked.

"Follow us, but stay separate. If you've been briefed, you know we're looking for something hidden on the property. We'll check the house first, but it's very possible it's hidden somewhere on the shore. That's why we asked you to bring the scuba gear and tools. What about keys? Did someone from our office get you keys for the property?"

"Duplicate keys are in my pocket. Don't ask where we got 'em, I'd have to kill you," Wyatt winked. "Scuba's here," he added, heaving a duffel bag onto the bed. "We going swimming?"

"I hope not," she said. "Your job is to rescue us if bad guys come. Once we're on the property, camouflage so no one knows you're there. Make sure no one can get to us from the road or any other direction."

"You really think someone's going to try?" Wyatt asked.

"I've been on this case a month," she said. "So far there's already been two killed in Panama, a dozen in France, a lawyer in Belgrade, three more in broad daylight in Cyprus plus an ex-MI6 agent in Greece and I've been almost killed a couple of times. Once we find this thing . . . "

"You're a target," Ryan said.

Wyatt picked up the M4, cradled it comfortably. "Daytime. Single lane road. We'll cover your ass," he said.

"Better watch your own too," Casey said.

CHAPTER FORTY-THREE

ROCKPORT, MAINE

THE HOUSE on Beauchamp Lane stood alone on several acres of rocky coast that jutted into the sea. It was a white two-story New England-style house, hidden from the road by tall hedges and stands of spruce and pine.

Casey and Brochard drove a private gravel road onto the property. The rain had stopped, but the air was wet, wind whipping drops of water from the trees. They got out of the rental car, leaving it parked on the cobblestone driveway. Brochard grabbed the duffel bag with the sea gear from the trunk.

Three minutes later, Wyatt and Ryan drove onto the property in a Ford Explorer. They parked in a stand of spruce trees, camouflaging the Ford with broken branches so it was virtually invisible from the road. Cradling M4s, armed with belts of equipment, ammunition, grenades, and pistols, they joined Casey and Brochard at the back of the house on the side facing the bay.

We must be close to the beach, Casey thought. She could hear waves breaking on the rocky shoreline. From where they were, she could see no other houses, only trees and the gray sky and the sea. The place had a lonely, foreboding feeling that Maine natives could've told her comes as winter approaches the coast.

They climbed the back porch steps and she felt in her handbag for the set of house keys Wyatt had given her before they left the inn, which he presumably got from Jerry Matthews, though she really didn't know who had arranged it. Maybe Arthur Dalton himself.

"You take outside. I'll cover inside till we know it's clear," Ryan said to Wyatt, giving Casey a blue-eyed "I'll protect you" look that if she was any judge had probably wilted female knees in half the bars in America.

"Take this," Wyatt said, handing a Glock pistol to Brochard, who carried it awkwardly, pointed upwards like an umbrella. Wyatt hopped down from the porch and crouching low, made his way around the side of the house back toward the trees in front to cover anyone coming from the road. Casey tried the keys on the back door. The second key worked and they went inside.

An alarm warning buzzer sounded. After a minute's frantic search, they found the alarm in a walk-in pantry in the kitchen. Casey pressed the key sequence Jerry Matthews had texted her via the automatic self-destruct app, Wickr and the buzzer stopped.

The house was nearly empty of furniture except for a sofa, a TV and a couple of arm chairs in the spacious living room, the hardwood floors making it seem even emptier. It had the feel of a place where no one had lived for a long time. The windows were large and every room gave unobstructed views of Penobscot Bay, but the house was unnaturally quiet. It gave Casey the creeps. Something bad had happened here. Get out as soon as you can, she told herself.

"Let's get started," Brochard said. He's feeling it too, she thought.

"I better go first," Ryan said, holding the M4 in a close-quarters combat shooting position.

They moved quickly from room to room, Ryan leading with the M4. After they verified that no one was on the ground floor, Ryan went down and checked the basement by himself. He came back up the stairs with a ladder.

They followed him up a staircase to the second floor and searched all the upstairs bedrooms, bathrooms, another sitting and TV room, closets, and second-floor decks. Ryan used the ladder to access the attic from the upstairs hallway. Casey followed. The attic was filled with odds and ends, tools and empty racks that looked like they'd once stored thousands of DVDs. Brochard reported no one in any of the rooms.

They met back in the living room. Casey and Brochard would now do a more thorough search, then explore the back part of the property along the shore. Ryan would go outside where he and Wyatt would cover to prevent anyone from approaching the house from the road. Casey told him she would text when they left the house to explore the shore. He would acknowledge by texting back: "*Tyrion*", his favorite character from *Game of Thrones*.

"So," Brochard said. "Where do we start?"

"I'll take upstairs. You search down here," she said, checking her watch. "If anything's hidden in the house, it's probably under or behind a board in the floor or a closet or something."

"But you don't think so?"

She shook her head. "Annabel Lee. The poem talks about a '*sepulchre there by the sea.*' I think Fleetwood told us exactly where he put it."

"But how, exposed to the water, the weather?"

"It'd have to be protected from the elements," she agreed and headed back up to the top floor.

She searched the closets, linen closets, rapping on the walls, closet shelves floorboards, looking for loose boards, a telltale line in a post or beam, a box, anything. Ridiculous, she thought, searching between the shelves in a linen closet. No man would ever hide anything in a linen closet. The walls were bare, with no wall paintings, nothing that might hide a safe; not even the outlines of spaces where paintings had once been. If it was anywhere in the house, it would be in the attic, but found nothing.

She went back downstairs but Brochard wasn't there. She looked in each of the rooms, then outside to the back porch, feeling the drizzle on her face and hair. Although it was mid-afternoon, the slate-gray clouds and sky made it feel later. A sense of urgency bubbled inside her. If they didn't find what they were looking for now, it might be too late. Where was Brochard? She pulled her Sig Sauer pistol out of her handbag. The only place left was the basement.

She opened the basement door. There was no sound. Something made her not want to go down there. Stop it, she told herself. Jessie's Rules: *Weakness comes from fear. Fear is a liar. Remember, we are the most dangerous creatures on the planet.* She tiptoed slowly down the stairs, one step at a time. Midway, a stair creaked and she froze. If anyone was listening, they must have heard her, she thought and came quickly down the rest of the stairs.

The basement was pitch black. She turned on the flash-light app on her iPhone. Boxes, tools, and old porch furniture were stacked in piles, only a narrow way between them. Moving carefully between the stacks, she came to a closed steel door at the basement wall. Why would Fleetwood have this here? She wondered. And where's Jean-Pierre?

She tried the door handle, opened it, and with the flashlight app and her pistol together in a shooting stance, stepped into another room. It looked like a library, except that the floor-to-ceiling shelves were bare. Above a desk by the far wall, the curling ends of cables suggested there might once been monitors or electronic equipment there. Brochard was sitting hunched at the desk. To his right, stood a row of metal file cabinets against a side wall. On the other side of the room was an open space with steel rings embedded in a concrete wall. A chain hung from a pipe on the ceiling.

"What is this place?" she said.

When he heard her, Brochard half-turned and said over his shoulder: "Not a good place."

"I couldn't find you," she said, coming over. "This place is creepy."

"No, evil," he said. She started towards the file cabinets.

"Don't bother, they're empty. But I found this under one of the cabinets. They must've missed it when they cleaned this place out."

She came over and aimed the flashlight app at what he was looking at – and then wished she hadn't. The photograph was an old-fashioned instant Polaroid. It must've been made years ago, she thought. It showed a naked young woman on all fours and two older men, one naked, the other wearing black jockey briefs and a leather mask. The naked man held her by a chain attached to a metal collar around her neck. The woman's face was obscured by her hair and distorted by a ball gag in her mouth.

Something about the man holding the chain gave her a

sick feeling of *déjà vu*. There was something familiar about the young woman too. *It couldn't be! Don't go there* – focus on the man. Had she seen him before? She examined the Polaroid more closely. No date or marking; nothing to tell when the photo had been taken. It had been at least a decade or more since they'd stop making Polaroid cameras and film. The company had gone out of business. She turned the photograph over again. There'd been at least three men in the room when it was taken. The two in the photo and the one who snapped the picture. Maybe more.

Then she saw it: metal rings bolted to the wall in the photo. It had been taken in this room. The idea made her sick; unspeakable things had happened here.

"You're right, Jean-Pierre. This place is evil. They took the photo in this room," she said, shivering. The sooner they got out of there the better.

"I know," he said.

"Wait," she said. The photo still bothered her. There was something about the man with the chain. She was certain she'd seen him before, bending closer to the Polaroid.

Was that a class ring he was wearing on the hand holding the chain? She used her iPhone's magnifier app to zoom in on the man's hand. A class ring, fuzzy, but unmistakable. Yale. She had seen him before, back when she'd graduated from HSI training. Back then he'd been a Congressman, part of a delegation. Now he was – of course! What idiots they were!

"It's him," she said, tapping her finger on the Polaroid.

"Who?" Brochard said.

"Thomas Fitzpatrick, Deputy Director of the CIA. No wonder everyone's going crazy," she said, putting the Polaroid into an evidence bag.

"These were important men – and there were others," Brochard said, gesturing at the Polaroid.

They went back upstairs and out to the back porch. Casey locked the door behind them. In the back of her mind a thought kept rippling: *Time is running out.*

"You don't think we missed something in the house?" Brochard said, hefting the duffel bag and slipping Wyatt's pistol into his jacket pocket.

"No. So far Fleetwood's been a hundred percent. We need to look where he told us to – somewhere on the shore – before someone beats us to it. We better hurry," she added looking up at the sky. "It gets dark early." She texted Ryan: "*Leaving house. Cover us.*"

Coming down the steps and out from under the porch roof, rain began to splatter on her jacket hood. It was coming down harder now, soaking her hair, despite the hood. I must look like a drowned terrier, she thought as they hurried on a stone path through cedar trees down toward the shore. They emerged on a rocky ledge just feet from waves breaking on the rocks.

"Damn," Casey said.

"What?" Brochard said.

"Ryan was supposed to text me back '*Tyrion.*' He hasn't."

"Are you sure your cell phone's working out here?" Brochard said, looking around. There was no one and nothing but the shore and the rain and the sea.

"I've got four bars, three-quarters battery. Something's wrong."

"I think we better get out of here. It's too dangerous to stay any longer," he said.

She looked around. "Might be twice as dangerous going back as staying," she said. The world was gray: sky and rocks and sea and rain. Water poured in miniature falls over the side of the rocky ledge down to a narrow strip of sand and pebble beach. Brochard took out Wyatt's pistol.

"What do we do?" he said, the side of his face suddenly lit like a camera flash.

"Get down!" Casey shouted, her voice lost in a clap of thunder.

CHAPTER FORTY-FOUR

HOG COVE, ROCKPORT

THEY CROUCHED on a narrow strip of beach, their heads tucked below the ledge of rock that formed a boundary between Fleetwood's property and the sea. Waves curled on the pebbles and rocks, dark and wet from the rain and the sea, just a few feet away. Brochard peered over the top of the ledge back toward the property.

"See anything?" Casey asked.

"Nothing. Maybe the text didn't go through. Maybe you should try again?" Brochard said.

"It went through," she said, not wanting to believe it. She'd seen these guys, Wyatt and Ryan. They were good, pros. Who was so much better than them that they could take them out so easily?

"I'll try again," she said, sensing she shouldn't. Still it would prove things, one way or the other. "*Left house. Do you copy?*"

Thirty seconds later came the reply text: "*Copy. Okay here.*"

"You get something?" Brochard said.

"Yes, but not what we agreed." Ryan would've responded, *Tyrion*. "Someone else has their phones."

"*Merde*, what do you think?"

"I think they're dead," she said, looking around as if there was help in the rain.

"What do we do? Call 112?"

"In America, it's 911. They haven't come after us yet. They're waiting."

"Till we find it?" he said.

"Probably."

"So where is it?" he asked. "It's not in the house. We have to do something. We can't stay here." He glanced at the surf. "What about the tide?"

"I checked the tide tables when I planned this." She glanced at her watch. "It's a little after three. This time of the month, we're at full moon. If it wasn't for the clouds, we'd see it tonight. Right now the tide's still going out, but in a few hours, where we are will all be under water."

"Maybe we should make a run for it?" he said, peeking above the ledge, gun in hand, then ducking back down.

"We wouldn't stand a chance. You cover me on the land side. Unless they're coming at us with a submarine – and with the ledges and shoals out there, it's too shallow – I don't think they're going to come at us from the sea. If you watch towards the house, you'll able to shoot first."

"We were supposed to do this together," he said, looking at her face and hair slick from the rain.

"Ryan and Wyatt are probably dead. This can't happen unless you cover me," she said.

They looked at each other as if they would never see each other again.

"Watch yourself," he said.

"If anything moves out there, it's hostile," she said. "Don't hesitate. Shoot."

Casey turned and crouching low, almost crawling to keep her head below the top of the ledge, moved along the narrow strip of pebbles and sand. Brochard positioned himself in a shooting position behind a rock on the ledge so he could scan 180 degrees to the landward side.

As she moved she kept her eyes peeled for anything that looked man-made, where something might be hidden. The smell of the sea, of shelled creatures, was strong. She traced her fingertips along the vertical face of the ledge and stony outcroppings; rocky surfaces that were normally underwater except at low tide. It had to be here, she thought, Edgar Allan Poe's line: "*In her sepulchre there by the sea,*" running in her head. But there was only rock.

She began to panic. Had she made an error? Why would Fleetwood keep anything hidden here where it might get ruined by the water? She'd been wrong. Stupid. *Stupid little Kimmy, she thought. Jessie would think she was an idiot, except Jessie was the only one in the world who wouldn't laugh at her.*

She had gone about half the length of a football field, when she came upon a large rock, almost a boulder, wedged into the granite ledge and embedded deep in the sand. It was shaped almost like a bird's wing, but flat on the side facing the sea. Could this be it? The *wingèd seraph*, she thought, heart pounding, remembering the lines:

"*With a love that the wingèd seraphs of Heaven
Coveted her and me.*"

A rock shaped like an angel's wing! How'd it get here? Glacier from the last Ice Age maybe, she guessed, This rock, like all the stony Maine coast, had been here forever. Or at least since Pangaea split into two pieces, North America and Africa right here, the very edge – water spilling into the gap to create the Atlantic Ocean. Dinosaurs have walked on these rocks, she thought, all the while her fingers felt like a blind person's on the rock's surface. Much of the time this rock would probably be underwater, except at low tide. What better place on earth to hide something?

Except there was no hiding place. Her fingers felt nothing. She had a sickening feeling. She'd been wrong. But no! It had to be here. This rock was perfect. The Edgar Allan Poe poem talked of the tide, of *"demons down under the sea,"* remembering the poem's last lines, embedded like a splinter in her mind after so many rereading's:

"And so, all the night-tide, I lie down by the side.
　　Of my darling—my darling—my life and my bride,
　　In her sepulchre there by the sea—
　　In her tomb by the sounding sea."

Except – of course! *"Demons under the sea. . . in her tomb by the sounding sea."* It's at the bottom, under the sand, under the sea, she thought, pulling the shovel and other tools, a hammer, chisel and crowbar out of the duffel. She glanced down the shore line toward Brochard, but she could no longer see him in the rain. She checked her watch: quarter to four. The tide had turned. This time of year in New England, it would be dark in a couple of hours. This would all be underwater.

She dug a ditch in the sand at the base of the rock. When it was about eighteen inches deep, she lay face down on the wet sand. Using the flashlight, she brushed away the wet sand and studied the rock face – and there it was. The top edge of a rectangular piece of dark metal. She deepened the ditch at that spot, digging out pebbles and sand to reveal a steel hatch with a lock embedded in the rock.

She tried the house keys, one at the time. The small one, that hadn't fit anything else in the house and they'd wondered what it was for, worked. The lock clicked, but the hatch cover wouldn't open.

Using the hammer and chisel on the cover's edge, she tried to pry it open, but it wouldn't budge. She couldn't give up now, she thought. Using all her strength, she smacked the chisel with the hammer at the edge and all at once, it gave. She pried the cover open. Inside was a plastic DVD case. She felt in the opening, but there was nothing else. It didn't matter. She had Dale Fleetwood's secret in her hand.

Suddenly she realized the water was lapping at her feet. The tide had turned. She had to get going. She hadn't heard a shot so hopefully, Brochard was okay.

Putting the plastic case into her handbag, she closed the vault cover and locked it with the key. In a little while, it would once again be covered by the sea. Using the shovel, she pushed sand and pebbles to fill in the ditch. By the time she put the tools back into the duffel, the waves were up to her ankles. Fleetwood found the perfect hiding place, she thought. Invisible from the land; unapproachable and virtually invisible from the sea.

Being careful to again keep her head below the ledge, she made her way back down the beach toward where she'd left Brochard. The surf hissed and splashed over her feet. Slinging the duffel and her handbag over one arm, Sig Sauer in her other hand, she made her way back along the shore.

Wiping the rain from her eyes, she peered over the top of the ledge to make sure she was back at the right spot. The rock outcropping and trees looked familiar. This was where she'd left Brochard, only he was gone.

CHAPTER FORTY-FIVE

HOG COVE, MAINE

FOUR FIGURES in wet suits emerged from the sea. Looking towards the house, Casey didn't see or hear them coming, the sounds of their approach muffled by the pounding of the waves on the rocks. One of them grabbed her from behind in a choke hold. Casey countered, twisting to shoot, but he was fast for such a big man. A strong hand twisted away her Sig Sauer as he slammed her against the rocky ledge. Before she could counter, he Sambo-kicked her middle, knocking the wind out of her. She barely had time to form the thought, *Spetsnaz,* when a leg sweep took her down. A second wet suit figure put a pistol to her head.

"Let's go in the house. We can talk without the gymnastics," a woman's voice said in American English.

They tied her hands with plastic flex and stood her on her feet. One of the men gathered her things: her handbag with the plastic case from the vault, the duffel bag, her pistol. Two others lifted her up onto the ledge. The woman kept a revolver on her as they walked up the stone path. Brochard lay on the ground beside the path, his hands and feet bound, tape over his mouth.

The woman signaled to one of the men, who cut the flex around Brochard's ankles, got him to his feet and shoved him towards the house. They climbed the back porch steps. It had been less than an hour since she'd gone up those steps with an intact team, thinking she was going to solve this thing, she reflected. A lifetime ago. She turned to the woman.

"Where are the other two, Ryan and Wyatt?"

"*Myortvy*," the woman said in Russian. *Dead*. I killed them, Casey thought bitterly, truly looking at the woman for the first time. There was something familiar about her, though it was difficult to tell because of the wetsuit. One of the men shoved Brochard toward the door.

"The keys are in my handbag. If you'll let me . . ." Casey said.

The woman ignored her. She poked through Casey's handbag, found the plastic case from the vault, the Polaroid photo, Casey's P238 pistol, and the keys. The woman tried several keys till she found the one that opened the door.

They went into the kitchen. The men and the woman stripped off their wetsuits. When the woman pulled off her hood, the moment she shook her hair free, Casey knew who she was. Natalya – Milena; the girl in the red mini-skirt from the Nice robbery.

And one of the other men, the tall one: Vincent the Cat! So Vincent had been in Cyprus. They'd been there together – and now here. Suddenly she understood how they'd tracked them, knew to come here to Fleetwood's place in Maine. They'd planted a GPS tracking bug on Brochard when he'd first arrived in Limassol.

No wonder she hadn't seen any cars following them from Portland. Once they knew she was in Maine and heading towards Rockport – and the FSB surely already knew Fleet-wood's properties – it was obvious where she and Brochard were going. She'd delivered Fleetwood's secret to them on a silver platter.

Their captors pulled jeans and sweaters out of waterproof packs, threw them on, then brought Casey and Brochard into the living room. One of the men told the smaller man in Russian to build a fire in the stone fireplace. Russians all right, Casey thought, but whose? Pronova's. The FSB? The Kremlin? Right now, odds were she and Brochard would be killed before she would ever find out.

The smaller Russian brought kindling and split logs and a fire was soon crackling in the fireplace. They seated her on the sofa by the fire, hands still tied behind her. It felt good, warm, after the cold and wet outside. They placed Brochard in one of the arm chairs, angled towards Casey and pulled the tape from his mouth. The woman Natalya and Vincent the Cat walked in. For a moment, no one spoke and with the fire going and the window view of the trees and the sea and the lights in Camden Harbor and the Russians with guns, it felt to Casey like a scene from a movie. Except that she'd soon be dead.

Brochard said something in French to Vincent the Cat, who snapped something back, ending with a sarcastic "*Monsieur le Procureur.*"

"I know you," Casey said in English to the woman.

"Do you?" the woman said.

"You're Natalya, Natalya Petrenko aka Milena Kolavitch, the woman in the red skirt from the Nice robbery. You were with Dale Fleetwood," looking around, "whose house this once was. Only now you've teamed up with one of the Blue Panthers, Vincent 'the Cat' Grumier," Casey said.

"So," the woman, Natalya said. The word was a bullet.

She called to the big Russian, Kostya, telling him in Russian to find them something to drink. The man poked behind the bar in the living room, went to the kitchen and came back empty-handed.

"*Nichivo*," Nothing, he told her.

"We'll use our own. Get it from my pack," Natalya told him. Kostya left and came back with a thermos and two plastic cups. Natalya poured cups for the two Russians, who downed them. She then took the plastic cups and poured for herself and Casey. Vincent watched.

"Vodka, Stolichnaya Elit. Cheers," Natalya toasted. She drank hers, held the cup for Casey.

"*Vashe zdorovye*," Casey toasted back. The vodka went down sharp, warm. The light outside was blue, nearly dark, clouds threatening more rain. Don't give away anything you don't want to, she told herself as Natalya took out an all-purpose tool with a knife attachment. She used it to remove a disk from the case. Removing a laptop computer from her pack, Natalya told the two Russians to wait in the next room as she slotted in the disk, leaving only Brochard, Casey, Vincent, and herself. After they left, she turned to Casey.

"I'm impressed by how you figured this out," Natalya said. "Not just which property, but exactly where. It was well hidden, but you went right to it like a homing pigeon. I told them, I insisted you should be kept alive."

"Where'd Vincent put the GPS tracking device?" Casey asked.

Natalya smiled. "Inside a pocket of Monsieur Brochard's carry-on at Limassol Airport. It's barely the size of a grain of rice. Unless you were really looking, you wouldn't find it."

"Who'd you tell to keep me alive? Sergei Mogilevich? The FSB?" Casey said.

Natalya smiled. "Mogilevich? He's not the most important. What's on this – " She held up the DVD. "You've shaken the tree to the very top."

"Are you going to let me see it too? I know things you may not. Important things."

"You're saying that so I shouldn't kill you," Natalya said.

"Let Monsieur Brochard go," Casey said. She couldn't see any way out for her, but maybe there was a chance for Brochard.

"He stays. If I let you watch, what can you tell me I don't already know?" Natalya said.

"Blue Madagascar," Casey said, gambling.

Natalya studied her. "So . . . " she said again, her voice trailing off.

"You've been on the trail a long time. That's why you were with Fleetwood. I'm guessing it wasn't his sex appeal."

At that, Natalya nearly laughed. "You know, he wasn't the worst I've ever had. He could be very interesting sometimes," she said, lighting a cigarette.

"You're FSB, not SVR, right?"

"Dale – we used his cover name, 'Layton Gary McCord' – was in bad shape when I first met him," she went on, not answering the question. "Living on cigarette butts in a rented room in the 10th *arrondissement*. But inside him was a terrible fire, his revenge. I knew if we could get our hands on it, it would give us enormous leverage over the United States.

"He was known to us from his CIA days. I stitched him back together, like a torn rag doll. We worked a few blackmail deals on some of his old colleagues, you know, '*Kompromat*'. That got him back in the money. To the outside, I was a trophy girlfriend, but I'm the one who set up the Luxembourg–Latvian–Serbian–Russian connection. The Dale Fleetwood everyone saw, the good and the bad, was a combination of the two of us." At that moment, for Casey another piece fell into place.

"You're the Jackdaw," she said. "I should've figured it out before, but we kept thinking *Spetsnaz*, 'a man'. You did the shooting in Limassol, didn't you? Why'd you save us and kill the Serbs? They were your partners."

"Kill you? That was the last thing I wanted to do. The others didn't matter. You were the one who could lead me to the prize. But don't you want to see this?" Waving the DVD. "Don't you have to know? Because I do."

"Very much," Casey said, leaning forward, almost forgetting her hands tied behind her as Natalya turned on the DVD. Casey glanced over at Brochard. His eyes were glued to the laptop screen. Natalya turned up the volume so they could all hear.

The video showed Dale Fleetwood in a hotel room, his face garishly lit by a lightbulb from a lamp with the shade removed. Probably the room in the Boulevard de Clichy neighborhood Natalya had mentioned. Fleetwood spoke directly to the camera.

"Before you can understand the footage on this DVD," Fleetwood began, "I need to provide context, so you'll know what the hell you're looking at and how I came to have it, what you might call its 'provenance'. The only other thing you need to know is that every one of the files on this DVD is authenticated with dates, locations, names of eye-witnesses, cross-references to other corroborating evidence and testimony. What I'm about to tell you is the truth, the whole truth and nothing but the truth, so help me God or whatever it is you do or don't believe in. I really don't give a shit."

Fleetwood took a deep breath. "So one night, this was in Pristina, Kosovo in 1999. Miserable night. Winter. Driving rain, coming down so hard it was almost Biblical. UNMIK, the UN security forces sent as peace-keepers, were having a party at some big monstrosity of a house on Garibaldi, near the Grand Hotel – and trust me, no matter what any official or general ever said – the UN and its forces weren't in the former Yugoslavia to protect anybody but themselves. Everyone was blitzed on Johnny Walker and *rakija*. And girls. Jesus! Up to our ears in girls.

"This Albanian piece of human excrement, Idriz, ex-KLA – that's Kosovo Liberation Army to you – a total scumbag, supplied the girls from a string of brothels he owned with his mother. No kidding, his mother. If you think he was a piece of work, you should've seen her. Dracula's mother would've taken one look and run a million miles in the opposite direction. Anyway, this Idriz promised a certain someone something special. And he delivered. Mother, did he deliver.

"Two really gorgeous girls, maybe sixteen or seventeen. One was Ukrainian, kind of a wheat-colored blonde. The other a brunette, I didn't know where she was from. Moldova, one of those Eastern countries. The blonde was exquisite. Creamy white skin, perfect little face and body, with this skinny white strap thingy dangling between her boobs. Sexy little thing. The brunette was even more beautiful, if you can believe it. Big dark eyes. Completely off the chart. I swear you'd have wanted to marry her. Compared to her, the Ukrainian girl was ugly. Both in these lacy tops and teeny mini-skirts even though it was pouring rain and cold as hell outside. And scared to death. You could see it in their eyes. It wasn't only they were so young; I don't think they'd been in it long. Just recently trafficked. In the Balkans in those days, anything went. I mean anything.

"But this person, for the moment, let's call him 'X', I'll tell you the truth, I didn't know who he was then, lit up like a Christmas tree when he saw them. Him and Idriz went upstairs with them. A couple of minutes later, Idriz comes down alone. I asked him what gives and he says, "No matter what you hear, he doesn't want to be disturbed, okay?"

"Why? What'd you do?" I asked. Something about the way he said it, set off a warning light in my head.

Idriz said "Just tied their hands. He wants to do a little bondage."

"That's when I should've done something, but the truth is, I wasn't paying attention. The thing was I was footing the bill for this little shindig. It wasn't philanthropy. With the Kosovo War winding down, though there was still fighting in the hills, UNMIK supposedly taking over but not really, and the Americans pre-occupied with Bill Clinton and Monica Lewinski, in the Balkans, it was the Wild West. With the amount of business we were doing, the few thousand for the party was chump change.

"So we're talking, me, Idriz, and a Serb – no kidding, a Serb from Belgrade. These two guys, an Albanian and a Serb, who would cheerfully massacre each other's whole families as soon as look at them, but when it came to money, they were close as two beads on a rosary – when we start to hear screaming.

"I don't mean screaming like scared screaming or pain screaming, I mean screaming like somebody being murdered. Everyone stopped, just stopped. Then Idriz, the human turd, stands up.

"'Listen guys. Everybody do what they want, okay? Girls, everything. You –' Idriz says to the bartender; guy with a mustache, looked like a Roma – 'No more *radija*. Only the best. Johnny Walker Gold for everyone!' Like he's paying for it, the son-of-a-bitch!

"So everyone went back to talking, but the screaming didn't stop. So here's a really interesting social experiment for any of you Seekers of Truth and Enlightenment, the Sixty-Four Billion Dollar Question, because it's really the only question that really matters: What do people do when they're at a party and they hear other human beings screaming in extreme terror and pain? Because that night, I can tell you, the people downstairs didn't stop; they just talked LOUDER to talk over the screaming. Only it didn't stop. The screaming went on; must've been another five, six, seven minutes. Finally, I couldn't stand it anymore. I got up.

"'I'm going up,' I told him.

"Idriz made as if to stop me, but when he saw the look in my eyes, we both went upstairs. The door was locked, but I knocked and when Mister X didn't answer, we smashed it open. Christ, I'll never forget it. Blood everywhere. All over the sheets, the floor. And here's our hero, Mister X, standing there naked, dick at full salute. And those girls, those beautiful girls. The blond girl, what he did to her breasts with a knife, Jesus! And the other one, even worse. I was sick to my stomach. Mister X looked at us.

"'It got a little out of hand,' he said.

"Out of hand! I wanted to kill him. Mind you, the girls were still alive. Not screaming since we came in, just whimpering like little animals.

"'What I do with them now?' Idriz yells. 'Who's going to want them now? You think everyone keep quiet about this? I got half of UNMIK downstairs.'

"'I'll pay,' Mister X said. The magic words.

"Idriz took care of it. At the time, I didn't want to know. I wanted no part of it. Idriz told me later they sent the girls back to wherever the hell they came from.

"Except about a year later, I heard from the Roma bartender – in those countries they call 'em 'Cigana'– that

Idriz killed the girls. He said they buried them in Taukbashce Park, near the Tennis Club.

"What was the truth? I wasn't sure. In this business, you hear a lot of stuff. I spent years in the CIA and I can tell you, probably forty percent of so-called 'intelligence' is bullshit and the other sixty percent is stone cold truth disguised as bullshit. But what happened that night, I couldn't get out of my head. I went back to Pristina. UNMIK was still running things and it was even more of a shit-hole than ever. The Roma bartender, his name was Nicu, was broke, like everyone else in the country. For two hundred bucks, he would've sold me his whole family: wife, son and three daughters. But he had something better, way better.

"Turns out Idriz, that Albanian human worm, had secret video cameras in the bedrooms of all his brothels, including the one on Garibaldi. He used it to blackmail politicos so he could run his sex and drug rackets free of interference. He had a video of every single thing Mister X had done to those girls. And there was more.

"Mister X didn't trust Idriz, as if anybody in their right mind would. To make sure Idriz really got rid of the girls, Mister X went with him to Taukbashce Park. And here's where it really gets interesting. It was Nicu the bartender who drove them and the girls – and, guess what? Nicu took secret photos in the park *as it happened*. And for two hundred bucks I had the only copy. Good thing because two years later Idriz was dead. Killed in some dust-up in Prizren with a Macedonian sex trafficker called 'Arslan the Wolfman'. Couldn't have happened to a nicer piece of garbage. So now I was the only person in the world with the evidence.

"In 2000, Kosovo wasn't a country yet. UNMIK was the country's acting police force. The Chief of police was a German, Thomas Stegen. I didn't tell him about the videos, just the bodies in Taukbashce Park. He'd heard rumors about that night, of course. There were a lot of people at that party.

"The Germans came with cadaver dogs, forensic equipment. I went along. Took them less than an hour to find the bodies. Right where Nicu said. Idriz and Mister X hadn't bothered to go far into the trees, right next to the soccer field where the kids play. They were able to identify the girls with DNA. Returned their bodies to Ukraine, Moldova or wherever. There's an official UNMIK report. It's in the files on this DVD."

"So now you know almost everything. Except Blue Madagascar." Fleetwood took a deep breath and looked straight at the camera. "First off, the thing they sent me to ADX for, I was framed, though I never claimed to be an innocent either. I've done bad things, but sometimes the worst are the things we don't do, like that night in Pristina.

"Blue Madagascar was the codename for a Kuwaiti deputy oil minister. His real name was Hamid al-Qahtani, not that it matters. At OPEC meetings, he'd always sit next to the Russian representative. Made it dead easy for them to pass stuff to each other. The conduit ran from a dead drop in Rock Creek Park in D.C. through my Greek company, LGM, AE to Blue Madagascar who passed it through the Russian OPEC rep to Pronova and the KGB. It was supposed to be phony intel we were feeding the Russkies, but they gave the Russians the real thing.

"Two Americans were the moles who used the dead drop in Rock Creek Park: first was that son-of-a-bitch who perjured himself to frame me because of what happened in Pristina and who'd been sitting there that very night slugging down Johnny Walker. Back then he was a U.S. Army Colonel liaison to UNMIK, today he's CIA Deputy Director Thomas 'Mastercard Fitz' Fitzpatrick himself.

"And now we come to Mister X, who became Director of the DIA, the U.S. Defense Intelligence Agency, and who instead of going broke in 1990 and disappearing into a sewer like he deserved, thanks to the Russkies got richer, way way richer. Between him and Fitzpatrick, they sold every military and defense secret America had. Bought and paid for by Pronova and Russian oligarchs headed by the Big Enchilada himself, a former KGB agent from Dresden who went on to become the President of Russia, Mikhail Slavin. They also sold to China, Iran, whoever would pay.

"Not to mention their little club of sex trafficking A-listers that included 'Mastercard Fitz,' the billionaire arms trafficker from Monte Carlo, Constantin von Holten, and last but not least, the star of the show, the one and only Mister X, who left the DIA to become governor of the great state of Texas and candidate for President of the United States of America, Governor Jeffrey Bryan 'Win with Jeff' Smullen.

"It was Jeff Smullen who shipped that C-4 to Saddam Hussein, him and Mastercard Fitz. They put me away to shut me up, they thought for good. But the dead don't always stay buried, do they?" Dale Fleetwood said, crossing his arms over his chest, a screw-you look on his face. The video ended. It was followed by Idriz's hidden security camera video of what had happened in the room with the girls.

CHAPTER FORTY-SIX

HOG COVE, MAINE

FOR A LONG MOMENT no one spoke, the only sound the popping of wood in the fireplace. They looked at each other dazed, like survivors of some terrible wreck, wondering how they got there. Casey wished she could unsee it, wash it from her brain.

"It's him in the video. Governor Smullen," Brochard said, breaking the silence.

Natalya clicked on the next file. It was a slide show of individual photographs, likely made with a hidden mini spy camera surreptitiously shot by the gypsy, Nicu in Pristina's Taukbashce Park, Casey reasoned. The photos were dark, disjointed from one to the next, sometimes slightly out of focus, but sufficient for evidence in court. They showed the two girls being led from the car by a man with a flashlight and a pistol to a dark stand of trees. The man had longish hair and a Stalin-style mustache. Idriz, Casey thought. The second man with him was Jeffrey Smullen. He was younger and wore a military overcoat, but it was unmistakably Governor Smullen.

One snapshot caught a flash in the darkness from Smullen's hand aimed at one of the girls. Literally, the murder as it happened. A second showed Smullen standing over the blond girl's body. Another showed Jeff Smullen, holding a shovel. The final photograph showed the two girls' bodies, next to a hole Idriz and Smullen were digging between the trees.

Next Natalya clicked on files that displayed documents, including an affidavit from Acting UNMIK Chief of Police Thomas Stegen, who'd found and identified the girls' bodies. Thomas Stegen was now a senior judge in the *Bundesgericht-shof*, the German Federal Court of Justice in Karlsruhe, the highest criminal court in Germany.

Natalya swiped through additional documents that included police reports of eyewitness statements from UNMIK officers who'd been there that night, fingerprints from the room, a ballistics report on Idriz's gun that matched the bullets in the girls' bodies, DNA evidence including Smullen's DNA from semen and hairs taken from the girl's bodies and clothes, military files showing dates from Smullen's deployment with UNMIK in Kosovo and phone records that conclusively placed him in Pristina that night.

They had the bastard cold, Casey thought. Fleetwood had spent fourteen years in ADX thinking about it and putting the evidence together. He'd tied it up for them with a ribbon.

"We should notify the FBI, the Kosovo State Prosecutor's office, Interpol, immediately. I can handle France. This man is a monster. He mustn't be allowed to become President," Brochard said.

Natalya took out her revolver, the OTs-38 Stechkin. "Those are not my orders," she said.

"I'm not going back to La Santé for thirty years," Vincent said, pulling the pistol from his belt.

Casey's heart pounded. It couldn't end this way – and even if she somehow got away, how could she trust Arthur Dalton or anyone in Washington with something explosive as this?

"We can't unsee what we just saw," she said.

"No," Natalya said. She aimed her revolver with both hands at Brochard.

"Wait!" Casey shouted, looking at Natalya. "We have to talk. Alone. If we don't, you'll never know."

CHAPTER FORTY-SEVEN

HOG COVE, MAINE

THEY STOOD in the mahogany-paneled library, the furniture gone, bookshelves bare. The room had the empty feel of a stage set after the actors have departed. Outside, it was nearly dark; the windows reflected back the interior of the room.

"I had a sister, Jessica," Casey said. "She disappeared when I was twelve. I never saw her again. She would've been your age. You speak English like an American. For a crazy second after Cyprus, I thought you might be her."

"I'm not your sister. I'm Russian," Natalya said. Casey stared at their reflections in the window; two female ghosts in an empty room.

"Why did you kill the Serbs and not me in Cyprus? You could've easily," Casey said.

"You were the way to Fleetwood's secret. I told them, whatever we do, don't touch her."

"Told who? Pronova? The FSB? That Constantin guy?" Natalya didn't answer. Casey saw a flicker, something unexpected in Natalya's face, something unexpected and incomprehensible, like a fish walking on land; inexplicable and yet it's strolling across the path in front of you. "There's another reason. Something you're not saying. What?"

"I saw what you did in Belgrade at the Women's Shelter."

"You were there?"

"I never saw anyone do that. Force those *ubliyudki*, those bastards to – " Natalya took a breath. "You saved those girls," she said, coming close and opening a knife, used it to cut the flex tying Casey's hands.

Casey rubbed her wrists. "How is it you speak English without an accent?"

"My parents were KGB agents in America. I spent the first years of my life in the U.S., in Bensonhurst in Brooklyn. When the Soviet Union collapsed, my parents were recalled to Moscow."

"How'd you get into . . . how'd you become the Jackdaw?"

"It's not a nice story."

"Neither is mine," Casey said.

"When we came back to Russia, my father went away. I don't know how or why. I never saw him again. We had no money. In those days, nobody had food, money, anything. My mother was drunk all the time, did drugs, heroin."

"Mine too. We have a lot in common. How'd you survive?" Casey said.

"They took me to a special school in Zelenodolsk, on the Volga."

"Who took you, the FSB?"

"Only later did I understand. For them I was perfect. I came from a KGB family, was athletic, pretty, spoke perfect American English. It was almost as if I'd been designed for this. As a young girl I was told 'You're not special because you're pretty, but we can make you special.' They taught me people are different around pretty women. Not just men, women too. Even when they pretend not to notice, it's different. People think it's a gift – but it's a gift with strings. One is you never know who you are. I often think I'm an ordinary girl."

"Trust me, you're not."

Natalya lit a cigarette. She took a puff and shared it with Casey. "There was a man, Maksim, he was very handsome – you know how that affects young girls, right? Of course you do." Casey nodded. "He was my teacher, my friend, almost a father to me. Later, when I was older, my lover. Don't think I resisted, I wanted him too, very much. They taught me everything. How to think, how to be sexy, how to seduce and manipulate men, how to spy, how to kill in a hundred different ways. They manufactured me the way you make a car." She stopped. "Men look at me and think, she's sexy, I like that. But this thing we do." She shuddered. "I'm hollow, you know. An empty bottle; there's nothing in me to drink."

"I'm not that different. There's a hole in me where my sister Jessica used to be."

"Maybe we are sisters in a way. We're half-made, both of us." Natalya gestured at their reflections in the library windows. "It's like a war. You and me, we're like soldiers in a night fog in no-man's-land," Natalya said. "We encounter an enemy – and maybe *this one time* we don't kill because we discover we have more in common with each other than with the assholes on our own side."

"I wanted you to be her. There was a connection," Casey said.

"I almost wish I was your sister. A sorority of two. I have a problem. I can't let you go – and I can tell you don't want us to kill the Frenchman. You have feelings for him?"

"We can't unsee what we just saw. We – I – have to do something."

Natalya exhaled cigarette smoke the color of fog. "I have orders."

"Your higher-ups are like ours, fools," Casey said. "They think they'll blackmail Smullen, manipulate him. But they don't know him. Once he's President, the law can't touch him. He could do anything, build concentration camps, nuke Russia if he wanted to. In my head, it's always been my big sister, Jessica and me. But now it's you and me. We can decide what happens with Smullen and the rest of those bastards. Not the Kremlin, not Washington. Us. You and me. We decide right here."

"How far are you willing to go? They'll kill us," Natalya said.

"I saw the same video you did. All the way. You?"

"Even if it means betraying your orders, your future?"

"This is bigger. Besides," Casey said. "I have an idea. I know exactly what we're going to do."

They walked back into the living room. Brochard and Vincent the Cat were talking rapidly in French, Vincent gesturing with his hands.

"Is there a way to solve this?" Brochard asked them in English.

"I have a plan," Casey said.

"So do I," said Vincent the Cat.

They said their goodbyes in the Logan terminal near the Air France counter. People pulling carry-ons, shouldering backpacks, checking cell phones walked by.

"You'll arrive in Paris in the morning?" Casey asked.

"The time difference," he nodded, putting his hand on her arm. She looked up at him. He really was the best looking man she'd ever met. Something told her she'd never see him again.

"Remember, you have to wait an extra day before you go into the office? And you have to pull the BOLO on Vincent?"

"The '*Appel à témoins*,' Be On the Look Out, yes, if the deal holds."

"What about Director Varane?"

"I'll speak to Marchand at the Swimming Pool? He'll deal with Varane, then I'll follow up. This Natalya is a strange woman. I don't think I've ever met anyone stranger," he said and she knew he was thinking about what had happened back at the house.

"If we hadn't done it, we'd be dead – and Smullen will become President. He'd take steps and we wouldn't be able to do anything, not to mention we'd be the first to be eliminated – in fact, it might be in process now. You have to go," she said.

"Natalya, you trust her?"

"Trust isn't something I do," Casey said.

"You've been very good. Not a word about us."

"You're leaving, Jean-Pierre. You'll be in Paris. Or Nice. Or whatever you and Gabi decide." There was a loudspeaker announcement of a flight boarding for Atlanta.

"We still shouldn't have done it," he said.

"What choice did we have?"

"Arrest them, like any other criminals. They killed the Americans who were supposed to guard us. We can arrest Smullen too," Brochard said.

"You have no jurisdiction here."

"You do. You could arrest Smullen."

"On what charge?" she said.

"Murder, assault, mayhem, torture, kidnapping, human trafficking. Multiple counts," he said, looking every inch a prosecutor.

"For crimes committed over twenty years ago? In another country, one that didn't even exist at the time? As for Blue Madagascar, once Smullen is President, he's legally untouchable. And with what evidence? My bosses – or theirs – would confiscate and destroy it." she shook her head. "But even before that something would happen to us. And the CIA, headed by the same bastards who are part of it would block it, just like they blocked you from finding out that Layton Gary McCord was Dale Fleetwood. Or they'll manufacture fake evidence proving Smullen was never in the Balkans or they'll say it's a political witch hunt. They'd eliminate all of us. Gabi and Juliette too."

"You really think – " he started, as someone with a backpack brushed by, nearly knocking him into her. She grabbed his arm to steady him.

"There's a long list of people with a good reason to see us dead: the Zemun Clan, Pronova, the Russian Mafia, the FSB, Mastercard Fitzgerald, Constantin von What's-his-name, the CIA. Not to mention the future President of the United States," she said. The glare of the air terminal lights made them seem like an airport couple, people who belonged someplace else. "Jean-Pierre, have you added up how many people have been killed since we started this case? The plan is our only chance."

"This woman, Natalya, 'the Jackdaw.' She's a killer," he said, making a very French face that expressed misgiving. "Be careful."

"All I ask is you hold off for two days. Do nothing till then." She looked up at him. "Can I kiss you goodbye?"

She reached up and pulled his head to hers, lips on lips and for the first time in her life, she shivered at a man's touch and the smell of his Prada aftershave and his clothes still damp from the rain and not wanting it to stop, she let go and watched him walk toward the security line.

"*Au revoir*, Jean-Pierre," Casey said as he disappeared into the security line.

Natalya was waiting in the bar at the Hyatt at a table overlooking Boston harbor. The lights of buildings across the water glittered in the cold night.

"Your Frenchman get away on time?" Natalya said. Casey nodded.

"And Vincent?"

"Gone. I'll be following shortly. We need to get paid," she almost smiled. "It's good you showed when you did. I've had so many men offer me drinks, the Russian Army couldn't walk out of here on its own two feet." Sure enough, the moment Casey sat down, a waiter came over indicating that a couple of men at the bar wanted to buy them drinks.

"I'll have a Sam Adams. Tell those guys at the bar we're lesbians," Casey said to the waiter.

"Are you sure? They're not half-bad," indicating the men at the bar. "He's handsome, your Frenchman," Natalya said.

"So's his wife and little girl. You have the original DVD?"

Natalya nodded. "Vincent has the other one. We're to meet in Europe; I won't tell you where. What about the clean-up?"

"It's taken care of," Casey said. She'd called Jerry Matthews to deal with the four bodies, two Americans, two Russians. "My guy wasn't happy about the Americans. Neither am I." That part made her sick. It was her fault.

According to Jerry Matthews, Wyatt and Ryan had been killed silently with the VSS Vintorez sniper rifle. They'd been prepared for an attack from the road or bordering properties, but the Russians had come from behind them, from the sea.

As for the dead Russians, back in the house, the three of them, Casey, Vincent the Cat and Natalya had walked into the kitchen, Casey with her hands behind her as if they were still tied. Vincent and Natalya fired at the same time, killing both men instantly, leaving them where they fell.

"It's war, people die," Natalya said in Russian.

"What will you tell your people?"

"The Americans were good. Professionals. They were waiting for us. Both statements true. I'll say we were lucky to get the DVD away from you and the Frenchman, Brochard, but unfortunately, when the Americans came in shooting, you both got away," Natalya said.

"Will they believe you?"

"They'll believe the DVD."

"By then, if the plan works, it won't matter," Casey said.

"God, I could use a cigarette," Natalya said, looking around. "What's wrong with Americans? Every place is No Smoking. It's like being surrounded by the Health Police. As for the plan, you'll have either dealt with things or they'll have dealt with you." At that, Casey smiled. "What's funny?"

"When Jessica and I were kids, she was always telling me what to do. She was the big sister. Now it's me making the plan," Casey said.

"You've grown up," Natalya said. She hesitated. "I've never had a woman friend before, if that's what we are."

"One of my sister Jessica's rules was: '*Boys don't matter – until they do. But sisters are forever.*'"

"Sisters are forever. I like that," Natalya said. "If you need to get hold of me, you know how. No one else, only you. As for your Monsieur Brochard, he'll close the case and drop the charges against Vincent? I was there when it happened. Nabil killed Fleetwood, not Vincent."

"Legally, you know that's irrelevant. Still, *you and Vincent the Cat*? Amazing,"

"Surprises me too," Natalya said, sipping her drink.

"What's the attraction? You like bad boys? The sex?"

"He's not boring."

Casey leaned closer. "What happens when he discovers you killed his crew? Does he suspect? He's not stupid."

"He had a chance to kill me in Athens. He didn't. I want a clean start. We'll have money and I'm hoping he feels the same."

"If he doesn't?"

"One of us will die," Natalya said quietly. From the way she said it, Casey suspected it was Vincent who'd be doing the dying. "You'll follow up with Monsieur Brochard?"

"He'll talk to the DGSE, also the Quai des Orfèvres, with the understanding that U.S. Homeland Security agrees and you and Vincent will never set foot again in France. No one wants either of you to ever testify in court or talk to the media. Where will you go?" Casey asked.

"Someplace warm, pretty. Palm trees, sandy beaches, where the food's good and they speak French – and allow people to smoke. Maybe the Caribbean. Both copies of the DVD are worth a lot. Vincent wants to open a *brasserie* on the beach. Someplace where he'd be sure to get a Stella and a decent *stufatu* lasagna like his *Maman* used to make."

"What do you get?"

"Drinks with umbrellas in them, the sound of the sea, a man who's actually a man, not a shit."

"And you said you're an ordinary girl."

"I plan to be a *rich* ordinary girl. What about you and Monsieur Brochard?"

"He loves his wife," Casey said, getting up. "I've got a plane to catch,"

As she started to leave, Natalya said "Casey." Casey stopped, looked back. "Jessica, huh?"

PART FIVE

THE NIGHT OF

"It's okay to forgive your enemies – after you destroy them."

JESSICA "JESSIE" MAKARENKO

CHAPTER FORTY-EIGHT

MIAMI, FLORIDA

"HAVE you any idea of the amount of shit we're in?" Jerry Matthews said. They were in a rented Caddy XTS on the Palmetto Expressway on the way back to Casey's hotel after meeting at a Cuban sandwich place at the Mall of America. "What were you thinking? You can leave bodies strewn around the state of Maine and nobody'd notice?"

"They weren't *strewn*, Jerry. Hidden, on a secluded property. You make it sound like a zombie apocalypse," Casey said, putting on sunglasses. The sun was shining, the temperature was in the seventies and her trench coat from Paris, now superfluous, was tossed on the back seat.

"Who do you think had to clean up your mess? A lot of fence-mending, too, Princess. The CIA's not happy. Those guys, Wyatt, Ryan, were S.O.G., CIA Special Ops Group. As for the dead Rooskies? You think the Kremlin won't notice they're gone?"

"Enemy combatants, Jerry. Or would you rather Prosecutor Brochard and me were dead?" she said.

"Brochard now, is it? Not Jean-Pierre, *mon cheri*. And how are my favorite Lovers Without Borders, *Les Amoureux Sans Frontières?*" Jerry Matthews said, puckering his lips and making kissing sounds.

"The only thing *sans* anything is how stupid you look. He's back in Paris, with his wife and daughter – where he belongs."

"So, are you okay?" he asked, glancing over at her.

"I'm fine. Just watch your driving. I don't want to die in Florida; it would be redundant."

Jerry Matthews glanced over at her. "Speaking of enemy combatants, Mr. Dalton wants to see you. He's not happy. Asshole!" he shouted, giving the finger to a Buick because the driver had honked when Jerry cut him off.

Casey knew about Arthur Dalton. He'd left three urgent cell phone messages to call him. She'd been busy that morning making copies of Fleetwood's DVD at a Fedex store. She put them into sealed mailers marked "URGENT!" addressed to specific news editors by name at the New York Times, Washington Post, AP, CNN, Fox News, MSNBC, Yahoo News, Google News, the Huffington Post, and the BBC News.

When the mailers were ready, she drove to a half-dozen secretarial services all over Miami, from SW 107th Avenue near the Mall to North Miami Beach to Hialeah to a little hole-in-the-wall on SW 8th in Alameda. She gave each office ten mailers with instructions to stay late that night till 11 PM. They were to do absolutely nothing except hold the mailers in their safe or their most secure holding area.

Casey instructed each of them, none of whom knew about the others, that if she didn't personally come back to retrieve all ten mailers – unopened, warning she would examine each mailer with a magnifying glass – from that office by eleven tonight, they were to mail all copies *Priority*

Same Day in the late night pickup. She gave them money to cover the expense, plus the extra hours for staying late. If she did come back and picked them up, after verifying they were untouched, they would each get an additional one thousand dollars cash, showing them the money in hundreds, so they'd know it was real.

Once everything was in place, she placed the call to Jerry Matthews that brought him to Miami. At the sandwich place in the Mall, his mouth full of Cuban pork, pickle and mustard, Jerry wanted to know, what gives?

"Come to my hotel room," Casey said.

"Thought you'd never ask," Jerry said, downing a Corona.

"To see the goods, Fleetwood's secret, Jerry. Close as you're getting to Paradise."

"People say that all the time. Next thing you know, they're married," he grinned.

With Jerry Matthews driving like the streets of Miami were the Monte Carlo Grand Prix, it didn't take long to get to her room at the Marriott. Jerry Matthews' expression changed after he saw Fleetwood's video.

"Unbelievable! Arthur'll want to see this immediately. Why're you delay – " he stopped when he saw the Sig Sauer pistol with the sound suppressor in both of her hands aimed at his chest. "Nice n' easy, Princess," he said.

"You take it easy, Jerry. If everybody's cool, Mr. Dalton'll see it soon enough."

"Is that really necessary?" he said, eying the pistol.

"It is, until you and I understand each other," she said.

"I hope you know what you're doing, Princess, 'cause you're falling off the edge here, " Jerry Matthews said, his face suddenly hard. No more good old Jerry. At long last we're seeing the real Jerry Matthews, Casey thought.

"If the polls are right, in six days, this filthy excuse for a human being is going to be elected President of the United States. I can't take the chance that Dalton or you might bury this or use it to pressure 'President Smullen' to get what you want. Can't risk it, Jerry."

"You won't trust us enough to even give us the benefit of the doubt?" Jerry Matthews said, glancing at the door.

Casey caught his look, stepped in the way. "Not on your life," she said, motioning with the pistol. "The Washington math says the smart play would be to let Smullen win and blackmail him. Mind you, Smullen wouldn't put up with it. He'd crush the lot of us: me, you, and Arthur Dalton. So I'm not giving you or him a choice – And taking me out – which is what you're thinking about right now – won't change the equation. I've set up a fail-safe. Anything happens to me, I disappear, I go to sleep and don't wake up, I hurt my little pinky – and I've got sixty separate channels to all the major media: New York Times, Washington Post, CNN, Google, you-name-it, who'll all have tonight everything you just saw on Fleetwood's DVD." she said.

"You don't need all that. I saw the video. I'm with you. We can't let it happen. The country won't survive. It wouldn't be America," Jerry Matthews said. "I'll cover you from Dalton till you report to him yourself. Whatever he does, that's him, not me."

"All right," she said, lowering the pistol. "We're going to need help. Who do you know in the Secret Service? Somebody high on the food chain."

Jerry Matthews thought for a moment.

"Brandon," he said. "Brandon Hillard, Deputy Assistant Director Protective Services."

"How well do you know him?"

"We were Army Rangers together, First of the 75th, Operation Desert Storm and Somalia. We were in deep doo-doo together in Mogadishu. Why? What do you need?"

Casey looked at her watch. "I need him here in four hours. Absolutely no one can know. Not his office, not ours. Off the grid. And Jerry . . ."

"Yeah?"

"I need a super-clean gun."

CHAPTER FORTY-NINE

BRICKELL, MIAMI

A CANDY-RED SUNSET cast the shadows of the high rises across Brickell Avenue. Jerry Matthews drove the Caddy into the parking garage of a bank building. When they were sure it was clear, Jerry got into a Ford. Brandon got behind the wheel as Casey moved from the backseat into the Caddy's trunk. She lay on her side, hoping none of the mat fibers got in her hair or on the black linen slacks and top she'd worn to make it harder for her to be seen at night.

The key to her plan, she'd explained to Brandon Hillard, a six-foot-four African-American in a Hugo Boss suit with a no-nonsense shaved head and shoulders that could take down a charging linebacker, was that none of them could exist. In order for it to work, it would all have to happen in the space of an hour and they'd leave no trace behind.

Luckily, Brandon was whip-smart. Though he refused at first, when he saw the video on her laptop he immediately understood why arresting Smullen wouldn't work. A veteran of Washington's inside-baseball, it was clear that unless they tried it her way, Smullen would skate away from this as he had from everything else in his life – only after the election he'd have the legal power and immunity of the Presidency. None of them doubted that as soon as he could, he'd eliminate them.

Riding in the trunk of the Caddy, Casey hoped that Brandon's rank in the Secret Service, his bigness, would as she'd expressed it to Jerry Matthews "work in the room." But what if it didn't, she worried. Smullen was an unknown.

And no patsy. Rich, powerful, protected, with extremely powerful friends. He wouldn't be afraid or intimidated by her – a nothing little *chica* from the *barrio*. Stop it, she told herself. That's fear talk. Jessie's Rules: *Don't let others define you. Who you believe you are is who you are.*

She felt the Caddy slow, stop, then resume. A toll booth? There was a curve, then the car headed straight with no stops. The road sounded different. They must be on the Causeway over the water to Key Biscayne. It must be dark by now, she thought. No moon yet. Time passed; more turns, stops. Finally, another stop. She heard muffled talking. Possibly Brandon flashing his Secret Service ID to the guard at the gated entrance to the Key Colony Beach Club.

Jerry would be behind by two or three minutes in the Ford, wearing a uniform from First Premier Security, the company handling gate security for the Key Colony Home Owners Association. He would relieve the gate guard, telling him the company had called him to fill in.

The Caddy started forward, moving slowly through the Club's private streets.

. . .

"I can give you ten minutes," Governor Jeffrey Smullen said, giving them his campaign smile, teeth whitened headlight bright.

Casey recognized him from television, except he was bigger, more of a presence in person. But it was all there. The familiar smile that never quite reached his eyes, the tanning-lamp complexion with a hint of five-o'clock shadow, graying hair combed straight back, the odd way he had of holding his head at an angle as if listening to music no one else was hearing; the man from a thousand campaign promos and Fleet-wood's video. The only difference being that instead of a business suit with an American flag pin in his lapel the way he usually appeared on TV, Smullen was casual in slacks and a pink polo shirt, a gin and tonic on the side table next to him.

They were in the living room of a luxury beachfront townhouse inside the Colony, decorated in rattan Margari-taville style, that Smullen was using as a getaway from his Florida campaign headquarters at the Four Seasons in down-town Miami. The patio glass doors and screens were open to the night air and the sound of the surf on the beach.

As they entered, a very young woman in a tight top and shorts, her face white as a sheet, was being hurried out by Josh Barsky, an assistant campaign manager, whispering urgently in her ear. Christ, he's still at it, Casey thought.

She and Brandon introduced themselves, showing their badges. Barsky came back in, but Casey said it was confiden-tial for the governor. Barsky hesitated, but didn't leave.

"What's this about?" Smullen said, still smiling. "I was told it was security."

"I have something to show you," Casey said, taking her laptop out of its carrying case and turning it on.

"Can't my staff handle it?" Smullen said.

"It's from 1999. Ring a bell, Governor?"

Smullen stood up. "Turns out I don't have time for this after all. We'll have to cut this short." he called out.

"Sit down. Your campaign is over," Casey snapped sharply.

"Who the hell do you think you're talking to? Mike! Deke! Lloyd!" Smullen shouted. Two Secret Servicemen and Smullen's personal bodyguard, an ex-NFL lineman came running into the room, hands on the guns in their shoulder holsters. Barsky moved toward them. Brandon Hillard faced the Secret Servicemen.

"I know you two know who I am," he said to the two Secret Servicemen. "You guys take a twenty minute break outside. When we're done, I'll call you." The Secret Servicemen glanced at each other uneasily.

"You sure, sir?" One of them said.

"That's an order," Brandon said. The two Secret Servicemen turned and left. Brandon showed his badge to Josh Barsky and Mike, the ex-NFL player. "I'm the Deputy Assistant Director of the Secret Service. What's happening now is classified Top Secret; a matter of national security. I need you both to leave the room for a few minutes." He turned to Smullen. "Governor, unless you want these guys to see something they can't unsee, I strongly suggest you tell them to leave at once. If you feel you need to, you can call 'em back."

"All right, get out," Smullen said, motioning his aides out of the room.

"Close the door and stay outside. You are not to call or speak to anyone while we're here. Stay off your cell phones. I promise we won't be long," Casey said. She waited till they left the room, then turned to Smullen. "Sit down please, Governor."

"I don't know who you think you're dealing with, but I'm

going to call the Attorney General and – " Smullen started, taking out his iPhone.

"You won't," Casey said.

"Oh? Why not?" Smullen said, his iPhone ready.

"Because you're not that stupid. I wish you were. Make it easier," she said.

"Maybe I am that stupid. Or don't take shit from anyone," Smullen said.

"All you have to do is watch something on my laptop. Just a few minutes. That's it. After that, you can call the President, the FBI, the Man in the Moon for all I give a damn, because if you are that stupid, you deserve everything that's about to happen," she said, watching his eyes narrow. Not used to having anybody talk to you like that, especially not a woman, she thought.

"She's right, sir," Brandon said. "I'm not sure you understand what's involved here. You owe it to yourself to find out."

"I don't owe anything to anyone. Get out," Smullen said.

Casey took a gun out of her handbag, the super-clean Glock Jerry Matthews got for her.

"You can either watch or be arrested, Governor. I don't care which," she said, locking eyes with Smullen.

"I'll watch," Smullen said after a moment, staring at their faces as if memorizing them. "I won't forget this – or either of you. When I'm President, your careers are over."

"You're not President yet," Casey said, planting the laptop on the coffee table in front of Smullen and starting the video.

She watched his face as he watched first Dale Fleetwood's video followed by the video of what happened in the room on Garibaldi. His face was expressionless, without emotion all the way through, but he blanched when he saw Nicu's photos of him at the killings in Taukbashce Park, followed by images of the DNA and forensic evidence presented by German

Federal Judge Thomas Stegen, UNMIK's former Police Chief. When it was done, Casey shut her laptop. No one spoke. The only sound was the surf on the sand through the open patio door.

"There are multiple fail-safes in place. If anything were to happen to the Deputy Director here or me, the whole world will see this," Casey said.

"How much?" Smullen said.

CHAPTER FIFTY

KEY BISCAYNE

SHE WALKED BAREFOOT on the beach in the darkness, the sand wet beneath her feet in the place where the surf ended. The full moon created a silver path on the dark water. At night in her black clothes, Casey was virtually invisible. I'm Asrael, the angel who brings the darkness, she thought, wondering where that thought had come from as she slipped on her sandals. Silent as a moon-shadow, she crossed the sand to the space between the hedges and the Key Colony's outer property wall.

Her only moment of exposure came as she was crossing Crandon Boulevard. A car stopped for her in the crosswalk. Instinctively, she turned her face away from the headlights and hurried into the shadows under the palm trees.

Brandon picked her up in the parking area of the mini-mall on Crandon and Sonesta. For a time, neither spoke. Driving on the Causeway, she again saw the orange Moon over the bay and the lights of Miami.

"I didn't know you were going to do that. We should've arrested him. In fact, I should arrest you," Brandon said.

"He'd've been out in twenty minutes, only then he'd be a martyr, claiming our evidence was a hoax. Once he's President, ordinary laws don't apply. We'd be the ones in jail – or dead."

"Even Presidents have limits. Impeachment, Special Prosecutors."

"That would require people putting country over politics. When was the last time you saw that happen? You saw the video. Don't you know who he is? He's the last candidate. There wouldn't be any more elections," she said.

Brandon dropped her off at her hotel and headed straight to the airport back to Washington. He would say nothing to anyone. Casey waited in her room for Jerry Matthews' two knocks, then two knocks again on the door. Pistol in hand, she let him in.

"You do it?" Jerry Matthews asked.

"We gave him the choice," Casey said. "Laid it out. Exposure, prison, loss of his fortune, his family broke, because we'd confiscate it all – or he ends it clean. His legacy stays intact. His family and heirs keep their fortune. He'd be famous forever."

"What'd he say?"

"Wanted to negotiate, buy us off. Wanted to know who I was?"

"What'd you tell him?"

Asrael, the Angel of Death; she'd wanted to say.

"It was in his eyes, Jerry. He wasn't going to do it. The second we left, he would've brought the wrath of God down on all of us."

"Jesus, what did you do?"

"I walked over to him, just a girl, no threat, put the

muzzle to his temple. *Bang!* Already had on my latex gloves. I pressed fingerprints from both his hands on the gun, made sure it had his print on the trigger. Fired a second shot out the open patio door straight out to the sea so his hand had gunpowder residue on it. Sand's less than a hundred feet wide there; bullet's somewhere in the ocean. Picked up the first shell casing, made sure to put another round in the magazine to replace the second cartridge, left the gun on the floor angled where it would've fallen if he'd shot himself."

"Well, Princess." Jerry Matthews eyed her. "You're not the little girl we hired."

"I never was," she said.

"What about his aides, the Secret Service?"

"They rushed in after the shots. Brandon handled the Secret Service guys. Told them it was a suicide. I dealt with Josh Barsky. Showed them the video. Said it was a joint CIA – Homeland Security op and if he or any of them ever said a single word to anyone about us, that we were ever there or even existed, they were dead."

"They bought it?"

"After the video, they understood. I think Barsky realized making Smullen a suicide and a mystery might even work better for his political career, the party. 'Tell you the truth, he was a prick,' he said."

They snacked on mini-bar pretzels and Corona and watched the TV as the news broke. In Key Biscayne, a local reporter, Cody Robinson stood in front of a police barrier, telling viewers that the Miami-Dade PD were a massive presence. "Crandon Boulevard near the Key Colony has been shut down in both directions. No one is being allowed anywhere near the site of this terrible tragedy," he reported.

Together, Casey and Jerry Matthews made the rounds of the secretarial offices. At each stop, she'd run in and retrieve the mailers – making sure each was still sealed – then watched them shredded in front of her before paying and going on to the next office. She paid each one the bonus with the money from Fleetwood's safety deposit box in Cyprus.

At the last stop, she told Jerry Matthews, "Tell Mister Dalton I'll bring him his DVD copy tomorrow personally."

"You took an awful lot on yourself, Princess. I don't know what Arthur's going to do. However it goes, you're an interesting person," Jerry Matthews said as they drove through Miami's night-lit streets.

"You know, Jerry, you're not as bad as you try to be."

"Now that's just where you're wrong, Princess. You keep underestimating me," he grinned.

That night in her hotel room, Casey dreamed about the orange moon over the water tower in Central L.A. Only this time, nothing bad happened. She came running out of the Florencia 13 house with the money. No one stopped her. The bike she'd hidden behind the Oaxacan restaurant on Pine was still there. She rode fast and free, wind in her hair, on the Slauson overpass over the 5 into East L.A. In the dream, she smiled and thought she'd have to tell Don Ernesto the next time she visited him at San Quentin.

CHAPTER FIFTY-ONE

"TEA ALL RIGHT?" Arthur Dalton asked. They were sitting in Dalton's office in Washington, sunlight filtering through the Venetian blinds into the book-lined room.

"You know I can't stand this jasmine crap. I like American coffee," Jerry Matthews said.

"Which comes from Columbia and Brazil," Dalton said. "About the Republicans?"

"They're supposed to have an emergency video Zoom mini-convention today. The heads of each state delegation to pick a new nominee, probably the Veep guy, Senator Phillips, now that the Dems agreed to delay the election two weeks," Jerry Matthews said.

"Phillips, another nonentity," Dalton said, stirring his tea. "This 'Invisible Woman' business is bubbling in the media? Did anyone see her?"

"A Nothing-burger," Jerry Matthews said. "I used our software on the hard drive for the security cameras. There's no video of the Caddy and the software fixed the time gap. She was dressed in black at night. No one saw her go in or out. Even if someone did, no one knows who she is, what she looks like. Secret Service won't talk. This Barsky guy? He already gave an interview to Fox saying suicide, that he was there a second after the shot. You could pull Brandon's fingernails out and he wouldn't talk. That just leaves Casey."

"You have concerns?" Arthur Dalton said, sniffing the tea, then taking a sip.

"Don't get me wrong. She's very good. But she was way out of bounds on Smullen – without authorization. We can't allow her to go rogue like that."

"Hmmm," Dalton murmured. "She didn't trust us. But then Jerry, why should she?"

"I don't get it. I thought you'd be furious."

"Once she and your Army chum, Brandon met with Smullen, the die was cast. As President, Smullen would've crushed us like bugs," Dalton said. "Our little Chicana may have saved the republic. Plus we can now go after Mastercard Fitz and the others, which'll give us leverage with the CIA, something we've long wanted," Dalton said. Not to mention taking his boss, Tommy Cociarelli's place, he thought. "Casey's a thoroughbred. If she'd grown up in anything resembling a normal family, she would've ended up on scholarship at Caltech or MIT. I'll give her a good scolding, but what's your real concern?"

"This whole thing about the Russkies," Jerry Matthews said. "Her being *simpatico* with this Natalya woman. Let's get real. Natalya Petrenko is the Jackdaw, the FSB. They run Natalya; they could also run Casey. And this weird thing she has about her long-lost sister."

Arthur Dalton sighed, putting down his tea cup. "You disappoint me, Jerry. Do you imagine we're amateurs here? You think I didn't vet the hell out of her? I know everything about that girl back to the day she was born: every God-forsaken foster placement, even that crack-house calamity of a mother, Anastasia Makarenko."

"What about the sister, Jessica? It's the real reason she does everything. It's how she has the lady-balls to walk into the lion's den."

"Old stuff," Dalton waved his hand dismissively. "Part of her original psychological profile; her prime motivation," Dalton said.

"So what happened to the sister? Do we know?"

Arthur Dalton got up and went to a framed photograph on the wall of himself with a former U.S. President in the Oval Office, swung it away from the wall and opened a hidden safe. He brought back a folder.

"If you ever breathe a word of what I'm about to show you, Jerry, you're done. I mean it. The only reason I'm showing you is because I need you on board," Dalton said. Inside was a single-sheet CIA file with the classification, "//TOP SECRET//X1: SPECIAL ACCESS / ORCON / NOFORN / 100X1", X1 designating the "Top Secret" classification level and "100" the number of years before the file could be declassified. The rest of the page was blank except for two lines: "Jessica Lynn Makarenko; DOB: 11/23/1985; Ht 5ft 7in, Wt Est 115 lbs, Race Cau Hair Black, Eyes Blue; disappeared Sunset Blvd, UCLA campus, 04/06/2006, approx: 6:05 – 6:45 am PDT, Los Angeles, CA 90024; X1:ref SIA391017-4B."

"What's SIA?"

"The Bulgarian State Intelligence Agency. Apparently one of the most corrupt intelligence services in the world."

"Bulgaria? The sister Jessica could be alive?" Jerry Matthews said.

"We don't know that. It's an ORCON Special Access file.

Special clearance, Originator Controlled distribution. One we can't see," Dalton said.

Jerry Matthews handed the page back to Arthur Dalton. "You going to tell her?"

"And remove her motivation? You said it yourself. Certainly not."

"Christ, I thought I was a cold son-of-a-bitch," Jerry Matthews said.

"Ah, Jerry, look at where we live," Arthur Dalton said, motioning at the window, his gesture somehow taking in all of Washington, D.C.

JESSICA'S RULES

1. Chance happens, but evil is a hunter. You can either be prepared or prey.

2. When it's time to act, go all the way, like jumping off a cliff.

3. Revenge will keep you alive when nothing else will.

4. Boys don't matter – until they do. But sisters are forever.

5. It's okay to forgive your enemies – after you destroy them.

6. Never show fear. What you feel is yours; what you show belongs to others.

7. Smile at your enemies. Never let them know you know who they really are.

8. *Weakness comes from fear. Fear is a liar. Remember, we are the most dangerous creatures on the planet.*

9. *Lying to others is what everyone does. Lying to yourself is suicide.*

10. *The only person you can ever really trust is yourself.*

11. *Emotion equals error. When a shooter wants to hit a target he holds his breath*

12. *The world is a maze filled with traps. The biggest trap is love.*
13. *Action without a plan equals failure.*

14. *Don't let others define you. Who you believe you are is who you are.*

15. *There's always a weapon. Find it.*

16. *If you dance with the devil, sooner or later you dance to the devil's tune.*

ABOUT THE AUTHOR

Andrew Kaplan is the author of two bestselling spy thriller book series: *Scorpion* and *Homeland*, the original prequel novels to the award-winning *Homeland* television series. His novel, *Homeland: Saul's Game* won the Scribe Best Novel of the Year award. His books have been translated into 22 languages.

A former journalist, war correspondent and business consultant, he covered events around the world and served in both the U.S. Army and the Israeli Army during the Six Day War. He has consulted with major corporations and think tanks that advise governments. His standalone novels include the NY Times bestsellers *Dragonfire*, *Hour of the Assassins*, and *War of the Raven*, cited by the American Library Association as "one of the 100 Best Books ever written about World War Two."

Kirkus Reviews hailed his writing as "Electrifying," *Publishers Weekly* called it "Smashing, sexy and unforgettable," and *Suspense Magazine* declared: "Kaplan's writing matches the be best work of the late Robert Ludlum and then surpasses it." His screenwriting career includes the James Bond film, *Goldeneye*.

CPSIA information can be obtained
at www.ICGtesting.com
Printed in the USA
LVHW030426310821
696476LV00004B/110